GOLD DUST

**BAEN BOOKS
by CATHERINE ASARO**

Skolian Empire: Dust Knights
The Down Deep
Gold Dust

Skolian Empire: Major Bhaajan
Undercity
The Bronze Skies
The Vanished Seas
The Jigsaw Assassin

The Saga of the Skolian Empire
The Ruby Dice
Diamond Star
Carnelians

Sunrise Alley
Alpha

To purchase any of these titles in e-book form, please go to www.baen.com.

GOLD DUST

CATHERINE ASARO

GOLD DUST

This is a work of fiction. All the characters and events portrayed in this book are fictional, and any resemblance to real people or incidents is purely coincidental.

Copyright © 2025 Catherine Asaro

All rights reserved, including the right to reproduce this book or portions thereof in any form.

A Baen Books Original

Baen Publishing Enterprises
P.O. Box 1403
Riverdale, NY 10471
www.baen.com

ISBN: 978-1-6680-7290-5

Cover art by Kurt Miller

First printing, October 2025

Distributed by Simon & Schuster
1230 Avenue of the Americas
New York, NY 10020

Library of Congress Control Number: 2025027740

Printed in the United States of America

10 9 8 7 6 5 4 3 2 1

DEDICATION

To everyone at Orange Theory Fitness, Port Jefferson
For being such great coaches, athletes, staff, and friends

ACKNOWLEDGMENTS

I would like to thank the many people who helped put together this book. Their input has been invaluable. My thanks to my Patreon subscribers for their support and encouragement, especially to readers Tamara Wiens, Mary Lou Mendum, and Duane Ebersole for their invaluable insights on the full manuscript, also to Stephen Aigles for his editorial input, and to Tim Oey for suggesting the title. Also to David Afsharirad and Josue Acosta for their input. To the amazing Kurt Miller for creating the exceptional cover artwork. To all the folks at Baen Books, including my superb publisher, Toni Weiskopf, and my dynamite editor Griffin Barber, to Carol Russo for going above and beyond, and to the amazing team there: Marla Ainspan, Alex Bear, Rabbit Boyett, Leah Brandtner, Jason Cordova, Joy Freeman, Christiana Sherrill, and everyone else who helped make this book possible. A special thanks to the Ethan Ellenberg Literary Agency for their excellent work on my behalf, including Ethan Ellenberg, Bibi Lewis, Lindsay Watson, Raelene Gorlinsky, Evan Gregory, Ezra Ellenberg, and Maria Santos. Most of all to my daughter, Catherine Kendall Asaro Cannizzo, and to my new daughter, Qisi Zhang, with all my love.

PART ONE
Raylicon

CHAPTER I
First Meet

"Go!" Mason shouted. "Come on! You can do it!"

Bhaaj stood in the coach's box of the stadium with Mason Qazik, Coach of the Raylicon Olympic Track and Field team, a lofty name for perhaps the worst Olympic team in human-settled space. Well, what did they expect? The world Raylicon had only the City of Cries to draw on, with a few million people, whereas the top teams recruited from worlds with populations in the billions.

The runners below were pounding around the oval track in the 800-meter race of the Cries Track and Field Meet. It was a small competition, five local teams, including Mason's Olympic hopefuls, a group of martial arts students from the Cries Tykado Academy, some kids from Cries University, another team fielded by employees from Abyss Associates, and the fifth sent by Scorpio Corporation. Although Bhaaj wasn't an official coach with Mason, she'd brought him many of her runners from the Undercity, swelling the size of his team from eleven athletes to over fifty, with hers easily besting the top runners from the City of Cries.

Below them, competitors from the five teams had reached the end of their last lap on the track. The crowd in the arena were cheering, calling out encouragement—

And booing.

Bhaaj scowled. Where did they get off booing athletes, particularly in one of the best races ever run in this spectacular but underused arena? The City of Cries thrived on the otherwise mostly uninhabitable world of Raylicon because of its historical importance and the wealth of its citizens. They'd spared no expense for the technology that made their city into an oasis in an otherwise stark desert, and the Athletic Center was no exception. If only they had a pool of athletes comparable to this remarkable facility.

That could change today as the Undercity runners pulverized the previous records set in this stadium. When the leaders below approached the finish line, the cheering from the crowd swelled—and so did the catcalls. The few holo-reporters covering the event jockeyed with more oomph than usual to record the winners, with Angel from the Undercity in first, Tayz Wilder from Cries in second, and an Undercity youth called Lamplight in third.

Given the informal nature of the meet, it didn't take long for Mason's volunteers to validate the results. As soon as they announced the medalists, repeating what everyone already knew, the crowd applauded and flashed their spark-sticks. The holo-casters converged on the winners, especially Angel. With her muscled build, great height, and tattoos, she looked about as angelic as a mountain basher. Gorgeous, yah, with her beautiful face and large eyes, but also a force of nature. Tayz Wilder seemed startled to come in second when in the past he'd run as the undisputed leader in everything, even the 800 meter, despite his preference for longer distances. He seemed more gratified than bothered, though. Finally he had a team worthy of his ability.

Several holo-casters were running toward Mason and Bhaaj. In the few moments of privacy they had left, Mason grinned at her. "The universe of athletics just changed forever."

Bhaaj didn't know whether to smile at his exaggeration or scowl at the booing from the stands. She didn't have time for either reaction before the reporters reached them.

"So, Coach Qazik," a woman said, shoving her holocam at him. "How does it feel to have gangsters from the Undercity beat your Olympic-trained runners?"

"This is the *Raylicon* team," Mason said. "All the runners working with me are trying out for our Olympic Track and Field team. I'm delighted to have such a strong showing."

"Yes, but most of them come from the Undercity," a man called out. "These kids live in one of the worst slums in the Imperialate. Are they qualified to run with the athletes you'll take to the Olympics next year?"

"Of course they are," Bhaaj said, exasperated. "You just saw them."

"You're Major Bhaajan, the Undercity coach, right?" another woman asked. "Didn't you earn a bronze medal in the classic marathon at the Olympics a few decades ago?"

"A silver medal," Bhaaj said. "I ran for the Pharaoh's Army team."

Another reporter spoke with suspicion. "That seems like too much of a coincidence, that you came out of the Undercity and made an Olympic team, and now you bring all these Undercity gang members here to destroy records in this arena. Cheating is immediate cause for disqualification."

For fuck's sake, Bhaaj thought. She said only, "Of course it isn't coincidence. Running well is a survival mechanism in the Undercity. We have no access to motorized transport. We travel with our legs." She met his gaze. "Most everyone in the Undercity runs every day of their lives." For her, that qualified as a long speech, but it was a better than cussing at the reporter.

"Surely your athletes have been altered," the first woman insisted. "Just look at them, at how long their legs are compared to their bodies. It seems unlikely *every* one of them just happens to have such a physique. Body augmentation is illegal for any natural-body meet, including the Olympics."

"Enough!" Mason said. "I always check my runners. None have augmentation of any form. Those who qualify for my team will represent Raylicon regardless of where they come from."

With that, he grabbed Bhaaj's arm in a flourish and stalked away from the holo-casters, headed for a tunnel into the interior of the stadium. As a coach's entrance, it had automated security sensors that blared at anyone who tried to use it without permission, including nosy reporters.

As soon as they were alone, Bhaaj said, "Booing. I can't believe it."

"I'm sorry about that." Mason grimaced. "I knew the Undercity runners would surprise people, but no way did I expect that reaction. So vicious!"

"You think that's vicious?" Bhaaj asked. "I saw a lot worse when I enlisted at sixteen."

"Sixteen?" Mason blinked at her. "I didn't think you could join the army that young."

"You can't fight. They put me in school." They'd intended for her to spend more than two years there, but she'd tested out early by doing far better than anyone expected, after which she'd applied for emancipated minor status. Given that she had no parents, and no one gave a damn about a kid from the Undercity, she'd had no trouble getting it. Soon after, she became a private in the bottom echelon of the military. They sent her out to fight alongside the drones and robots and other low-value soldiers, those considered expendable.

"I didn't realize you'd enlisted." Mason's ever-expressive face became confused. "People call you Major Bhaajan. Doesn't that mean you served as an officer before you retired?"

"That's right." She felt like saying, *Not this again,* but she held back. She'd come to like Mason this past season since her runners had started to train with his team. "It's possible to go from the enlisted to the officer ranks."

"But you're from the Undercity—" He winced. "Sorry. Now I'm doing it, making all those stupid assumptions."

His embarrassed response helped Bhaaj warm toward him. "I don't think anyone expected me to succeed. But I did. When they found out how well I could run, they delayed my commission long enough for me to represent the army at the Olympics." She could have competed for many more years, except the Olympics didn't allow biomech augmentation, and army officers received the biomech upon their commission. After she'd fought so hard for her rank, she hadn't wanted to risk delaying her commission another four years. Instead, she'd put away her track and field shoes and become Second Lieutenant Bhaajan.

"It was worth the work," she added.

He gave a friendly laugh. "Your usual taciturn answer, yes? I can only imagine the history behind those words."

Bhaaj almost smiled. She didn't because in the Undercity you never smiled at someone unless you trusted them. But she did nod to him.

A group of their runners appeared around a curve of the concourse, laughing and talking. At least the Cries athletes were talking. The Undercity kids gave terse responses or said nothing. Some had trouble understanding their Cries teammates, given the different dialects they spoke. It helped that Angel had experience with above-city culture, enough that she knew how to interact with the Cries competitors.

As the runners gathered around them, Angel nodded to Bhaaj, and Bhaaj nodded back, just barely, but enough to acknowledge the team's accomplishment.

Mason beamed at them all. "Nice work today! The medal ceremonies will start soon!"

Tayz Wilder, the Cries team captain, scowled. "I can't believe those people were booing."

"I understand you're all upset," Mason said. "But don't go down to their level. Choose your words with care."

"Yah." Strider, one of Bhaaj's athletes, spoke in the Undercity dialect. "Got good words for booers. Fucking ass-bytes."

Some of the runners laughed, Cries and Undercity both, then stopped when Mason glared.

Hyden Laj, another leader among the Cries athletes, spoke in an aloof tone. "Of course we get such gems of wisdom from the Undercity. In refined language, no less."

Rockjan, the largest of the Undercity gang members, turned to him. "You can go—"

"Enough!" Bhaaj said, in the same instant that Mason said, "Stop it, everyone. Show respect, all of you, to each other and to your opponents. Always, no matter how the crowd reacts."

The Cries athletes squinted at him, and the Undercity kids turned impassive. None of them liked the booing, but neither did they want to ruin the high of doing so well at the meet. Before anyone thought of a response, a muted roar came from the track.

"What the blazes?" Mason said, looking at the sports band on his wrist.

Max, Bhaaj thought. *What's going on?*

Checking. That came from Max, the Evolving Intelligence, or EI, in her leather-and-tech gauntlets. When she thought with enough force to Max, it fired bio-electrodes in her brain, which sent signals along biothreads in her body to the gauntlets on her wrists where Max lived. His signals followed the reverse path, letting him "think" to her.

The first runner from the classic marathon has reached the stadium, Max thought. **It's Tam Wiens. She's doing her final lap.**

"Tam just entered the stadium," Mason was saying, reading the tiny holos above the sports band around his wrist. "It's too soon."

"Come on," Bhaaj said. "Let's go look."

They headed back to the entrance where they'd escaped the reporters, and their curious runners followed. Technically, the athletes weren't supposed to use that tunnel, but neither Bhaaj nor Mason said anything. They came out into the tiers to see a young woman on the track below, headed for the finish line. An orb the size of a soccer ball floated above her, verifying her progress as it had done throughout the city. Two cool-carts wheeled along the track, one with officials getting human verification of her progress and the other with holo-casters recording her win.

"How can Tam be so early?" Mason said. "She must have taken wrong turn."

"No, look at her stats," Bhaaj said. "She's done the full route." The numbers continually updated on a holo-scoreboard above the track, which took its data from the monitor on Tam's arm. She crossed the finish line accompanied by an appreciative roar from the crowd. Actually, "roar" exaggerated the reaction, given the stands were only about one-fifth full and a few people persisted with the jeering catcalls.

"We've never seen anything like it!" the stadium announcer exulted, his voice coming from media orbs spinning above the stadium. "Tam Wiens, a runner from the *Undercity*, just crushed the previous marathon record here. Anyone could've told you that's impossible, and yet here she is, her run verified by both human and drone monitors. First place, in two hours and three minutes. Times have steadily improved over the past decades, but if this meet were an Olympic qualifier, that result would put Wiens on the team—ho, *look!* The second-place runner just entered the stadium, *another* Undercity athlete, the man called Ruzik. Yes, that's right, another gang member—wait, I'm getting a note—they call these runners Dust Knights, a syndicate known for their aggressive fighting."

"I don't believe it," Bhaaj said. "Do they just make up this shit?" She'd promised herself to clean up her language here, but this announcer made it too easy to forget.

"We need to get better descriptions out there about your runners,"

Mason told her. "But look at Ruzik! He's going to hit an Olympic qualifying time, too."

"So he is," Bhaaj said, gratified but not surprised.

"It's a new game, folks!" the announcer enthused. "Raylicon may field a respectable team in track and field at the Olympics next year. Who'd have thought so much talent could come from homeless thugs squatting under the city!"

"Enough already with the insults," Bhaaj growled.

"I'll register a complaint." Mason sounded sincere, but far less annoyed. "He's right about the team, though. What a group!" He grinned at her. "I had no *clue* you had so many spectacular runners down there in the Undercity."

"At least you don't call it a slum."

"I'll call it whatever you want." Mason beamed with unabashed delight. "You can't scare me with all your scowls and growls, Bhaaj. I know you're happy."

She couldn't help but smile. "The City of Cries better look out. We're coming."

Angel stood on the podium with Tayz Wilder to her right and Lamplight on her left. She felt good. The official who put the gold medal around her neck neither smiled nor spoke, a relief given how above-city types did both far too much. As they put the medal on Tayz, though, they were all *Congratulations, Del Wilder, Well done*. It hadn't taken Angel long to realize the title *Del* indicated honor, which they gave to Tayz and not her.

Even so. Angel liked Tayz. He worked hard and gave respect. Not like so many others, with their we-hate-the-Undercity biz, jeering her for winning a race that didn't even go anywhere, just around a big circle. Well, tough. She'd keep beating their entitled asses. She loved running. Strange, that they'd taken a means of survival—racing for your life—and turned it into a game.

"The Lost Sky" played while they stood on the podiums. Angel, her husband Ruzik, and Bhaaj had chosen that music to represent the Undercity last year when they competed in The Selei City Marathon on the world Parthonia. Angel and Ruzik had gone to Parthonia to help Bhaaj with one of her private investigator cases, so they figured why not try the race? When the officials had asked what song represented their people, they chose "The Lost Sky." Since no recording of the song had existed, Ruzik had sung it, the only one of them whose voice wouldn't kill a desert lizard.

After the medal ceremony, Angel went to where Bhaaj stood talking with Mason. Bhaaj nodded to her and said, "Good run," a fine response indeed, two words to indicate honor.

Ah, but Mason. Oh, yah. Mason.

"Incredible! Just amazing!" he enthused. "Our team is dynamite! Well, what do you expect! Of course we're the top team on Raylicon. Fine job, all of you!" And on and on, full of words and verve and thrill. Angel wondered that he didn't pass out with all that energy. He meant well, though, and he never scowled when Undercity kids outdid his Cries runners. He genuinely didn't care where they came from. They were *his* team. Actually, the Undercity kids considered Bhaaj their coach, but she told them to honor Mason, so they did. In this past season, since they'd trained with his team, he'd earned their respect.

While Mason talked, the setting sun stretched shadows across the track. Although sunsets still bemused Angel, the passage of "days" no longer bothered her. She'd started sneaking above ground years ago, to explore the desert and look at Cries from a distance. Gradually she'd become used to the astonishing sky, how the sun came and went. Runners who'd never ventured above ground before had a tougher time when they joined Mason's team last season, but they liked to run more than they wanted to avoid sunlight, so they came, gawked at the sky, and outran the slicks.

On the podium, the medal ceremony for the marathon had started. It gratified Angel to see Tam receive the gold. Good person, Tam. She never had a bad word for anyone. And Ruzik with the silver. Yah, a fine figure of a man, this husband of hers. He stood tall and impassive, the tats on his arms vivid in the slanting sunlight. The third-place finisher, a guy from the Cries Tykado Academy, got a bronze medal.

Bhaaj was speaking to Mason. "If you'd put Tayz Wilder on the marathon today instead of the 800-meter, I'll bet he'd have medaled instead of that kid from the tykado academy."

"Yes, absolutely." Then Mason added, "Wild wanted to try the shorter race, though, just for practice. For the Olympics, I'm thinking of Tam, Wild, and Ruzik on the royal marathon. Who else? That is, if we qualify anyone else. I've got to get this team out to interstellar meets. So far, Wild is the only one who has officially qualified for *any* Olympic event."

"Wild?" Bhaaj asked. "You mean Tayz Wilder?"

"You bet! Everyone calls him Wild." Mason chuckled. "It's because he's so wild about training. He never lets up."

Listening, Angel almost laughed. Tayz was about as wild as a fluff-pup, given that his every word and action whispered, *I'm a rich city slick*. The team even had a member of the royalty, Azarina Majda. She had none of the arrogance so ingrained in the older Majda women, though. Except for her straight black hair and aristocratic features, you'd never know she was a Majda. Not that the royal Majda family reigned on Raylicon anymore—unless you included their financial biz, an empire of wealth far more powerful than any realm their barbarian queens had ruled thousands of years ago.

The Undercity and Cries athletes mostly kept their distance. At least they hadn't come to blows. They took their cues from their leaders, Wild as team captain, and Ruzik as Bhaaj's second for the Dust Knights. Angel discreetly watched Ruzik and Wild. Strange that, to see a Cries man talking to an Undercity athlete. That never happened. Yet here they were. Wild didn't seem fake, either. Angel felt his emotions, not as strong as with Ruzik, but enough to read his mood. However impossible it seemed, he and Ruzik got along.

She hoped it lasted. If putting Undercity runners and Cries slicks together on one team was going to work, they needed to pull together instead of wanting to pulverize each other.

CHAPTER II
Cartel Jump

Strider, Lamplight, and Zee ran along the canal, their feet pounding the dusty ground. Strider reveled in the exertion, her mind one with the Undercity, this world she loved, even more now that she'd glimpsed what lay above, too much heat and brightness in an eerie city of mirrored towers.

Today they ran in a medium-sized canal, one about twenty-five paces across but tall enough that the three of them could stand on each other's shoulders and still not reach the ceiling. About halfway up the walls, midwalks ran along both sides of the tunnel. They could run single file up there, but today they felt like going side-by-side, so they stayed on the bottom of the canal despite the dust they stirred up. It swirled around them, red with flecks of blue.

They couldn't see the colors, of course, given that they only wore dim lamps. She knew the details from when this place blazed with light from torches set out by their circle. Their kith and kin. As a dust gang, they protected their circle, who in turn made a home for them all.

Sadness swept over Strider. They no longer had a full dust gang. Jasin had died, killed in the cave-in of a collapsing tunnel last year. Now they had only three.

Running at her side, Lamplight laid his hand on her arm. She nodded, and he nodded back, then withdrew his hand. They didn't need touch to share their grief; it flowed from his mind to hers, just as it flowed to them both from Zee, their third, who ran on Strider's other side.

We need new fourth, Lamp thought. Normally Strider only picked up his moods, but with thoughts this intense, she caught more.

A thought came from Zee, lighter, more fluid. *Crinkles maybe.*

Crinkles too young, Lamp thought. *Baby.*

Strider sent a silent laugh. *Not baby. She twelve. Almost adult. But yah, too young.* Besides, Crinkles had her own group, several other twelve-year-olds who'd someday protect their own circle. Crinkle's sister Darjan would've been a good choice at seventeen, well into adulthood, younger than Jasin by four years, but savvy. Damn good fighter, and not just in what Bhaaj called "street rumbling," though they had no streets here, only canals that had never carried water. As a Dust Knight, Darjan was working toward her first-degree black belt in tykado. Yah, she'd be perfect, except she already had her own gang.

Not get third fem, Lamp protested. *Need man.* Dryly he added, *I outnumbered.*

Strider smiled. He had a point. She knew of no dust gang without that balance, two women, two men. He even used a three-syllable word, *outnumbered,* to emphasize his point.

Then again, the word came in his thoughts, not his speech. Aloud, they used as few words as possible. Those with more than two syllables became jokes, or more rarely showed honor or emphasis. Sure, they thought in a more complex style, including words with many syllables, but they didn't need to waste energy by saying all that talky-talky aloud. They felt what they meant in their moods.

Maybe Nic, she thought. He was working on his brown belt in tykado, and he could run like nobody's business. He'd make a good addition to Coach Mason's city-gang of runners, if anyone could convince him to join.

Jasin would've loved Mason's team.

Strider ran harder, trying to outpace the grief. Lamp and Zee matched her speed, and together they sprinted in honor of Jasin's memory.

After a while, they slowed again, steady and endless, running, running, running.

Nic not good fit, Zee eventually thought.

Yah. Strider knew what she meant. Like them, Nic was also a mooder, what city types called a *Kyle-operator.* He only felt moods a little, though, and he'd never picked up their thoughts. For all that they felt hollow without Jasin, having a fourth who didn't fit would be even worse, like dying of thirst even as they stood in front of water.

A new sense came from Lamp, an unease that prickled up Strider's back.

What? Strider asked.

Someone follows, Lamp thought.

More than one, Zee added.

Strider let her senses expand. Yah, she felt it, people creeping in the canal walls, moving through hidden passages that networked the stone. *Drug punkers,* she thought, pissed off. They didn't need a bunch of raggedy-assed dealers sneaking around Dust Knight territory.

The attack came with no warning. Supposedly. Strider was ready. The punkers slipped out of cracks in the walls above, and two of them jumped down in front of her. In her side vision, she glimpsed more lunging at Zee and Lamp. Ho! A lot more!

With no pause, Strider grabbed one punker and hurtled her into the second. They shouted and attacked, using the rough-and-tumble. She easily countered, rolling one of the punkers over her hip in a tykado move and slamming her onto the ground amid clouds of dust. As the second punker barreled into her, a third grabbed her from behind, and a yet another one socked her in the stomach, so hard she doubled over with a grunt. Somewhere Lamp shouted and Zee groaned. Strider felt their fear; their attackers far outnumbered them.

Strider kept using tykado for the advantage it gave her, uncaring that half her moves were illegal. The hell with slick rules that could cost your life. She bashed the punkers any way that worked, but they kept coming, working her over. She found herself on her knees, choking as she gasped in dust-laden air. While three of them held her down, a woman in front of her drew back her arm, her fist clenched—

"Nahya!" a man shouted. "Stop!"

To Strider's unmitigated surprise—and yah, that word deserved all five syllables—the punker in front of her froze, her fist high in the air. Strider looked past the gritty curls straggling into her eyes to the scene beyond. The punkers were more visible now in light from their tech-mech gauntlets. They all brandished the symbol of the Vakaar cartel on their clothes, a red orb with a white slash. One of them, a man of eighteen, stood on a rock stump. He looked familiar somehow.

"Not fight these three," the guy told the punkers. "Friends." He seemed startled, apparently just recognizing them now that he saw them in brighter light.

Harsh laughter rumbled through the other punkers, all eight of them. Add in the guy on the rock stump, and that made nine attackers.

"Not friends," a woman of about seventeen said. "Dust Knights."

"Maybe," the man said. "But they runners. In Cries. On Mason team. We all on team."

Ho! *Now* Strider recognized him. Dice Vakaar, heir to the cartel queen Hammerjan Vakaar. He was one of two punker kids who'd joined the track and field team. Incredibly, he put that even above beating the shit out of Dust Knights.

A grumble went through his punkers, and they shifted their feet, scowling. Then the three holding down Strider let her go, giving her a rough shove. Standing slowly, stepping back to keep everyone in sight, she gave a wary nod to Dice. He returned it, then motioned to the other punkers. With that, they took off, scrambling up the walls of the canal. In seconds they'd disappeared into the hidden byways of its walls.

"Shit," Lamp muttered, getting back on his feet.

Zee came over to them. "Dice."

"Yah." Strider scowled. "Dice."

"Felt his mind," Lamp said. "He mooder. Like us."

"Yah, I sense, too," Zee said.

"Tough," Strider said. "This *our* land. Punkers not belong." She'd never known them to invade duster places this way. Her dust gang fought to protect their circle or to get food and water. Cartels fought to kill people. They left the dusters alone because it kept the balance; if war broke out between the gangs and the cartels, it could destroy the Undercity.

Why had the punkers broken that unwritten law? They had their own food and water, more than anyone here in Dust Knight territory. The people they addicted to their shit would trade anything to get what they craved.

"Need warn Knights," Strider said.

Damn it all to hell, Ruzik thought. They didn't need this, the cartels destroying the balance that the gangs and punkers had lived by for centuries. The Dust Knights had risen out of the dust gangs, established with Bhaaj's leadership, making it even riskier for the punkers to invade their territory. Yet here they'd come in force, ready to fight, maybe kill.

He sat on a rock stump in the cave he used for meetings while Strider and her gang reported the attack. Ruzik's brother, Byte-2, sat on a sawed-off stalagmite. The third in their gang, the woman called Tower, leaned her muscled self against another rock formation. Just as Strider's gang had one person missing, so did Ruzik's, though for him it was temporary. His wife Angel had gone to her job with the Kyle Corps in the City of Cries.

Odd, that. Cries ignored his people if they stayed in the Undercity or threw them in jail for no damn reason if they went above. At least they used to. Now, with Mason's team and Angel's job, they were trickling out of the Undercity. The Kyle Corps insisted anyone who could mood-feel could join them. Of course no one here wanted their jobs. Slicks only offered life-threatening, menial labor to Undercity folk.

Except.

This Kyle Corps seemed different. They considered Angel's job high-powered, even elite. Besides, someone had to spy on the slicks and figure out their sudden interest in the Undercity. Who better than Angel? Damn smart, that wife of his.

Strider's gang had no such comfort for their loss. A year had passed since Jasin's death, but nothing eased their grief. As much as they needed a fourth, finding someone whose Kyle abilities matched their strength wasn't easy. Even in the Undercity where Kyle traits supposedly occurred at more than three thousand times normal human populations, few existed as strong as Strider, Lamp, and Zee. Ruzik understood; he, Angel, his brother, and Tower shared a similar bond.

"Not see why punkers invade us," Strider was saying.

"Hungry, maybe," Ruzik said. "They not as rich as before war."

"Ass-bytes," Lamp said. "Nine of them, three of us. We get more gangers, go hit back."

"Nahya," Ruzik said. "Not fight." The cartel war from four years ago still remained vivid in his memory, how it had devastated the Undercity, killing people and collapsing two major canals, those "architectural wonders," as city types called the ruins here. They'd cared more about the canals than the people. That was before they discovered those same people might be the most important resource they'd ever found.

"Cartels weak now," Ruzik said.

"Not enough food," Byte-2 said.

"Not enough good water," Tower said.

Zee crossed her arms. "*We* need our food. Our water. Got less than them."

"Used to be that way," Strider spoke thoughtfully. "Now? Maybe not."

Lamp scowled. "Nahya."

"Mason gets us food," Ruzik pointed out.

Zee spoke with disgust. "We not take *char-i-tee*."

As much as Ruzik understood how they loathed handouts, his people needed good food and filtered water. Toxins saturated the water on this world with its failing terraforming, where the best places on the surface had become deserts and the rest of the world grew more hostile to human life every generation. Down here, chemicals and minerals in the rare underground grottos and streams poisoned anyone desperate enough to drink the untreated water.

"Not charity," he told Strider. "Bargain. We run for Mason's team. He give water and food."

"Dice let us go," Strider mused. "Say Mason's team like circle."

Ruzik motioned toward Tower and Byte-2. "We look into it."

Strider nodded. "And we say if we learn more."

"Yah. Good." Rumors always swirled in the Whisper Mill, the Undercity version of what above-city types called *social media meshes*, except here the whispers were all verbal.

After Strider's gang left, Ruzik sent Byte-2 and Tower to sleuth out if anyone else had rumbled with the cartels. It worried him. His gang protected the largest Undercity circle, including single adults, families who looked after children, and his best friend, Hack, a cyber-rider who could best any Cries tech with his genius. People in his circle tended to live longer, well into their twenties, even thirties. He meant for it to stay that way.

The odds for survival in *all* circles had improved in recent years, and even more since Mason started providing food to the Undercity athletes after practices. Vegetables and fruit. And steak! As much as the nutritionists who worked with Mason's team cautioned against too much meat, Undercity athletes craved it. They hunted pico-lizards and mousites down here, but those were scant and stringy in their flesh.

At first, the rich Cries diet had made Ruzik queasy. Plants here lived mostly in the dark. If you cobbled together a power source, you could use LED lights to grow some species. Those helped provide food, also oxygen and humidity, but no way could they produce enough for a place this large. After stealing time on the Cries university meshes, he'd realized some of their plants survived in the dark by getting cozy with bacteria, taking energy from chemical reactions. Oxygen also came from algae that grew in the poisonous water, but humans couldn't eat it. They did cultivate edible fungi, like the sweet-meat mushrooms that thrived in the dark. He loved the taste, especially when cooks in his circle grilled and spiced the delicacy.

Still, he had a lot to consider in his job as second in command for the Dust Knights. The plants alone couldn't provide enough oxygen for everyone to breathe or take away all the carbon dioxide they produced. Their survival also relied on a vast network of ancient conduits that spread throughout the Undercity and circulated air from the desert above. These past years, he'd worked to strengthen the ranks of their rock-riders, the Undercity diggers who kept the ventilation systems in good repair. They had more than enough good air, but even with Mason's help, they still barely had enough food. If the cartels stole their scant resources, they'd starve. They needed a better solution for circles and cartels both. No one wanted charity.

"Charity, hell," Ruzik muttered. Until recent years, the Cries doctors had refused to treat his people, not even the most basic care *everyone* in the city received. Well, no more. The Undercity deserved the same resources that slicks took for granted. He and Angel had traveled to the planet Parthonia last year to help Bhaaj solve a case—and they'd found paradise. Pure water, free and unlimited. You needed only turn on a "faucet," and out it came. Flowers, trees, bushes, and vines grew everywhere, fragrant and beautiful. Goddess, that such a place could exist.

Yet everywhere they'd gone, he'd heard shit about the Undercity, how his people were less than human, dirty, ugly, stupid, all homeless drug addicts and criminals. The Skolian Imperialate, a civilization that claimed thousands of worlds and habitats, had no idea about the true Undercity, the great beauty here. Yah, they also fought crushing poverty and drugs, but they needed resources to fix those problems, not demonization. They'd lived here for thousands of years, ignored and dismissed. They didn't like Cries any more than Cries liked them; they kept to themselves, protecting their fragile culture against the outside universe. But that meant the rest of humanity knew nothing except the ugly stories that trickled out about the drug cartels, the only group in the Undercity with even scant offworld connections. His people had long ago become convenient villains for a star-spanning media.

Except then it all changed.

The military discovered the Undercity had something they wanted, something they needed desperately. Over a third of Ruzik's people were full-fledged Kyle operators, carrying in their DNA certain neurological mutations that had become almost extinct among the rest of humanity—traits so valuable to the survival of the Skolian Imperialate that the authorities refused to let anyone know what existed here, lest that knowledge endanger their priceless Undercity resource.

Yah, charity be damned. It was time his people took their place among the vast, star-flung civilizations of humanity, one they belonged to just as much as anyone else.

Change was coming.

CHAPTER III
Kiro

When Kiro reached the track in the Cries stadium, many runners had already arrived, chatting and warming up. He held back, unsure what to do. In the meet yesterday, he'd run with the Abyss Associates team, but they'd barely managed even to get here. Afterward, he'd had to listen while they complained about the Undercity runners winning so many medals. Seriously? If they wanted to win medals, they ought to try practicing. No rules prohibited Undercity athletes from running better than everyone else.

Kiro wanted to run that well. He hoped to qualify for the Olympics next year. Hell, he'd wanted it all his life. No chance of that existed if he stayed with the Abyss team. They only got together when they wanted to party, then complained when they came in last at the local meets.

So today, he showed up to practice with Mason's Raylicon Track and Field team. It didn't even sound overblown for Mason to name his Cries team for an entire world, given that almost no one lived on Raylicon except in this city. He ran the Olympics trials here and trained the athletes who would represent Raylicon at the Olympics.

Kiro had heard Coach Mason would let anyone try out with his team, but now he had doubts. He felt out of place. Awkward moods swirled around the runners as the Cries and Undercity athletes watched each other. As always, Kiro avoided people, especially those with intense emotions. His reputation suffered from what many called his "standoffish" nature, but he'd learned to live with it. They had no idea how it felt to soak in everyone's mood until you wanted to disappear. Sometimes he thought he'd go crazy. He feared to let anyone know his weakness, even his parents.

He had no siblings to share his moods. His parents had followed the unwritten rules, limiting their progeny to conserve resources on this dying world. If not for the great wealth of the Majda family, the terraforming on Raylicon would have failed so badly, no one could live here. But this planet had been the original home to a group of humans long ago displaced from Earth, and it remained home to one of the most powerful families in existence. Even the Majdas couldn't redo an entire world, but they kept this region livable, including their mountain palace and the City of Cries.

On other worlds, Kiro knew he probably couldn't make the Olympic team. Here, he might. He'd worked hard for years, mostly on his own, running through the beautiful, nearly deserted streets that wound into the foothills of the San Parval Mountains, an isolation that protected his mind from the onslaught of human emotions. His best events weren't distance, though, but sprints. He practiced those constantly. With his self-training, he'd managed to increase his speed until he could almost reach an Olympic-qualifying time. Although it made him the best athlete on the Abyss team, that meant almost nothing. So today, he showed up uninvited for Coach Mason's practice.

Orbs spun in the air above the runners, and a man's voice came from one of them. "All right, folks. Get to your lanes. Okay, well, I know we haven't assigned anyone a lane. Just find a place. We'll start with an easy run. I don't recognize a lot of you, so I'd like to see how this fits together. Have fun! No pressure, enjoy yourselves."

Kiro smiled. That sounded like Mason. Although he didn't know the coach well, he'd always liked what he sensed from him. Mason seemed a good person, relaxed and welcoming, without the arrogance and ingrained assumption of privilege Kiro felt from so many of his peers at Cries University. Not everyone at school came across that way, but enough that in his accounting classes, he usually tried to find a seat with no one nearby, or else he attended via the mesh as a holographic student. He preferred running to math and databases, anyway.

Kiro jogged toward the starting line glowing on the track. Other

"What happened, Abby boy?" Hyden taunted. "You get kicked off your crappy Abyss team? Got nothing left to join but dust rats, hmmm? Get in at the bottom of the barrel."

Kiro scowled, but before he could answer, even if he'd known what to say, an Undercity runner said, "Shut mouth, ass-byte."

"You talking to me, dust rat?" Hyden asked.

"Enough!" someone said. Kiro turned with a jerk to see Coach Mason a few steps away. He spoke to them all, Cries and Undercity athletes alike. "If you want to run with my team, you treat each other with respect. *All* of you."

Hyden gave him a dismissive look. The Undercity runners kept their faces impassive, but Kiro sensed their mood toward Hyden. Yes, *fuck you* applied just fine.

A beautiful woman stood with Mason, as tall and as striking as an ancient warrior queen. She had an Undercity look, the same features, dark trousers, and a tank top, what they called a muscle shirt. However, she carried herself with an ease in her surroundings that suggested she came from Cries. She seemed familiar, but he couldn't figure out why.

Wait. Now he remembered. Coach Bhaajan, the retired army major who led the Undercity team. Of course! He'd heard of her, not only at the meet a few days ago, but also from holo-casts. She was the Undercity native who'd escaped the slum, joined the army, done the impossible by becoming an officer, and then retired to work as a PI for the Majdas. No wonder she seemed more at home here than the other Undercity athletes. She'd dealt with the Imperialate elite for decades.

The coaches withdrew and Mason called a start. When one of the orbs produced the bark of a starting gun, the Undercity runners literally jumped, then lunged into an explosive start, leaving Kiro behind. He sprinted after them, trying to catch up. The girl who had greeted him glanced back, then slowed to run with him. Her two friends followed suit, so they were all together. Startled, Kiro stumbled, then caught his balance. He couldn't figure out what they were doing, but if they wanted to run with him, that helped speed him up, since their natural pace seemed faster than his. They fell into a rhythm, running in step.

Kiro managed to stay with them for the first lap around the track. As he flagged in the second lap, they gestured at him, urging him to speed up. Shaking his head, he motioned them forward. So they all sped up, like three cogs in unison. An odd pang came to him, a sense of loss. Strange. He wished he could have kept their pace.

It had felt right to run with them.

"They all seemed tense out there today," Bhaaj said, an understatement if she'd ever uttered one.

"No kidding." Mason settled into a plush chair in his big office, the extravagant place the stadium officials had provided him inside this amazing sports center. Like everything else in Cries, it operated as an elite facility for an elite city—with almost no elite athletes to use it.

"The animosity felt so thick, you could've cut it with a knife." Mason winced. "Maybe I shouldn't say knife? Though I'd swear, Bhaaj, some of your kids looked like they were carrying. I don't mean to stereotype, but this team won't work with so much hostility among the athletes."

Bhaaj felt too wound up to relax. "I'm worried what will happen when some Cries athletes lose their shot at the Olympics because Undercity runners did better in your qualifiers."

"With so many people trying out this year, I have to pick a training team. I have good resources, but not enough to prepare this many athletes at the level they need for the Olympics." He suddenly grinned, his face transforming. "Bhaaj, you brought me a gold mine. The talent of your athletes is obvious. It won't be a problem. Everyone knows I can only take the top contenders."

You have no idea, Bhaaj thought.

Her thought must have been more intense than she realized, toggling her communication with Max, her EI. **Tell him,** Max thought. **He needs to know.**

Bhaaj exhaled. The more she could overcome her ingrained tendency to say as few words as possible, the better for her runners. "Maybe you should consider taking more than twenty-five people for the training team. Cries athletes might be less willing to lose a spot to mine than you realize." During her early army days, too many people had assumed that because she came from the Undercity, she should get the worst assignments. If she excelled, it didn't change their minds, it just pissed them off. "We need to find some way that encourages these kids to like each other."

"A party!" Mason beamed at her. "We'll invite everyone to a meet-and-greet right here in the stadium. It will be great! They'll have fun."

Bhaaj didn't know whether to laugh or stare with disbelief. "Mason, Undercity kids don't want to party with Cries kids. They wouldn't come, except maybe Angel and Ruzik. Even if anyone else did show up, it wouldn't be long before the taunts started on both sides." Dryly she added, "It could end up in fights. My kids would pulverize yours."

Disappointment washed over his face. "Why would they want to, uh, pulverize mine?"

"It's how they act when they're uncomfortable."

He crossed his arms. "If any of your runners fight any of mine, they are *off* the team. I don't care how well they do. It's zero-tolerance. You make sure they know that!"

"They know." She chose her words with care. "For thousands of years, my people have kept to themselves. Sure, every now and then you hear about a secret love affair, or someone sneaks into the Undercity and gets mugged. But willing participation, my people invited to join with yours? This is a first." Bhaaj paused, awkward with so many words. Still, she had to speak; this was too important. "We're setting a precedent. We need to do it right."

Mason rubbed his chin. "Your runners do seem uneasy here."

"They feel like interlopers." She reviewed the day in her mind. "It was odd, though. Strider and her gang asked that kid from your team to run with them."

Mason blinked at her. "Who is Strider?"

"Sorry, I shouldn't give her name. The girl in the green muscle shirt with vine designs."

Mason's forehead wrinkled. "Why shouldn't you give her name?"

"We never do in the Undercity." As much as Bhaaj disliked having to reveal so much about her people, the more Mason understood, the more chance they had that this would work. "You don't give your name unless you trust a person. It's considered an honor. Same with smiles. That's why it looks like my runners are always glowering."

Mason spoke wryly. "I think they look that way because they *are* glowering."

She gave a dry laugh. "Yah, could be."

"So how do you suggest we improve matters?"

Bhaaj wished she had an answer. "I think for now, we need to let them decide. Partially. Let them follow the lead of Tayz Wilder among your people and Ruzik among mine."

"Partially?"

"We also need to stop any fights before they start."

"Like today." Mason scowled. "What the blazes am I going to do with Hyden Laj? He's a great runner, but saints that man can be a pain."

"Who?"

"Laj. The fellow who trash-talked your athletes." He paused, squinting. "Actually, I think he was trashing one from Cries. It's that kid from the Abyss team, their top runner. What's he called?" He snapped his fingers. "Kiro! Laj was trashing him for starting with your runners."

"Laj?" Bhaaj tried to remember where she'd heard the name. "Don't they run Scorpio Corporation?" Given the cutthroat universe of high-stakes finance, enough turnover existed in the top positions to make it hard to follow if it wasn't your interest.

"That's right." Mason blew out a gust of air. "Not the easiest family to deal with, but I need to. They're the biggest supporter of the team after the Majdas. They expect Hyden to go to all the major meets with us." When Bhaaj started to scowl, Mason held up his hand. "He's an excellent marathoner. He'll qualify, including against your runners."

"Some of my runners do look lousy out there," Bhaaj admitted. "Yah, they're fast, but they have bad habits. We have our work cut out for us."

"Ah. Hmm." He shifted in his chair. "Yes."

She regarded him warily. For Mason, that qualified as a markedly terse response. "What?"

"About coaching—"

"Yah?" Remembering herself, Bhaaj switched into the Cries dialect. "Yes?"

"You said 'we' have a lot of work to do."

Oh. Of course. "Sorry. I meant you. I don't mean to intrude. I've been working with them in the desert because they need to adapt to running outside instead of underground. And to learn how things work." She grimaced. "Like the starting orb. I had to make sure they knew no one was shooting at them."

Mason squinted at her. "Shooting at them?"

Bhaaj didn't want to go there, but she wanted even less to see problems with the team. "You can find guns all over the Undercity, including ancient ones. To them, the noise your starter orb makes sounds like a weapon."

"I hadn't realized." He considered her. "I'm beginning to understand the Majdas' position."

"What position?"

"Well, yes, you see, that's why, um, I need to talk to you. I know you're busy and all, that you've a lot of work elsewhere, I mean, I'd never assume, but they insist. The Majdas are our largest donor, especially these past few years since Azarina joined."

"I've heard." Mason had recruited Angel because Colonel Lavinda Majda suggested it after seeing Angel win the Selei City Open on Parthonia. "But what does that have to do with me?"

"You work for the Majdas."

"As a PI." Right now, her only case involved digging up secrets in some abstruse financial thing.

He cleared his throat. "I understand. But uh, they insist."

"Insist what?" She scowled at him. "That I don't involve myself?" That could be a problem, given that her runners didn't trust anyone here. She'd have to talk to Lavinda, one of the three Majda sisters who ran the family empire. Bhaaj knew Lavinda better than the other two sisters. The oldest, Vaj, the Majda Matriarch, also served as General to the Pharaoh's Army, making her one of the most powerful human beings alive. Not exactly approachable.

"It's the opposite." Mason tried to regard her with an impassive look, an impossible quest given his expressive face. He obviously felt ill at ease. "They want me to make you a team coach."

Bhaaj didn't get the problem. "I already work with my runners."

"They want you added as an official Olympic coach. They don't think I know how to handle your athletes." Leaning forward, he spoke intently. "I'll tell you what this is about. They're tired of sponsoring one of the worst teams in the history of track and field. Goddess, what do they expect? Look at the planet Metropoli. They have *ten billion* people, and they only send three teams. For the *entire* planet. How can we compete against that?" Sitting up, he waved his hand. "I'll tell you how. The Undercity. It's like you're genetically altered to go fast.

Except you aren't! We can prove it's the genuine gene pool, not illegal tinkering, especially given that no doctors ever went to the Undercity until recent years. We didn't even know you existed. I mean, we did, sort of—"

"Mason! Stop." Bhaaj held up her hand, laughing. "I get the idea. And sure, put me as an official coach. You have to stay as the primary, though. You're the one with the experience."

He sat back with undisguised relief. "Well. Good. Yes. Thank you."

It did make sense. Bhaaj had spent more than four years on retainer for the House of Majda, not only because she did her job well, but also because only she could solve cases for them that involved entry into the elusive, secret world of the Undercity. If they wanted their track and field team to do better, it made sense to have their liaison with the Undercity work with the athletes.

Even with her help, though, they had no idea where this divisive situation might lead, as the Undercity dust gangs mixed with the Cries elite.

CHAPTER IV
Cries

Too many people.

When Angel walked into the lobby of Selei Tower in Cries, she found it crowded in a way she'd never seen before. Execs in glossy suits stood around talking and drinking stuff in crystal goblets. It looked like what these people called a "reception."

Ignoring the gathering, she headed for the lift across the lobby. As she reached it, a woman stepped in front of her, a guard in the uniform of Selei Tower Security.

"You stop right there," the woman said. "This building is off-limits to the public. You have to leave. *Now*."

Angel spoke in the Cries dialect. "I'm going to work." She indicated the badge on her belt. "I'm in the Kyle Division."

The guard frowned at her. Then she tapped the high-tech gauntlet on her wrist, bringing up small hieroglyphics that floated above its screen. She glanced at Angel's badge, then tapped her gauntlet again, rewarding herself with more holos, what slicks called holicons.

"Huh. Your ID is in the system." Rather than relieved, the guard seemed angrier, as if Angel had robbed her of a satisfying moment. She jerked her head toward the lift. "Get up there and don't bother anyone. Just do your cleaning or whatever and mind your business."

Angel knew she should just nod and leave. This guard pissed her off, though. Seriously, what did she think? Drones did cleaning, not people. You didn't need to feed drones, except recharging them every now and then. Instead of just going on her way, Angel said, "I'm a telop, not a cleaner."

The guard rested her hand on the pistol holstered on her belt. "What did you say, girl?"

Be cool, Angel reminded herself. *No punching*. When she'd started this job, she'd held back because she promised Bhaaj not to get into fights. Now she did because she enjoyed seeing slicks get bent out of shape when she confounded their assumptions. She made herself sound pleasant. "I don't mean disrespect, ma'am. You can check it in my ID."

The guard squinted at her, then went back to her gauntlet, tapping away. "I don't believe it," she muttered. Looking up, she spoke harshly. "Go on. Get out of here."

"Thank you." Angel felt like saying more, a lot less polite, but never mind. The lift had picked up the signal from her badge and opened its glass doors. After she went inside the waiting car, it closed its attractive but breakable self and headed up the tower. The guard stood below, watching, her upward-tilted face visible through the reinforced dichromesh-glass floor. Then she shook her head and walked away, back to guarding the slicks in their glossy suits.

Angel wondered about the party. The people looked like execs, an occupation that had never interested her. Learning how to use her brain to access the ancient Kyle tech—now *that* she wanted. Most slicks couldn't do it. Even her trainers didn't do it well. No matter.

She'd learn regardless of what they knew. Or didn't know.

Kiro jogged home from practice, thinking over the day. He'd kept up reasonably well with the other Cries athletes; if they were his only competition, he'd have a good shot at making the training team. But where had all those Undercity runners come from? He'd counted thirty-eight, plus two preteens who should be working with juniors. Realistically, though, no one else would take Undercity juniors. Mason was an outlier, which was one reason Kiro liked him. The coach didn't fake his acceptance of the Undercity runners; he considered them no different than anyone else.

Except they *were* different. The vague impressions Kiro picked up from them suggested their mental landscapes were far more active in words, thoughts, and images than their terse speech. Despite their impassive exteriors, their minds felt rich with moods. They seemed like sleek cars with hidden capabilities. He had no idea why he interested Strider and her friends, whose names he'd figured out from their minds, but he looked forward to seeing them at the next practice.

He soon left the city behind. The streets became boulevards shaded by droop-willows, like feathery lace created by nature. Except nature hadn't made these trees, at least not here. He'd learned about them in his terraforming class at Cries University. Nothing lived on Raylicon except spiky, drought-resistant vegetation and a few flowers that bloomed at night. The rest of their flora came from offworld. Biogeneticists adapted it to Raylicon, but the plants still needed water without poisons. The city farmed water from below ground, purified it, and doused the greenery until it thrived, thick and lush. That wasn't only for beauty; no one wanted a lawsuit if someone ate a plant and got sick or died due to some toxin it had absorbed from unfiltered water.

Kiro kept running, going higher into yet more secluded areas. The houses became mansions on acres of land and then vanished from view, set too far back from the road to see. Eventually he came to an archway framed by a trellis heavy with pink and red flowers. Jogging under it, he entered a pathway bordered on either side by an artistic jumble of shrubs that looked natural, except he knew the gardeners spent hours coaxing them into that "wild" beauty.

After a few kilometers, the path widened into a circular driveway that curved in front of a mansion. Kiro avoided the driveway and took a pathway around the side of the house. He didn't stop until he reached a vine-draped archway with a wooden door. He'd realized years ago that most houses here didn't use wood because trees didn't normally grow on Raylicon. You had to import the material or else cut down valuable trees designed for beauty. He didn't know why his parents chose wood, but he liked the effect. Opening the door, he walked into a pretty foyer tiled with white squares, each with flowering vines painted around its edges.

"Identity verified," the house EI told him. The door closed and clicked as its locks activated. The security seemed overdone to him; people rarely came this high in the Willow District, and no one bothered to follow the long pathway to the house. Even so. His mother wanted it that way, so that was what they did.

A small cleaning bot hummed by him, cleaning up whatever it

found on the floors. He saw nothing of the drones that took care of the walls or ceiling. His parents even had a few human servants, and he almost never saw them, either.

As Kiro walked down the hall, he thought about the practice. He'd missed more classes at the university today so he'd have time to warm up at the stadium. It meant that tonight he'd need to watch holovids of the lectures and do his neglected course work. He had to keep up; if he failed out of school, his parents would make him stop running. He didn't much like the accounting major they'd urged on him, but he disliked the idea of giving up running even more, so he crammed in his studies around his training schedule.

"Kiro, is that you?" a woman called.

Following her voice, he walked into the kitchen and found his mother sitting at the center island with Jasmin, their full-time chef.

"Heya, Hoshma." Kiro sat across from them. "Sorry I'm late. I ran home."

"You should let me know," his mother said. "I was worried."

"I will." Sometime in the past few years, he'd stopped being annoyed when she scolded him, probably because she treated him like an adult now instead of a kid.

"Would you like dinner?" Jasmin tilted her head toward the cooler. "I kept a plate for you."

"Thanks." As much as he loved her cooking, he couldn't eat so soon after working out. "I'll have it later."

Jasmin glanced from him to his mother, then said, "I'll leave you to it, then."

"You have a good evening." Kiro's mother sounded preoccupied. After Jasmin left, she said, "Kiro, make sure you eat. You're too thin."

"I will." He was more concerned about her. She looked exhausted, her dark eyes hollow from a lack of sleep. "Are you all right?"

"Of course." She shrugged, an elegant motion, like everything else about her, from her tailored grey suit to her minimal gold and diamond necklace. She had tech-bracelets on her wrists far more complex than any Kiro owned, and his had cost thousands of byte-bucks. As always, she wore her hair in a graceful coil on her head.

"Did you work late again?" he asked. Although he rarely saw his father, a commercial starship captain, his mother was usually here. Except not so much lately.

"Unfortunately." She exhaled. "We're fighting a takeover attempt by Scorpio Corporation."

"Ah." Kiro didn't know exactly what that involved. Despite majoring in accounting, he'd never quite figured out what his mother did. Sure, he knew her title: Predictive Analyst. Something with databases that she rarely talked about. She usually wanted to talk about his life instead.

His father remained less interested in his running. He'd only say, "I don't understand what you *do* with it." Given that he was almost never here, though, they didn't get into arguments, especially after Kiro outgrew the stage where he defied them just because they were his parents. Seriously, how had they put up with his teenaged self? He was probably as glad as them that he'd finished that angsty stage of his life.

Right now, he worried more for his mother. "You need to get more rest."

"So do you." Her gaze turned curious. "What did you think of Coach Mason's team?"

"It's a good workout. I felt less..." He stopped, unsure how to describe feelings he didn't understand that well himself. "Less isolated. The runners are more like me."

Concern shaded her expression. "Did you have any problems? Any panic attacks?"

"Mother, for flaming sake. I don't have panic attacks."

She raised an eyebrow. "Really? What would you call them?"

"I get tense, that's all. It's like—" What could he say, that other people's emotions pushed on his mind until he had to escape or else have a convulsion? Right, sure, that would make him sound real stable. Instead, just said, "I felt fine."

"Good." She didn't look convinced, but she let it go. They talked a while longer and then he headed off to his portion of the mansion. He lived by himself, secluded in his wing. Although he'd considered moving into a dorm at the university, he gave up the idea when he realized he'd live close to a lot of other students and share a room. He couldn't bear the proximity to so many other people. Besides, he had everything he needed here.

You're a spoiled asshole, he thought. He'd seen the way the Undercity kids wolfed down the food Coach Mason provided after practices, and how they packed away extra supplies for later. He couldn't imagine how their lives worked, living underground in... in what? Caves? It went beyond his ability to comprehend. Yeah, he was an asshole, taking his advantages for granted.

He had no idea what to do about it, though. The Undercity runners kept to themselves, silent and impassive. The three who invited him to run today had given the only hint that any of them might want to interact. Well, except that fellow Ruzik. He and Tayz Wilder seemed on good terms. The thought of talking to someone like Ruzik so intimidated Kiro that if he *had* been the type to have panic attacks, it could have started one. The guy looked ready to kill someone, with all those scars, muscles, and tattoos.

Ruzik had implanted circuit designs, too, but those couldn't last. Coach Mason had told everyone to get rid of *anything* that might disqualify them. The only approved aids were the health meds everyone carried in their bodies. No one expected athletes to risk their health. Still, the meds had to meet the standards set up by the Interstellar Olympic Committee, with no illegal enhancers.

You need to check yours, he reminded himself. His meds were high enough in quality that they might look like augmentation. He'd talk to Coach Mason. Of course, any meet where they competed would also test the athletes for enhancement, including drugs, genetic tinkering, implants, or anything else designed to give them an edge. Kiro had no interest in those extras. He wanted to succeed on his own merits.

Eventually he reached his rooms, a pleasant suite paneled in sunwood. After he showered and changed, he sat at the desk in his office with its holoscreen, holo-readers, virtual-reality setup, and library mods. He'd cram in as much studying as he could tonight before he fell asleep sitting here, like he did most nights, living in his introverted world, with no one to share his life except his preoccupied mother, distant father, and servants he rarely saw. He stayed safe from the universe, lost in his own world—

And so very, very lonely.

CHAPTER V
The First Tunnel

The grotto normally made Ruzik feel peaceful. Today, it didn't work. Yah, sure, crystals in the rock glittered, the water gleamed with phosphorescence, and the graceful sculptures shone. Light from torches on the walls lit the place, drawing sparkles from the rock, turning it into a place of magic. Or whatever. Today he couldn't stop worrying.

"How many punkers?" Bhaaj asked. She was sitting on a rose-quartz bench the sculptors in Ruzik's circle had carved to resemble a giant pico-lizard.

"Strider say nine," Ruzik said. After spending his time in Cries, using their endlessly wordy dialect, it felt good to talk like a normal person. "All punkers. Like Dice."

Bhaaj grimaced. "And if Dice not there? Punkers kill Strider's gang?"

"Not sure," Ruzik admitted. "Maybe. Maybe just crush."

"Why?"

Good question. "I think for food. Water."

Bhaaj rubbed her chin, her face thoughtful. Dust had drifted over her hair, and the lights in the grotto drew glints of blue and red from the grains, making her curls glitter. On days when Ruzik came here with Angel, this place soothed them both. Today, none of that mattered. They needed to figure out why the cartels had invaded their territory before someone got killed.

"Dice is Vakaar," Bhaaj said.

"Yah, Vakaar. Not Kajada." So far, no one from the Kajada cartel had showed up.

Bhaaj gave a dry laugh. "We could go ask cartel."

"Yah, sure." Ruzik snorted. "Might as well just walk up, ask them to beat on us."

"I ask Dice," Bhaaj decided. "At next practice with team."

"Could," Ruzik allowed. "Better I ask. You head of Knights." It seemed less confrontational to start with him instead of Bhaaj, their biggest metaphorical gun.

"Yah. Good." With satisfaction, she added, "Strider and them—they bash punkers, eh?"

"Yah. Hard. Vakaars not ken tykado." He grimaced. "But it nine on three. Bad odds."

"Cartels not like Dust Knights."

No kidding. Bhaaj made the Knights swear off drugs. Ruzik had smoked hack as a kid, and he hadn't wanted to give it up at first, but it turned out she had a point. He did feel stronger now, especially on Mason's team.

They all knew Bhaaj had run with a gang in her youth, one led by Dig Kajada, the daughter of the Kajada cartel boss back then. Bhaaj and Dig, they'd been like sisters. Dig had never punked drugs—until the previous Vakaar queen murdered her mother. After that, Dig took over the Kajada cartel and went on a rampage against Vakaar. Bhaaj had already left for the army, and by the time she came home, Dig had become the most notorious cartel boss in Undercity history. The war exploded not long after, killing both Dig and the Vakaar queen. Ruzik felt Bhaaj's grief. She mourned her sister, both her death and what she'd become.

He said only, "Dust Knight Code, it honor the Dig you knew."

Bhaaj stared out at the shimmering grotto. Ironic, that water with such beauty could kill any human foolish enough to drink it. "Yah," she murmured.

Enough said. He understood.

She turned back to him. "Good that punkers not know tykado. Not need them get better at whacking people."

"Plenty good at it without tykado." As long as Bhaaj kept the prohibition against drugs in the Code every Knight had to swear, no punkers could join her tykado classes. Of course, that made the cartels want to break the Knights even more, especially Bhaaj.

Except.

The current Kajada cartel queen, Cutter Kajada, considered Bhaaj family. Sort of. Ruzik had no doubt that if Bhaaj stirred things up too much, Cutter could change her mind. Bhaaj hadn't done shit, though, except help coach a sports team with a bunch of slicks from Cries.

"Shiv Kajada on Mason's team too," Ruzik said.

"Kajada not bash any Knights."

"Not yet."

"Maybe Angel talk to Shiv at next meet," Bhaaj suggested.

"Yah. Good." If he talked to Dice and Angel talked to Shiv, they might figure out what was up with the cartels.

Bhaaj's voice lightened. "How Angel like new job?"

"Says okay."

"They treat her right?"

"In Kyle Division, yah." Ruzik shrugged. "Others, not so much." As much as he wanted to crack anyone who dissed his wife, he also wanted to prove Undercity natives weren't the vicious thugs everyone in Cries assumed. Besides, Angel was perfectly capable of taking care of it herself.

Ruzik wondered how Bhaaj had managed when she enlisted. Now the Undercity had her as their liaison, and she had the ear of the most powerful people on the planet. When Bhaaj had started out all those years ago, she'd had no patron, no Majda, no nothing. She rarely talked about that time, but he'd seen the haunted look she usually managed to hide. Whatever had happened, she'd survived. Hell, she'd beat the slicks at their own games and then some.

Now they had new work to do, to make sure the cartels didn't blow apart their lives.

Angel liked her office in the Kyle Division. She never tired of staring out the windows, which wrapped around two walls. Sunlight poured through them and showed Cries spread out far below, all gleaming buildings and greenery. Beyond it, the desert stretched to the horizon in dunes of sand, sand, and more sand, red and gold. In the east, mountains towered above the city, sharp like knives in the pale sky. The Majdas lived up there in their palace.

Angel squinted against the glare. "Too bright," she told the room.

"Increasing polarization of glass," an androgynous voice said, the EI that served her office. It called itself EI-142. Every now and then she thought of giving it a more creative name, but only when it annoyed her, and those names didn't seem fair given that most times it did a good job. Besides, she was trying to clean up her language around slicks, so they'd quit thinking she wanted to beat them up. Or weird variations of that concept. One time, a fashion exec had asked if she'd model for their "rough-n-tumble" line of clothes. They said she fit the look they wanted, "gorgeous and ready to kill." Angel told them no. She had no current plans to kill anyone.

Today EI-142 changed the tint of the windows enough to dim the glare but still leave her office full of sunlight. "Is that sufficient?" it asked.

"Yah, good." Angel could stare all day at that view. She didn't, because she liked doing her job more, but right now she let sunlight bathe her face as she sat in her smart chair at her smart desk with her smart console. Very intelligent office. Especially the console. Cyber riders in the Undercity made consoles unlike anything in Cries, cobbling them together from tech-mech they stole, salvaged from Cries, or got on the shadow market that dealt in stolen goods. This one was brand-sparkling-new. It worked, too, mostly, and if it had problems, she needed only to comm someone from "IT-Mesh" to fix it. These ITM slicks were like junior cyber-riders. They didn't have the know-how and creativity of a rider, but they could repair city tech like no one else.

"Angel?" a voice asked.

Looking around, she saw a woman in the arched doorway of her office. "Eh, Gabrial." Two words for a greeting, a lot, but Gabrial was good people.

Gabrial smiled amiably. "Do you ever close this door? It's always wide open to the hall."

"Not need." Back home, where she and Ruzik lived with their circle, they had no doors, only walls. Closing a door never occurred to Angel, besides which, almost no one ever walked by.

Gabrial looked sunny today, in her golden tunic and trousers. The bright color offset her dark skin and eyes, and the straight black hair that poured over her shoulders. "I'm going to the training center to work on the mesh connectors," the young woman said. "Don't you have an appointment today to meet your new tutors? We could walk there together."

So many words just to say, *Testing, eh. Come with?* Even so. Angel enjoyed her company. She went over to the delicate Gabrial, aware of her greater height. They were the same age, mid-twenties, but Gabrial seemed so fragile. She'd never last in the Undercity if she showed up there alone. Then again, she'd never come to Undercity, so no need to worry.

An odd thought occurred to Angel. Maybe Gabrial *could* visit sometime, meet her circle.

"You still here?" Gabrial asked after Angel had stood thinking for a while.

"Eh?" Angel focused on her. "Yah. Let's go."

They left the office in companionable silence.

"Just tell me what you see," Angel's new Kyle tutor repeated. He was pretending to be patient, but she could tell he believed she had a brain smaller than a scuttle-bug. Enough already. She'd answered his questions over and over again.

"Round," Angel said. Again.

The tutor, a man in his thirties, stood in front of a large mesh screen that glowed on the wall. It showed a simple image, a round blue tunnel that looked as if it extended back into the screen, going on forever, shrinking to a point in the far distance.

"Round like what?" the tutor asked. He held a console plate with holos floating above it. Every time Angel answered, he flicked his fingers through the holos, making them jump and flash.

"Like round." Angel couldn't figure out what he wanted. It wasn't square, hexagonal, triangular or any other shape.

"A lot of things are round," he said. "Can you be more specific?" His thought came through to her clearly. *Goddess, she's stupid. Why the blazes did they hire her?*

Angel blinked, startled. Normally she only picked up thoughts from Ruzik and their dust gang. With slicks, never. Then again, this guy wouldn't be in the Kyle division if he didn't have the mood thing more strongly than most people. Impressive, but he was still being an ass-byte.

"Round like circle," Angel said.

He set his film on a nearby stool. "Can you tell me something?"

Probably not. "What?" she asked.

"How did you get this job?"

"Majda invite."

His forehead furrowed. "Could you repeat that? I can't understand your accent."

I don't have an accent, Angel thought. *You do.* "Army offer me job. For my Kyle rating."

He frowned at her. "What Kyle rating?"

Angel just looked at him. She didn't see the point of this conversation. If he hadn't looked up her rating, or if he didn't believe her preliminary results, that was his problem, not hers.

After a moment, he said, "We're done for today."

Good. Angel stood up.

As the fellow walked across the room, two other testers joined him, a man and a woman. Although they spoke in low voices, Angel had no problem hearing. You needed that skill to survive, just like you needed to run fast. She could also pick up moods from these testers better than with most people. It made figuring out their conversations easy.

"I'm *telling* you," the man who didn't like her repeated. "She's *not* a Kyle. She's failed every test. Her rating is zero."

"Are you sure?" the woman asked. "According to her records, she has a rating of eight."

"Eight?" the second man asked. "That would be one of the highest here in the Division."

"It's fake," the first guy said. "She tricked whoever tested her. Besides, she lacks the brains to work as a telop. She can barely even form a sentence. Obviously she has a sub-human mind."

Yah, well, screw you, too, Angel thought. She went over to the trio and spoke to the annoyed guy while she indicated the mesh screen. "You left up tunnel. Should turn off when done."

He stared at her, his face turning red. "Don't give me lip, dust rat."

The other man focused on Angel. "What did you say?" A strand of his hair fell into his eyes like the fur on a fluff-pup, so she thought of him as Fluff-Pup.

"Screen on," Angel repeated. "Pics burn if they stay too long." She always had trouble with that when she used the cobbled together screens in the Undercity. They didn't have as many built-in safeguards as the tech-mech here in the city.

"Yes, we'll fix it," the woman said. "But we didn't mean that. You said something about the image on the screen. What did you see?"

This again. Reminding herself to be patient, Angel said, "Round. Circle."

"You didn't say circle, though." Pup seemed intrigued. Interested.

Angel thought back to her response. "You mean tunnel?" It meant the same thing.

"Yes!" The woman waved her hand with agitation. "That looks like a tunnel to you?"

"Yah." Why were they getting so excited? "Round tunnel."

"Can you give more details?" Pup seemed fascinated now.

Before Angel could respond, the original tutor said, "Round tunnel?" He seemed angrier, furious even. What for? He treated her like an idiot, cut her session short, insulted her with a slur, and now he thought she dissed *him?*

He spoke as if he were pinching off his words. "What other kind of tunnel is there?"

Angel switched into the dialect used by the Majdas, which resembled Undercity speech. Maybe these three could understand that better. "Where I live, we use tunnels to get places. They honeycomb the Undercity. The tunnels have different shapes, depending on whether they are part of the ruins, we built them, or they developed over time from erosion or dripping water. If we need to give directions, we specify both the direction and the shape of the tunnel."

"What the hell!" the angry man said. "Where did you learn to speak Iotic?"

Angel blinked at him. "I'm speaking the original language of my people. The dialect we use now is a terser version of it."

They were all gaping at her. Finally the woman found her voice. "You're speaking classical Iotic. It's a dead language. Royalty and nobles, like the House of Majda, use modern Iotic."

Angel shrugged. "You understand me, so it can't be that rare."

"We all learn Iotic," Pup told her. "We have to, because we deal with the Houses. Modern and classical Iotic are close enough that if you understand one, you usually understand the other."

Interesting. Supposedly these Houses carried the highest concentration of Kyle operators, more than the general population. Compared to the Undercity, though, the Majdas had almost no Kyles. She didn't want to make more trouble, so she just said, "My people went down to the Undercity thousands of years ago, back when our ancestors all spoke what you're calling classical Iotic. Our dialect developed from that tongue."

The original tester had tensed up so much, his mood felt like a clenched fist. Angel frowned at him. "Why are you angry at me?"

"Don't be foolish and over-emotional," he told her. "I'm not angry."

The woman spoke carefully. "We're all getting it, Georj, even with your barriers up."

It never stopped amazing Angel how careless folks from Cries were with their names. The woman didn't even seem to realize she'd just revealed a secret about Georj that he'd *never* tell Angel if he came from the Undercity. Now she had an advantage. Given how little slicks understood, though, probably none of them realized or cared, which sort of negated the advantage.

Georj spoke tightly. "I'm concerned about her motivation in hiding her ability to speak properly. Who knows what else she might be up to?"

Yah, right. Like *she* was the one who couldn't speak well. If he didn't quit dissing her—no, damn it, she'd promised Bhaaj she wouldn't punch any slicks. Even if she hadn't given her word, she couldn't risk it. She could get "fired" from her job or kicked off Mason's team. Besides, even a child could tell these people were defenseless.

So instead she continued in Iotic. "Why would I speak to you in this language under normal conditions? It isn't my natural dialect or yours." The language everyone here seemed to speak, what they called Skolian Flag, sounded similar enough to Iotic that Angel could understand them, but Iotic came more easily.

"If it isn't your normal language," the woman asked, "why use it now?"

Angel met her gaze. "Because people here treat me better when I do."

Pup winced. "Point taken." He indicated the glowing blue circle on the screen across the room. "Can you describe in Iotic how that image looks to you? In detail."

"It's a round tunnel," Angel said.

"In your usual language, that's giving a lot of information, yes?" Pup asked.

"That's right." What more did they want? "Why?"

"What you're looking at is a Kyle-generated image," Pup said. "A telop here is creating it in real time. Someone with Kyle ability sees the image differently than someone without. The greater your ability, the more details you can see."

Angel hadn't wanted to insult them with too much talky-talky, but it sounded like they genuinely needed to know more. "It looks three-dimensional," she said, "Like a tunnel that stretches back into the screen. It's luminous. Glowing. The color comes in shades of blue, lighter at the opening and darkening as it goes back. It eventually reaches a point of perspective where the blue turns so dark it looks black. It's as if the tunnel goes on to infinity." She paused, more intent. "When I focus, the tunnel rotates. The harder I concentrate, the faster it goes." Ho! Look at that. "Right now, I've got it spinning." Pleased with this new effect, she added, "It's pretty."

"Goddess above," Pup murmured. "I've never heard such a vivid description of a Lock Corridor except from a Ruby operator. And spinning? That's new."

"I'm not a Ruby," Angel said. From what she understood, only members of the Ruby Dynasty had that rating, which, surprise, was why people called them Ruby operators. The endless Kyle Division orientation she'd slogged through claimed Ruby operators had ratings off the chart. They were also called Rhon psions, as if slicks didn't already have enough words for stuff. "My rating is about eight," she added. "Maybe nine."

"That's incredibly high," the woman said. "Why would you hide it?"

Angel squinted at her. "I'm not trying to hide anything."

Georj regarded her with suspicion. "You pretended you didn't see anything but a flat circle."

"Georj, wait." Pup sounded annoyed, not at Angel, but at Georj. He didn't seem at all fluffy now. He looked like a wolf. "She speaks a different language. It has different meanings." To Angel, he said, "You don't need to give details to Kyles among your people, right? It's why your language is so terse. When you speak, you're often communicating as empaths, even telepaths. Is that it?"

Yah, good, he got it. "That's right," Angel said. "I speak Undercity to you."

"Undercity?" Georj demanded. "You're *deliberately* trying to cause problems—"

"No, wait!" The woman sounded far happier than the situation warranted. "It's an honor, right?" she asked Angel. "When you speak to us in your dialect, you're showing that you consider us part of your—your—" She stopped, seeming to run out of words. "Team?" she finally asked.

Although Angel hadn't thought about it that way, she realized the woman had the right of it. They were like her, mooders.

"Yah," she told the woman and the fluff-wolf. She ignored Georj.

"Angel?" a woman asked next to her. "Is everything all right?"

Startled, Angel swung around, her fists clenching. She relaxed when she discovered Gabrial standing next to them, a step back as if she wasn't sure she should approach.

Angel unclenched her fists. "Yah, fine." She glanced at the others. "We done?"

"We've just begun!" the woman enthused. "Now that we understand, we've so many other exercises, interviews, tests—"

Pup spoke quickly. "No, that's fine for now. We can continue later." An odd sense came from him, as if he didn't want to put off Angel, not because he looked down on her, but because he believed she had great value to the Kyle Division. Interesting.

Yah, she had work to do here, not just with Kyle biz, but learning what these slicks wanted.

CHAPTER VI
Willow Runs

Bhaaj pushed aside the bead curtain and entered the waiting room of Karal Rajindia's Undercity clinic. Undercity artisans had created the curtain, just as they made the other artworks in the clinic, their way of giving back for her medical services. No one paid Karal with byte-bucks or opto-credits. They didn't trust a currency you couldn't touch. Their economy worked on trades of goods and services.

As Bhaaj let go of the curtain, the beads clinked in ripples of sound. It reminded her of the gilded-wing fliers that sailed on air currents created by the ventilation system that networked the rock all the way to the surface. The tiny critters resembled pico-lizards, but more fragile. The fluttering of their wings in unison sounded like music.

Inside, artists had smoothed and polished the cave surfaces until they resembled the marble halls of a Cries mansion. Tapestries graced them, woven in rich colors, and golden rugs warmed the floor. Stone carpenters had sculpted the furniture from a rock called air-pumice, which had so many air bubbles that it weighed less than its wooden counterparts on other worlds. Embroidered cushions rested on the furniture, and a second beaded curtain hung in an archway across the room.

As Bhaaj entered, Karal Rajindia came through the other curtain. The doctor smiled with the ease of her above-city background. "My greetings, Bhaaj. What brings you here today?"

Bhaaj needed a moment to absorb the unexpected speech. In the three years since Karal had set up this clinic for the Undercity, the doctor had learned to speak their dialect well and used it most of the time, though with the Iotic accent of her aristocratic background. Unlike most members of the noble Houses, however, she showed no arrogance. She had the straight black hair, large black eyes and dark skin of the nobility, but she acted like an unassuming healer.

Bhaaj? Max asked.

Distracted, Bhaaj thought. *What?*

You're just staring at Doctor Rajindia.

Oh. Yah. Taking her cue from Karal, she answered in the Cries dialect. "My greetings. I wondered if you had time to meet. If you're busy, I can come back later."

"No problem. I don't have any patients right now." Karal motioned at a bench sculpted from the wall, with scalloped legs and cushions embroidered with rose vines. The wall itself formed the "back" of the bench, engraved to resemble an Undercity grotto. A stone table carved in the same motif stood before the couch holding a delicate decanter and several blown-glass goblets, lovelier glassware even than what many of the Cries elite owned—the same crowd that assumed Undercity natives were crude brutes who lived in squalor.

The supposed "Undercity goods and art" sold on the Concourse consisted of cheap work created by slicks. It had little worth, except that the Cries merchants upped the price by claiming it came from the Undercity. Their customers had no idea how the true Undercity works surpassed what the city merchants sold. Getting a license to sell on the Concourse posed problems for Bhaaj's people because no one wanted them there, but they could overcome the problems with enough effort, as already done by Weaver, the husband of Bhaaj's best friend Dara. Bhaaj hoped to convince more Undercity merchants to market their goods on the Concourse, once they realized how much tourists would pay for such exquisite work.

"Bhaaj?" Karal asked as they sat down. "Are you all right?"

She mentally shook herself. "Yah. Good."

"You seem preoccupied."

She switched mental gears to her reason for coming here. "I've been thinking about our runners on Mason's team."

"Ah, yes! I heard." Karal beamed at her. "I'm glad they feel more like they can go into the city. They need to take precautions with the sunlight, though."

"They're careful." Bhaaj spoke her greatest concern. "They need health meds."

Karal didn't look surprised. "Convincing people here to let me inject them with *anything* is difficult. The idea of meds in their bodies they can't see—well, most won't hear of it."

"That's what worries me." After the government had discovered their wealth of Kyle's here, they'd encouraged Karal Rajindia to do whatever she could for the Undercity. The military desperately needed healthy Kyles to run ancient machines from the Ruby Empire that helped defend the Imperialate. Part of what gave Bhaaj's people their unusual neurological traits came from how they lived. It was why their ancestors had retreated to the Undercity all those millennia ago, choosing an isolation that protected their empathic minds. Their ways had become so ingrained over the generations, however, and their trust of Cries so low, that they adamantly resisted change.

"Here's the thing," Bhaaj said. "Olympic rules allow athletes to have health nanomeds. It's considered a necessity. Going without them puts my athletes at a disadvantage. But so far only Ruzik and Angel have agreed to them."

"I can give anyone meds at their request," Karal said. "But I can't force them."

"Mason is pushing for it." On other teams, athletes *wanted* to upgrade their meds to the edge of the legal limit, seeking any advantage they could gain. "It doesn't guarantee they will, though."

Karal spoke thoughtfully. "I'll keep working to convince them. When they see how well it helps their Cries teammates with sickness, fatigue, minor injuries, all that, surely more of yours will agree."

"I hope so." Bhaaj turned to a concern that worried her even more. "We also need to get them vaccinated against this new strain of carnelian rash." In Cries, the rash had long ago become only a childhood disease, one easy to cure. In the Undercity, it often proved fatal. Last season, a new variant had almost wiped out the population of the Deep, an area well below the Undercity where about three hundred people lived. Or had lived. Nearly a quarter had died in the outbreak.

"Most everyone in the Deep has agreed," Karal said. "After

surviving a plague that virulent, they've been more willing to accept treatment. But here? Not so much." She pushed back a lock of hair that had escaped her ponytail. "Even after recovery, some people from the Deep have long-term effects. Fatigue, no appetite, muscle aches." Her voice lightened. "On the plus side, the birth rate is up. I think epidemics have hit that population on a regular basis, maybe for thousands of years. It bounces back because the virus interferes with the birth control they use."

"Some sort of tea, isn't it?" Bhaaj's nanomeds had provided her with top-notch birth control for so long, she tended to forget how she managed in her youth, before she left the Undercity.

"Yes, from a plant that secretes phytoestrogens," Karal said. "Those can block fertility. The tea-plant only grows in the Deep, though. It can't survive in even the minimal light here."

Bhaaj thought of her only living blood relative, a cousin from the Deep. "Some Deepers wanted to join Mason's team, but they can't come to the city because of the sunlight."

"Yes." Concern filled Karal's voice. "How are the Undercity runners managing?"

"It affects us, too, just not as much." With a grimace, she added, "It's too hot in midday for *anyone* to go out. We do outside practices in the morning before it heats up or in the evening after it cools down. During midday, we work inside the stadium."

"That sounds sensible. And no worries, I'll get meds and vaccines for your runners."

Bhaaj nodded, relieved. "Good."

She left the doctor feeling more optimistic. If only they could as easily treat the hostility between the Cries and Undercity athletes.

"Not good," Rockjan grumbled, sitting next to Ruzik. "Stupid."

Ruzik glanced at her, amused, but said nothing as he went through the exercises Mason had given them. He and the other distance runners had settled in a grassy area in the center of the Cries track, stretching their muscles. He sat with one leg straight out and the other bent while he lowered his head to his knee, loosening up his hamstrings. It felt good, like his tykado warm-ups. Many of the runners were grumbling, though, both those from Cries and the Undercity.

Rockjan reached her hand toward the foot of her outstretched right leg. "Ah, *shit!* This im-pos-see-ball." She made the four-syllable word an insult, though who she was insulting, Ruzik had no idea. Maybe her leg.

He rested his head on the knee of his outstretched leg and continued to stretch.

"That's fucked," Rockjan told him.

He turned his head to look at her, his ear on his knee. "Feels good."

"Pah. You crazy. This crazy. Ca-ray-zee."

He sat up again. "I do this a lot, for tykado. Gets easier."

Rockjan snorted. She did go back to the stretches, though.

As Ruzik switched legs, he looked around the field. Angel had finally arrived and sat a few meters away, also warming up. When he smiled, she grinned, then went back to her hamstring stuff.

How job? he asked.

Strange. Her thought came with more strength than usual. That often happened after she'd worked at the Kyle center, as if she exercised her brain there like how they exercised their muscles here. She added, *Slicks not ken much.*

They think same about us, he answered.

Yah. So they say. All the time. Although a sense of amusement came from the surface of her mind, he felt her anger simmering.

Not let them get to you, Ruzik told her. *Stay calm. Ignore stupid shit.*

Yah. She sent the mental image of lifting her hands in a shrug. *Job easy. Look at pics today. Blue tunnels.*

Ruzik stretched out both legs and rested his forehead on his knees. *Why?*

Not know. But they pay me to do it. Lots of byte-bucks just to look at pics. Weird.

Well, *that* was a change. Before she'd started this job, above-city currency had never interested her. He hadn't cared about it either, until he joined the Dust Knights and Bhaaj insisted they get schooling as part of the Code. The learning bored him at first, simple stuff he already knew. Then he discovered "economics." Ho! City slick magic with numbers and digital systems. It could make you rich. Some people, like the Majdas, got so fucking rich, they controlled entire planets. When he learned to invest, he loved it. Angel hated it, so he set up and managed city accounts for her income from the Kyle Division.

Got your bykes rolling into your accounts, he told Angel. Slicks called digital credits byte-bucks, or bykes for short. A hundred bykes made one opto-credit.

Our accounts, Angel thought.

Yah. Make us rich.

She sent him the image of a grin. *All for looking at pics. Silly slicks.*

He sent back a smug smile. *Maybe not. Bhaaj invest. So do Majdas. And execs. Now us.*

Saw herd of exec slicks at job today. In lobby.

Why there?

Not know.

Mason's voice came over the stadium speaker. "All right, kids. Line up on the track. We're practicing sprints today."

Angel stood up and came over to Ruzik. "Kids?" she said.

He rose to his feet. "Just thing he says. To all, young or old."

"Eh." She looked past him. Following her gaze, he saw Strider and her gang headed for the starting line. Except they were four now instead of three.

"Who Strider fourth?" he asked.

"Not know." Angel squinted at the group. "That a slick? Can't be."

Ruzik didn't sense anything unusual from the dust gang, just mild tension, what happened when you put people together who didn't know each other well but who wanted to. Angel spoke true, though, it did look like a slick with three Dust Knights. Bad sign? Or good? He didn't want friction with above-city types to put off the Undercity athletes, particularly given that a lot of them still hadn't decided if they wanted to be here.

Ruzik loped through the cooling evening in a residential area high above the city. He liked this better than the weird exercises Mason gave him, like "walking lunges," which meant kneeling with each step, or jumping up and down on a box, or other biz Mason called "plyometrics," whatever that meant. Actually, Ruzik knew what it meant after he stole time on the Cries meshes to look it up. All those quick, strong motions were supposed to increase his speed, power, and efficiency. He didn't like them, but he tried anyway. And ho! He got stronger and faster.

The best, though, came when Mason said, "Now just go run." He wanted the improvement to become second nature, not anything

Ruzik needed to think about during a race. So this evening he just ran, enjoying the hills. The towering plants called "trees" kept it cooler here. He couldn't see the mansions; they were too far from the road, hidden away. Instead, he ran past endless thriving plants, a form of riches far greater than invisible houses.

Sprays of water fed the greenery and misted across him like a piece of heaven. It bothered him, too. All this filtered water squandered while his people were dying because the Undercity struggled to build filtering systems for their poisoned water. Here you could stand in a sprinkler and just open your mouth. Except if anyone came here from the Undercity, city drones would arrest them for trespassing. The only reason no one stopped him was because he wore the tech-mech belt Mason had given everyone on the team, devices that granted them permission to run anywhere.

For now, he forgot about plyometrics, oxygen volume levels, EI-assisted holographic studies of his stride, and everything else Coach Mason came up with to analyze what he needed to improve. He ran for the sheer joy of running.

Up ahead, he glimpsed another runner half-hidden by the trees that shaded this winding road. Ah. Good. His hunch may have borne fruit. He sped up until he reached an intersection and turned right onto a road with even more trees. There! He caught another glimpse of the other runner going around a bend. Yah, the rumors held true, that Dice Vakaar liked to run up here after practice.

Ruzik sped up, taking longer steps, what Mason called his "world-devouring stride." It made him want to laugh. Yah, he had long legs. He'd never felt the inclination to eat any planets, though.

As he rounded the curve, he saw Dice up ahead, loping along. Droop-willows shaded the road and met overhead, their lacy foliage turned red in the blaze of a sunset Ruzik couldn't see. He liked it better here under the trees than down in the stadium. With the branches arching over the road, it almost felt like the most spacious canals in the Undercity.

It didn't take long to catch his target. When he was a few paces behind, he said, "Eh, Dice."

The Vakaar man glanced around, his hand dropping to the sheathed knife on his belt. When he saw Ruzik, he stopped drawing his weapon.

"Eh." Dice slowed until Ruzik caught up, then fell into pace with him. They ran together, their strides in synch, their silence appreciated.

Eventually, Ruzik said, "Got to talk."

Dice glanced at him. "We not bash Strider gang. We stop."

"Yah. But why start?"

He expected Dice to make some abstruse response or not answer at all. Instead, the cartel heir simply said, "Hungry."

"We not got enough to give you ours," Ruzik said. "But Coach Mason can help."

"Char-i-tee." Dice over-enunciated the three syllables, turning the word into a deep insult.

"Not charity," Ruzik said. "We got what they want. Good runs. They win honor, respect, shit like that because of us. So they give us food, pure water. Good bargain."

"Bargain with slicks?" Dice scowled. "Not like."

"Yah," Ruzik agreed. "But why slicks got so much, and we got none? They use us to make them look good. They *owe* us."

Dice's face relaxed as if he meant to smile, then stopped himself. He and Ruzik were far from trusting each other. But he did say, "Running fun. Slicks make bargain for fun. Silly for them, good for us."

"Yah," Ruzik said amiably. "Food good. Water good. Can take more. Enough that Vakaar not starve." Bhaaj had been discussing it with Mason. "And Vakaar not beat on Dust Knights."

Dice slanted a look at him. "Not like Dust Knights."

Yah, well, we don't like punkers. Ruzik kept that thought hidden because he did like Dice, even if he had no intention of admitting it. Instead he just grunted.

They continued together, two cogs in a mental and physical machine working in synchrony.

Kiro sensed the runners before he heard them. One? No, two. They were in the hills nearby. He kept running, not reaching out but not shuttering his mind either. Gradually they drew nearer, until he felt certain they sensed him. When they caught up and fell into stride with him, he nodded to them. Ruzik and Dice. They nodded back, and the three of them kept running, needing no words.

Eventually Ruzik and Dice headed down to the city and Kiro to his home. It wasn't far; their run had taken them into the Willow District. It always intrigued him that the city planners named the most exclusive and isolated area of the city after a simple tree. Then again, maybe that was the point. Only the people wealthy enough to import and maintain the willows could live here. In his youth, Kiro had taken this all for granted. No more. He said nothing about his home to his peers, none of whom seemed to like him much anyway. No, that wasn't all true. Ruzik and Dice had just run with him, and Strider, Zee, and Lamp actually sought his company.

As he entered the house, he heard his parents talking in another room. So. Father had come home. Following their voices, he ended up at the Gold Hall, an expansive living room with golden chandeliers and wood furniture. Brocaded cushions in hues of gold and ivory gleamed on the white upholstery, and a glass-enclosed hutch stood to one side with crystal plates inside. His parents were relaxing on one of the couches, sipping red wine in crystal goblets rimmed with platinum.

"Ah, Kiro." His father stood up, smiling. "I was wondering when you would get home."

"My greetings, Father." Kiro went over to him. "It is good to see you."

"Yes. Absolutely." His father lifted his hand, indicating a plush couch next to where he and Kiro's mother sat. "Join us, please."

"Of course." Kiro sat on the edge of the gilt-edged couch, wishing he could disappear to his side of the mansion. His clothes had nanobots worked into them that cleaned the cloth, but he still wanted to go change. He wanted more to see his father, though. "You look well," he said. It was an understatement; his father looked fantastic, as perfect as always. He had straight black hair and black eyes like a nobleman, even though he had no known connections to any House. His captain's uniform, with its crisp blue cloth and gold braid, made him look like a hero. Which, Kiro supposed, was the point. His father piloted star cruisers for the wealthy. He had to look heroic.

"Did you have a good practice at the stadium?" his mother asked.

"Yes, great." Kiro hesitated. "And I ran up here with a couple of people from the team."

"Ah. Good. Very good." His father nodded. "I'm glad you're making friends."

Kiro wondered how he'd react if he knew Dice and Ruzik came

from the Undercity. He'd started to wonder about a lot lately. "I've a question for the two of you," he said.

"Really?" His father gave him an indulgent smile. "Ask away."

"I hope this doesn't sound foolish." Kiro hesitated. "Do either of you—do you ever feel as if you know someone else's mood?"

"You mean as an empath?" his father asked. "A Kyle operator? Goddess, no, never. We've been spared that shame."

"Shame?" Kiro squinted at him. "What do you mean?"

"For saint's sake, Nial." Kiro's mother scowled at his father. "It isn't shameful. It's a vital gift prized by an entire civilization."

"That's bullshit," Nial said. "The government claims it's a gift so people will admit they're empaths. It's only because they need Kyles, and no one wants to be one. Can you imagine having to sense what other people feel all the time? What a nightmare."

Yes, it is, Kiro thought. Except not with Strider, Lamp or Zee. Or tonight, with Ruzik and Dice. He noticed it with Tam, too. She showed empathy to everyone, even city slicks like him, treating them all as if they mattered. And Rockjan. She'd terrified him when he'd first seen her, hulking around the track, huge and muscled, ready to kill someone. After a while, he'd realized she just looked that way. She didn't go around killing people. Dust Knights swore off killing, at least for vengeance. It had something to do with a Code of Honor. Kiro wanted to know more.

What he *didn't* want was for his father to feel ashamed of his empath son. So he said, "I just wondered. One of the Undercity women on the team works at the Kyle Division in Selei Tower."

His father made a *hmmmph* sound. "You stay away from her. No good will come of adding dust rats to the team."

"Nial, stop it," Kiro's mother said. "I won't have ethnic slurs in this house."

"What slurs?" he demanded.

"You called them rats," Kiro said.

Irritation washed across Nial's face. "How is that a slur? It's what they call themselves."

"They call themselves Dust Knights," Kiro said. "It's an organization that protects the Undercity population."

"Whatever." His father glanced at his mother. "Gwen, I'm spent. I haven't slept in thirty hours, what with this last run to the Metropoli star system." He set down his wine glass, then stood and stretched his arms. "Time to call it a night."

Kiro rose to his feet, at a loss. His father would be off on another starliner run after he slept, which meant this was the last Kiro would see of him for many days. He spoke awkwardly. "It was good to talk to you." Even semi-arguing with his father was better than never seeing him at all.

"Yes, indeed." As an afterthought, Nial added, "I hope school is going well."

"Yes. Very well." Another questionable statement, but he doubted his father cared. He'd never notice unless Kiro did something drastic, like fail out or get expelled, neither of which seemed likely. He did enough to pass his courses and spent the rest of his time training. "The marathon tryouts are tomorrow morning."

"Strong body, strong mind, heh?" With that, his father left, going off to his privacy.

Kiro sat again, watching his mother. She looked so tired. "Are you having trouble at work?" he asked.

"No, nothing."

"Mother, I can tell something is wrong."

For a moment she just looked at him. Then she said, "Never believe, Kiro, that shame exists in being a Kyle operator. Is it a gift? Maybe." She finished her wine, then set the empty goblet on a side table by the couch. "Empaths can learn to barrier their minds against the onslaught."

"Learn?" He wanted so much to ask more, but the words wouldn't come.

She spoke softly. "Otherwise, it's like living without your skin, always vulnerable, until you have to retreat from everyone, choose a life path that doesn't involve people, a job that you can do alone or virtually." Her gaze never left his face. "Or become a runner, always training alone."

He stared at her, his face heating. "I don't—I can't."

"Not everyone feels like your father." Her voice gentled. "You can get training to deal with the onslaught. If you do, you'd have your choice of prestigious, high-earning careers. A job like your teammate has, as a telop." Dryly she added, "Even if your academic record is less than stellar."

Kiro winced. "It's not that I don't want to do well. Training just takes time." He spoke with pain. "I don't think I can qualify for the Olympics. I'm right on the edge, and with those kids from the Undercity blasting through all the team records, how will I manage?"

"You work hard." She gave him an encouraging smile. "You can make it."

He wished he felt that confident. "I hope so."

"You avoided the rest of what I said." Although she spoke lightly, her gaze never wavered.

"You think I'm a Kyle." Before she could answer, Kiro added, "Because you are."

She answered simply, with no evasion. "Yes."

"Does Dad know?"

"We've been married for twenty years."

"He doesn't, does he?" Kiro doubted his father would notice unless his mother hit him over the head with it. "Why did you marry him, anyway?"

"Kiro! What kind of question is that?" When he didn't say anything, just looked at her, she said, "We loved each other."

Could have fooled me, he thought. Choosing tact, he said nothing. He didn't miss that she used the past tense, *loved*. He could imagine how it must have been for her, a shy data analyst having the attention of a glamorous starship captain. He knew people wondered why his father married his mother. He hated the way they disdained her as neither beautiful nor powerful enough for his father. To Kiro, her beauty was inside, far more compelling than any model, queen, or high-powered exec that his father might have chosen. Maybe Nial sought her out for that very reason. Sometimes Kiro thought more lurked under his father's glossy surface than he let show.

"Have you always known you were an empath?" he asked. It didn't surprise him, given how she'd always sensed when he needed comfort as a child.

"My father knew even before me," Gwen said. "He got me training."

"Discreetly?"

"He didn't want the military to know." She spoke quickly. "Not that it's a bad thing. It's more that once they know, they pressure you to work for them." Now she had the intent look again. "They train their telops, Kiro. Show them how to protect their minds. And they can give empaths a—I'm not sure how to describe it. A community? When you're with other empaths, it's easier, at least if you get along. You can sense each other."

A sudden thought hit him. "Ho! If I'm an empath, then Dad must be too."

She gave him a singularly unimpressed look. "And you came to the conclusion how?"

"You know how. The traits are genetically recessive. You can't be a Kyle operator unless you get the alleles from both parents. That means Dad must have the DNA for an empath."

"Yes. But he wouldn't be an empath unless he carried at least some of the DNA paired, from both his parents." She hesitated. "Maybe he does. I just can't—" She stopped, but Kiro knew what she meant. He never sensed from his father what he felt from the Undercity athletes, and he knew his father far better than Dust Knights he'd only met this season.

"Do you think I could get training?" he asked. "Secretly, I mean. I'd rather not tell anyone about it just yet." He stopped, then added, "If ever."

"It's your choice." A smile warmed her face. "And yes, we can do it discreetly." She stifled a yawn. "We can talk more tomorrow, yes? I'm beat."

"You look wiped out. Seriously, Mom, what's going on at work?"

After a hesitation, she spoke tiredly. "Scorpio Corporation is attempting a hostile buyout of Abyss Associates. Zaic Laj, the Scorpio CEO, is lobbying our shareholders to sell him their shares. His son, Hyden, also just purchased a slew of Abyss stock. If they gain control of enough Abyss shares to dominate a board vote, Abyss becomes theirs."

"Can they really do that?"

"Oh, they're savvy, no doubt." Now she sounded annoyed. "Laj is trying every trick, holding elite parties, offering employees better jobs if Abyss become a Scorpio subsidiary, throwing around wealth, all that business." She scowled. "Well, damn them. They won't get Abyss."

Kiro had forgotten how intense his mother could get about her job. He hoped the people who ran Abyss Associates appreciated her dedication. Scorpio also annoyed him for another reason. Hyden Laj ran on Mason's team. Sure, Hyden did well and would have no trouble qualifying. But he could be a narcissistic shit. When Kiro found himself close enough to pick up Hyden's mood, he found somewhere less unpleasant to go.

"Abyss will defeat Scorpio," he assured her.

"I hope so." Gwen shook out her hair, letting the black locks fall around her shoulders. Straight black hair, like his father.

"Um... Mom." He brushed his hand over his close-cropped hair. "Why do you always say I should keep my hair so short?" He looked ready for the military.

"Isn't it better for your running?"

"I suppose." He paused, then added. "It also hides my curls."

She tensed. "What do you mean, 'hides'?"

"No one else has curly hair."

"Sure they do. Just not here. You've relatives from offworld. It comes from them." She smiled. "I've even seen people with red hair. Once I saw yellow!"

He smiled. "Kids at school get tattoo jobs on their hair to make it all sorts of colors."

Gwen made a *hmmmpf* sound. "What, are you planning on dyeing your hair?"

Kiro couldn't help but laugh at her very parental reaction. "I don't care enough to do anything with it." Then he mused, "I should look up our family tree. I'm curious about our relatives from offworld." He paused. "Or from the Undercity."

His mother froze. "What did you say?"

"Everyone in the Undercity has curly hair."

She stared at him for several seconds before she said, "That has nothing to do with you."

"I suppose," he said, copying her standard answer when she knew more remained to say on a topic. "I'll look at the family tree, though."

"You won't find anything for the Undercity."

Her conviction gave him pause, mainly because he also felt it from her mind. Then again, maybe she had learned to protect herself so well, she could hide even her moods. "I have long legs, too, relative to my body," he added. "Like the Undercity kids."

"That's why you run so well." Her face relaxed. "That, and the way you train so hard."

He could tell he wouldn't get more out of her, if anything more remained to get. With a sigh, he said, "I should get some sleep. We're having the final tryouts tomorrow for the team."

Her forehead furrowed. "I thought you were already on the team."

"Coach Mason is letting me train with them. He's been doing tryouts all season for all the track and field events. He'll take the top forty athletes to train for the Olympics."

Her look turned protective. "Is that why you think you could get dropped?"

He shrugged, pretending he didn't care. "Right now, I'm ranked forty-first, based mostly on my short distance runs. Those are my best events." He especially liked the 800-meter race. "Coach Mason said if I don't make the top forty, I can be an alternate and keep training with his team. The Olympics only comes every four years, but I could go to other meets." He hesitated. "Or I suppose I could go back to the Abyss team."

"The Abyss team is terrible." His mother grimaced. "I pass the field when I go to lunch. They just sit out there drinking and partying."

Kiro laughed. "Yah, they like that." It had been fun sometimes, when he didn't stay long, but he liked Mason's team far better. "I just hope I do well tomorrow. It's twenty kilometers. Almost half a classic marathon."

"I thought the marathon was eighty kilometers."

"That's the royal. The classic comes from Earth. A little more than forty kilometers."

She frowned. "Why would Mason make you qualify in a marathon? You run sprints."

"He doesn't expect everyone to do well in everything. His ranking emphasizes our best events. He wants everyone to try the half marathon, though, just to see how we do." His voice lightened. "I like long distances. That's why I run in the hills after practice. And Mason rewards hard work. If I do well tomorrow, I could move into fortieth place."

"You'll qualify," she said. "I have faith in you."

"Thanks." Kiro wished he had that much faith in himself.

CHAPTER VII
The Cliff

Bhaaj stood high in the tiers of the stadium, savoring the dawn. The air felt cool, neither the blistering cold in the depths of night nor the killing heat of midday. The runners had gathered below at the starting line for the twenty-kilometer run, over a hundred hopefuls today. It happened every time Mason had an official tryout event, bringing in athletes who didn't normally train with the team. Bhaaj wished he could take everyone who wanted to participate, but he'd be lucky to find twenty who could qualify for elite-level meets. Opening it up to forty was optimistic, but all those extra spaces helped ease resentment against the Undercity runners.

Mason stood near the starting line. When he saw Bhaaj, he waved her down. As she headed toward him, she checked the snap-bottle on her belt. It felt secure, full of filtered water.

When she reached Mason, he said, "Don't push them too hard on the pace."

Bhaaj gave a dry laugh. "Trust me, I won't. My days at the elite level are over."

"Hah! You don't fool me, Bhaaj. You came in fifth at the Selei City Open last year, just behind Ruzik."

"He's gotten better since then." She watched Ruzik checking to make sure all the Undercity runners were ready to start.

"A lot better." Mason motioned at Hyden Laj. "Him as well. He wants to run the classic."

"It's a good fit." Bhaaj indicated a tall woman from Cries. "What about Helyne Tallmount?" Although only in her mid-thirties, Tallmount was older than most of the other athletes. She worked as a junior exec at Scorpio. These days, it wasn't unusual for elite athletes to compete into their fifties, even their sixties or beyond. Raylicon, however, had a markedly young team. The strict laws of the Imperialate, which put the age of majority at twenty-five, made all the Undercity kids minors. Only Angel and Rockjan would be twenty-five in time for the Olympics. Among the Cries athletes, only Tallmount and Jon Casestar were in their thirties, and Hyden would turn twenty-five a few days after the Olympics.

"Yes, Tallmount also." Mason spoke carefully. "We need to make it clear that Hyden earns his place on merit only."

Bhaaj slanted him a look. "Why?"

"After the Majdas, his parents are the largest contributors to the team. Actually, the support comes from Scorpio Corporation. Zaic Laj, Hyden's father, is the CEO."

"You're right, this shouldn't be about money. Besides, you're swimming in it." The Raylicon team had the dubious honor of being the best-funded lousy team anywhere.

Mason smiled. "Nobody on this barbecued planet is swimming in anything." When she glowered, he said, "We don't have as much as you think. Our food bills have skyrocketed. Without the Scorpio donation, I couldn't keep the banquet open for your Undercity runners to take as much as they need." His voice gentled. "Your runners need to eat. So do their families. I'll gladly give them the extra food, but you know they won't take anything that feels like charity."

"Yah." She thought of Dice and his punkers attacking Strider's gang. "But if they can't find, grow, or steal enough food, they might kill for it."

He stared at her. "*What?*"

She motioned toward the runners. "Before they came here, none of them ate enough. And this heightened training takes its toll. They eat constantly and need more good water than they've ever had available in their lives." In her youth, she'd lived with starvation. She'd never forget. She invested her money like a demon now, fanatical about protecting it because she never wanted to experience that grinding poverty again.

"I'm not going to cut off the banquets. You have my word." He exhaled. "But that means Scorpio is paying for the food."

"Don't tell Zaic Laj that." If Hyden learned his behavior from his parents, she didn't want to imagine how Zaic would react if he knew his support went to feeding Undercity kids.

Mason spoke wryly. "I tell him it helps provision the team."

"That works." She changed the subject to something less intense. "I should go out there now."

He indicated a cool-cart hovering by the track. "The med-station will go with you. Push the runners on the pace, but not so hard that they injure themselves. After five kilometers, my assistant coaches will take over as pacers. They'll change it out every four kay."

"No worries." With that, she headed to the track, where she'd be a few meters ahead of the athletes when the race started.

At first it had surprised her that Mason let the team practice with pacers. Most elite meets these days didn't allow formal pacers. Still, it seemed a good idea here. Setting a strong pace helped push the kids to their best. Bhaaj's runners took naturally to the idea, given that they often ran in groups, anything from two friends to gangs as large as Dice and his punkers.

At the track, Ruzik nodded to her and Tayz Wilder waved. She nodded to them both, then took her position to one side. A moment later, Mason called out the start, a pistol sound cracked through the air—and they were off!

Bhaaj ran in long, loping strides. Glancing back, she saw Angel and Wild in the lead, followed by Ruzik, Tallmount, Tam, and Hyden. The other runners spread out behind them. They soon left the stadium and headed into the city along a route laid out for the team. A few people gathered on the sidelines despite the early hour, cheering as if this were a real marathon. Bhaaj waved at several she recognized. When she glanced back, she saw Cries athletes running close enough to the barriers to brush the outstretched hands of friends or family.

At the five-kilometer mark, assistant coach Linsi took over as the pacer, a young Cries woman with a shorter stride. Too slow, though. As Bhaaj left the road, she sent a focused, directed thought to Tam. *Help pace?*

Tam glanced at her—and sped up. When she started to pass the pacer, Linsi also sped up, moving ahead. It was why Mason had each pacer only do four kilometers, so they could keep the world-class pace of elite runners even if they couldn't do the entire distance at that speed.

It gratified Bhaaj to see Tam with the team. The young woman had lost so much. Her mother had died giving birth to her, and Tam had lost her father a few years later to a drug overdose. Five years ago, Tam lost her only sibling, an older sister, to the carnelian rash. As a child she'd lived in the same circle as Ruzik, but they'd drifted apart after she joined her own dust gang. They hadn't yet formed a circle, so Tam had only the other three members of her dust gang as family, and they hadn't joined Mason's team.

Bhaaj stood by the roading, watching the runners go by. *Max,* she thought. *Why am I so tired? It feels like long-term effects of the carnelian rash.* She didn't have time to get sick.

You're tired because you just ran five kilometers, Max thought.
I do that all the time.
Yes, but not that fast, at least not anymore. You're getting older.
Ouch. *Not feeling tactful today, eh?*
I'm an EI. Not a diplomat.

Bhaaj smiled. That sounded like how she would answer. Regardless, she needed to stay in better shape. She wasn't old, only fifty, and her health meds delayed her aging. She felt and looked thirty. Well, okay, maybe late thirties. But still.

After a few moments, when she'd rested, she took off running again, taking a shortcut through the city. She could have asked someone for a ride, but she liked the run. Besides, she knew back roads that would get her to the end of the course well ahead of the team.

Mason was already at the finish line when Bhaaj jogged into the cleared area beyond it. A makeshift arch curved above the line, and vibrant holos saying *FINISH* glowed along its curve. The area beyond the arch formed a cup in the foothills of the Saint Paravel Mountains.

They'd arranged a scoreboard showing the times of the runners and a real-time holo-movie of the athletes. If runners had previous times on this course, those appeared next to their current time. A third entry showed their top time ever recorded. The second and third columns were mostly empty, given that most of the runners had never done an official twenty-kilometer race. Only Wild, Tallmount, and Hyden had previous times.

The holo-movie currently showed the lead runners, with Tam well ahead of everyone else, followed by Ruzik and Angel running together, then Wild, Tallmount, and Hyden. Beyond them, Bhaaj could just see Rockjan pounding along.

She went over to Mason. "Eh."

He turned with a start. "Who gave you a ride? We couldn't find you."

"I just ran."

"Seriously?" He gaped at her. "You aren't even out of breath."

"I took a shortcut." She glanced at the holovid, which had shifted to show runners farther back in the group, including the two twelve-year-olds. They loped along, synchronized like metronomes in unison. Although Bhaaj hadn't heard of them forming a gang, it wouldn't surprise her. They were training together to become Dust Knights, and she rarely saw them apart. Probably the only reason they hadn't formed a gang yet was because they needed to find a third and fourth they liked.

The list on the scoreboard shifted as Tallmount's name moved ahead of Hyden. Not that it mattered; they were both within the top fifteen and would have no trouble making the team. Some of the other names startled her, though.

"Mason, look at that." Bhaaj indicated the board. "Crinkles and Full-up are in the thirties."

"The thirties are full? What does that mean?" He peered at the board. "Oh. I see. Those are the names for two of your athletes." He beamed at her. "A lot of yours will make the team."

"Not these two." She motioned at the movie. "They're the pair on the left, the two younger girls. They're only twelve."

"Well, durn! I can't take them to adult competitions." He thought for a moment. "I'll see if I can find a juniors team for them."

"They'd like that." She'd known Crinkles for years, the daughter of her best friend, Dara, who tended bar in the Undercity's only casino.

The vid switched again, this time showing Strider, Lamp, Zee, and Kiro. They'd never be top marathoners, but they held their own. Their lives consisted of doing long distances every day. The difference was that they rested more than athletes in training, which meant they rarely had injuries. They didn't push it unless they were vying for bragging rights—or running for their lives.

"Kiro works hard," she commented. When he'd started with Strider and her dust gang about two months ago, he struggled to manage their pace, but now he seemed fine.

"I don't know much about him. He keeps to himself." Mason spoke in a confiding voice. "I didn't think he'd make it this year. When he tried last year for the team I took to the Interstellar Championships, he came in close to last. But look at that. He's fortieth out of one hundred and six." Studying the list, he added, "Lamp is twenty-first. Strider and Zee aren't far behind."

"Good." It gratified Bhaaj to see Strider's gang do well. After the death of their fourth last season, they'd grieved so deeply that she'd feared for their health. Since joining Mason's team, their spirits had lifted. She hoped Kiro qualified; they seemed to like him.

"The leaders are coming up on the cliff." Mason fiddled with his hand device, and the movie shifted again, showing a steep cliff with no path, just a lot of jutting rock. "Anyone who does the royal marathon will have to go up a cliff like that, except higher."

"We can enter four in the royal at the Olympics," Bhaaj said. "Assuming we qualify four."

"Angel already has, sort of," he said. "Just barely, but her time coming in first on the Selei Open is one second above the qualifying time. That isn't an official Olympic qualifier, though."

"I'm not sure she wants a marathon," Bhaaj said. "Have you seen her sprints? She's tearing it up." Then she added, "Mason, most of these kids aren't going to qualify for a marathon."

"I know," he admitted. "I just want to see how they do in longer distances. And on the cliff."

Bhaaj had no concerns about the climb. Her runners scrambled up far worse in the Undercity all the time, especially in regions where the tunnels had collapsed. This cliff was tame enough that they didn't even need safety harnesses.

"Tam's almost there," she said.

Now Mason looked worried. His expressions changed so fast, she had trouble keeping up with them. "You think she'll be all right?"

Bhaaj held back her grin. "Just watch."

Sure enough, when Tam reached the cliff, she leapt up to catch her first handhold. Like a mountain lizard scrabbling over rocks, she went from spike to crack to foothold with surreal speed. She had a lean, long build, enough that she didn't carry as much weight as more muscular athletes.

"*Ho!* That's incredible!" Mason gaped at the screen. "Look at her go!"

"Yah." Bhaaj nodded, preoccupied. Angel and Ruzik had reached the cliff. Although Ruzik started first and went faster than Angel, both used the same techniques as Tam, climbing with confidence. Bhaaj remembered her days as a runner with the Pharaoh's Army Olympic team. She'd done the same. Above-city types didn't know how to climb.

"Bhaaj, Bhaaj, Bhaaj!" Mason looked ready to burst. "They're going to pulverize the record on this course. Destroy it, I tell you!" He grabbed her shoulders and shook her. "Goddess almighty! We have a team! A *good* team."

Bhaaj couldn't help but laugh. "Mason, let me go."

"Oh! Sorry!" He dropped his hands. "Sorry, sorry, I can't help it. I've never had so many athletes of such high quality. Who'd have guessed that some of the most talented runners in the Imperialate lived right below my feet all these years?"

"Don't get ahead of yourself," Bhaaj cautioned. "Right now, they're relaxed. They don't know what it means to do elite athletics." She had no idea how they'd react in the interstellar arena. Just getting them to accept health meds was difficult, and that was only one step in many necessary to compete on an Olympic level. They'd need to handle the stress of going to worlds with different gravity, air, day length, and so much more. They'd also interact with athletes who had different customs, languages, and cultures. When faced with too much input, her runners tended to withdraw or become hostile. Goddess only knew what would happen.

Mason tried to hold back, but as he watched Tam reach the top of the cliff and vault over the edge, back onto the road, he was practically hopping up and down. A moment later, Ruzik came over the edge, followed by Angel and then Azarina Majda. The road after the cliff had one last curve, and then the runners would come in view of the finish. Bhaaj waited there with Mason, the assistant coaches Linsi and

Tena, a med-tech in case anyone needed help, and another tech making sure the holo-movies and scoreboard worked.

Linsi came over to them. "Shall we stretch a holo-tape across the finish?"

Mason grinned at Bhaaj. "Think Tam would like that?"

The idea appealed to her. "She'll have no idea why it's there. But yah, sure, go ahead."

Within moments, Tam came around the curve and headed for them. Linsi and a tech pulled a tape radiant with *finish* holos across the line. Tam didn't seem the least bit fazed by a strip of glowing stuff in her path. After working steadily with both Bhaaj and Mason, she ran better now than Bhaaj had ever seen, and she'd already been one of the best in the Undercity.

Then Tam kicked.

All the Undercity runners had a big kick, the extra speed they added at the end of a race. In a world where your ability to out-sprint your enemies could mean the difference between escape and getting beaten or killed, they kicked *hard*. When Bhaaj suggested they use it in races, they'd just stared at her. Why kick when you were running in a circle, with no enemy in sight, unless you counted city slicks who couldn't fight worth shit? So she asked them *Do you want to lose the race to the slicks?* Ho! They hated the idea. It was in their blood, their genes, the generations of survivors who'd learned that the faster you went, the better you survived. If your opponents outnumbered or outgunned you, that kick could make the difference between life and death.

And yah, Tam could *kick,* even after a long distance. She tore down the final stretch, her bleached white hair gleaming, her worn shoes beating the ground, her arms pumping. With no fanfare, she tore through the holo-tape, ripping it apart as she raised her arms in victory.

"Tam, yes!" Mason shouted. "Fantastic! Excellent! *YES!*" Grabbing Bhaaj's arm, he pointed at the screen. "*Look* at her time! She beat the all-time record on this course set by Garnet Jizarian thirty years ago!"

"Uh, Mason." As Bhaaj disentangled her arm from him, Tam watched with amusement. She kept walking, breathing deeply and taking the water bottle Linsi offered. The assistant coach burbled over with enthusiasm too, so Tam nodded amiably to her, then drank half the water.

Bhaaj glanced at the track. "Here comes Ruzik." He'd appeared around the curve, racing down the final stretch. He also kicked, that Undercity burst of speed that had saved countless lives.

"Incredible!" Mason exulted. "Where do they get that energy after twenty kilometers?" He peered at the scoreboard. "This is his best time yet."

It didn't surprise Bhaaj. "And Angel," she said, as Ruzik's wife came around the bend.

Mason frowned at the scoreboard. "She's not improving like Ruzik and Tam."

"It might be her job with the Kyle Corps. She has less time to train."

Mason nodded, intent as Ruzik crossed the finish. "Way to go!" he called. "Dynamite!" He stayed back, which Bhaaj appreciated. It hadn't taken him long to realize Undercity runners hated being crowded. Angel soon pounded across the line, then Wild and Azarina. Within a few more minutes, Tallmount finished, followed by Hyden Laj and then Rockjan rounding out the top eight.

The holos in front of the board shifted. Although Tam beat everyone at longer races, Angel was the strongest at short distances. Ruzik, Tayz, and Hyden also excelled at long distances and Ruzik liked jumping hurdles. Azarina excelled at middle distances, the 1500-meter and 5000-meter races. Rockjan, with her upper body strength and notorious weapons skill, beat everyone at javelin and discus. The final ranking ended up with Ruzik first, then Tam, Angel, Wild, Rockjan, Azarina, Tallmount, and Hyden.

Mason peered at the vid that showed the athletes still on the course. "Look at Strider and her crew. They're synchronized." He glanced at Bhaaj. "Don't they realize this is a race?"

"Yah. They just like to work as a team." Dust gangs ran together because it helped protect them. Strider, Lamp, and Zee had held their own against Dice's punkers long enough for Dice to recognize them because her group worked together so well.

"Why are they with Kiro Caballo?" Mason asked. "I don't want him to hold them back."

"Actually, they've pulled him up to their level." Bhaaj studied the evolving stats on the scoreboard. "He's improved a lot."

Mason followed her gaze. "If he keeps this up, he'll make the team."

The quartet soon approached the cliff. Lamp reached it first and sprung up for a handhold, then scrambled up the wall. Strider followed with Zee and Kiro. They climbed fast, with that surreal situational awareness of what to grab. Kiro kept up—

And then lost his grip.

The moment Kiro started to slide down the cliff, Bhaaj knew he'd just lost his hope to make the team. Even if he managed to redo the climb, he was already too close to last—

Without pause, Zee and Strider grabbed Kiro by the arms, hoisting him up as they kept climbing. With a grunt so loud, it came through over all the noise of the runners in the finish area, Kiro grabbed a projection and resumed the climb. It happened so fast, they lost only a few seconds.

"What the blazes?" Mason said. "That's not legal."

Bhaaj thought back to the endless compendium of Stuff she'd inflicted on herself to read, all the rules and regulations of every event in every track and field tournament the team might attend. She had to make sure she didn't miss anything because to her runners it *all* seemed arbitrary. Without guidance, they'd end up breaking who knew how many rules.

"Actually," Bhaaj said. "It's legal. Nothing in the rules for this event at this stadium say competitors can't catch another competitor who is falling." She suspected that was more of an oversight than anything else, given that most top meets prohibited competitors from helping others during an event. "Even if it did, you can make exceptions for good sportsmanship. Which is what Zee and Strider showed. If you disqualify Kiro, you have to disqualify them, too."

"It's not the same." Mason frowned. "Without their help, he wouldn't have made the cutoff. He should be able to on his own." Watching the evolving scores, he said, "Right now, the only reason he's in fortieth place is because he had help. It wouldn't be fair to add him to the team."

Bhaaj thought it a shame, given how hard Kiro had worked. But she deferred to Mason. He was the one who had coached this team for decades.

As more runners crossed the finish, the area became crowded. Voices flowed while the standings shifted. The top positions became static; none of the runners arriving now had any chance of dethroning the top fifteen. When Strider and her group arrived, Kiro still ranked fortieth, but then the word *disqualified* appeared next to his name, allowing another Cries runner to make the team instead. The names of the two twelve-year-olds appeared in the top forty, but without a rank, which allowed two older runners to place, one from Cries and one from the Undercity.

The last runner eventually stumbled across the finish, a Cries woman Bhaaj didn't recognize given that she'd never attended a single training session. Some of the athletes were exuberant, chatting among themselves, relieved and happy. Some had to sit down, resting while the med-tech checked them over. Others had become quieter, their disappointment obvious. The names of the team qualifiers turned a luminous blue color on the board.

Mason tapped a link on his sports band, connecting to the floating orbs that sent his voice to the runners. "All right, everyone! Excellent job by all! You've done fantastic work, every single one of you. I wish we had the resources to work with you all. Those of you in the top forty, please report to Coach Linsi to get your documents for the team. And to everyone, you all deserve those medals Tena is passing out. All of you! Completing an Olympic-level qualifier is a great accomplishment. Congratulations, and I hope you come back next year to try out again. Absolutely!"

The disappointed athletes perked up a bit as Linsi and Tena put medals around their necks. In her youth, it had puzzled Bhaaj that in marathons, everyone got a medal. It wasn't the gold, silver, or bronze of the winners, but still. Running was a matter of survival, not gifts. She understood it better now, the celebration of completing such a difficult event, but back then, she'd thought they ought to give water instead. Still, her runners seemed satisfied. Of the thirty-six Undercity kids who'd tried out, twenty-six made the team. All thirty-six had already qualified for Bhaaj's desert team and could continue work with her if they wanted, just as Dust Knights trained with her and Ruzik in tykado. She suspected most of the Undercity athletes who hadn't qualified for Mason's team hadn't wanted to. They came for the food and did the training because that was the agreement. In their minds, they'd finished this weird thing she'd arranged. Bargain completed.

Except.

Three of them did NOT look happy. Strider, Lamplight, and Zee were standing across the crowded area, surrounding Kiro. All three had their arms crossed and were staring at Mason with implacable looks that suggested he rated lower than a pico-lizard scuttling in the sand. Kiro seemed heartbroken. He tried to leave, but Strider grabbed his bicep and held him in place.

"Bhaaj." Mason was also watching the quartet. "What's wrong? Why won't those three take their documents for the team?"

"Goddess almighty," Bhaaj murmured. "I don't believe it."

Mason glanced at her. "What?"

A strange sense swelled up within her, one hard to define. It felt like amazement, disbelief, confusion, and joy mixed up together. "They've taken him as a fourth."

"Yes, well, they can't." Mason scowled. "He didn't qualify."

Bhaaj glanced at him. "They don't agree."

"They don't *agree?* They don't *get* to agree. I'm the coach. Kiro fell. They caught him, but that doesn't mean he didn't screw up."

"He only fell, Mason. It happens." She spoke without doubt. "They won't join your team without him. And they're good runners. We don't want to lose them. Especially on the relay, *including* Kiro. You saw how well the four of them work together. They're top notch."

Mason squinted at her. "I can't. I already disqualified him." He motioned at the scoreboard. "What am I supposed to do, tell that kid in fortieth, 'Oh, sorry, I changed my mind, you don't qualify after all?' No. I can't do that."

Fix this, Bhaaj told herself. No dust gang had ever chosen a member who didn't come from the Undercity. It was impossible. Except Strider and her gang didn't know that, so they had gone ahead and done the impossible.

She spoke quietly. "This is big, Mason, bigger than you know. We don't want to lose this, and I don't just mean for the team, I mean for Raylicon. It's a step forward in bringing my people and yours together." She willed him to understand. "I can cover the cost of a forty-first team member. That way, no one gets dropped." With what the Majdas paid her as a retainer for her PI services, she could manage the funds.

He regarded her uncertainly. "You really think I should do this?"

"Absolutely." She tilted her head at other Undercity runners who were also watching them now. "If you don't, you could lose more of my runners than Strider's group."

"Yah," a man said. "I think Tam would leave."

Bhaaj turned with a start. Ruzik stood a few paces away, listening. Angel had stayed back, respecting his position as the Undercity captain, but she remained intent on them, as did many of the other Undercity runners. If Tam left, many of them would, too, given how much they admired her.

"Huh," Mason said. "All right. Kiro can join." Looking around, he motioned to Linsi, who was also listening. "Drop the disqualified note on Kiro's name and add him to the team. But leave the forty-first person up there in blue."

Although Linsi didn't look pleased, she didn't protest. Bhaaj sensed her reaction, though. Had Kiro been from the Undercity, she wouldn't have accepted the situation so well.

Mason lifted his speaker and his voice boomed out of the media orbs. "One correction to the line-up. The disqualification of the athlete who fell is removed since no rules forbid other athletes from catching someone. However, we have left the forty-first athlete as a member of the team." On the scoreboard, Kiro's name turned blue, leaving forty-one names glowing with triumph.

For the first time since the Undercity runners had started training with Mason, one of them smiled at him. Ho! Strider's grin flashed even as Lamp gave Kiro a hard slap on the back. The Cries youth stumbled forward, and Zee caught him, all four of them laughing. Kiro looked happy, and Bhaaj sensed something deeper within him. She'd never wanted to be an empath; she had enough trouble dealing with her own emotions. But when she felt Kiro's hidden reaction, his great joy and the silent tears he wouldn't shed in front of his new friends, it gratified her. His friends. Three Undercity kids.

"He's an empath," she commented to Mason. "A strong one."

"You think so?" Mason sounded preoccupied as people gathered around him.

Bhaaj stepped back, letting Mason deal with the questions pouring in. Ruzik and Angel nodded to her. Strider and her gang, Kiro included, were with coach Tena, filling out their team documents. Bhaaj knew that she and Ruzik would have to go over it all with her runners, but for now seeing them accepting the holo-slates was enough.

It's a new age, Bhaaj thought. The impossible had happened.

Where they would go from here remained to be seen.

CHAPTER VIII
Fourth

"Hey, this is good," Kiro said after he swallowed his bite of spice stick. Breezes ruffled the cloths on the table where Mason's helpers had set out food and water.

"Eh." Strider finished her water, set the self-cleaning bottle on the table, then stuffed two full snap-bottles in her pack. Zee was choosing various morsels, most of which went into smart pouches from the table and then into her pack. Lamp took extra food and water both. Normally Kiro went home after a practice, so he'd never snacked here. It hadn't taken him long to realize this food was for Undercity runners, not him, someone who came from a family with a full-time chef who made him gourmet meals. Today, though, he wanted to be with the three people who had kept his Olympic dreams alive. Saints only knew why they wanted him on the team, but it felt good.

"Got meeting when we get home," a woman said behind them. "Not forget."

Startled, Kiro turned around. Bhaaj stood there, towering in her wild beauty. If Strider and her friends personified young fighters, Coach Bhaaj embodied a warrior goddess incarnate. Her warrior self, however, hadn't noticed him. Her focus remained on the Undercity kids.

"We come," Strider told her.

"Good." With that, Bhaaj took off to talk to Undercity athletes farther down the table.

Lamp showed Strider his full pack. "First we bring food to circle, eh?"

"Yah." Zee joined them, shouldering her crammed pack. "Kiro, you come with."

Kiro blinked at her. "Come where?"

"To meet." Strider spoke as if to say *Of course to the meeting. What else would you do?*

"There." Lamp motioned toward where Bhaaj was leaving with Ruzik and Angel. The other Undercity runners straggled after them.

Strider took two more water bottles and handed them to Kiro. "You carry."

"Uh, okay." Confused, he went with them, bringing the bottles.

The Undercity kids began to run. None went fast; they all seemed tired. Kiro didn't want to run, but he wanted even less to get left behind. They went slow enough that once he started, it felt more like a cool-down than a struggle.

Only a few Cries citizens were out now, during this time in the eighty-hour day when most had their midday sleep. The few pedestrians they passed stopped to stare. Kiro felt their disapproval. Not from everyone, though. Some found it intriguing to witness the unprecedented event of Undercity athletes jogging through their streets.

Eventually they reached the plaza that bordered the city. No one stopped; they ran across the expanse of pale blue stone, passing a fountain that sent poisoned water arcing into the bright sunlight. At the far edge of the plaza, they ran down the wide steps, never breaking stride—

Until they reached the Concourse arch.

Everyone stopped. Hot breezes tossed Lamp's black curls across his face, and the blazing sunlight heated the top of Kiro's head. The arch rose out of the desert, a solitary object in the flat landscape. Kiro almost never came here; the Concourse was a tourist trap for people who wanted the thrill of experiencing the Undercity or a trendy night spot.

"Day too bright," Zee muttered.

"Yes." Kiro agreed one hundred percent.

The athletes ahead of them were going under the archway. An opaline shimmer filled it, but they walked through as if it were nothing. Curious, Kiro followed. The shimmer dragged along his skin, and then he came out on a landing at the top of a wide staircase.

"Huh," he said. "That's a molecular airlock.

Lamp stopped next to him. "What?"

"A molecular airlock. It's used on ships to keep in the air." Its presence here had to be symbolic. No way could one airlock affect a place as vast as the Undercity, which surely had hundreds, even thousands of ways for air to circulate, enter, and escape.

"Mo-lec-u-lar." Strider laughed as she walked past him.

Kiro smiled. He hadn't figured out why they found multisyllabic words so funny, but he got a kick out of their reaction.

They filed down the stairs to a lobby with vending stations where people could buy drinks, food, and souvenirs. Kiro headed for a wide archway across from the stairs. Beyond it, tourists and young people wandered the spacious boulevard, walking past upscale cafés and boutiques.

"Nahya." Zee caught his arm. "We not go there."

Kiro stopped. "Why not?"

"Key clinkers throw us in jail," Strider said.

"The police won't let you go to your own home?"

Zee laughed bitterly. "We not live there."

"Fake Undercity," Strider told him. "Only for rich slicks."

Kiro thought of the kids he knew at the university who came here for the night life, hanging out at purple-light clubs or getting in trouble at the dance bars. They would never patronize this place unless it catered to the wealthy. "Where do you live, then?" he asked.

"We show." Strider motioned him toward a rack of easy-cycles that tourists could rent to get around the Concourse, which prohibited other vehicles.

They didn't rent the cycles, though. Instead, they went past the rack to a gate hidden in a corner. Designed with scrolled metal strips and vine designs, it looked pretty but unused.

Puzzled, Kiro followed them through the gateway into a lane behind several buildings. Holos of adorable kit-lits with fluffy blue tails ran up the wall of one, morphed into glyphs spelling *The Kit-Lit Club* and then turned into a waterfall of pale blue light that poured down the building.

"Pretty," Strider commented. They set off at a jog along the hidden lane, past the back walls of clubs and restaurants. The athletes up ahead rounded a turn that led away from the main Concourse, but when the four of them reached the curve, the place looked empty.

"Where'd they go?" Kiro asked.

"Here." Strider kept jogging, heading to the wall of the Concourse, which hid in shadowy back alleys that the glitzy types on the boulevard never saw. She stopped at the barrier. It stretched so far above their heads that it became lost in the shadows, a blank expanse of grey casecrete. As she pressed a series of cracks in the wall, Kiro watched, memorizing the pattern.

A click came from within the wall. Strider pushed—and the wall scraped inward, stone grating on stone, granting entrance into the darkness beyond.

"We're going in there?" Kiro didn't know whether to be intrigued or alarmed.

"Come with," Zee said.

So Kiro went with them, through the opening. Once they gathered inside the wall, Strider pushed the door closed, leaving them in darkness. Kiro raised his finger to tap the light on his designer tech-mech band, but then paused, wondering if it would seem boastful.

A dim golden glow appeared around them, coming from a light stylus Strider had hung on a string around her neck, a button on the gauntlet Zee wore on her wrist, and what looked like a cobbled-together light hanging from Lamp's belt.

"Oh." Kiro tuned his light to its lowest setting, modulating the color to match their lamps.

"Good glow," Strider told him, then set off running again.

Intrigued, he went with them. Nothing this interesting had happened to him in ages. He was going to miss his differential equations class, but he didn't mind. Sitting through the lecture almost never helped; he always had to study the play-back in slowed-down detail to figure it out. He'd finish it later tonight, even if he had to miss the next sleep period when he got home. He had to make doubly sure now that he made passing marks, so his parents didn't object to the hours he spent training with Mason's team.

Kiro put out his hands, trailing his fingers along the walls. This run felt surreal, like a dream. Gradually he noticed glints of light as the tunnel widened. Shadowed stalactites hung from the high ceiling like rock icicles, and stalagmites rose in cones of rock from the ground. Their path curved to the left, into view of—

A miracle.

"Goddess," Kiro breathed.

They were running through a wonderland of sparkles, white, gold, green, blue, and pink, all glittering in the dark. Except it wasn't dark any longer. Dim light filled the cavern they'd entered, coming from natural rock formations embedded with crystals in so many colors. And *ruins?* Yes, human-made arches supported the ceiling. Statues stood here and there, some ancient, others newer. Kiro wanted to stop, to explore these wonders, but the others kept moving.

They passed under a large arch at the back and entered another tunnel. Or corridor? Its walls looked too smooth to be natural. Engravings covered them, geometric tessellations more beautiful than the loveliest arches in the homes of his parents' friends. He knew those families because his parents took him to visit people with kids his own age, trying to bring him out of his shell. He suspected one reason his mother supported his Olympic dreams was because she hoped he would make friends on the team. Well, he had, though probably not what she'd intended.

More light came from ahead, warm and golden. When they turned a corner into the radiance, it took Kiro a moment to reorient. They'd entered a *huge* tunnel about twenty meters wide and twice as high. In single-file, they ran along a walkway against one wall of the tunnel about halfway up from the ground to the ceiling. Torches filled the area with golden light. Down below, people had gathered, fifteen or so of them, talking, laughing, and—fighting? He winced as one girl threw down another so hard, surely it must have injured her opponent. But the other girl just jumped up and went back to their fight. No, their *training*, he realized. They were practicing throws.

Other people had settled up here on the walkway. Strider slowed down as they approached a group of three teens, two boys and a girl tending a small fire in a circle of rocks. They'd set a grate over the flames and had two pots simmering on it, one filled with bubbling soup and the other with sauces that wafted delicious aromas to Kiro's nose. Tendrils of smoke curled up from the fire, rising toward the ceiling high above their heads. Given that no smoke accumulated in the canal, this tunnel must have a ventilation system, another aspect of Undercity life that had never occurred to Kiro.

"Eh." Strider knelt by the group. "Got food." She slipped off her pack and handed out the contents to the trio, fresh vegetables and fruits, containers with meat or grain, and spice sticks.

"Good," the girl said, relief in her gaze. "Need good water, too. Ran out."

"Here." Zee emptied her bag, including her snap-bottles of water. "All filtered."

"And this." Leaning past Zee, Lamp gave them the contents of his pack as well.

When Kiro glanced at Strider, she gave the slightest nod, so he edged forward and handed his bottles to one of the youths. The boy watched Kiro with curiosity, but none of them spoke to him or offered their name. He felt their moods, though. They wondered where Strider had found a fourth ganger.

Ho! They thought he was a *gang* member? Couldn't they tell he came from Cries? True, he had on old clothes, but his running shorts and tank top didn't look like what people here wore. He also had on an exorbitantly high-end wrist band.

As soon as the thought came to Kiro, one of the boys glanced at his wrist, and his mood changed from bemused confusion to suspicion. The other two at the fire also tensed. It didn't show in their faces or bodies, but Kiro *felt* it.

Strider tilted her head toward Kiro as she spoke to the trio. "With us."

They nodded, relaxing. "We not pinch," the boy explained. "Hear about in Whisper Mill."

Kiro squinted, trying to figure out what they meant. He thought they'd just assured Strider that they wouldn't try to steal Kiro's wrist band, but that they already knew about it. Although he hadn't seen anyone before they reached this tunnel, he'd sensed people watching from secret places. This all felt dreamlike, as if this place existed as a fantastic land hidden from Cries.

Strider indicated the supplies they brought. "You three in charge. Get food to all, yah?"

"Will do," the girl said.

"We got meet with The Bhaaj," Strider told them. She stepped past the trio and set off running again.

Startled, Kiro followed her. Surely Strider and her friends didn't live this way. Where were their parents? No one here looked older than their early twenties, and most were teens or younger kids. Confused, he ran behind Zee and Lamp, the four of them going single file, staying on this path about two meters wide and set halfway up the wall of the tunnel.

Midwalk, Strider said.

"What?" Kiro asked.

Called midwalk, Lamp told him.

We in aqueducts, Zee added. *All here, Undercity, the Deep, all places, we call it aqueducts.*

Ah, no. It *couldn't* be true. They spoke in his *head.* He had no enhancements, no bio-threads, no tech, no nothing. This was the real thing.

Not panic, Strider thought.

Sorry, Kiro answered, too shocked to react with more than one word.

Not say sorry, Zee scolded. *Sound weak.*

Uh—okay. This felt too strange.

They kept running, nothing more to say, mental or verbal. The glow from their lamps sparkled off crystals in the walls, ceiling, arches, and rippling curtains of rock. So beautiful. So incredibly *beautiful.*

For some reason they allowed him to see this miracle. He'd never heard of anyone from the Undercity inviting someone from Cries to their world. The rumors at school about kids sneaking into deeper areas of the Undercity were nothing like this. People said they couldn't find anything below the Concourse except empty tunnels. Usually they got mugged before they made it even a few hundred meters. Sure, his peers went to the Concourse to shop or enjoy the glitz clubs, but never this far below the surface.

The real Undercity, Kiro thought. *This is the real thing.*

Yah. That thought washed across his mind from Strider, then from Lamp and Zee.

The attack came out of nowhere. Someone shoved Kiro off the midwalk so fast, he had no time even to grunt. He flailed as he fell through the air and crashed into the ground below, crying out as pain shot through his body. The thick dust cushioned his fall, but it still hurt like hell. The swirling grit made it almost impossible to see. One thought blazed in his mind: if someone injured him, he might never get to the Olympics.

Dazed and angry, Kiro struggled to his feet, but before he could regain his balance, someone hit him in the stomach and someone else grabbed his wrist with the tech-mech band. Furious, Kiro punched out, hitting air instead of his attackers.

"Ho!" Strider's shout echoed through the canal.

Someone yanked away the person trying to steal Kiro's band. Someone else hit Kiro, and he doubled over, groaning. He swung his fists wildly, trying to fight back. Although he could see now, at least enough to aim at the man attacking him, the guy easily evaded the blow and struck back. When Kiro dodged, the punch hit his shoulder. Somehow Kiro knew which way to go; otherwise, that blow could have hit his throat, maybe even broken his windpipe. Desperate, he shoved at his attacker. He *sensed* his opponent's location and managed to throw him into the canal wall. The guy slammed against the rock, sending up a swirl of dust. He started to lunge forward, then froze, his gaze going to a point to the right of Kiro.

Gasping, Kiro tried to get his bearings. The place looked like a scene of some hell. Strider was standing over a motionless body, clenching a knife. A drop of blood fell off the blade onto the face of her fallen opponent. Lamp and Zee were watching over two other people, one who lay on the ground groaning, the other who stood nursing a bleeding arm. The guy Kiro had shoved remained intent on Strider. He'd obviously figured out who to fear, and it wasn't Kiro.

"Fuck you, assholes," Strider told them. "My land. You invade."

The guy Kiro has pushed glowered at her, then spoke to Kiro. "Whisper Mill say you pinch from slick." He motioned at Kiro's tech-mech band. "Our biz."

"What?" Kiro could barely understand him.

"You a stupid shit or what?" the guy asked Kiro.

"*You* fucking stupid," Lamp told the guy.

Strider pointed to the fighter collapsed at her feet, a woman, and spoke to the man who wanted Kiro's wrist band. "You pay price, Cojo." She waved her bloody knife at him. "Got your first stabbed."

The man, Cojo apparently, walked over to Strider, though he kept some distance between them. "You kill my first? You pay blood oath."

"Not kill," Strider told him. "Got Knight Code. Not murder."

She spoke the words as if they left a bad taste in her mouth. "Except to protect. You kill my fourth, ass-byte? Try again, I call blood oath on you."

"Yah, well, fuck you, too," Cojo told her. "Your fourth is id-jee-ot."

The woman Strider had stabbed moaned and opened her eyes. "Eh."

Cojo held out his hand. As the woman grabbed it, he pulled her to her feet. Tall and muscular, with cyber implants on her face, she glared at Strider. "Not kill me, bitch."

"Not invade my canal, bitch." Strider turned to Cojo. "Get out."

Kiro expected the others to threaten or attack again. He wasn't sure, though. It sounded like they'd violated some pact. Strider's gang had bested them, despite Kiro being an idiot, so now Cojo and his gang had to leave.

Except they didn't. Instead, Cojo said, "What take?"

Strider considered him and the woman she'd stabbed. Then she looked at the woman near Lamp. Finally, she turned to the guy Zee had knocked over, who had also climbed back to his feet. Strider pointed to an ornate dagger the man held. "That."

"Like hell," the guy told her.

"Lost tumble," Strider said. "Pay price."

The guy let loose with a string of profanity that would have startled even Kiro's most garbage-mouthed peers. Then he threw his knife, and it hit the ground near Strider. Lamp scooped it up, then handed it to her.

Strider lifted her chin at Cojo. "Now get out."

He glowered, but he and his people took off running, vanishing into the shadows.

"Holy shit," Kiro muttered.

"You okay?" Strider asked him.

"Yeah. Fine." His head hurt, but he didn't think he had a concussion. Any minor injuries, his health meds would treat.

"Bleed." Zee motioned at his head.

"I am?" Touching his temple, he felt a sticky liquid. "Oh." He wanted to throw up, but he wanted even less to humiliate himself, so he managed to hold it back. Or maybe his health meds kept him from upchucking all those spice sticks he'd eaten earlier. Exhaustion flooded him, followed by fear as his shock of adrenaline eased. He had *no* idea where he was, how to get home, if he had any injuries that needed treatment, or *what*—

"Not panic," Strider murmured. "We take care of our own."

Kiro watched her in confusion. "But—I'm not your own. I'm a—an intruder, right?"

Strider came over and laid her hand on his shoulder. "You Kiro. You honor us with your name. Not worry. We invite. You can stay. Or if you want, we take home. Your choice."

"Got team meet," Lamp reminded them. He tilted his head at Kiro. "Should come." Then he added, "If not want that, I take home. Strider and Zee go to meet."

Kiro couldn't humiliate himself by running home when they all planned to continue as if nothing had happened. "It's, uh, is fine. I stay." He was stuttering, trying to use their dialect. He'd heard rumors that Coach Bhaaj had paramedic training. Maybe she'd know if the fight had injured him enough to threaten his chances of staying on Mason's team.

"Good." Strider nodded with approval. "We go."

They set off running in the glittering darkness.

Torches and lamps lit the cavern more brightly than anywhere else Kiro had seen in the Undercity. More than forty people had gathered here, including the runners from the practice today, all of them, not just the qualifiers. Coach Bhaajan was there as well, talking with Ruzik. They'd entered a huge room, a cavern with polished walls covered by exquisite mosaics in coppery, bronze, and golden tiles, tessellated patterns that looked like geometric art.

A man Bhaaj's age stood near the wall, watching, dressed in black, with black hair and eyes. A scar snaked down the side of his face, and he had cyber implants on both arms. They glinted in the torchlight, calculating who knew what for this silent, threatening stranger. If those four gangers who had attacked Kiro were proto-thugs, this guy ranked as a criminal king.

Bhaaj looked over as Strider's group walked in, and relief showed on her face—until she saw Kiro. She froze then, staring with what felt like shock to him, though her face remained neutral. For an instant he felt sure she'd tell him to get out. Then she took a breath and walked over.

"Why late?" she asked Strider.

"Cojo and his crap-sucking ass-shits," Strider explained.

"You rough-tumble?" Bhaaj asked.

Strider tilted her head toward Kiro. "They want his tech-mech."

Frowning at Kiro, Bhaaj motioned at his wrist band and spoke in the Cries dialect. "You can't bring that here, not where people can see. It's like you're daring them to steal it."

Strider looked embarrassed. "Should have said," she admitted to Kiro. "Forgot."

Kiro almost said sorry, then remembered he wasn't supposed to apologize. Instead, he took off the band and stuffed it in a pocket of his shorts.

Bhaaj tilted her head toward the thug king. To Kiro she said, "Come with."

As much as the guy intimidated Kiro, he had no intention of arguing, so he walked with her. Strider and her group went to talk with their friends, and everyone else either pretended to ignore the guy or else just didn't care that Bhaaj wanted Kiro to talk to him.

When they reached the man, he scowled at Kiro and spoke in a perfect Cries dialect. "What the fucking hell are you doing here?"

"Uh, Strider invited me," Kiro said.

"Yah, right," the man said. "Don't lie to me, asshole."

"Jak, don't," Bhaaj said. "He's telling the truth." She lifted her hands, then dropped them as if she didn't know what to do. "Strider, Lamp, and Zee picked him as their fourth."

The man stared at her. "They *what?*"

Kiro finally found his voice. "They wouldn't join the Olympic training team unless Coach Mason included all four of us."

Jak spoke to Bhaaj. "We can't have Cries intruders here. It's not safe, not for him or us."

Bhaaj glanced at Kiro. "It's true, you're in bad shape."

"It's all right." With his adrenaline going before, Kiro hadn't felt much, but now everything hurt, especially his head and his side where he'd slammed into the rocks. His legs ached, too, though whether that came from all the running he'd done today or the fall, he had no idea.

"You need a doctor to look at you." Bhaaj raked her hand through her hair. "Jak, can you get Doc Karal? She wants to talk to the team anyway."

"Yah. Will do." He gave Bhaaj the barest hint of a smile and then set off without a lamp. Kiro wondered what it would be like to see that well in the dark. No wonder Undercity natives had such large eyes.

Bhaaj turned back to him. "You need to be more careful. You don't want any injuries to sideline you from the Games."

That sounded like she believed he had a chance to qualify. "I'll be careful. I promise."

"Good." Her tone warmed. "And yes, you've a chance, assuming you keep improving."

Kiro tried not to feel flustered that she caught his thought. Maybe she'd just made a good guess. "To qualify, we have to meet an Olympic standard at an official meet, yes?"

"That's right." She motioned toward where Strider, Zee and Lamp had sat on a bench carved like a dragon. They kept an open space on the long seat next to Zee, waving off anyone who tried to sit there. "Go join them. We're going to talk about all that." She watched him intently. "You'll hear some of this twice, once down here and again from Mason."

Kiro suspected she had a lot to say that wouldn't occur to Mason. He nodded, then headed to the others. As he approached, Zee patted the open space. After Kiro sat down, Strider leaned out past Zee and Lamp and spoke to him. "Bhaaj chiz you out?"

Kiro shrugged. "Said be more careful."

"Yah," Lamp stated. Enough said, apparently.

Bhaaj went to stand on a rock stump and spoke to everyone. "Okay. All here. We talk team."

A rumble went through the waiting athletes. "Hungry," someone said.

"Thirsty," several others added.

Bhaaj glanced to the side. Following her look, Kiro saw Ruzik standing there. Whatever silent communication went between him and Bhaaj, Ruzik nodded and moved away.

Bhaaj turned back to the gathering. "We get you food. Water. Take what need." She spoke firmly. "But not stuff selves. Not get sick."

Not get sick? Kiro wondered what she meant.

"Some here on high team," Bhaaj continued. "Some on reg team. High team meet with Coach Mason in Cries. Reg team meet with me in desert or down here."

"We Dust Knights now?" someone asked, an athlete who hadn't qualified for Mason's team.

"You got invite," Bhaaj told them. "Still got to learn ways of Knights. And swear to Code."

"Dust Knights better than high team," someone else said. "Harder to make."

Kiro blinked. It had never occurred to him that people had to qualify for the Dust Knights, or that they'd consider it even more exclusive than making an Olympic team.

"Not want to run," a girl said. "Rather do tykado. Fight like Knight."

"Not have to run with team if not want," Bhaaj said. "Bargain done."

"Still want to do reg team," a guy said. "Get better for next time."

Another kid gave a dismissive grunt. "Get black belt. Better than running team."

"Do either or both," Bhaaj suggested. "You decide."

"Bargain done?" someone asked. "We not get water from now on? Food?"

"Still get both," Bhaaj said. "As long as high team got, you all got."

Kiro spoke to Lamp in a low voice, trying the Undercity dialect. "Not ken bargain."

"We make bargain with Coach Mason," Lamp explained. "Come to practice, get food. Even if not make team, still get food as long as train with The Bhaaj."

Kiro still didn't get it. "Why make bargain for food?"

"Need," Zee said. "Why else?"

"And water," Strider added. "Good water. Not make you sick or kill you."

"You mean—you don't have that?" Kiro asked.

Lamp shrugged. "We good dust gang. Most times, we find enough for circle."

Somehow Kiro kept his voice calm. "And if not find enough?"

"Stay hungry," Zee said. "Or pinch food from Concourse stalls."

"Key clinks not like," Lamp added. "Catch us pinching stuff, put us in jail."

"Goddess," Kiro whispered. He felt like a monster, sitting here well-fed and pampered while these runners, who'd qualified far more easily than him, managed it without enough food or water. His parents could feed everyone here for days on what they spent for one meal from their chef.

"I can bring good food," he said in a low voice. "Good water."

Lamp scowled at him. "Not take char-it-ty." He made the last word an insult.

"I ken," Kiro said. And he did get it. He'd never liked how some of his peers assumed they deserved to get whatever they wanted through their privilege rather than earning it. The Undercity athletes accepted food from Mason by making a bargain with him. It couldn't be cheap for the team, feeding so many people. Maybe his parents could discreetly help fund Mason's spread. Except, the way his father talked, it sounded like he'd rather jump in a lava pit than help the Undercity.

Kiro decided to try his mother first. He wondered about her too, though. It had upset her more than he expected when he mentioned the Undercity, enough that he worried how she'd react if he told her about this visit. She treated him as an adult and no longer asked him where he went, but he didn't want to hide his friendships. He needed to find the right way to approach his parents.

"Not fight," Bhaaj was telling the gathered athletes. "Not get hurt. Can't do team if hurt."

Strider spoke up, her voice tight with anger. "Might need to fight. Not have choice."

"Dust Knights not on team will stay with you," Bhaaj said. "Twenty-six of you on high team." She motioned at the crowded cavern. "That why we got so many Knights here."

"*We* Dust Knights," Zee said. "Not need Knight to protect Knight."

"Yah, need." Bhaaj spoke firmly. "Not fight. Ass-byte throw you off midwalk, they maybe break your arm. Your leg. Your damn neck." Dryly, she added, "You die, you not on team."

Zee squinted at the thought and said no more.

"Big thing, this team," Bhaaj told them. "Big in *all* places. And you outdo slicks. Is good."

"Yah!" Agreement rolled around the cave, coming from everyone, including the Knights assigned to the athletes. Kiro couldn't imagine what it was like to live in a place where you needed hulking tykado bodyguards to protect you from getting broken or killed.

Tam spoke up. "High team go to Olympics?" She said the three-syllable word *Olympics* with respect.

Interesting. Kiro had assumed using a word with more than two syllables showed scorn or ridicule. Given what he felt from Tam, though, it could also indicate honor. Come to think of it, they used Undercity or aqueducts to name their home, never with ridicule. Their lives, their culture—it meant more to them than his people knew or understood.

"Not sure we all get to go," Bhaaj cautioned. "Need run at big meets. Get high scores."

"What meets?" a man asked. "Like today?"

Kiro tried to remember the man's name. Dice. That was it. Dice. He had a second name, too, which seemed unusual here. Kiro couldn't remember it, though.

"Meet today not count," Bhaaj said. "Not big enough."

Rumbles went around the crowd, including derisive whispers of the word *important*. Bhaaj hadn't sounded mocking, though. She used those extra syllables to stress her point.

"Go to other places," Bhaaj said. "Places with more runners. Compete against them."

"So high team got to make more-high team," another guy said. His name eluded Kiro until he remembered his mnemonic. This man with the arm scars that looked like cracks in stone was called Rockson, son of the rocks. The woman with cracked-stone scars on her arms was Rockjan, daughter of the rock. He stored their names in his memory; Rockjan had joined Mason's team, and Rockson considered becoming a Dust Knight more coveted than qualifying for the Olympics.

"Yah, so," Bhaaj agreed. "We go offworld to make more-high team."

Silence met her words. Finally someone said, "What that mean, offworld?"

"Leave Cries," Bhaaj said. "Go other places."

"Why?" a woman asked.

"Cries tiny," Bhaaj told her. "These other places, they got more gangers. Lot more."

Disbelieving rumbles rolled around the room. Zee spoke to Kiro in a low voice. "That true?"

"Yah," he said. "We go to worlds at other stars."

Lamp blinked. "What 'stars' mean?"

"Other solar systems."

Zee snorted. "Jib."

Kiro scowled at her. "Not gibberish. Other worlds. They go around star like Raylicon go around our sun."

"Ray-li-con. Star-star-star." Lamp flicked his hand. "You make up."

"Not make up," Kiro growled.

"Stop make noise," Strider muttered at them. "Bhaaj talk."

"—you need to choose," Bhaaj was saying. "Which events you do."

Zee spoke up, her voice loud and clear. "Run. Throw. Climb. Three events."

"More than three," Bhaaj said. "Many ways to do each." She motioned at the people to her right. Angel stood there and Ruzik had returned. So had Jak, with a woman who looked familiar, though Kiro couldn't place why, except that she had straight black hair instead of curls.

"We break into groups now," Bhaaj said. "Ruzik and Angel help as Undercity coaches." She indicated the woman with Jak. "Doctor Rajindia talk to you about med stuff."

Ho! Kiro gaped at the woman. *Rajindia?* That name belonged to the House of Rajindia, one of the highest among the noble houses. They didn't just produce doctors, they specialized in treating Kyle operators. Psions. Empaths. He knew now why she looked familiar. Even though she dressed in Undercity clothes, simple trousers and a blue top, and wore her hair pulled back in a ponytail, she had classic Rajindia features, the aristocratic nose, the high cheekbones, the large eyes. Yet even she seemed to defer to this Jak person, the king of thugs.

Lamp spoke under his breath. "He king of cards, dice, all that."

"Eh?" Kiro asked.

"Jak run Top Mark," Lamp said. "Only way slicks come here. 'Cept you." With a soft laugh, he said, "All those rich slicks, they lose bad in Mean Jak's place."

Oh. Of course. Even Kiro had heard of the Top Mark casino, an elite establishment you could visit only by invitation, with guides who blindfolded you, muted your hearing, and more, all to hide its location. He'd heard that the proprietor even periodically changed its name to make it harder to find. The glitzy casino catered to the wealthiest, most powerful clientele on the planet. Unfortunately, Raylicon also had the distinction of being the only world in the Imperialate where gambling was illegal. *Seriously* illegal.

"How Bhaaj know him?" Kiro asked.

Lamp laughed and Strider gave Kiro a look that plainly said, *maybe you're a stupid fuck after all.* When Kiro glared, Zee relented and said, "Bhaaj husband."

Kiro gaped at him. Coach Bhaaj, retired army major and personal PI for the House of Majda, had married one of the most notorious crime bosses on the planet? Yes, today was certainly one of the most interesting days he'd had in a long, long time. Like ever.

As the athletes broke into smaller groups, Jak led Doctor Rajindia to Strider's group. They all stood up, Kiro included.

Jak motioned to Kiro as he spoke to Rajindia. "Strider's fourth. Got jumped. Check, yah?"

Rajindia nodded, her focus on Kiro. Flustered, he nodded to the doctor. *Empath* doctor. Something was up with the Kyle operators here in the Undercity. Supposedly the noble houses had more Kyle operators than the regular population, yet Kiro had sensed more empaths after only a few hours in the Undercity than in the rest of his entire life.

After Jak left, Rajindia said, "All four of you in fight?" She spoke the Undercity dialect with almost no accent.

"We fine," Strider informed her.

The doctor motioned them back to the bench. "Have seat. I check." Glancing at Kiro, she frowned. "Who?"

Before Kiro could give his name, Strider spoke sharply to the doctor. "Nahya."

He stopped, confused. They didn't want him to give the doctor his name?

Rajindia didn't seem surprised. She spoke to Kiro in the Cries dialect. "Do you come from the city? I can't tell. You look Undercity, but I'm not sure." Her gaze flicked over his clothes. "I recognize that designer logo on those world-class running shoes you're wearing."

"Yes," Kiro said. "I'm from Cries." The shorter he kept his answers the less chance he'd say something stupid.

"What the blazes are you doing down here?" Rajindia asked.

Before he could respond, Strider said, "Our fourth." To Kiro she added, "If you want."

He wanted to grin, smile, give her a thumbs up, anything. Somehow he restrained himself and just nodded, Undercity style. "Yah. Is good." He had no clue what she meant, but he trusted her. He sensed Strider, Lamp, and Zee more than he ever had with anyone else, even his mother, whose thoughts he had never picked up. He'd find out what fourth meant soon enough. He just hoped it didn't get him killed.

"Interesting," Karal Rajindia said.

The doctor checked them using equipment she carried in a backpack, state-of-the-art med-tech. Sometime during it all, she told Kiro he could call her Karal. It honored him, not only for what it indicated in the Undercity culture, but also because Imperialate nobles gave out their personal names even more rarely than people in the Undercity.

The four of them were in reasonably good shape, though the knife wound in Zee's arm needed a smart-bandage that would dispense nanomeds to speed its healing. Kiro had a lot of bruises and cuts and a sprained wrist, but his feet, ankles and legs—his running tools—were fine.

As they finished up, Bhaaj returned. "They okay?" she asked Karal.

"They'll live." Karal frowned at them. "No more fight. I help heal, but you need be careful."

They looked back at her, nothing said, but no protest, either.

"Did you check my health meds?" Kiro asked, switching to city dialect before he realized it.

"They're operating well," Karal said. "Why do you ask?"

"I was worried they might be too much for the Olympic regulations."

She tapped a monitor on her medical wrist band. Apparently no one down here mugged the doctor for her tech. "Let's see...." She peered at the data scrolling above its small screen. "Yes, that's good... fine... not sure about that." She brought up more glyphs, nothing Kiro could read upside down, but they included the five rings of the Olympic logo. Finally, she looked at him. "You're good. If you qualify for the Olympics, make sure you have them monitored by the team doctor, in case the IOC makes any changes in the rules."

Relief washed over him. "I will. Thank you."

"Too many words," Lamp grumbled at them. "Just say, 'You good for now.'"

Bhaaj laughed, which made Strider, Zee, and Lamp all glare at her. The doctor also smiled. She left them then, off to check other athletes.

"So," Bhaaj said. "We need talk about what events you do."

"Run," Strider told her.

"Run what?" Bhaaj asked. "100 meter, 200—"

"Not need numbers," Zee informed her.

"We run all," Lamp stated.

"That so?" Bhaaj inquired. "How? Got less than year to make even one."

"We try all," Strider said.

"You try too many, you end up with none," Bhaaj told her. "Get tired. Maybe hurt."

"We fine," Zee said.

"You good runner," Bhaaj agreed. "Top slicks better."

Lamp snorted. "They suck."

"You not see best in Imperialate," Bhaaj said. "Raylicon need get better."

"Im-per-i-a-late," Strider said. She, Zee, and Lamp burst out laughing.

"Ray-li-con," Lamp added, and they laughed more.

"Yah, enough fucking joke," Bhaaj said. "You want be on team, you learn right words."

The trio regarded her with impassive expressions. *Almost* impassive. Kiro felt them trying not to laugh. He wanted to ask Bhaaj what events she thought he should specialize in, but if he did it now, it would sound like he was ass-kissing. Instead, he kept his mouth shut.

Strider glanced at him. Then she turned back to Bhaaj. "What you think we should do?"

"Good question." Bhaaj stopped looking annoyed. "The relay." She considered them. "Four-hundred-meter relay. You four."

"Not marathon?" Kiro asked.

Bhaaj shook her head. "You better at sprints."

He just nodded, but relief flooded him.

"Like short runs better," Lamp said.

"Which like best?" Bhaaj asked.

"Shortest," he said.

"You good at that. Do 100, maybe 200 too." Bhaaj glanced at Kiro. "You do 400?"

"Yah, good." He liked both the 400- and 800-meter races.

Zee said, "Not got water on short run," evoking more laughter from the others.

Bhaaj squinted at them. "What?"

"When jump over water," Strider explained. "Is silly."

"Oh." Bhaaj stopped looking confused. "You mean the steeplechase."

Kiro had heard of the steeplechase, but he didn't know much about it, just that it included jumping over both hurdles and pools of water.

"Steeple, weeple." Zee laughed. "Is silly, put water under sky."

"Water always under sky on other worlds," Bhaaj said.

They regarded her with dubious expressions, much the way they had when Kiro tried to talk to them about stars. Unexpectedly, Lamp said, "Astronomy."

Strider smirked. "Talky-talky jib-jib."

"Nahya," Lamp said. "Learn about in school stuff."

"Good," Bhaaj said. "Need learn."

"Ass-trah-nooooo-mee," Zee said, and burst out laughing.

Bhaaj sighed. "You think about which races you like," she told them. "Now go home. Get sleep." She glanced at Kiro. "You stay here?"

Kiro hadn't thought that far ahead. He couldn't stay; he had no place here. Home was such a long way, though. He had no idea how far or deep they'd gone into the Undercity.

"Can stay with our circle." Strider was watching him with a look he recognized now, as she sensed his mood. Normally it went no farther; those moments when he'd picked up their thoughts had felt unusual. His head throbbed, too, which made him wonder if he'd used his Kyle senses too much. Maybe his mind had a limit, just like doing too many exercises could wear out his body.

As much as he wanted to go home, though, he didn't want to insult them. He just said. "My thanks. I stay with circle." She must mean the people they'd met on the way here.

Watching him, Strider's expression gentled. "Is okay. We take you back if you like."

"Nahya." He sensed how tired they felt. "Here is fine."

"Don't worry," Bhaaj told him. "I have to go upside anyway. I'll bring you home."

Kiro couldn't imagine spending that much time with this Undercity goddess. He'd be tongue-tied the entire time. He couldn't tell her no, though, so he managed, "Thanks."

"All right." To the others, she said, "Not go on patrol for circle without Dust Knight guard. Not get hurt. Keep legs to run. Ken?"

"Yah," Strider said, echoed by Lamp and Zee. That they didn't even protest told Kiro far more about how tired they felt than if they'd used words.

With that, he and Bhaaj left.

CHAPTER IX
First Visits

While Kiro gave the flyer's autopilot his address, Bhaaj leaned back and closed her eyes. Normally she'd have run the kilometers from the Concourse to her penthouse in the city, but she felt too tired tonight. Mason would have her hide for letting the kids jog home after a half-marathon. He didn't get it, though. For them, an easy jog felt like a walk. Or at least she'd have thought so on any other day. Right now, she wanted to collapse.

First she had to make sure Kiro got home. What the blazes was Strider thinking? She had to know Kiro couldn't act as their fourth. Bhaaj doubted he wanted to move to the Undercity, not if the hints she'd seen of his wealth gave any indication of his lifestyle. Yah, sure, his clothes looked worn, but their logo belonged to one of the most expensive sports lines in existence. That tech-mech band of his had to be worth thousands.

Besides, he couldn't fight worth shit. True, he didn't have to be a Dust Knight to join a dust gang. Cojo had never wanted to join the Knights or keep their Code. It was one reason, however, that Strider, Zee, and Lamp had trounced his gang. Kiro had been lucky to slow Cojo's attack for the few moments Strider needed to stop the fight. Then again, maybe it wasn't all luck. If he shared an empathic bond with Strider's gang, he'd probably sensed their awareness of Cojo. That could explain why they chose him as their fourth. Kyle sensitivity outweighed everything else.

Bhaaj opened her eyes. Kiro had sat by the window and was staring out at the city as it baked under the blistering noon of Raylicon's eighty-hour day. He looked as tired as she felt.

"Long day," she commented.

He turned with a start. "Yes, very." His voice cracked on the second word, and he winced.

She wondered why she made him so nervous. "You had a good run today."

"It was generous of Coach Mason to allow me on the team after I fell." More to himself, he added, "I'd have been fine if I hadn't lost my grip on that blasted cliff."

Bhaaj understood all too well. "It could happen to anyone. And he wasn't generous, Kiro. You deserve your place on the team. You and Strider's gang will make a strong relay, much better I suspect than if Mason tried to find someone else as their fourth."

"Thanks, Coach." With diffidence, he added, "Your runners seem good at all the distances."

"Ah, well." Bhaaj doubted this was the time to talk about how poverty and violence had bred them to run well. Besides, Kiro had earned her respect. Not only did he show his teammates honor regardless of where they came from, but he'd accepted their invitation to the Undercity and never once complained, not even after another gang mugged them.

She glanced beyond him, out the window to the lushly forested neighborhood below. They'd reached the foothills of the Saint Parval Mountains, which in most places had almost no greenery, just spiky vines. Yet here in Cries, a verdant forest thrived on a planet where a significant portion of the population was dying for lack of purified water. Goddess, what a waste.

"It does seem like a terrible waste," Kiro said.

Bhaaj jerked, caught off guard.

"My apology." He reddened. "I didn't mean to be rude." Then he winced again. "Sorry. I keep forgetting I'm not supposed to apologize."

"How did you know I was thinking about the trees?" Even suspecting he was a Kyle, she hadn't expected that sensitivity. She'd learned to protect her mind by using thoughts that changed her neural firing patterns, damping the Kyle processes in her brain. Not only did it protect her from picking up moods, it also made it harder for other empaths to sense hers. Only someone with an exceptionally high rating could have caught her thought.

"Your thoughts?" He blinked with confusion. "I don't know what you mean."

"I didn't say that about the waste aloud."

He seemed to withdraw, as if he'd closed a door. Bhaaj recognized his bland look. She used to do that herself, before she admitted she needed to learn how to handle being an empath rather than suppressing it. If Kiro had the strength he'd just hinted at, that put his ability as rare as one in ten million, maybe even one in a hundred million, at least outside the Undercity.

"You must have spoken," he said.

"Kiro, don't." She felt too drained to deal with his defenses. This was too important to bungle, though, so she softened her tone. "You're obviously an empath. Maybe a telepath."

His posture went rigid and his face paled.

"It's not a crime," Bhaaj added. "It's a gift." She hoped that last didn't sound sarcastic.

"Are you going to report me?"

"For what?"

"I don't know." He hesitated. "Doesn't the government want Kyles to work for them?"

"That's true." They'd hit dangerous territory. She was about to go exactly where Jak feared when he warned her that Kiro posed a threat to the Undercity. "But I won't say anything. It's your business." She spoke carefully. "The same is true for any interaction you have with Strider, Lamp, and Zee. It's private. Do you understand? Anything you sense in the Undercity, any bonds you form with our people—it's private."

"Yes, of course." Now he looked confused. Or maybe she sensed his reaction with her own abilities, which she didn't want any more than he apparently wanted his.

"You'll also have to sign a non-disclosure agreement," she added.

He gaped at her. "*What?*"

"Actually," Bhaaj said. "You'll need a security clearance with the government."

Panic flashed across his face. "What are you talking about?"

Bhaaj wished she had the energy to do this better. "I'm sorry," she said, using a Cries-style apology, which went a long way with slicks. "The military and the government have an interest in the Undercity. By linking with Strider's circle, you got yourself involved."

His surprise vanished. "I see."

Bhaaj regarded him warily. "See what?"

"A lot of people in the Undercity are Kyle operators," Kiro said. "The authorities want them to work for the military. Or the government. That's why Angel has that high-powered job."

Smart kid. It didn't surprise her; with all those extra neural structures, Kyle operators tended to rate high on measures of intelligence. They had the neurological make-up needed to use the ancient tech that protected the Skolian Imperialate. It didn't come down to just one trait; the more Kyle DNA a person carried, the stronger their abilities. Only one in a million had the strength to operate the ancient machines. The side effect? It made them more sensitive to neural signals from other humans. They rated as empaths. One in a billion could even pick up a few words in thoughts.

Except in the Undercity. Almost one third of them were empaths. One tenth were telepaths.

Bhaaj spoke carefully. "I'm going to trust you to say nothing about it while I get you the clearance. This isn't a small thing, Kiro. If you betray my trust, you'll end up in prison."

"I won't. You have my word."

"Good."

Curiosity seeped into his voice. "Is it always this way, that when you're around other Kyles, it heightens what you pick up from people?"

"Essentially. You both send and receive better than the normal population."

"But what good is it?" His question sounded genuine, not cynical. "I mean beside helping the military use ancient tech they don't understand to stop the Traders from conquering us."

"You just answered your question," she said dryly. "That's a damn big use."

"I mean what's the use to *us*." He didn't try to hide his pain. "It makes your life hell. Being an empath feels like living without your skin. The only escape is to hide from the rest of humanity." With longing, he added, "Don't take Strider, Lamp, and Zee away. They're the first people who've ever seen me, I mean really *seen* me, like a light in the darkness."

Her voice gentled. "I won't. You need to learn how to protect yourself, though."

He got The Look, that universal expression known throughout history, that of an adult child putting up with a parent's scolding. "That's what my mother tells me."

Bhaaj held back her smile. "I'm not surprised, if she and your father are empaths."

"My mother is. I'm pretty sure my father isn't, though."

"The genes are recessive. You won't show the traits unless you get them from both parents."

He sat thinking. "If my father carried the genes unpaired, he wouldn't be an empath, but he could still give some of them to me."

"Well, yes." Bhaaj spoke carefully. "It doesn't usually work that way, though. Given your strength, your father must have a lot of them. And *none* are paired?" It seemed unlikely. Not impossible, but still. Kyles sought each other, looking for mates who shared their neurological sensitivity. "Are you sure he's not an empath?"

"I suppose he could be." Kiro didn't sound convinced.

"He might have repressed it." She didn't add, *Or maybe he isn't really your father.*

Are you talking to me? Max asked.

What? Oh, no. Actually, yes. Can you analyze Kiro's face?

It should be possible. If I link to the biomech lenses in your eyes, I can get images of him. What are you looking for?

In the Undercity, people seemed uncertain if he came from Cries. But usually we know right away. It's more than how someone dresses, carries themselves, or speaks. It's a look we have.

You want to know if Kiro has Undercity heritage.

Can you tell?

I can't do much just using your lenses. But I can get a rough idea.

Thanks. Let me know.

"Coach Bhaaj?" Kiro asked. "Are you all right?"

"Sure, fine." She realized she was just staring at him. So she said, "I think we're at your house."

Kiro turned to the window. "Oh. Yes. Of course." After a hesitation, he added, "Would you like to come in? I think my mom would enjoy meeting one of my coaches." His tone became apologetic. "My dad isn't here. He's gone most of the time."

Bhaaj wanted to say no. She felt too tired. However, her job as a coach extended to the entire team. With the Undercity kids, she'd assumed the title of guardian for those who'd lost or never known their parents, which included most of her athletes. However, meeting the parents of the Cries athletes also mattered. Mason wanted good relations with everyone.

"I'd be honored to meet your mother," she said.

His face relaxed into another of those smiles he gave so freely. "Great. Thanks."

The flyer settled on a long, curving driveway. Ho! That was a *huge* mansion, surrounded by who knew how many acres of forest. Magnificent trees shaded the house. The place shone, all blue and white with windows and skylights everywhere, glistening in the streaming sunlight.

They disembarked into the burning heat of midday. That lovely sunshine felt like a furnace.

Kiro grimaced. "Come on. Let's get inside."

He took her around the side of the mansion, along a rustic path under trellises heavy with flowers shaped like pink and white trumpets. They entered the house through an arched side door. Once inside, they walked along corridors paneled in wood. *Wood.* It must have cost a fortune. How could they bask in such extravagance while her people died below the desert?

Kiro glanced at her, his face subdued. "I'm sorry."

"What?" Bhaaj focused on him. "What happened?"

He started to answer, stopped, then said, "Nothing."

An androgynous voice spoke into the air. "Del Kiro?"

Bhaaj looked around. "Is that your house EI?"

"One of them." Kiro raised his voice. "My greetings. Are my parents here?"

"Your mother is in the north-wing living room. Would you like me to tell her you're home?"

"Yes. We'll be there in a moment."

They followed halls, climbed stairs, went through an entertainment room, and then down a curving staircase. Bhaaj wondered how many people lived in this huge place. "Is there a staff here?"

"Mostly droids." Kiro sounded nervous, unsure how she'd react. "We also have a live-in chef and a human gardener."

"Ah." She didn't know what else to say. Only the wealthiest of the wealthy could afford human staff.

Eventually they entered a living room with sleek, modern-style furniture in blue and white. Sunshine poured through the windows. A woman with straight black hair was sitting at a piano, picking out a tune on the keys.

"Hey, Mom." Kiro ambled over to the piano.

The woman turned with a start. "My greetings, honey." Her smile vanished. "Kiro! What happened? Where did you get that bruise on your face?"

"It's nothing." He spoke casually. "I slipped during the cliff climb. But I'm fine. A team doctor checked me out and gave me some extra meds for healing."

"You need to be careful." Worry lines creased her forehead. "Did it stop your race?"

His expression lit up as if the sun came out. "No! I made the team!"

"That's wonderful!" Relief washed across her face as she jumped up and hugged him. "I'm so proud of you!"

Kiro hugged her back, then let go, looking self-conscious. "Some friends helped me."

"That's lovely. You should invite them here."

"Um, yes. I'd like that."

Such irony, Bhaaj thought to Max. *With all his advantages, he and his mother feared he couldn't make the team, yet for all our poverty and struggles, none of mine worried at all.*

Some don't even seem to care.

They will, once they better understand what it means to be an Olympic athlete.

"Look who's visiting." Kiro stepped aside. "This is Coach Bhaajan."

Bhaaj gave a slight bow. "My greetings, Goodwoman Caballo. I'm pleased to meet you."

Gwen nodded. "I am pleased to make your acquaintance."

Unexpectedly, Kiro chuckled. "Eh. Too talky."

Bhaaj couldn't help but laugh. He sounded just like Lamp.

"What?" Gwen looked from her son to Bhaaj. "Is something funny?"

"Team joke," Kiro explained.

"Ah. I see." She didn't look like she saw at all, but she seemed happy. Lifting her hand, she invited them to the plush couches in the living room.

After they settled into their seats, a gleaming drone brought glasses of wine and little rolls of some sweet that tasted heavenly, like chocolate, cream, and spice sticks mixed together. They talked for a while, casual chat about the team.

"It sounds exciting," Gwen said. A sense of gratitude ran deep within her mood, also a feeling of... what? Joy. It overjoyed her to see her son happy instead of lonely.

The realization hit Bhaaj like a hammer. Kiro spent most of his time alone in this huge, echoing house. He used his isolation to protect his empathic mind. She sensed a few mental barriers he'd instinctively built, but he'd never developed them. It differed dramatically from the Undercity, where if you didn't protect your mind or repress your abilities, life damaged you beyond repair. Some drug punkers, surrounded by their vicious reality, became warped beyond healing. Cutter Kajada, the Kajada cartel boss, had gone from a bright, curious child to a sociopathic adult.

"Your run today sounds great," Gwen was saying. "Much better than my exec meetings."

"More corporate politics at Abyss?" Kiro asked.

His mother grimaced. "I swear, it never stops."

Bhaaj's interest perked up. In her job as their PI, the Majdas had her investigating a takeover attempt of Abyss Associates by Scorpio Corporation. Scorpio controlled the utilities of entire planets, including Metropoli, a world with ten billion people. Abyss built skyscrapers and had recently taken over water production from Suncap Industries. Normally water offered a less lucrative market than utilities, but on parched Raylicon, it was everything. If Scorpio absorbed Abyss, it would become the most powerful corporation in Cries. With substantial holdings in both companies, the Majdas stood to gain no matter what happened. Why they wanted her to spy on this specific financial war, she had no idea, but she suspected they favored the Scorpio takeover.

Curious, Bhaaj spoke to Gwen. "You're an Abyss exec? That must be exciting."

"I'm just a data analyst." Gwen relaxed as she talked about work. "I do predictive studies."

"I've never much understood what analysts do," Bhaaj said. It wasn't true; in the army, she'd specialized in analyzing and improving military strategies. But she wanted to encourage Gwen to say more about her work.

"I figure out what most profits the company," Gwen said.

Well, that was vague. Bhaaj put on a confused look. "Ah. I see."

"I analyze trends," Gwen explained. "I look at what other companies are doing, especially how that might affect Abyss, and then I project futures for the company."

"I had a friend at university who was a whiz organizing databases," Bhaaj said, even though what Gwen described went far beyond the work her friend had done. She wanted to spur Gwen to say more.

And indeed, Gwen did look miffed. "It's more than just using databases. I project the development of the economy as it affects Abyss. Even how it affects the planet." Dryly she added, "Which essentially means how it impacts the Majdas."

"Huh." Kiro yawned, trying to hide it behind his hand.

His mother's expression gentled. "You look tired."

"It's been a long day," he admitted.

Taking the hint, Bhaaj stood and nodded to Gwen. "My honor at our meeting, Goodwoman Caballo." To Kiro, she added, "See you tomorrow at practice."

He jumped to his feet. "You bet!"

After Bhaaj left, it only took moments for the flyer she called to arrive. She moved slowly as she boarded and settled into her seat, feeling the proverbial "under the weather," whatever that meant. If you felt healthy, did that put you on top of the weather?

Max, she thought as the flyer took off. *Are my health meds working?*

I don't detect any problems. Why?

I feel stiff. Achy. And like I have a fog in my mind.

That sounds like the long-term effects of carnelian rash.

That can't be. The rash had never affected her, at least not the way it hit other people.

You should get checked. The virus can mutate.

I guess so. She didn't have time to be sick. *Did you finish your facial analysis of Kiro?*

Yes. It took a while because you were mostly looking at his mother. But I was able to use their family pictures.

And?

I'd guess he's about half Undercity. He's had some minor work on his face that makes him look more like a Cries citizen, but it's superficial.

Hah! I knew it.

I checked his records. His parents married about seven months before his birth.

You think they wanted to make him legitimate? In the highest levels of Imperialate society, where inheritance meant everything, legitimacy took on a meaning most people didn't care about.

It's hard to say. Kiro doesn't look like his father, but I'd say Gwen Caballo is his mother. Maybe she couldn't marry his true father.

Interesting. She had a new trend for her PI investigation, figuring out if and how Kiro's mother fit into the scheming on Raylicon, financial or otherwise.

Georj settled the neural cap on Angel's head, and her scalp tingled as the cap extended delicate strands into her skull. Disconcerted, she took off the cap slowly, giving the strands time to retract. She frowned at Georj and the other two people standing around her control chair, Fluff-Pup and the woman she'd met before. It turned out that Pup called himself Darin and the woman was Bayley. Such slick names, not strong at all. Angel couldn't help but think of Darin as Pup.

Georj scowled at her. "You can't work as a telop if you won't wear the gear."

"Not like in head," Angel told him in her dialect, not for honor but because it annoyed him. Then she thought, *Oh, stop it. Just because he's being an ass-bat, you don't have to be one too.* She switched into Iotic. "It bothers me to have threads extend into my brain."

"A lot of people feel that way about the caps," Bayley said. "You'll get used to it."

"If you'd take a biomech web in your body," Georj said, "you wouldn't need a cap."

"I couldn't go to the Olympics then." Angel savored all three syllables of *Olympics*. Except she felt how much Georj hated that she was training for the Games. He believed she deserved neither her position on Mason's team nor this job. He assumed she got them only because someone had decided to promote her people over his, leaving him at a disadvantage. Angel didn't understand. How could he envy someone whose people had nothing, who were dying from starvation, violence, diseases, and poverty? She had no idea how to react to him.

"Olympic athletes can't have any augmentation in their bodies," Pup said.

Georj snorted. "Giving her biomech that detects neural firings won't make her run faster."

"You never know," Bayley said. "People come up with all sorts of cheats."

"You know," Angel said, "I'm sitting right here."

Pup reddened. "Sorry. We didn't mean to be rude."

"Eh." It never stopped amazing Angel how often slicks apologized. In the Undercity, people would've flattened them a million times by now for sounding weak. They meant well, though, at least Bayley and Pup.

"The thing is," Bayley said, "We can't link you to the Kyle mesh without the cap."

Pup pulled over a chair so he could sit next to Angel. "It's how you enter the Kyle gate."

Angel wanted so much to slip into her dialect. Iotic felt less comfortable, especially when she became this tense. But they were trying, including Georj even though he *really* didn't like her. So she said, "I still don't get this Kyle biz. I read the orientation, but it doesn't seem real."

"What a surprise," Georj muttered.

Angel kept her *Fuck you* to herself.

Bayley grabbed a chair and sat next to Pup. Georj continued standing.

"It's not real," Bayley told her. "At least not in the way we experience space and time."

"Kyle space is outside of space-time," Pup said. "The gate lets you access it with your mind, but we can't physically go there."

Angel motioned at the training lab. Everyone else in the cavernous place was intent on their own consoles, often with colorful holos floating in the air. "All of this, every place we know, that's what we call space and time, right? How can Kyle space not be part of that?"

"It's complicated." Georj sounded like he was trying, in his own way, to be nice. "Don't worry that you can't understand. You don't need the math to do the work." Under his polite facade, his thought was so intense, Angel even caught the words. *You're too slow to get it.*

Irritated, Angel spoke in the Undercity dialect. "That mean *you* not know how it work?"

Georj stiffened. "Don't insult me."

"You not ken it," Angel deduced.

His face turned red. "You need to learn your place, dust rat."

"Enough!" Bayley said.

Angel switched into Iotic and spoke to Georj with a courtesy she didn't feel. "I know you don't mean offense," she lied, "But please stop calling me a dust rat. My people consider it a slur."

"It's just a word," he told her. "No need to be a sensitive flower."

Angel almost laughed. People had called her many things, *blunt, aggressive, hard,* and other less repeatable names, but *sensitive flower?* She wanted to be pissed, but the description was so funny, she couldn't get worked up. Instead she spoke to them all. "This Kyle place, it's about eigenfunctions." Let Georj chew on that rudely polysyllabic word.

Bayley gaped at her. So did Pup and Georj. Huh.

"Uh, yes," Bayley stammered. "You've studied quantum physics?"

"A little." After Angel had finished the first few years of the college biz Bhaaj insisted she do, she'd branched out. "It's not my favorite subject, but I've a friend who loves it." Hack, the cyber-rider for their circle, spent his days playing in his weird lab making weird stuff using weird math he got off the meshes in Cries or figured out himself. It was why he'd never tried out for Mason's team even though he ran as well as Angel and Ruzik. He only had time for one extra pursuit besides his lab, and he preferred training for his second-degree black belt in tykado.

Pup spoke with curiosity. "How much do you understand the theory?"

"Not much," Angel admitted. "You can describe stuff by a wave function that solves the Schrodinger equation." That was as far as she'd gotten. She had no idea how to do the math.

"She's just parroting back words she's heard," Georj said.

"I'm not a bird," Angel said. "Why don't you tell me what it means?" She leaned forward, watching him with what she intended to appear as polite interest. It didn't work. Georj thought she looked ready to beat them up, Bayley wondered how hard she worked to keep those muscles, and Pup thought she looked like a glam-ad for marines in the Advance Services Corp.

"Uh, yes, well, um." Georj shifted his weight. "It's not my job to teach you physics."

Pup spoke quickly, before Angel could poke at Georj more. "It's true, wave functions describe everything in our universe. Matter is both solid and a wave."

Yah, that sounded like Hack's hallucinatory talk. Angel told them what Hack had said to her after she informed him that she wasn't a fucking wave. "Our wave lengths are too small to see, eh? You can only measure them for tiny stuff, like atoms and electrons."

"Well, yes." Bayley looked as surprised as Georj. "That's right."

"When I think," Angel said, "the quantum wave functions that, uh, describe the molecular behavior of my brain change." All these rudely named processes were giving her a headache.

Pup looked pleased. "That's right. Let's say at a certain place and time, you have a thought. Like now. Your position is fixed, but your thoughts are changing."

"In Kyle space," Bayley said, "your thought is fixed but your location changes. The closer your thoughts are to what someone else is thinking, the closer you are to them in Kyle space."

"Well, good for us," Angel said. Hack wasn't the only one who sounded like he'd taken drugs when he talked about physics.

They all exchanged looks. Finally, Pup said, "Angel, it's important. It gets around the problems we have with communicating across interstellar distances."

That did sound useful. She still didn't ken it, though, so she just said, "Eh."

"Almost instant communication across interstellar distances," Pup added, watching her. When she continued to wait, he said, "Only the Skolian Imperialate has it. That's huge. It's the only reason our military can stand up to the Traders. They have no Kyle mesh. Either they try to steal time on ours without trained telops, which is as hard as hell, or else they're stuck using starships to carry messages. That takes far longer."

"Starships go fast, though," Angel said. "They go into complex space, yah?"

"Yes!" Bayley leaned forward. "If you add an imaginary number to your speed, that makes it a complex number. It removes the problems with light speed. It's like you're on a road blocked by an infinitely high pole. That pole is the speed of light. You can't climb it to reach the other side. But! You can leave the road and walk *around* the pole. The road is real space. Leaving the road is like going into complex space. When you come back to the road on the other side of the pole, you've gotten around the problems at the speed of light. You're going faster than light there."

After having seen the many pages of math on the subject, Angel liked that Bayley reduced it to a few words. "It still takes too long, though, yah? Because ships can't violate—" What was the word? "Causality!" That was it. "Space and time switch around at speeds faster than light. You can go backward in space here. In complex space, you can go backward in time. Except it can't—" Can't what? She wished she'd read the relativity stuff better in the last physics class she'd hacked. "Everything that happens must be consistent no matter what your frame of reference. You can't go into the past and do something like stop yourself from being born, because in another reference frame, you've already been born."

"Hey," Bayley said. "That's a good summary."

Angel was glad she liked it, because that exhausted what she knew. So she just said, "Eh."

Pup seemed happy with her, though. "Even in complex space, the time it takes to travel is still essentially distance divided by speed. Sure, relativistic effects come into it, but you can't travel anywhere near as fast as we can communicate using Kyle space."

It almost made sense. Angel wondered why Georj had gone silent. Maybe he didn't ken it that well, either. She was still irked at him, so she said, "Yah, okay. I get it." Which was sort of true.

Bayley motioned at the lab. "We use the tech here to access Kyle space. We act as conduits to other operators. If we're thinking along similar lines—having a conversation—we're next to each other in Kyle space no matter where we are in this universe."

Angel motioned at the neural cap that Pup held. "And that lets me use this Kyle tech?"

"Absolutely." He indicated her seat. "It links you to this control chair."

Well, what the hell. When she'd agreed to take health meds in her body, they'd helped, so she might as well try this, too. Unlike the meds, she could remove the cap whenever she wanted.

"Okay," she said. "Do it."

Angel forced herself to sit still while they fastened her into the cap. A visor lowered over her head, and everything went dark. Then the view lightened until she found herself in a stone room with bare walls, ceiling, and floor.

"Eh?" Angel asked.

Bayley's voice came out of the air. "Can you hear me?"

"Yah. Hear fine. Not see you."

"The mindscape responds to neural firings in your brain," Bayley said. "Imagine how I look, and I should appear."

Angel envisioned her, and sure enough, Bayley morphed out of the air, standing in the room next to a chair.

"Okay. You here." Angel looked around, trying to find herself. "I not here."

"That's normal your first time," Bayley said. "You don't usually look at yourself, after all."

Interesting. Angel had seen her reflection in metal or water, but never well. She thought of Ruzik, imagining his sexy, muscled self. He didn't appear, though.

"I see you because you also linked to Kyle tech," she told Bayley.

"That's right." Bayley lifted her hand, revealing a thread that went from a socket in her wrist to her chair. "I have a biomech web in my body that links to my neural system."

Like Bhaaj. Angel wished she could read about it more with the online library—

The room suddenly changed into a bright cave with flecks of crystal in its polished stone walls, benches, and tables. Many shelves stood farther back in the cavern. Console films lay everywhere, rolled out on the carved tables, every film whole and gleaming, with none of the dark splotches like the ones she used back home. Stained glass windows high in the walls added color to the scene, as they often did in the Undercity. Bayley sat at a table across from where Angel stood.

"Eh," Angel said.

"Hey!" Bayley said. "What did you do?"

"You see what I see?" Angel asked.

"I'm not sure. Did you just make a library in a church?"

"Yah. Nahya."

"I'm sorry. I didn't understand what you said."

"I make library. This looks like real room, though. Library is just stuff on mesh."

"Libraries used to be real places," Bayley said. "Your sim is incredible."

Huh. Interesting. *Chair,* Angel thought. A cloud formed and morphed into a chair across the table from Bayley. It consisted of a rock stump veined with rose quartz and sculpted like a giant hand opening palm-up to the ceiling. Nice. As Angel sat down, she finally saw her body, at least a blurry view of her legs and arms. When she tapped the table, a film appeared, gleaming and flat.

"Gods," Bayley said. "Who taught you how to do this?"

"Me," Angel said. "This first time I come here." She spoke to the film. "You got biochem?"

An androgynous voice answered. "I have access to every public civilian database in the City of Cries, and any military databases available with your level of clearance."

Angel scowled. "Jib."

"I'm sorry, I don't understand," the voice said. "Do you wish texts about biochemistry?"

"Later." She considered Bayley. "I get in trouble for using this place?"

"Why would you get in trouble?"

"To use school meshes, I got to steal time on them."

"Library accounts are free," Bayley said. "You just sign up for them."

"Not us."

"Anyone can," Bayley insisted.

Angel scowled at her. "Nahya."

"Here." Bayley spoke to the rose-quartz table. "Bring up the library entrance portal."

A pleasant garden appeared on the table, with flower-draped trellises framing an arched door. *Cries Library* appeared above the arch in soft colors that matched the flowers. Sunrise colors. Angel had never known that word in her youth, given that she'd never seen either a sunrise or such big flowers. Lately, though, she'd gone early to the stadium to train before work and witnessed a sunrise every morning, as well as the flowered bushes along the way. Pretty.

"Open access for new account," Bayley said.

The words *Full name* appeared floating above the table.

Bayley started to say, "An—"

"Nayha." Angel put up her hand to stop her. Then she said, "Jumper." The name belonged to a man who'd lived in her circle. He'd passed away from old age a few years ago, a rarity, except people in her circle tended to live longer because their dust gang looked out for them so well. Jumper had made it to forty-six.

"I have no record of anyone called Jumper," the library informed them.

"Not alive," Angel admitted. "Die five years ago."

"I have no record of anyone named Jumper living in Cries, now or in the past."

"Live in Undercity."

"I have no records for anyone in the Undercity."

"You give free account to all," Angel told it. "So make me account."

"I am happy to give you a free account," the library said. "Please provide your ID."

Angel frowned. "Not got ID."

"Sure you do," Bayley said. "You can use your Kyle Division—"

"Nahya." Angel held up her hand again. "Me, true. Most of my people, not true." Then she added, "Library, I not got ID. Still make me account?"

"You can go to the civic center to obtain an ID," the library told her. "You will need your birth certificate."

"Not got birth cer-ti-fi-cut." Angel stressed all four syllables to express her low opinion of slick documents, though she doubted the library cared.

"The hospital where you were born can provide one," the library informed her.

"Not born there," Angel told it. "Born in cave."

"Ask the doctor or midwife who delivered you."

"Not got doctor or midwife. Just mother."

"You can still use the record of your birth to get an ID."

"Not got record."

After another pause, the library said, "What you describe is impossible. My authentication routines have determined that this is a prank call. If you persist, I will notify the authorities of your inappropriate use of this portal." With that, the pretty garden disappeared.

Angel raised her eyebrows at Bayley. "Not prank."

Her tutor seemed confused. "You couldn't have been born in a cave with no one attending."

"Brother there." At least, he claimed that. He'd only been four. "He wait outside."

"But—why didn't your mother call a doctor? Nurse? Midwife?"

Angel regarded her impassively. "Not got doctor-nurse-midwife."

Bayley seemed at a loss for words. "I don't understand."

"Same for all Undercity." Then she amended, "Get a doctor now. Doc Karal. Bhaaj bring."

Her tutor went silent, her avatar staring at nothing.

Eventually, Angel said, "You okay?"

Bayley's avatar came back to life. "Sorry. I was trying to look up Undercity birth records. None seem to exist." She regarded Angel. "Is that really true? You give birth in caves?"

"Yah."

Bayley waited, as if she thought Angel would say more. After a moment, she said, "But it's so dirty. Doesn't that bother your people?"

Anger stirred in Angel. "Not dirty."

Bayley grimaced. "It's disgusting. Not just the cave, but that you don't try to do better."

Yah, screw you, too. Angel almost spoke out loud, then reminded herself she was an "ambassador" for the Undercity. Instead she told Bayley, "This what you call dis-gus-ting."

She imagined her home.

The library vanished, replaced by the cathedral-like space where her circle lived. The cavern had polished walls hung with tapestries in pleasing spirals of color. Rippled rock curtains bordered the main room, creating private areas where people could sleep or be alone. In the central area, columns supported arches that blended into the roof. Human artists had sculpted the columns into warrior goddesses holding up the ceiling or handsome men in the robes of ancient princes. Crystals glittered on swords the warriors carried or in the medallions worn by the princes. Light filled the cavern, coming from glowing candles and figurines holding lamps.

Artisans had sculpted furniture from the walls, benches shaped like dragons with flat backs, their heads raised at one end and their tail curled around the other. Embroidered pillows softened the seats. The sculptors designed the movable furniture from air-pumice, chairs with circular seats, round tables, and a round dais with a table where they held meetings. Another table had glazed plates and blown-glass cups waiting for a meal. Too often they didn't have enough food to fill those plates or enough filtered water for the glasses. The food from Mason's banquet helped support their circle without them needing to fight other gangs for supplies.

The weavers who made the tapestries and cushions had chosen gentle colors that matched the pumice, hues with names like rose, lavender and azure. Angel would've said wimpy red, wimpy purple, and wimpy blue, but what did she know. Her skills involved beating people up and running fast, which seemed paltry compared to gifts of the artisans who made this cavern a home.

"Goddess," Bayley murmured. "This is *gorgeous*. Is that where you live?"

"Yah." Angel spoke tightly. "Not dirty."

"I'm sorry." Bayley sounded mortified. "So, so sorry. I had no idea."

Angel said nothing, resisting her instinct to attack someone who sounded weak. She appreciated what Bayley meant with the apology.

After a moment, Bayley tried again. "You must have a large family."

"Circle." Angel's voice thawed. "Not know my blood family. Parents die when I little. Two brothers, one still alive. Ruzik and me, Tower and Byte-2, we protect circle. We Dust Knights."

"Dust Knights," Bayley mused. "I've heard the term. A fighting force, yes?"

"Yah." Angel left it at that. This conversation cut too close to her private life, which she had no wish to share with anyone from Cries. "We work now?"

"Ah. Yes." Bayley seemed to mentally shake herself. "Okay. Back to the Kyle. When you work as a telop, you're accessing a mesh in Kyle space that the Ruby Dynasty Kyles created."

"Why only Rubies make it?" Angel asked.

"They're the only ones strong enough. If you or I tried, we'd fry our brains."

Angel frowned. "What that mean, 'fry brain'?"

"It means—actually, I've never tried to explain." Bayley thought for a moment. "Our brains have organs called the Kyle Afferent Body and Kyle Efferent Body. KAB and KEB. Everyone has them, but undeveloped. In Kyle operators, they develop more. The more Kyle DNA you have, the larger your KAB and KEB. Your brain also produces a neurotransmitter called psiamine. Its presence can indicate you're an empath even if you don't show any traits. Does that make sense?"

"I think so." Angel switched into Iotic, which had words that didn't exist in her own dialect. Also, multisyllabic language didn't sound foolish in Iotic. "My KAB picks up brainwave activity from other people, right? It sends signals to, uh—" To what?

"To para organs in your brain," Bayley said. "They interpret the messages."

"It's why I feel moods, yah? And my KEB does the reverse? Sends out signals. Most people can't pick up such weak activity. Only strong Kyles." Like Ruzik, Tower, and Byte-2.

"Essentially," Bayley said. "Even most Kyles can't decode signals as complex as human thought."

"I still don't ken what 'fry brain' means."

"Maybe that's the wrong phrase." Bayley paused. "All that neural activity can overload your brain. It's like an electrical firestorm, which causes a convulsion. If you go into a state called status epilepticus, or back-to-back seizures, it can kill you."

Angel hesitated. "You think that might happen when I train?"

"Not according to your exams." Bayley spoke with reassurance. "I think you're ready to take your first Kyle steps. Want to give it a try? If you notice problems, I'll pull us out."

"Try what?"

"To enter the Kyle mesh."

"How?" Angel saw no mesh, just her home. She thought of the bare stone room that had appeared when she first came here, and the cavern faded, turning back into that first place. She and Bayley sat at a stone table, and a display of colorful holicons floated above the table.

Bayley flicked her finger through a holo. "How did you know I needed this menu?"

"Didn't." That wasn't quite right, though. "I think the Kyle place knows from my mind."

"Interesting," Bayley mused. "Whatever you did, it looks like the Kyle mesh interpreted it as a command to provide my teaching tools." She waved her finger through the holo of an arched doorway. "Angel account, Kyle Division."

A holo of Angel appeared in the air and a voice said, "Telop trainee Angel, do you give permission for telop Bayley Barrows to access your account?"

"Eh," Angel told it.

"Is that an affirmative?" the table asked.

Angel switched into Iotic. "Yes, go ahead."

"May I access your gateway into the training space of the Kyle mesh?" it asked.

Angel liked that it talked *to* her instead of *about* her to Bayley. "Yes, sure."

"Gateway activated." The holo of Angel turned into the image of an archway shaped like a giant keyhole with a stained-glass window in its top. Mosaics in gold, blue, and silver bordered the entrance, similar to the ancient archways in the aqueducts.

"Why arch look Undercity?" Angel asked.

"The system here is responding to your mind to an unusually high degree," Bayley said. "More than for most of us."

Angel liked this telop biz. She could create things just by thinking. "What I do now?"

"Go through the gate."

"How? Not real. Just light pic."

"It represents the entrance into psiberspace."

Angel scowled. "Jib."

"I'm sorry, what?"

Psiberspace? Angel thought. It sounded like a gibberish word.

"It means Kyle space," Bayley answered.

Angel stiffened, startled. "How you know what I think? You say you only sense moods."

Now Bayley looked confused. "You spoke. You said the word sounded like gibberish."

"Nahya. I just think that."

Bayley's avatar froze. After a moment, she came back. "Okay. Our link through the Kyle lab enhances our interaction. It seems your signals are strong enough that with additional augmentation from the tech, I can even get a few of your strongest thoughts."

Huh. Angel didn't need augmentation with Ruzik, his brother, or Tower.

Bayley was watching her. "Go ahead. Think yourself through the gate into Kyle space."

"Not see any Kyle space."

"I know. Just try. You need to align your mind with the gate."

At a loss, but too embarrassed to admit it, Angel glared at the holo. *Open up, silly arch.*

A thought came into her mind with the cool, flat sensation of a machine. **Gate accessed.**

Angel blinked. *Eh?*

Is that a command? the arch asked.

Take me to Kyle mesh, Angel thought.

The room faded to blackness. When it lightened again, she was floating above the desert. Except the red sands that spread out below seemed gentler than the scorching Raylicon dunes. Glimmering lines intensified within the landscape, forming a mesh that reached to the horizon in every direction. The area below her swelled into a smooth, symmetrical peak glowing with gold light. Other peaks showed in the distance.

A new peak rose next to hers, not as high, and rose-hued instead of gold.

Angel? the peak asked, with Bayley's voice.

This Kyle place? Angel asked.

Yes! Bayley sounded pleased. *Nice work.*

What work? So far she'd done exactly squat.

Let's start with something simple. I just sent a comm message in real space to Georj, asking him to access another Kyle gate in the lab. He's thinking about his breakfast. Can you find him?

Angel imagined him in her mind, then thought, *Georj, what you eat today?*

A grey light flashed in the distance.

Angel squinted at the intermittent light. *Georj, that you?*

The grey light rushed toward them, morphing into a peak as symmetrical as theirs, silver at the bottom and shading into a grey so pale, it looked white at the top.

Hey, Georj thought.

Eh, Angel answered.

Let's stick with work questions, Georj sounded different here, less... what? Less certain? Not exactly. He just didn't come across as strong in Kyle space. Neither did Bayley.

I got work question, Angel said. *Not see point of this. We talk fine in lab. Why need this?*

It's practice. Georj didn't mask his annoyance. Or maybe in Kyle space he couldn't hide it.

Okay, practice done, Angel said. *Now we do real stuff.*

You don't know enough yet, Georj told her. Although he didn't say more, she picked up his mood. He thought she wanted to avoid the practice because she was lazy.

Why you think I not want to learn? Angel asked, all patience today. Not that she had any choice. It wasn't like she could punch anyone in this Kyle place.

Bayley started to say, *I don't think it's nec—*

Telops contact people offworld, Georj interrupted.

Fine, Angel thought. *I do that.*

Georj laughed, an ugly sound here where it seemed harder for him to hide his true opinion. *Right, dust rat.*

Angel sent a deceptively mild thought. *Told you not call me that.*

Maybe we should call this a day, Bayley said quickly. *Tomorrow we ca—*

Look, Georj interrupted. *You want a task? Fine. Contact the Orbiter space station.*

Georj, stop it! Bayley said.

Angel imagined herself in a hidden cavity deep within the Undercity. It surrounded her, cutting her off from Bayley and Georj. Then she thought, *Kyle gate, you talk to me private?*

I am the Kyle Division training EI, a disembodied voice thought. **The gate is only part of my function. And yes, we are now in private mode.**

Fine. Connect me to Orbiter.

I cannot. Neither of us has the clearance. Also, the Orbiter has

millions of nodes. Even if you had access, you would need to specify which one.

They got guest node? Every network she'd found so far had them.

No.

Who can get me there?

You need someone cleared to access the Orbiter web.

Who I know got access?

Do I have permission to check your personal data?

Yah. Go ahead.

General Vaj Majda can give you access. I estimate zero chance that she would do so.

Angel could just imagine how the hard-assed general would react. *Anyone else?*

Colonel Lavinda Majda. I estimate a 1.4% chance she would agree.

Ho! Of course. Lavinda. *Okay. Link me with Colonel Majda.*

Colonel Majda is not currently in the Kyle net.

But you can link me to her regular comm, yah? Angel imagined the archway icon for the Kyle gate. *You can go back out like we came in.*

You are correct that I can use the Kyle training web to reach comm systems in real space, such as when I send reminders to trainees of upcoming sessions. However, I cannot contact Colonel Majda. The best I could do would be to reach an aide of an aide of an aide to her. I doubt you could make it past the first level.

I got link that goes straight to her.

That isn't possible.

Why not?

Colonel Majda would not give a telop trainee a direct link to her comm.

Well, she did. Here. Angel envisioned the code in her mind. *Try that.*

Very well. After a moment, it said, **I have Colonel Majda on your interface with her personal mesh. She is currently in her office at the Selei Tower.**

Angel's hiding place vanished, replaced by an office much bigger and more high-tech than anything she'd seen before. It looked like what she'd imagined for the execs at that party in Selei Tower. Lavinda sat behind a large desk with the window-wall at her back showing a panoramic view of the city. Holicons floated in front of her, above a desk screen.

Angel had last seen the colonel when Lavinda visited the Undercity, with Ruzik's gang as her escort. Today Lavinda wore the same crisp uniform and had her black hair swept back. Her large black eyes and high cheekbones had an aristocratic quality Angel couldn't define but knew when she saw it. The colonel's dark skin looked smooth, none of the lines, scars, and tattoos someone her age would have in the Undercity—if they lived that long. Lavinda was fifty, the same as Bhaaj, but with all the advantages of her position, including health meds that delayed her aging.

Lavinda regarded her as if Angel sat in a chair across the desk. Looking down, Angel saw her body in detail, including the soft grey tunic and trousers she'd worn today to work.

"Angel?" Lavinda sounded puzzled. "Are you contacting my console from the Kyle mesh?"

Angel looked up. *Yah,* she thought. Except it didn't come out that way. Instead, she said, "Yes, ma'am." She spoke with respect in Iotic. "I could use your help, if you aren't too busy."

"Help with what?" Lavinda seemed baffled.

"I need a link to Orbiter," Angel said.

Lavinda stared at her. "What's going on? What happened?"

"My Kyle trainer thinks I'm too stupid to be a telop," she explained. "I told him I'm not, that he should give me task and I'd do it. So he told me to contact Orbiter. My trainee EI says you are the only person I know who can help. Well, you and General Majda. You seemed the right choice." To put it mildly. Vaj Majda could flatten her into a pancake with just a look.

Lavinda scowled. "What the blazes is a tutor doing, telling you to contact the Orbiter?"

"He thinks I can't do it."

"Of course you can't. No one in your position could. What's the name of this tutor?"

"I don't want to make trouble for him." Angel could handle Georj herself. "I'd just like to show him that he's wrong."

"Angel, this isn't a small ask," Lavinda said. "The Orbiter is one of the most secured places in the Imperialate. It's a military center and home to some members of the Ruby Dynasty."

No wonder Georj thought she couldn't do it. "I ken. I will show honor." The colonel knew enough about the Undercity to understand the significance of that vow. Angel would keep it even at risk to her life.

"All right." Lavinda nodded to her. "I accept your oath."

Angel nodded back, sealing the bargain.

"You do actually have the clearance for a low-level link," Lavinda said. "Normally a trainee doesn't, but you needed clearance as my escort when I visited the Undercity. And eventually, if you rise in the Kyle Division, you will need the ability to link to the Orbiter networks."

Fair enough. "How I make this rise?"

"Well, showing initiative, resourcefulness, and a high Kyle ability is a good start."

"Okay. How I do that?"

Lavinda smiled. "You already have." She flicked her fingers through holicons above her desk, bringing up new menus. "Let's see... not that one... there!" Looking up, she said, "I'm giving you access to the Tribune holo service, the Orbiter version of the news you can get for free here at any terminal." She paused. "Angel, this is an interstellar link. Do you know what that means?"

"It goes to another world." It had been a year since she and Ruzik had traveled to Parthonia to help Bhaaj. Since then, Angel had stolen time on the university mesh to figure out some astronomy. Weird subject, but fun.

"It's not another world, not exactly," Lavinda said. "Astronomical engineers designed and built the Orbiter. It's what we call a space station."

"I ken," Angel said. "I've read about them."

"Good." Lavinda went back to work, flicking up menus. "All right. There you go."

A new voice spoke, one that sounded like the Kyle training EI. "Access to the Orbiter general news feed granted to telop Angel."

"Eh." Angel liked that it called her a telop instead of a trainee. She nodded to Lavinda, expressing her thanks. The colonel nodded in return, using the exact same motion.

"All right," Lavinda said. "You go back to your work." With that lengthy good-bye, she tapped a panel on her desk and—

Ho! Angel once again stood in her secluded hiding place. *Kyle EI,* she thought. *Take me back to Bayley and Georj.*

Privacy mode deactivated, the EI answered.

The grid with its people-peaks reformed around Angel. The rose hill for Bayley and the silver hill for Georj hadn't moved.

Where did you go? Bayley sounded worried.

She fell apart when I gave the Orbiter command, Georj answered. His thought felt so smug, Angel wanted to smack him.

Instead, she did the Kyle equivalent. *I make Orbiter link,* she told them. Then she added, *Kyle EI, activate my link to the Orbiter.*

Done, the EI answered.

A new thought came with the feel of a machine, but larger somehow than the EI. **Welcome to the Orbiter Tribune broadcast service. Would you like to see a menu of our stories?**

Show latest news, Angel thought.

A virtual scene formed, a city unlike anything she'd ever imagined, a place where pathways, bridges and arches moved as if they had their own minds. A menu of news stories floated within the scene.

Holy shit! Georj thought. *That's the news feed from the Orbiter.*

Angel shrugged. *You tell me link to Orbiter. So I make link.*

Bayley said, *How?* in the same moment Georj said, *How the hell did you do that?*

Can't say. Is secured. Angel doubted the news feed was confidential since they could get similar stories from the Raylicon feed, but she'd promised to respect Orbiter security, and she could take that promise to whatever extreme she wanted, like not telling them squat.

Suspicion flared in Georj's thought. *You cracked the Orbiter? That's treason!*

Seriously? Angel thought. *First you act like I'm too stupid to do anything, and now you think I can hack one of the most secured networks in Imperialate. You can't have it both ways.* In a more courteous tone, she thought, *I got permission to make the link.*

From whom? Bayley sounded more curious than alarmed.

Angel was tempted to say *it's secured* again, but then she relented. *Majda.*

Yeah, right. Georj's thought felt derisive. *We have to report this.*

Go ahead, Angel told him. *I'm sure Colonel Lavinda Majda would love to talk to you.* Then she added, *I didn't tell her which tutor wanted me to reach the Orbiter. And she asked, Georj. She doesn't know. If you go reporting it—which is fine with me if that's what you want—but if you do, she'll know who gave me a task they thought was impossible. And she was pissed.*

Gods damn it. If a thought could growl, he was doing it. With more caution, he asked, *You really know Lavinda Majda?*

Not well, Angel admitted. *She's the one who recruited me for the Kyle Division.*

Cool. Bayley's thought rippled with approval.

Still, Georj said. *I'm not comfortable with this. I'm pulling out of the web.*

It is getting late, Bayley said. *I think we've done enough for today.*

Angel wanted to stay; she loved this place. But she needed to go practice with the running team. She was already late. *Okay. I go too.*

And thus her first visit to Kyle space ended. She'd only just begun to figure out what she could do here, but the possibilities intrigued her.

Yah, this would be *interesting*.

CHAPTER X
Hidden Paths

"We need to go offworld," Mason said. "Get the team into an official meet." He stood with Bhaaj in the stadium watching their athletes practice on the track below with the assistant coaches.

Bhaaj couldn't imagine taking so many Undercity kids offworld. As much as they weren't ready to face the universe of elite athletics, though, they had no choice. Less than a year remained to get them qualified for the Olympics, and they couldn't do that on Raylicon. They had to enter a track meet approved by the IAC, the Interstellar Athletics Committee, a meet where they didn't also have to qualify for *that* competition. Given their short time frame, they had few options.

"Which meet did you have in mind?" she asked.

"It depends." Mason was peering at his holo-pad, frowning as holicons rotated above it in luminous colors. "Does Tam want to do the royal marathon or the classical?"

"The royal. She loves ultra marathons." At 80 kilometers, it was the longest Olympic race, also the one with the most elevation, even more than the cliff climb. The classic marathon founded by the Earthers was considerably shorter, about 42 kilometers. "Ruzik wants the royal, too."

"And Wild." Mason flicked his finger through several holos, saving data to a file.

"Wild has improved. Ruzik, too." She watched the two young men running together below. "They need to vary their training more, though. Like with cross-fit."

Mason nodded absently, then looked up from his holos. "Where is Angel? She's late again."

"It's her job." It seemed to take more and more of Angel's time lately.

"Can she ask for shortened hours?"

"I'll talk to her." Bhaaj wasn't sure Angel wanted less time at work. She'd taken to the job more than Bhaaj expected.

"What do you think for her distances?" Mason asked. "The classic marathon?"

"Actually, no. She's built more for shorter distances, don't you think? She loves to sprint. She suggested the 200 and 400-meter races."

Relief washed across his face. "Absolutely. I wasn't sure how she'd feel about it, given how well she did at the Selei City Open last year." He went back to his holos, partitioning athletes into events. "Some of yours are great jumpers, and most like to throw, at least weapons, but they aren't ready in those events. The point isn't to attack. They need more training than they can get in time for this Olympics."

Bhaaj thought over her Dust Knights. "Rockjan might qualify. She's always loved throwing."

Mason grinned. "I swear, she's built like a powerhouse. And scary! She just glares at the discus and the terrified thing flies across the field."

Bhaaj couldn't help but laugh. "That's true."

"Ho!" Mason was looking past her shoulder. "I don't believe it."

Startled, Bhaaj turned. The last person she'd expected to see walking toward them was Lavinda Majda, crisp and impressive in her army uniform.

"Colonel Majda." Mason bowed as Lavinda came up to them. "You honor us with your presence." He fell silent, seeming at a loss despite his usual bottomless well of words.

"Thank you for coming to the practice," Bhaaj said, as confused as Mason. Lavinda had no reason to come here. Sure, the House of Majda was their largest donor, but that didn't translate to sending one of the senior sisters to a practice.

Lavinda glanced down at the athletes. "They look good."

"They've been working hard," Mason said. "A great group! Motivated, strong, everything you'd want in a team." He was getting his mojo back. "You'll be proud of them, Colonel. Your family is helping to make this possible. We're exceedingly grateful."

Lavinda inclined her head to him. "You're welcome." She turned to Bhaaj. "Do you have a moment?" She indicated a tunnel entrance into the stadium not far from where they stood.

"Yes. Of course." She glanced at Mason and he nodded, his face easily readable. He might as well have spoken out loud: *See what she wants. Make a stellar impression.*

After they reached the tunnel, Lavinda drew her to a stop. "I had an odd talk with Angel."

Bhaaj stopped, even more confused. Angel had no reason to meet with Lavinda. "Isn't she training with the Kyle Division today?"

"That's right." Dryly, Lavinda added, "She used their Kyle training EI to contact me at my office on my personal comm."

"How did she manage that?" Blast it, what was Angel thinking?

Lavinda seemed surprisingly sanguine. "She still has the private code I gave her when she served as one of my bodyguards during my visit to the Undercity last season."

"Yah, but she shouldn't have used it." Bhaaj went into damage-control mode. "I'm sorry she disturbed you at work. I'll have a talk with her."

"No need." Lavinda sounded more intrigued than annoyed. "After we talked, I looked at the record of her session. Bhaaj, it was her *first* time in Kyle space. I've never seen anything like it." The colonel frowned. "She doesn't have the right trainers. One wants to believe she's incapable. The other two mean well, but they don't have a clue what she can do or how to teach her."

It didn't surprise Bhaaj. She'd run into similar when she enlisted. A difference existed here, though. Angel had allies. "What do you suggest?"

"We need to get her a trainer who has worked with top-ranked telops." Concern came into Lavinda's voice. "I think she needs to look after her health, too. She seems tired."

"Yah." Bhaaj exhaled. "She's over-extended, trying to work full-time in a demanding job and train with the team here." Not to mention her work as a Dust Knight. "It worries me."

Lavinda thought for a moment. "I can find her more suitable teachers. I could help arrange a more feasible work schedule for her, too, until the Olympics. She could work partial shifts. Do you think she'd go for those changes?"

"I think so. I'll talk to her about it."

"Good." Lavinda spoke thoughtfully. "Just before she contacted me, I caught an image from her through the Kyle, something about a reception in the lobby of Selei Tower."

Bhaaj hoped this new Kyle tutor also trained Angel how to protect her privacy better. "Don't they do that sometimes, entertain people in the lobby?"

"I suppose. It struck Angel as notable for some reason." Her face took on the inward quality that happened when she accessed the private node implanted at the base of her brain. "I didn't get much more than a blurred image. It looks like Scorpio execs."

"That does seem off," Bhaaj said. "Why entertain Scorpio suits in Selei Tower? It's a government building, not a corporate location."

"The army does have contracts with Scorpio. Nothing to do with Selei Tower, though." She focused on Bhaaj again. "Any news about the Abyss-Scorpio business?"

"I've connected with an analyst at Abyss. She's predicting how the takeover could affect Abyss Associates." Bhaaj thought back to her talk with Kiro's mother. "My gut instinct? She very much *doesn't* want the takeover to succeed."

"What's her name?" Lavinda asked.

"Gwen Caballo. Ring any bells?"

"I've never heard of her. Keep looking into it."

"Will do."

After Lavinda headed back to wherever aristocratic colonels spent their days, Bhaaj returned to Mason, lost in thought. She had new business to investigate with Abyss and Scorpio.

Kiro listened with growing excitement as Coach Mason outlined their plans, gratified that said plans included him. Yes!

"It's called the North-Metro Track and Field Meet," Mason continued. "It's an IAC-sanctioned event, which means all the events meet the standards for Olympic qualification."

Everyone had gathered on the velvet-lawn enclosed by track. Kiro stood with Strider, Lamp, and Zee. As Mason continued, Strider glanced at Kiro and tilted her head as if asking a question.

"We need show we run fast," he said in a low voice. "We do well, we go to Olympics."

Her puzzlement vanished. "We do today?"

"Nahya. Go to other planet."

"In Cries?" Zee asked.

If only it were that easy. "Not here. Far away."

"How get there?" Lamp asked.

Good question. Kiro had no clue. "Listen. Coach say."

So they listened, and eventually Mason said, "For your travel, we'll make the arrangements and cover those expenses. Also your room and board."

Zee scowled. "Jib."

"Not jib," Kiro said. "They take us there, give food, water, place to sleep." Anticipating their reaction, he added, "Bargain. We run, they feed. We go to planet, they get us place to stay."

Alarm flashed on Lamp's face. "Not leave home!"

"Not live there," Kiro assured them. "Just short visit."

Mason's voice cut through to them. "Kiro Caballo, do you have something to share with us?"

Mortified, Kiro jerked his attention back to the now scowling coach. Bhaaj stood at his side, her focus also intent on him, though she seemed intrigued rather than annoyed.

"My apologies, Coach," Kiro said. "I was telling them about Metropoli."

Laughter rippled through the Undercity athletes, along with murmurs of, "Meh-trah-po-li."

"Enough," Bhaaj told them. They all just looked at her, but they stopped laughing.

"Here's the thing," Mason said. "The air on Metropoli is different than here. We have less oxygen in our atmosphere than other human-settled worlds. Living here, it's like you've trained at high altitude all your life. That could help you on Metropoli, but we need to get there early enough to let your bodies adapt."

Up near the front, Rockjan spoke in her gravelly voice, which sounded threatening even when she talked in her normal tone. "What that mean? Ox-y-gen. Al-ti-tude. Is all jib."

Mason glanced at Bhaaj, and she gave the slightest nod, then spoke to everyone. "Metrop not same as here. Air rich. Make dizzy. Need adapt. But is good air! Help you run better."

None of the Undercity runners looked convinced, but Kiro suspected they'd like it once they got to Metropoli. Although he'd only visited once, on vacation with his parents, he'd never forget. The air had exhilarated him. The gravity was lower, too, not much, but maybe it could help them get better times. It could also make it harder to time their steps, though, which could slow them.

Before Kiro had a chance to remember that he hated talking in front of people, he waved at Mason.

The coach squinted at him. "Yes?"

"How much time will we have on Metropoli to acclimate?" Kiro asked. "To adapt to the atmosphere, gravity, and shorter day?"

"Ah. Good question." Mason nodded. "We can manage two standard tendays before the meet."

Zee spoke to Kiro in a low voice. "That enough time to 'adapt'?"

"I think so." It had only taken a few days on his last trip, but he hadn't been in a sports meet.

Hyden Laj spoke from where he stood to one side. "Coach, are you taking everyone here?"

"That's right," Mason said.

"How?" Hyden asked. "Where are you getting the funds?"

Awkward silence followed his words. Then Mason said, "We have enough to cover the team."

"Do you?" Hyden asked. "A substantial portion comes from Scorpio Corporation."

Kiro swore under his breath. He knew exactly where Hyden was going with this. What if his family didn't want the Undercity representing Raylicon at a major tournament?

Mason spoke tightly. "We'll cover the expenses," Before anyone could ask more, he motioned at the whole group. "All right. You all have your training program for today. Let's go."

As everyone started to talk among themselves, Lamp turned to Kiro. "Why you mad?"

Kiro's voice tightened. "Hyden not want us at Metrop."

"So what?" Strider said. "Not stop us."

"Hope not." Kiro had never understood the high-stakes universe his mother inhabited, but he knew this much: Scorpio could wreak havoc on the team if they wanted.

"It's not up for debate," Mason repeated. They'd gathered in his office: Mason, Bhaaj, and Zaic Laj, the Scorpio CEO. Sun rays slanted through the windows, casting late afternoon light across the three of them, the comfortable furniture, and the pictures of meets where Mason's teams had competed. None of that serene atmosphere mattered. Everyone stood stiffly, no one sitting, no one smiling.

"I'm sorry," Zaic said. He didn't sound in the least bit apologetic. "Scorpio can't support a team that takes a pack of Undercity dust rats to represent our world to the rest of the Imperialate."

"Stop with this 'dust rat' business," Bhaaj said. "That's considered a slur among my people."

"Fine." Zaic met her gaze with a cold stare. "Take your drug-addicted 'knights' off the team and they won't have to hear any words that offend their delicate sensibilities."

"Enough!" Mason said. "No one on the team takes drugs. We monitor them. And everyone goes to Metropoli." He regarded Zaic steadily. "If that means Scorpio withdraws its support of the team, then so be it."

Zaic stared at him, his expression hard. Bhaaj had no doubt he hadn't expected *that* response. "If you persist in this abomination, I will also withdraw my son. And don't tell me you don't care, Mason. You know damn well he's one of your best runners. Only Tayz Wilder can beat him."

Mason met his gaze. "Your son is welcome on the team, and yes, he's an excellent athlete. However, if he wishes to withdraw, that's his prerogative. Either way, I won't drop the Undercity athletes." Then he added, "And by the way, at least four of them can beat Hyden. Maybe more."

Zaic's face contorted with anger. "What did you do, give them biomech enhancements? You get caught doing that, and your career is over."

"That's ridiculous," Bhaaj said. "Not only do my runners have *no* augmentations, many don't even have health nanomeds."

Zaic gave her a long, appraising look, then turned away as if her comments were so far below his notice, he had no need to respond. "Make no mistake, Mason. You go through with this, and you'll find yourself—and your dust rats—in a world of trouble."

With that, he turned and strode from the office.

Bhaaj stared at Mason, and he stared back at her. "Shit," he said.

"You really think he'll pull the Scorpio funds and Hyden?"

"I don't know. But I won't have anyone telling me who I can and can't take." Mason took a steadying breath. "Hyden won't like it if his father takes him off the team."

"He's twenty-four. He can make his own decisions."

"Yes," Mason said. "But legally, he doesn't reach majority until he's twenty-five."

"Yah, well, that's ridiculous." It had always annoyed Bhaaj. In the Undercity, she'd become an adult at fourteen. Earthers set the age at eighteen. So did most Skolian employers and the military, as well as most bars, dance clubs, love-link sims, and hack-smoke shops. "I wouldn't be surprised to see him defy his father. He *really* wants this."

Mason pushed his hand through his disarrayed hair. "Zaic has connections everywhere. It wouldn't surprise me if they extend even to the Olympic committee."

She thought of when she'd competed, decades ago. "They pride themselves on their neutrality. The Olympics are the only interstellar venue where all of us—the Skolian Imperialate, the Eubian Concord of the Traders, and the Allied Worlds of Earth—come together in peace. If the committee can stay neutral with the Eubian Aristos, they can hold their own against angry corporate billionaires."

"I hope so." Mason didn't sound convinced. "Without Scorpio's support, I don't know how we can afford to take all these kids." He cracked his knuckles with frustration. "We *must* get them to at least one IAF-recognized meet or no one except Wild will qualify for the Olympics."

"I can donate more," Bhaaj said. With her retainer from the Majdas, her obsessive fear of ending up in poverty again, and Max's investment savvy, she'd accumulated far more wealth than she'd ever imagined possible in her youth. She wanted to help her people in ways that opened doors they could walk through on their own. Sports offered just such an opportunity. "I'll cover the starship fare to Metropoli for the Undercity kids."

"I can put in some too," Mason said. "And maybe the Majdas will contribute more."

"They already cover a quarter of our expenses." She spoke uneasily. "If we aren't careful, they could turn this team into their own little empire."

He pulled himself up straighter. "Then we'll find new sources."

"We will." They had to figure this out. To disappoint the Undercity athletes after she'd finally convinced them to trust Mason would be a miserable betrayal. Her people would never trust anyone from Cries again, not for sports, not for cooperation, and not to work as telops.

Kyle space surrounded Angel in a luminous grid, golden here at the hill of her identity and shading into different colors in every direction, each hue blending harmoniously with the next. Other hills showed in the distance. The "sky" spread in a radiant expanse of light, white overhead but shading into violet at the horizaon.

Pretty, Angel thought.

A new hill rose nearby, deep blue in color. *Yes,* her new tutor thought. *It's beautiful.*

Eh. Angel didn't know what to think of this woman who'd showed up today to replace the flustered Bayley, Georj and Pup. From their reaction, Angel gathered they all knew this stranger, at least by reputation. They seemed in awe. So far, Angel had no opinion, except for two things. One, this stranger didn't talk too much, and two, she didn't condescend.

What do you see in the distance? her new tutor asked.

Angel concentrated on a part of the grid far away. A ripple appeared in the air there and raced toward her, faster and faster. Before she could react, it pounded her mind with abstract data, strange and unpleasant, like someone had hit her in the head.

Not good, she thought.

You made too many neural links at once, her tutor said. *You need to control how fast you take input. Otherwise, you could have a seizure.*

Angel thought back to the reading she'd done last night, at the behest of this new tutor. Neurons and more neurons. They wanted her to learn "brain anatomy." She didn't see how that helped anything, but at least it had proved interesting.

Angel focused on where the ripple had originated and saw another hill, one so far away she could barely make it out. As she concentrated, the peak raced toward her.

Too fast, she told it.

The hill slowed, but kept approaching until it became clear, a silver peak with blue grid lines. It arrived and washed over Angel with curiosity. A new thought came into her mind, one with warmth and a sense of age. *My greetings, Angel.*

Who? Angel asked.

I am Sailor, he answered. *That is my title.*

Good. A title rather than a name. She sent him a sense of approval. *Why you here?*

You and Tutor are on a different planet, Sailor answered. *You've accessed a gateway for the Kyle mesh that serves Imperial University in Selei City on the planet Parthonia.*

I ken Selei City, Angel thought. *Visit there with The Bhaaj.*

Yes, I see that in your files, Sailor said. *You impressed Colonel Majda on that trip.*

She offer me this job, Angel said. *Why you talk to me?*

As a telop, you will need offworld access, Sailor answered. *Your duties will include setting up communications for people who aren't Kyle operators. They can't access psiberspace without you.*

How I do that?

That's what we'll work on today, he thought.

Angel focused, trying to resolve him into something other than a hill. The grid faded, turning into a comfortable den with several well-used armchairs, four consoles, and an older man relaxing in a control chair. He had no neural cap. Instead, prongs on his console plugged into sockets on his wrist.

Nice office, Angel commented, her version of "small" talk. Very small.

You can see my office? The man sounded like Sailor.

Yah, Angel answered. *You sit in chair by console. You got a lot of consoles. Four.*

Tutor responded. *Good work.*

You knew she could form simulations on her own? Sailor asked Tutor.

She did it with Colonel Majda, Tutor answered.

This how you look? Angel asked Sailor.

I don't know. Sailor seemed intrigued. *How do I look to you?*

As Angel focused on him, pain sparked in her head. *You got grey hair. Straight. Black eyes. Too skinny. You need food.* She thought of the banquet Mason provided them. *You not get enough? Maybe we can help.*

A sense of a smile came from Sailor. *Thank you. But I have enough to eat. I'm just thin. My spouses tell me the same as you.*

You got more than one spouse? It amazed Angel how much personal stuff slicks revealed when you'd just met them.

Indeed, Sailor said. *I've a husband and two wives.*

Huh. That seemed very busy to Angel. Since he'd offered her the honor of personal details, she decided to reciprocate. *I got one husband.*

Ah.

Angel waited, but they seemed done with the little chatting. Good. She had questions. *I can use this mesh to go see people on other worlds? Like you.*

That's the intent, Sailor said. *I'd suggest we start with a warm-up exercise. How about creating a sim of something you've already seen? Pick a memory.*

Angel thought of the slicks in the reception at Selei Tower. As she strained to recall the party, her headache got worse. Damn, it *hurt*—

Do you wish to leave the training mesh? the Kyle-training EI asked.

Angel eased back her thoughts. *Nahya. I just need a memory. Can you help?* Maybe this Kyle place could fire her neurons in a way that focused the memory. Or something.

Sailor's den rippled, faded—and snapped out of existence, replaced by a chaotic grid with ragged peaks morphing, shattering, zooming with harsh noises. Too much!

There! The scene stabilized, becoming the reception in Selei Tower. Angel tried to see faces of the people better—if she just didn't feel so dizzy—too *much*—it was breaking apart—

Make record! she thought, desperate to hold onto what little progress she'd managed. She had a sense of the memory pouring into a jar—*ah, nooooooo*—

Angel silently screamed as the scene disintegrated, throwing her back into the chaotic grid. The hill that defined her in Kyle space exploded—*so much pain*—

With a gasp, Angel found herself back in her control chair in real space. She groaned as people around her yelled things like, "Get her out of the mesh NOW!"

Angel reached for the neural cap, intending to yank it off, but someone was already removing it. She sagged back, dimly aware of blurred motion and noise all around her chair. Closing her eyes, she tried to calm her raging headache.

A voice spoke. "Angel?"

Angel opened her eyes, wary and slow. Tutor was standing in front of her, surrounded by screens that had risen around the chair, horizontal plates with holos above them. Tutor looked like a female version of Sailor, with grey hair, a lined face, and black eyes. And too thin. So strange, that these people, who had plenty to eat, didn't do it enough.

"Are you all right?" Tutor watched her with concern.

"Head hurts," Angel admitted.

"How did you do that?"

"Eh?"

"You cut your connection with both me and Sailor."

"Sailor say get memory," Angel said. "So I try."

Tutor's wrinkled brow furrowed even more. "I don't understand."

Angel switched into Cries speak. "I wanted to look at a memory from work. It was nothing."

"A memory?" Tutor scanned the holos above one of the plates. "This says you hacked security files in Selei Tower and downloaded one of them, the record of a reception in the lobby."

"Eh," Angel informed her.

Tutor frowned. "How did you do that?"

"Do what?"

"Get into files you had no business accessing."

"Not know," Angel admitted. "Want see mem. Thought Kyle space might help."

"Mem?"

"I was trying to remember details of the reception," Angel said. "I thought maybe being in Kyle space could help make my memory better."

"I don't see why that would improve your memory." Now Tutor was reading holicons above her gauntlet screen, comparing them with those by Angel's chair. "When you asked for help getting the memory, the Kyle mesh interpreted your input as instructions to access security files for this building." She focused on Angel again. "Where did you learn to break into secured networks?"

Angel regarded her guiltily. "Not do that today." It was true, after all.

Tutor wasn't fooled. "Not today? Then when? And how?"

Angel spoke carefully. "I wanted to get an education. However, in the Undercity, we have no access to Cries meshes. The only way I could teach myself was to, um, 'borrow' time on the university meshes." She warmed to her subject. "Right now, I'm studying quantum mechanics. Bayley, Pup, and Georj tried to explain Kyle space to me, but I didn't get the math. So I'm reading more." With a grimace, she added, "It's weird. I mean, I like probability math, odds and all that, but fuck-all with the partial differential equations."

Tutor blinked. "You're teaching yourself the mathematics of theoretical physics?"

That was certainly a rude mouthful. "Say what?"

Tutor studied Angel as if trying to decipher her. "Do you have a diploma or a degree?"

Angel had no idea what that meant, which made the answer obvious. "Nahya."

"How did you learn enough physics to study quantum mechanics?"

"Told you. Pinch time on school mesh. Teach self."

"Goddess," Tutor murmured. She spoke in a business-like voice. "You don't need to steal access. You get it free through your account here. Sailor can set up any classes you want."

Angel liked this new development. "Not have Kyle account that long. Rest of life, no access."

"Then you hacked into the city meshes without a valid account."

Angel would have bristled, except Tutor didn't make it sound like an accusation. She just stated the fact. So she said, "Yah."

Tutor rubbed her chin. "Most of your people are off the grid, right?"

"You mean the meshes?" Hah! No wonder she saw Kyle space as a grid. "Yah. Not have grid."

"That's why you didn't have a Cries account. You needed a city ID."

Angel scowled at her. "My people not get ID. Not want city spy on us."

Tutor didn't look surprised. "Ah, well. That's a huge debate itself."

She considered Angel. "But you're the one spying here. How did you hack our security?"

"Not sure," Angel admitted. "Asked training EI for help."

"It should have refused." Tutor brought up more holos above her gauntlet. "Huh. Interesting. It picked up neural patterns from your brain related to the university and applied those to our mesh."

Angel had no answer, at least not one she wanted Tutor to know. Hack had taught her how to break into meshes. He knew far more than city techs, and he came at it from different directions than them, which made it easier to find holes in their protections. She rubbed her temples, relieved her headache was fading.

Tutor watched her with concern. "You pushed yourself too hard today. If you overdo your training, it can cause brain damage."

Angel grimaced. "Not ken what happened."

"We need to teach you control," Tutor said. "You're like fireworks going off in the Kyle, bam, bam, bam. You have to slow down so you don't harm yourself." Quietly she said, "Or anyone else."

"Not want hurt anyone," Angel assured her. She just wanted to play with this Kyle biz.

"I know." Tutor became stern. "You also need to follow the rules. You can't blast around Kyle space breaking laws. You'll end up in prison." When Angel started to speak, Tutor held up her hand. "I'm not talking about a night in jail. I mean a high-security prison for high-level crime." She thought for a moment. "Imagine someone with your physical strength in a shop full of glass vases."

Angel squinted at her. "Why I do that? Not need wimpy vases."

Tutor smiled—and Angel discovered it didn't bother her. Interesting. Her mind had apparently decided to trust Tutor.

"Just imagine it," Tutor said. "A store with all these fragile items on thin glass shelves."

Angel scowled. "I move, I break stuff." Although she'd always appreciated her strength, especially when it came to fighting, it left her clumsy around anything flimsy.

"Yes! Exactly." Tutor looked relieved. "Your mind is like that in Kyle space. You've huge mental muscles, but if you aren't careful, you could cause damage there, too."

Angel had to admit, it made sense. "Okay. You teach me not break stuff." She winced. "But no more today, eh? Head hurts."

Tutor nodded. "You go home to rest. We'll meet again tomorrow."

"Got team practice." The thought relieved Angel. With her new schedule, she could leave early today and get to the practice on time.

"Are you sure?" Tutor asked. "Olympic training isn't what most people consider rest."

"Is for me." She loved the exertion.

"Oh. Well. Good." Tutor seemed more flustered by Angel's enjoyment of sports than anything else her student had done today.

"You not like to run," Angel decided.

"Even less than I'd like having my teeth pulled out." When Angel started to ask why the fuck she'd want her teeth pulled out, Tutor laughed. "It's just a saying. It means no, I don't like to run."

Angel had no idea what to say. Or maybe she did. "You got good build for it. Long legs, lean." She stopped, distracted. Pup had come up to the chair.

"How did the session go?" he asked. He sounded like he cared, which made her like him more.

"Was fine." Angel pushed out of the big chair and stood up. Yah, she felt steady.

Time to go run.

The world sparkled around Kiro as he jogged with Strider's gang along the midwalk. Torches in ornate scones burned at intervals along the walls. The four of them also wore light-pens on cords around their necks. It all shed a golden glow over the canal, catching blue glints from azurite crystals in the red dust. Sculptures of Strider's gang icon appeared on the ground a few meters below, the shimmerflies carved in detail. Kiro had helped them make the sculptures from dust they hardened using glue mixed with poisoned water from underground streams.

"When we get there," Strider was telling Kiro. "You let Bhaaj say."

"Get where?" Kiro couldn't fathom this journey they'd invited him on today, in a new region of the Undercity. He'd had the map-EI in his wrist band record the trip, but they insisted he also memorize it, so he could find his way without depending on any tech.

Strider just said, "Eh."

Lamp caught up with him, jogging in the space between Kiro and the edge of the midwalk. "You fight like shit," he informed Kiro.

Kiro scowled at him.

"Yah," Zee said behind them, ever helpful. "Like lizard-crap."

"You fall off midwalk," Kiro growled.

"Not fall," Lamp said. He slowed down, though, enough to move back behind Kiro.

Eventually they reached a cavern with many statues. With so much more space, Zee came to run with Kiro while Lamp went ahead with Strider. Stalactites filled the cavern, formed by eons of mineral-laden water dripping from the ceiling until they solidified like stone icicles. Stalagmites under them rose from the floor in narrow cones. Sculptures showed everywhere, carved from columns that formed when a stalactite and stalagmite joined together. Instead of the ancient deities depicted elsewhere in the Undercity, these showed people as they lived now. Many were in fighting poses, wielding knives, guns, or maces, but others were holding children.

"Lot of stone people," Kiro commented.

"Shows wealth," Strider said.

"Yah?" Kiro stopped by a statue of a man with a child. Both wore Undercity clothes, trousers and tank tops. Even Kiro dressed that way now. Lamp had traded the clothes to him for several bottles of the power drink Kiro gulped down after workouts. Neither the father nor the baby in this statue had anything that implied riches, no necklace, bracelets, or tech. No water or food, either.

Strider came over and laid her hand on the baby's back. "Wealth."

"Ah." He liked that the Undercity considered their children their wealth. For all their poverty, they seemed rich in ways he'd never known, with their close circles of kith and kin.

They resumed their jog, rounding a rock outcropping carved like a dragon in flight. Soon they reached a large arch with tiled borders, a glory of geometrical designs in sunrise colors. Beyond it, Knights stood in rows, listening to someone he couldn't see. He couldn't make out the words, either.

Strider stopped and gave Kiro a stern look. "Not talk inside, yah? Just do what Bhaaj say."

"I ken," he told her, wondering what the blazes they'd gotten him into.

They entered the cave, a huge, hexagonal box with its six walls and vaulted ceiling polished until they gleamed. Rather than carvings on the walls, artists had tiled them in patterns that evoked fighters, some in martial-arts forms. The scuffed floor looked worn but not slippery, and dumbells lined the walls.

Everyone had turned to Strider's gang. Or no, not the gang: they all stared at Kiro.

"Eh," a woman said to his right. "You late."

Startled, Kiro turned. Bhaaj stood there, dressed in worn trousers and a tank top.

"Teach, yah?" Strider said, tilting her head at Kiro.

Bhaaj nodded, and that was that. She just said, "Third row."

Confused, Kiro went with Strider and the others to the third row. As they took up positions at its end, Bhaaj continued speaking to the group. "In five days, we do tests with Cries Acad." She motioned at someone, and Kiro glanced over to see a man he vaguely recognized. Who? Hack. Yes, that was his name. He was some sort of cyber genius from Ruzik's circle.

"Hack test for second degree black belt," Bhaaj was saying. "Same for Angel and Ruzik." She turned to Lamp. "You go for first degree black, yah?"

"Yah." Lamp nodded to her.

Bhaaj continued, verifying or suggesting what belts people should go for. Apparently she had an arrangement with the Cries Tykado Academy to let her students do official tests. The longer Kiro listened, the more out of place he felt.

Soon they started the class. The first part gave him no trouble. It felt like a mix of calisthenics, cross-fit floor exercises, and the stretches Mason had them do every day. Once they finished the warm-up and started "round-house kicks," though, Kiro felt like an idiot. No way could he keep up.

After about ten minutes, Bhaaj motioned to one of the most advanced students, a man in the front. He came up to take her place and began drilling the group on punch sequences.

Moving off to the side, Bhaaj beckoned Kiro. Relieved, he went over to her.

"Ever do tykado before?" she asked.

"Never." Then he amended, "Well, once. A few years ago, I tried out for the track team fielded by the Cries Tykado Academy, so they let me take one class for free."

She didn't look surprised. "You're in good shape, Kiro, and you pick up the moves well. But no way are you ready for this class."

Kiro grimaced. "I figured."

"You should start at a white belt." She considered him. "It won't take you long to work through the beginning levels."

"But—" He hesitated. "Is this part of my training for Mason's team?"

"Well, no." She paused. "I assumed, when you showed up, that you wanted to learn tykado."

"Strider brought me."

"Ah." She glanced to where Strider, Lamp and Zee were practicing kick and punch combos. "Did they explain?"

"Sort of." Dryly Kiro added, "Lamp says I fight like shit."

She smiled, a natural expression, gentle rather than derisive. "That sounds like Lamp." Her tone became serious. "Do you understand what these classes represent?"

"Uh... martial arts?" He didn't see what else they could mean.

"These are the Dust Knights." She regarded him steadily. "If you train here, you're learning to become one of them. It means you will swear to live by our Code. You're giving Strider, Lamp, and Zee your oath to be their fourth, that their circle will become your circle, to protect and cherish." Her voice remained firm. "They consider this their home. You don't. You come from an immensely wealthy background and attend Cries University, an elite school. Could you live here even part-time? Even if you wanted to, when would you, after your Olympic training and college classes?"

Kiro stared at her. "I have no clue."

She spoke with a respect he didn't feel he'd earned. "Strider's gang has accepted you. They *want* you to become a Knight. No one from Cries has ever done that. We've never invited anyone to." Dryly she added, "Nor did I ever intend to."

"Do you want me to leave?"

"No. Not unless that's your choice." She spoke carefully. "Do you want to become their fourth in more than just word, but in actuality?"

"I'm not sure," he admitted, his voice low. He doubted the others could hear, but he took care just in case. As much as he didn't want to disappoint them, he didn't know if he could commit the way Bhaaj described. "They mean the world to me. But all these changes—I need to think about it."

She nodded to him. "That sounds like a good idea."

"So... should I leave?" Strider must realize he couldn't continue with this class. He wasn't sure where to go, though. "I think I could find my way out. They insisted I memorize the route."

"It's up to you." She regarded him with curiosity. "You're letting your hair grow."

Self-conscious, Kiro pushed a curl out of his eyes. "I thought I'd see how it looks."

"Looks Undercity." She waited as if expecting an explosion.

Kiro thought back to his mother's words. "I've relatives from offworld. That's where I get it."

"Maybe." Bhaaj continued to wait.

"Do you ever wonder...?" Kiro paused, uncertain how to phrase his question.

"Wonder what?"

"About your parents."

The moment she stiffened, he knew he'd hit a forbidden subject. She said only, "I never knew them." After a pause, though, she added, "And you?"

He understood all too well the import of her question. They both knew he had no reason to wonder about his parents. No obvious reason.

You suspect, Kiro thought. His heart raced and he suddenly felt hot, then cold. *You know.*

Bhaaj jerked as if he'd struck her. "Goddess," she murmured. "Your mind is like a furnace."

Flustered, he said only, "What?"

I don't know if you can pick this up, she thought. *But if you can, then yah, I think your father comes from the Undercity.*

"Can I find out here?" he asked in a low voice.

"Find out what?"

"If my biological father comes from here." There, he'd finally said it out loud.

"Doctor Rajindia has genetic profiles on many of our people," Bhaaj offered. "She could do a search if you'd like." She paused, and he had a sense she was trying to decide how much to trust him. After a moment, she added, "Not many locations exist where a Cries woman could meet with an Undercity man. However, I know the likeliest place where it might happen. That could tell you more beyond a DNA profile. Do you want to look into it?"

"Yes." He swallowed, feeling as if he had a lump in his throat, though nothing was there. Just his emotions. "I'd like to find out."

"I'll take you."

With that, they left the cavern, headed out into the enigmatic Undercity.

CHAPTER XI
The Highest Mark

Bhaaj had forgotten the impact Jak's office could have on someone who'd never seen it before. Its polished black surfaces gleamed in the light from his fixtures, not just the bars embedded in cubic patterns on the ceiling, but also the niches in the walls. Each contained an obsidian sculpture of a skull with gem-like lights for eyes. She had always found it artistic in a stark sort of way. Given the way Kiro hung back as they entered, though, she doubted he felt the same way.

Jak sat sprawled in his big chair behind his big desk. Gold and black patterns swirled on its surface, and holos floated above it, rotating, morphing, or tumbling in ways that looked random but undoubtedly meant something to him. He'd brought up images of the main room downstairs, packed by gamblers. The place glittered with holographic displays of wheels, cards, dice, and more, sparkling in the air of his infamous casino. It baffled Bhaaj why people gambled in games controlled by an EI system. The EI could win any time it wanted, and so it did, over and over and over, only letting the gullible humans score when it calculated that they needed a success to keep them playing.

When Bhaaj and Kiro arrived, Jak looked up with no hint of surprise. Only Bhaaj could reach his office without his security stopping them. He considered them from his big chair, looking every bit his notorious reputation, all in black from his torn sleeveless pullover to his heavy tech-mech gauntlets to the way he'd slicked back his night-black hair.

"Eh, Bhaaj," he rumbled, a two-word greeting, indicating an extra welcome. He glanced at Kiro, then back at her, his gaze becoming hooded. "Got problem?"

"Eh, Jak," Bhaaj said. Kiro stayed close to her side, or more accurately, partly behind her, as if she offered a bulwark to protect him from the Undercity's infamous criminal kingpin. "Here." She pulled Kiro onto view. "He need show you pic."

"Um, I...not...I—" Kiro hung back.

"It's all right." Bhaaj nudged him forward. "Show Jak."

Stumbling, Kiro tried to activate the viewer on his wrist band. His shaking fingers slipped, and the image of a fluff-pup came up instead, a frisky critter jumping up and down with excited barks while someone, Kiro it sounded like, made encouraging comments off screen.

Jak's laugh rumbled. "Cute pup. You want bet it? Roulette takes pet bet if you out of bykes."

"Nahya!" Kiro stared at him with undisguised shock. "Mine!"

"He make joke," Bhaaj told Kiro. She scowled at Jak. "Bad joke." She knew he was only teasing Kiro, but this wasn't the time.

"Not pup—here—this—" Kiro fumbled with his band until a holo of his mother appeared, an elegant woman with straight black hair wearing a blue blazer, white blouse, and blue slacks.

"Not take her as bet," Jak said with a perfectly straight face. "Not trade people here."

"Jak, stop it." Bhaaj went over and brushed a panel on his desk, making his holos disappear.

Jak stood up and met her gaze, eye to eye. They were both the same height, six feet tall. "Not do that," he growled.

He didn't fool Bhaaj. She knew he was intrigued rather than annoyed. "Not make fun of my guest," she told him.

"Why bring him here?" Jak asked. "He bored with games?"

"Oh." No wonder. He thought Kiro was gambling in his casino, and he never invited slicks to his office. He only let Kiro visit because he came with her. "Nahya," she said. "Strider's fourth."

"Yah. Recall." Jak peered at Kiro. "If you not come for Top Mark, why you here?"

Kiro stepped closer, showing Jak the image of his mother. "Bhaaj thought maybe you know?"

Jak glanced at her. "Know what?"

Bhaaj motioned at the holo of Kiro's mother. "She ever come here?"

"Maybe. When?"

"Twenty-five years ago."

He thought about it. "Too long to recall."

Bhaaj tapped his desk, which included a state-of-the-art mesh system he'd arranged through the shadow market. "Maybe got record?"

"Why you want know?" he asked.

Bhaaj glanced at Kiro, sending him a sense of a question.

"Is okay," Kiro said. "Can tell him."

Turning to Jak, she tilted her head at Kiro. "Mother from Cries. Father maybe from here."

Jak's gaze seemed to gleam. "Big scandal, eh?"

"Big secret," Bhaaj said. "Hoshma say his curly hair come from offworld kin."

"Maybe. Maybe not." Jak motioned at Kiro's holo. "Got more?"

Tapping his band, Kiro brought up a few more holos of his mother. After peering at them, Jak sat back down and went to work. Lights from within his desk played across Kiro's holos, blurring them, and glyphs flowed across the desk, three-dimensional images. Their top surface defined words, and their other dimensions encoded nuances of meaning, like certainty or uncertainty.

Jak looked up at Bhaaj. "Doc Karal check his DNA?"

"Yah." They'd contacted Karal Rajindia on their way here. "She searching. Nothing yet."

Jak went back to the glyphs. "Nothing here either..." After several moments, he sat back and considered Kiro. "Shadow mesh search could take a while."

Kiro spoke awkwardly. "I ken."

Bhaaj nodded to the youth. "You go to main floor, eh? Enjoy Top Mark." She doubted he would; he seemed about as likely to frequent a gambling den as to bounce on his head. Even so. She wanted to talk to Jak in private, besides which, it wouldn't hurt Kiro to get out a bit.

"Uh—" Kiro reddened. "Not sure how get there."

"Not problem." Jak touched another desk panel, and a figurine in a niche on the wall behind him came alive, a statuette of a beast with six clawed arms and mechanical wings that unfolded as it launched into the air.

"Ah!" Kiro stumbled backward with a lurch as the critter arrowed toward him.

Jak looked as if he were trying not to laugh. "Not hurt you."

Bhaaj glowered at Jak. "Stop it."

"Eh." He spoke in a friendlier voice to Kiro. "Just a bot. Lead you downstairs. You enjoy."

"Not play games too much," Bhaaj warned Kiro. "You lose."

"Not tell him that," Jak said. "Let the boy have fun."

"You not cheat him," Bhaaj said.

"Is okay." Kiro started to smile, then stopped himself. "I not do much."

Jak waved his hand at the youth. "Go. Enjoy."

So Kiro went, following the drone as it whirred through the air. The door opened, then shut noiselessly, leaving Bhaaj alone with Jak.

"What's up?" He regarded her curiously. "That boy really Strider's fourth?"

"Not sure," Bhaaj admitted. "They invite. He think on it."

"Not get it," he said. "Why you take shine to this boyo?"

"He's a good kid," she said, switching into above-city speech. The two of them interacted with Cries enough that they went back and forth between the two dialects with ease, whichever seemed to suit their subject better. "That's not what I wanted to talk to you about, though."

"Here." He motioned to a chair against the wall, a chrome affair with black cushions. While she pulled it to the desk, he settled back into his big seat.

"Angel sent me a file," Bhaaj said as she sat down. "It's a security record from Selei Tower. I'm trying to decode some patterns in it."

Curiosity flickered in his gaze. "Why tell me?"

"You've some of the best spyware on this planet. Hell, anywhere." The Top Mark didn't just serve the Cries elite; it also brought in offworld tourists seeking a taste of his notorious casino. "Something is going on with Scorpio, something to do with a hostile takeover of Abyss Associates." Then she added, "Majda hired me to find out more."

"Send me the file." He tapped a finger-tip panel on his desk and new holos appeared, showing images of neural synapses in the brain.

Bhaaj blinked, startled. "You got a psiphon prong with this rig?"

"Yah, sure." He tapped again, and a small panel slid open in front of her. A prong lay in the cavity below, attached to the desk by a translucent cord.

Bhaaj clicked the prong into a tiny hole in her gauntlet, which let it extend into the socket in her wrist. From there, it connected to biothreads in her body and sent signals to the bioelectrodes in her brain, causing her neurons to fire. Tech-induced telepathy.

Max, she thought. *Allow Jak's office mesh to link with my biomech web.*

Done, Max answered.

Jak was reading the glyphs scrolling across his desk. "Okay, we're linked."

Send him the file from Angel, Bhaaj thought.

The holos above Jak's desk disappeared as if a wave had washed them away, and a new one formed showing the lobby of Selei Tower. People filled the place, talking, sipping from crystal goblets, or enjoying sumptuous holo-displays of scenes from Cries. They looked like corporate execs out for an afternoon function, dressed in business chic.

"It's just an office party," Jak said.

"For what office, though? They're in a Tower dedicated to military Kyle services."

He looked up at her. "A lot of the corporations in Cries have military contracts."

"Angel said it felt wrong."

"Wrong how?"

"She couldn't explain." Bhaaj focused on the holo. "The resolution is lousy."

Jak spoke to the air. "Royal? Can you clean up this image?"

"I'll see what I can do," a man answered, the deep voice of Royal Flush, Jak's EI. He'd named the EI after the legendary poker hand that won him enough wealth to start the Top Mark. Royal's words seemed to come out of the air, but he "lived" in Jak's gauntlets and used their comm. He could also access all of Jak's extensive office systems. The recording of the reception in Selei Tower sharpened as if someone had turned up the focus.

"Thanks, Royal," Bhaaj said.

"My pleasure." His words had the same sensuous quality that was always her undoing with Jak. Lifting her head, she pretended to glare at her husband. "Your EI needs parental controls."

He laughed, a deep, husky sound. "Just for you, Bhaajo."

She smiled, then motioned at the holo-vid. "You recognize any of those people?"

"A few." He studied the holo. "Isn't that Zaic Laj, the Scorpio CEO?"

"Yah, well, fuck him," Bhaaj said.

"You got a problem with Laj?"

"He pulled his support of Mason's team because of the Undercity athletes."

Jak's expression darkened. He brought up a new image, Zaic standing by the glimmering holo of a roulette wheel rotating in the air. "He comes here. Likes to bet big, throw around optos."

"Maybe not let him come, eh?"

A dangerous smile spread across Jak's scarred, handsome face. "Let him come all he wants. Too bad if he loses, eh? *Really* lose. Bad."

It would serve Zaic right. It wouldn't dent his fortune, but it could ruin his night.

Jak brought back the holo of the party at Selei Tower. "Who is he talking to there?"

"Not sure." Zaic looked sleek in an elegant grey suit, surrounded by other execs. "Max, who is that woman talking with Zaic Laj?"

Taking his cue from her, Max spoke aloud, using her gauntlet comm. "Her name is Abber Isles. She's an exec at Para-Abyss on the planet Parthonia."

"Para-Abyss?" Jak asked.

"It's a subsidiary of Abyss Associates that develops psibit chips," Max said. "She's their Chief Financial Officer."

"Psibit chips," Bhaaj mused. "That's odd. Abyss doesn't do Kyle research. They plan cities."

"Here, yah," Jak said. "Their offworld subsidiaries, maybe not."

Bhaaj considered the woman. She had dark eyes, dark skin, and dark hair like most everyone on Raylicon, indeed on any Skolian world. Her face had a subtle difference, though. "Max, can you tell where she originates from?"

"I'm not sure, given this vid's mediocre resolution, but I'd say the world Foreshires Hold."

"Why is she here?"

After a moment, he said, "I'm not finding anything. Do you want me to dig deeper?"

"Yah, Max," Jak said. "Go hack and crack."

Exasperated, Bhaaj said, "Not tell my EI to break laws."

Jak regarded her with an innocent look. "I would never."

"Shall I proceed with my search?" Max asked. "It's legal."

"Go ahead." Bhaaj had her doubts, but Max never admitted going beyond the law.

"Isles lived on the world Foreshires Hold until a few years ago," Max said. "She was the CFO for the Research and Development Division of Suncap Foreshires. Abyss lured her away with the lucrative position on Parthonia." He paused. "Well, look at that. Interesting."

"What?" Bhaaj asked. She didn't ask how he'd dug it up. Plausible deniability and all.

"I found a message between Isles and someone named Patrik Laj on Raylicon," Max said. "Something boring about an event they both planned to attend. It was decades ago, when she still worked as a Suncap exec on Foreshires. No obvious link to Zaic Laj, but I'll keep looking."

"Suncap has a subsidiary here on Raylicon, doesn't it?" Jak asked.

"A big one," Bhaaj said. "They control the water farms in the desert." It was why she never invested in Suncap. Those farms employed Undercity natives—and it could be a death sentence. They used humans because getting sand in their bodies didn't make people break down as much as robots. But people required more "upkeep." So Suncap saved by giving their underpaid laborers almost no food or filtered water and working them until they collapsed. Until recently, when Bhaaj became a liaison for the Undercity, her people hadn't realized they could file cases of wrongful treatment. She intended to change that, which didn't endear her to Suncap.

Today she said only, "None of that explains why someone held a party for execs in a tower for scientists and military types."

"Actually," Max said. "I did find a reason. Isles is meeting with people here at Abyss to talk about new directions for their research. They're also going to make psibit chips for the Kyle mesh."

Bhaaj still didn't get it. "Then why would she meet with Zaic Laj?"

"It could be just a chance meeting," Max offered.

"Maybe." She didn't buy it, though.

"Kyle development is a tricky market," Max said. "And a big one."

Bhaaj had no arguments there. Star-spanning civilizations couldn't exist without the fast communication across interstellar distances that the Kyle mesh provided. It made possible star-spanning governments, militaries, industries, or anything else that required real-time interactions. "I get that the demand is high. But Scorpio's involvement with that market is small."

"Maybe Zaic wants a bigger share of it," Jak suggested. "To do that, he needs telops."

"I don't see why," Bhaaj said. "You don't need electrical engineers to get involved in markets that involve classic computer tech, or qubit engineers for quantum tech markets."

"Yah, but that's different," Jak said. "Us ordinary humans can use regular tech fine. Not so with the Kyle. How do you develop the market for components you can't see or use?"

"You need a telop," Max said. "You can't test the components without access to Kyle space, and you can't access Kyle space without a telop."

Jak motioned at Abber Isles and Zaic Lak. "Just look at them plotting about it."

"Talking to each other at a party hardly qualifies as plotting," Bhaaj paused, then added, "Still... it's odd to see the Scorpio CEO so deep in conversation with an Abyss CFO."

"Judged from their body language, facial expressions, and what I can get of their words," Max said. "I'd estimate a thirty to ninety percent chance exists that they already knew each other."

"Well, that's precise," Bhaaj said.

"Wait, I can fine-tune it." After a moment, he said, "I've narrowed my estimate to a seventy-four to ninety-eight percent chance that they know each other and are discussing business."

"What kind of business?" Jak asked.

"I can't say," Max answered. "The audio quality isn't great even with Royal's cleanup."

"Are most of those execs from Abyss and Scorpio?" Bhaaj asked.

"Actually, no," Max said. "They come from many places. The

common thread is that they're all involved in Kyle research or production."

"I suppose that makes sense, given the location." It still didn't feel right, though she couldn't say why. The military qualified as the largest user of Kyle applications. Of course they'd woo the geniuses involved in its development. "Can you read their lips?"

Royal answered. "Only partially. We can't get a clear enough image."

"It's strange," Max said. "Why isn't the resolution better? Selei Tower has top-notch systems."

Jak spoke thoughtfully. "I'll bet it's a ruse. If someone erased the file, it'd be obvious they tampered with it. But mediocre resolution? It's far less likely to raise flags." He flicked his fingers through the holos like a maestro playing a shadow-market Stradivarius. "Maybe I can compare it to vids from other days... damn it!" An array of red siren horns appeared on his desk, blaring loudly.

Bhaaj jerked, startled. "What did you do?"

"It's the security at Selei Tower." Dryly Jak added, "Apparently it's good enough to keep even me out." Another flick and the noise and sirens vanished.

"They catch you spying?"

"Nahya. The horns are my warning system. Not theirs."

"Yet somehow Angel hacked her way in through Kyle space?" Bhaaj didn't see how, if even Jak's top-notch systems had trouble with it. "She thinks the training EI took patterns in her mind from when she hacked the library at the university and used those to hack security at Selei Tower. But that shouldn't work. The university has lousy security. Selei Tower is just the opposite."

Sitting back, Jak rested his elbows on the arms of his chair and steepled his fingers. "What else is unique about Angel?"

"The Undercity," Bhaaj mused. "We're so far off the grid here, most of our people don't even know the Kyle mesh exists."

"The security EIs probably never encountered neural patterns like hers."

"I suppose." It didn't seem enough to explain what happened.

"She's training for the Olympics," Jak offered.

"So are forty-one other people. They couldn't break into—" She stopped, then spoke slowly. "Hyden Laj is on the team."

"I thought his father pulled him off."

"Hyden still comes to practices. If he's no longer a member, no one told us. Or him."

"Okay. What do we have?" Jak held up his hand and tapped his index finger. "Zaic Laj talking biz with an Abyss exec." He tapped his middle finger as if showing it to Laj. "Someone fiddled with the record enough to hide details of their chat." Next tap, his ring finger. "Hyden Laj is on Mason's team." He spread his hands apart as if giving up. "I don't see a link. I mean, sure, he's Zaic's son. But so what?"

Bhaaj didn't see what that got them either, but something tugged at her thoughts—ah! "Angel was in Kyle space."

"So?"

"So your proximity to someone there goes by how similar your thoughts are to theirs."

"Yah, but Angel was looking at a *recording* of a conversation. Holo-vids don't think."

"That doesn't mean Zaic wasn't thinking about it, too." Bhaaj shifted the puzzle pieces in her mind. "The more important the conversation to Zaic, the more often he'd think about it. His and Angel's mutual connection to Hyden would increase the strength of her response to him. And she's one hell of a strong telop."

"She wasn't looking for Zaic," Jak said. "She just wanted a record of that party."

"Yah," Bhaaj mused. "Maybe Zaic was in Kyle space, talking with someone about the party. It wouldn't surprise me if Angel ended up close to him."

"Maybe. But he'd have security." Jak motioned around his office. "Like I have here. Top-of-the-line. I don't see how Angel could break into his system."

"She was in the Kyle, thinking about the reception... Hah!" Bhaaj snapped her fingers. "I'll bet the poor resolution isn't tampering. Othrwise, a system as advanced as yours could compensate better. It's Zaic's *memory*. That'd explain everything. Angel was thinking about the reception at the same time as him, so she hacked his memory."

Jak didn't look convinced. "She'd practically have to be on top of him in Kyle space for that."

"Yah." Another problem occurred to her. "She never said she recognized Zaic at that party. So why would she be thinking about him?"

"Actually, that makes more sense," Jak said. "When I'm in the Kyle, it picks up things I don't even know I'm thinking and moves me all over. Without a telop, I'd end up in a mess."

"And Angel's a beginner," Bhaaj said. "It wouldn't surprise me if she bounced around."

"So let's say she thinks about the reception and recalls Zaic, maybe subconsciously."

"Jak, you're right," Bhaaj said. "It wouldn't be unusual for him to be using the Kyle. If his talk with Isles was important, he might have been thinking about it later. Hah! Good point."

He laughed. "Don't look so surprised, Bhaajo."

"Not call me Bhaajo," she pretended to growl.

He grinned, giving her that devastating look someone should've registered as an illegal drug long ago. "You come back here tonight to convince me, eh?"

"Could." She sometimes spent her nights at the penthouse the Majdas had given her in the city as part of her retainer. It offered a good base for her investigations, or at least it did after she outwitted all the spy biz they put there to monitor her. But other times—well, the Top Mark could be more like home than home. "Might do that."

He started to add something, then stopped.

"What?" Bhaaj asked. It wasn't like him to hold back his opinions.

"You look tired."

"I need to upgrade my health nanomeds. They aren't doing their job."

"What's wrong with them?"

"No sure." She finally said aloud what had worried her for days. "I may have a long-term effect of that carnelian rash variant that killed so many people in the Deep."

His forehead creased. "I thought you were immune."

"Not immune. I have a protein in my body that blocks the virus from hijacking my cells. If it can't get into my cells, the virus can't use them to replicate."

"That means it doesn't make you sick, right?"

"It didn't then. But it was in my body, and it mutates fast." She grimaced. "Or maybe I stayed on the surface too much today during noontime. It gets bloody *hot* out there."

Jak watched her with a concern he rarely revealed. "You need to take care of yourself."

"I'm fine."

"You always say you're fine," he growled. "Even when you're dying."

"Seriously, Jak. I'm sure it's nothing." Then she said, "Max, ask my health meds."

"I can't literally," Max said. "Their piconet works on atomic transitions. They can transmit messages to each other, but I'm not part of that."

"You talk to them all the time."

"In a sense. I send signals through your biomech web that spurs them to, say, release medicine in your body or help repair an injury. I don't interface directly with their pico-system, but I can generally tell what they're up to, based on their behavior." He paused. "Ah. I see. Earlier today they gave you a medicine used for symptoms of carnelian rash such as fever, nausea, or aches. I'd suggest checking with Doctor Rajindia. She might have better treatments for its effects."

Jak was watching her. "Don't put it off."

"I won't." Bhaaj meant it. Even if the rash couldn't kill her, it could make her life miserable.

"Good." He turned to his desk and brought up views of the main room downstairs. Motioning to a holo-roulette table, he said, "Look there."

Bhaaj peered at the vid, which showed several drunk young people wearing skimpy clothes with stylish rips that still managed to look expensive. They'd gathered around a wheel that spun in the air with sparkly numbers. Pretty—and crooked. She'd never figured out why it didn't bother people to lose so much money for nothing except to watch that wheel spin, but these kids seemed happy. Either that, or they were too boozed out to care. Didn't they have work or school in the morning? Good thing her athletes weren't down there—

"Oh, fuck," she said.

"Yah." Jak smirked at her. "Want me to make him lose?"

"You already make them lose." What she wanted was for Hyden Laj to get out of Jak's casino, go home, and sleep off his high so he could function tomorrow at practice. But there he was, laughing too loud and as drunk as a dump. "What is he thinking, putting that shit in his body?"

Jak crossed his arms. "Leave him alone. Besides, you just sent that other kid down there."

Good point. "Can you find Kiro?"

He panned through other parts of the main room, then stopped at a table where patrons were playing the card game blackjack. "That looks like him."

Bhaaj peered at the view. Yah, there was Kiro, standing back, watching the game instead of playing. "Huh," she mused. "He chose the one game on that main floor that your patrons have a chance at winning, if they play well enough."

"Meaning what?" he demanded. "If they count cards? I'll kick them out."

"You counted cards all the time as a kid," She didn't relish the memories. "And I was the one who had to bandage you up after they beat the crap out of you for it."

"That was different."

"And why, pray tell, was that different?"

"Because it wasn't my casino." He motioned at the blackjack table. "The only reason I have that on the main floor is because some people don't want to go to the high-stake poker games in the back rooms, but they won't play games of pure chance, either."

"Well, fuck, Jak, I wonder why."

He scowled at her. "Don't start with me."

She exhaled. They'd never get anywhere with this argument. Jak wanted this life, and nothing would change that. She wasn't even sure she wanted him to. He reminded her of an Earth legend, a fellow named Robin Hood who stole from the rich and gave to the poor. Jak employed only from the Undercity, offering the best jobs available, good wages, plenty of filtered water, and even health benefits, especially since Karal Rajindia had set up her clinic. He also kept violence out of the Top Mark, with none of the cruelty that ran in the drug cartels or among the more vicious dust gangs. Yet he also dealt in what, for some, was an addiction just as soul-parching as the cartel drugs.

She couldn't deny another truth, however, one that rose above the others. They'd known each other since they'd been three years old. They'd become lovers long before the above-city considered them adults. Their relationship had survived her two decades in the military and another years-long separation when she either had to accept that he would always live on the edge or else leave him. In the end, she'd come home. They always came back to each other. He was part of her and she of him, and nothing would ever change that truth.

"Bhaaj?" He was watching her with that intent look he got when he wanted to figure her out.

"I'm tired, that's all."

He touched her cheek. "We'll deal with the rest, eh? Always find way."

She took his hand and curled her fingers around his. "Yah. Always."

"Well. So." A gleam came into his gaze. "Now we go get this Scorp boyo."

CHAPTER XII
Glitz Clubbing

The main floor of the Top Mark never looked the same. Jak used top-of-the-line nanobots to create the place, and they could tear down and rebuild the entire casino in hours. He moved it regularly, sometimes even changing the name, keeping its location a secret from everyone except his employees and a few select others. No one came unless he invited them.

If a potential client did wrangle an invitation, they couldn't just walk in. Jak's thugs came for them and used shadow-market tech to make them blind, deaf, and unable to smell during the journey through the Undercity. Lately he'd even used suits that blocked their ability to feel textures. They couldn't remove the tech until they were inside the casino. If the clients balked, their guides took them home. Period. They had no visit, not then, not ever. Jak took no chances.

Tonight, the glitz had a noir quality. Purple holos sparkled in the air, wheels and tumbling dice, as if twilight wanted to descend but couldn't because of the glitter. Music swirled in the background, low and slow, glit-glow jazz. It put Bhaaj on edge. Not for its sensuous sound, which she liked, but because Jak encoded subtle messages in the music and holos to make people want to gamble. It didn't work on her; not only had the army trained her to resist subliminal signals, but she'd long ago added a series to her meds that dampened her response. She could have them block the effects of alcohol, too, but right now she had no intention of drinking. Save that for when she could enjoy herself with her kingpin husband instead of worrying about misbehaving athletes.

The patrons glittered as much as the casino, either elite tourists dressed for their scandalous night out at Jak's infamous establishment or his Cries regulars, who wore the latest styles in decadent wealth, torn glit-shirts and miniskirts with abstract holos washing over the fabric. A few newcomers were trying out the casino for their first time. Like Hyden Laj.

He'd moved to sit at the blackjack table, seeming oblivious that Kiro stood in the shadows, watching. A youth in the silver shirt of a dealer was giving out cards, managing to look classy and cool at the same time. Bhaaj recognized him; he lived in the Oey circle protected by Pat Cove's Dust Knights, one of the larger kith-and-kin groups in the Undercity.

The dealer glanced up, his dark gaze sharpening as he saw Jak across the table, standing behind six players who sat on its curving portion. Hyden had taken the rightmost seat. When he saw Jak, he stiffened, alarm washing across his face. Almost as fast as it came, his reaction vanished, masked by his usual look of boredom.

Bhaaj went to stand with Kiro, hidden in the shadows with him. He spoke in a low voice. "Did you bring Hyden here, too?"

"Not me." She also kept her voice low. "Someone he knows must have finagled an invite."

When the dealer nodded to Jak, the players in front of him turned to look—and did a double-take. Although everyone tensed, no one said or did anything other than incline their head to Jak. Good. This group knew better than to try engaging the casino's notorious proprietor.

The game resumed, and Jak just stood watching them play his namesake. It didn't take Bhaaj long to realize Hyden sucked at blackjack. She felt like metaphorically thumping him upside the head for coming here.

In a game, each player started with two cards, both face up. The dealer also had two, one face down and one face up. For each round, a player could ask for another card or let his hand stay with no additions. The goal seemed simple; Hyden just needed the sum of his cards to be greater than or equal to what the dealer held without going over twenty-one. The value of the cards went from one to ten, with the face cards, the queen, jack, and prince, each counting as ten. A player could make an ace either one or eleven. If they got twenty-one on the first round, it won them more money.

Blackjack offered one of the few games in the casino Bhaaj enjoyed, because it involved skill. If you kept track of the cards, your chances of winning increased. In Jak's youth, with his nearly photographic memory for cards and his killer knack for probabilities, he'd cut a swath through every poker den he frequented. Back then no casino existed in the Undercity, just informal games, but the people running them hadn't liked Jak's talents any more than he liked it from players here. Unlike in those dens, though, Jak didn't have his thugs beat up people for winning, at least not if they didn't cheat. If they won too much, he kicked them out and didn't invite them back.

Each of the six players had put several chips in a small rectangle woven into the green cloth that covered the table. Hyden's bet was way too large for a kid his age, but given the wealth of his family, it didn't surprise Bhaaj. If he lost, it went to the house, which meant Jak used it for the people of the Undercity, who needed it thousands of times more.

After giving out cards for a new round, the dealer glanced at the player to his left, a woman with a four and a six showing. She scratched the table, asking for another card, and he dealt her a six. The player next to her, a man with greying hair, had an ace and a seven. He waved his hand over his cards, palm down, indicating he didn't want another card. The dealer continued with the other players, either giving them a card or not according to their signal.

Hyden had a queen and a six showing, not the best hand, but not bad given that the dealer would have to take cards until his hand reached at least sixteen, which meant the dealer had a relatively good chance of busting, or going over twenty-one. Watching Hyden, Bhaaj thought, *Don't ask for another card. Stand with what you have.*

When Hyden scraped the table instead, Bhaaj scowled. Sure enough, the dealer gave him a seven, for a total of twenty-three. Bang. He went bust and lost his bet to the house. The dealer smoothly collected his cards and chips and continued with the game.

During the next few rounds, Hyden glanced at Jak several times. He tried to be discreet, so he could pretend he didn't notice the casino boss watching, but Bhaaj could tell Jak rattled him. Hyden kept making too-large bets and losing them, dropping a fortune. If he played this badly with the only game he had a chance at winning, Bhaaj didn't even want to imagine how much he'd lost at holo-roulette.

"Enough," she muttered.

Bhaaj went over to Jak and stood with him, glaring at Hyden. The youth glanced her way—and froze. In a loud voice, he said, "What the bloody hell?"

She crossed her arms and jerked her head the way she did during practice when she wanted the runners to get moving. He scowled at her, but when she just stood, glaring, he threw down his cards and stood up. Everyone at the table shifted, looking irritated or confused. Ignoring them, Hyden went over to Bhaaj and spoke in a low voice. "What are you doing here?"

"I could ask the same of you. You need to quit losing money and go home. We've got practice in a few hours." She glanced up as Kiro joined them. "Both of you. No more screwing around."

Kiro opened his mouth as if to protest, probably since Bhaaj had sent him here, but when she gave him an implacable look, he closed it again.

Hyden blinked at Kiro. "How did you get here?"

Bhaaj could tell the dealer and the other players were getting irked with the noise. Jak didn't show any reaction, but he didn't fool her. He found this hilarious, damn him.

"Come on." She motioned toward the far wall of the casino. "We're leaving."

Hyden said, "I don't want—"

"You heard her," Jak interrupted in his low, gravelly voice. "Your coach wants you to leave."

Hyden jerked, looking from Bhaaj to Jak and back to Bhaaj. "Fine." With no more ado, he set off across the casino, headed for who knew where. After two steps, he stopped and turned back to them, his forehead creased with confusion.

"Going somewhere?" Jak inquired.

"Uh, no," Hyden said. "I meant no disrespect."

"Jak, leave him alone," Bhaaj said. She headed across the main room, motioning for Hyden and Kiro to accompany her. They both got into motion, moving fast to keep up with her.

"I'll take you out," Bhaaj told them.

"What about the guides?" Hyden asked.

"You mean Jak's thugs?"

"I wouldn't want to insult anyone—"

"Why not?" Kiro asked. "You do it all the time in practice."

"Kiro, cut it out," Bhaaj told him.

Hyden turned to look at where Jak had stood. The casino boss had left the blackjack table and was wandering the main room, watching the games. For all appearances, he'd forgotten them.

Hyden turned back to Bhaaj. "Is he going to do anything to us?"

"Not to Coach Bhaajan." Kiro smirked at Hyden. "He's married to her."

"Yeah, right, asshole."

"I'm not joking."

Hyden squinted at Bhaaj. "He's kidding, right?"

"No, it's true." Bhaaj kept her voice bland. "Jak is my husband."

"Holy shit," Hyden muttered. He waited until they reached the edge of the main room, then spoke in a low voice. "You're an Olympic track and field coach. Isn't it illegal for you to marry a casino owner? At the least, it's bad publicity for the team."

"Why do you care?" Kiro asked. "You and your family have nothing to do with us anymore."

"I'm still on the team." Glancing at Bhaaj, Hyden added, "Right? I am?"

She drew them both into an alcove. As the door slid shut, the small room hummed, its engines setting it in motion like an elevator that moved horizontally. Niches in the walls glowed, and the skulls within them glittered with red lights for their eyes.

"Yes, you're still on the team," Bhaaj said. "If you come to practices ready to work." Dryly she added, "And rested."

Relief washed over his face. "Good." He looked around the room. "This is weird."

Bhaaj ignored the distraction. "Hyden, legally, you're a minor. As far as I'm concerned, you're an adult, but if your parents want to pull you from the team, we can't override them."

"They won't stop me." He peered at a skull in one of the niches, then shook his head and turned to Bhaaj. "They think Coach Mason will relent about the Undercity."

"He won't," Kiro said. He seemed far less disconcerted by the room, probably since he'd already seen it when Bhaaj brought him here.

Bhaaj tapped a code into a discreet panel, and a subtle change sounded in the low hum of the engine, the only sign that she'd changed their destination.

"Coach, why are you angry?" Hyden asked. "My gambling has nothing to do with the team."

She turned to him. "You just lost as much in one night as a season's worth of your father's pledge to support the team. And you did it after he withdrew that support."

"You must realize we can't send Undercity gang members offworld to represent Raylicon." Hyden spoke awkwardly. "It's worse than you marrying one of the worst criminals on the planet. With the team, we can't hide it the way you do with your marriage."

"For flaming sake," Kiro said. "How can you be such an asshole?"

Hyden swung around to him. "What, you think you're one of them now because you made a few friends? They'd turn on you in a second if anyone here attacked you."

"Actually, someone did," Kiro told him. "Strider and them defended me." With a grimace, he added, "Now they want me to learn tykado, so I can defend myself."

"I don't get it," Hyden said. "Why do you hang out with them?" After a hesitation, he added, "You even look like them, especially since you let your hair grow. Why would you do that?"

"Why wouldn't I?" Kiro inquired.

"Because." Hyden spoke awkwardly. "You come from good stock, Kiro. But if people think you're Undercity, they'll spit on you."

"Hyden, enough," Bhaaj said. "Do you have any idea how much respect you squander with these cracks?"

He considered her. "You know, my father had you checked out when you joined the team. You aren't really Undercity, right? His investigators say you're richer than sin."

Bhaaj made her expression bland. "So?"

"So why do you act like you come from here? You even curl your hair." He spoke with incredulity. "And you *married* that casino guy? I don't get it."

She took a moment, counting to ten, then spoke in a calm voice. "I was born here. Jak and I grew up together, same age, same gang, same everything. By common law marriage—which is how we do it in the Undercity—we've been married since we were kids. I enlisted at sixteen and shipped out after I finished school. Shall I continue?"

"But—that can't be." He didn't sound angry or condescending, just confused. "You retired as a major. Almost no one can jump from the enlisted to the officer ranks. Certainly not someone born and bred in the Undercity. And you work for the *Majdas*." He took a breath. "No. It's impossible."

"Stop being dense," Kiro told him. "She's so famous here, they make statues of her. If you quit being an ass-byte, I'll show you one."

Hyden turned his disbelief onto Kiro. "How would you know where to find it? No one can come here without all that tech they put on us to hide the way."

"I come all the time," Kiro boasted. When Bhaaj glared at him, he amended, "Well, a few times so far, with Strider's gang."

A low buzz came from one of the skulls. Both Hyden and Kiro jumped.

"Time to go," Bhaaj said. A door across from them slid open with an almost inaudible hiss. Blackness showed outside, just barely lit by the dim light from within the alcove.

"Don't we need an escort?" Hyden regarded her uneasily. "The guides who picked me up in Cries told me that if I didn't follow their rules, I'd end up, uh . . . in bad condition."

"You're with me. That's enough." Bhaaj left the alcove, exiting into a dead-end. As they followed her, the door of the casino snapped shut, leaving them in complete darkness.

"Shit," Hyden muttered.

"Yah." Kiro no longer sounded so cocky.

"You can turn on your lamps," Bhaaj said.

A golden light appeared around Kiro, created by the light stylus he wore around his neck. Zee had given it to him as a gift. Interesting. One situation existed where someone would offer a gift instead of a bargain, no strings attached. Bhaaj smiled. Did Zee have a soft spot for Kiro? He was a good-looking kid, especially with that new mop of curls, and he had a charming personality.

Hyden tapped on his wrist band, which produced a bright light. Bhaaj winced at the glare.

"Can you dim that?" Kiro asked. "It hurts my eyes."

Bhaaj expected Hyden to make some crack, like he always did in front of his friends, but he only said, "Just a sec." He tapped more and the light dimmed until it matched the intensity of Kiro's stylus. Bhaaj activated her gauntlet light, using the same intensity and golden hue.

The area around them looked nondescript, just a dead end with a tunnel stretching to their left. Bhaaj didn't move, however. Instead, she stood considering Hyden.

"What?" he asked.

"Don't try to come back down here," she said.

"I had no intention of it."

"Jak is going to move the casino, so even if you wanted to find it, you couldn't." Bhaaj spoke bluntly. "This isn't something we do, allowing outsiders into our world. You're many levels below the surface. Normally you couldn't even get one level down without protectors."

"Why would I want to?" Hyden asked.

"Are you kidding?" Kiro said. "It's like magic here, a secret place you can never reach unless someone gives you the key. And the keys are like spells. They don't work unless someone here teaches you how to use them."

Hyden shifted his feet. "If we're so far down, aren't tons of rock above us?"

"I suppose." Bhaaj rarely thought about it. "Passages network a lot of it. Or caves, ancient ruins, air conduits, and underground canals with buttresses that have supported them for millennia."

"The aqueducts," Kiro said. "Not just the Undercity, but everything down here."

"Aqueducts? Canals?" Hyden squinted at them. "You mean water is down here?"

"Just poisoned streams," Bhaaj said. "No water flows in the canals. They're too big."

Hyden spoke wryly. "That sounds real magical. Dry canals and poisoned streams."

"You'll see." Kiro glanced at Bhaaj. "Can you take us out? I don't think I could find my way back to the main areas."

"Sure." She led them to the tunnel, headed into the maze of passages she knew by heart.

✢ ✢ ✢

Bhaaj jogged with Hyden and Kiro along the midwalk of a large canal. She'd brought Hyden via this route to let him see one of her favorite Undercity places, a garden of bioluminescent plants. Instead of one midwalk on each side of the canal, this one had walkways at many levels, from near the ground all the way to the ceiling. Staircases spiraled up the walls, and hidden crevices and passages also networked the stone, allowing people access to all the levels.

Plants glowed everywhere with green and blue luminescence, some with pink accents. Wall carvings spiraled in artistic patterns that the gardeners used to direct the plant growth. Delicate veils of fungi draped the walls like living lace, pleasing to touch, yet so strong that they only vibrated when she brushed her hand across them. Graceful trees with translucent leaves pulsed gently with internal light like a radiant heartbeat.

The value of the gardens lay in more than their ethereal beauty, however. Microbes in the foliage helped clean the water and air. Humans still needed to purify the water before they could drink it, but the process became easier with the liquid already partially filtered. Those lovely veils of bioluminescent life contained microbial fuel calls, living batteries that created energy by undergoing chemical reactions with the dust or dying plant life.

On the ground below, algae grew in a series of pools, adding blue luminance to the tunnel. The algae created oxygen, especially in the radiance from LED lights powered by the microbial cells. The LEDs fit so well into the engraved artwork, Bhaaj could barely see them. Such lights had always existed in the Undercity, a remnant from the ancient Ruby Empire. Cyber-riders had passed the knowledge of how to repair them from generation to generation, but in the past few centuries they'd relearned the LED tech, until now they could make new, better lights.

Far above, close to the surface, poisoned water trickled through rocks heated by Raylicon's killing sun. Rock-riders, the Undercity version of structural engineers, used stone conduits to direct that water down here, where genetically engineered plants with thermoelectric properties could generate energy from the heat. The ceiling of the canal arched high above them, fading into shadows, barely lit by luminescent mist rising from the heated pools.

"Goddess," Hyden said. "This is beautiful, like something out of a fantasy world."

"Yah," Bhaaj murmured. "Don't drink the water, though. It's poisonous."

He looked around. "Why is it so empty?"

"Not empty," Kiro said. He had that serene look of a runner lost in the zone. "People here."

"What?" Hyden squinted at him. "You know, lately sometimes, you sound like them."

"Like Undercity," Bhaaj said, falling into the cadences of her own dialect. Kiro had the right of it; people were following them, using hidden passages in the walls and ceiling.

Hyden had no comment, so they continued in silence. Somewhere a distant clatter of falling pebbles crinkled the silence. The air smelled faintly sweet, a trace of aromatic compounds created by microbes clinging to the blue azurite that glinted in the otherwise red, iron-heavy dust.

A whistle came through the air. Kiro whistled back.

"Hey," Hyden protested. "Kiro, what are you doing?"

"Zee," Kiro explained.

"Zee what?"

"She comes—" He stopped, peering at the midwalk ahead. "Is that her? Wrong place." In the distance, a shadowy figure had stepped out from the wall.

Bhaaj grabbed Hyden's arm, jerking him to a halt. Kiro went another couple of steps, then stopped and looked back at her.

"Wait," Bhaaj told them. To Max, she thought, *Turn on my ear augs.*

The air suddenly seemed full or rustles, clicks—and yah, she heard it, the grate of metal on stone, like the accidental scrape of a knife. Bhaaj knew that sound. Punkers made it as they crept along unfamiliar paths. This canal belonged to the Dust Knights, not them.

The shadowed figure strode toward them, resolving into a man. Another figure stepped out from a nearer crack in the wall, a woman. As they came into the light, Bhaaj recognized the Kajada symbol of a giant lizard on their gauntlets.

"Fuck," Bhaaj muttered. She stepped ahead of Hyden and said, "Kiro, get back here."

While Kiro moved back, Bhaaj spoke in a sharp voice to the approaching duo. "What want?"

The figures faltered, their walk slowing. "Who?" the man asked.

"The Bhaaj." She identified herself by title rather than name. "You?"

The punkers stopped in the light of a torch. They looked in their late twenties, hardened by what the Undercity considered their advanced years.

"Got no shit with The Bhaaj," the woman said. She had a narrow face, craggy with scars and tattoos. Circuit diagrams snaked up her arms, embedded in the skin.

"Got no shit with Kajada," Bhaaj said. With Kiro and Hyden here, she couldn't take risks.

The man motioned at Hyden. "Got rich ass-byte."

"Got runner," Bhaaj told him. "Runs with team. With Shiv Kajada."

"Eh." The Kajada man raised his large dagger. "We take his biz."

"His tech," the woman said. "He give, we let go."

Bhaaj couldn't tell Hyden to give them his tech-mech band. If she let these punkers win, it would race all over the Whisper Mill, not only that they beat her, but that you could get away with challenging her if she brought slicks here.

Max, combat mode, she thought.

The rest of her senses heightened. She could feel the blood pumping in her body as her biomech web activated her bio-hydraulics and skeletal augmentations, giving her two to three times the speed, strength, and reflexes of a normal human.

She spoke in a low voice. "Kiro, you ken your way out from here?"

"Yah," he murmured.

"When I move on punks, you take Hyden. *Run.*"

"Will do."

"Good. *Go!*" In that same instant, Bhaaj lunged at the punkers, going so fast that she reached them before either had a chance to react. Grabbing the man by the arm, she swung him into the woman, shoving them both off the midwalk. As they plummeted to the ground below, she whirled around and found Kiro and Hyden gone. Without a pause, she jumped off the midwalk, turning in midair toward the punkers. She felt the impact as she hit the ground, but her knees bent by just the right amount to ease the landing, and her enhanced musculature and skeleton absorbed the shock.

The Kajada woman lay in the dust, but the man was climbing to his feet, his face contorted with fury. He leapt forward, trying to catch Bhaaj with a street move. She easily pivoted and grabbed his leg, bracing her shoulder against his body as she threw him down. Although he shouted and struggled, she held him pinned to the ground.

"Not fucking invade Dust Knight places," she told him.

"Not your fucking place," he ground out.

"Yah. *Mine.*" Bhaaj was angry enough to lay claim to the entire region controlled by the Knights. They treated her as their leader, with Ruzik as her second. This was Oey territory, adjacent to the region claimed by Ruzik's gang, the two largest circles in the Undercity. When the punkers invaded these canals, they invaded her home.

Bhaaj didn't want to kill the guy, but when she eased her grip, he managed to wrench free and jump to his feet. He went at her again. Or he tried. Although he knew the rough and tumble well, he couldn't match a trained combatant with a sixth-degree black belt in tykado. She easily countered every move he tried. This time when she knocked him down, she kept him on his back while she pressed her arm against his throat. As he fought her hold, his face paled and his struggles grew more labored, until finally he stopped resisting and gasped for breath.

"Not kill," he whispered.

"Not fuck with me," Bhaaj said. "You ken?"

"Yah." He barely got out the word. "Ken."

She let go and jumped back with enhanced speed. Far more slowly, he climbed to his feet, turning just enough to check on the woman who had come with him. Although she still lay on her back, she lifted her hand. Relief washed over Bhaaj. She hadn't wanted to kill anyone. Her people lived by their own laws, untouched by Cries. Here, you could kill in self-defense or to protect your territory. Even after her time in the military, though, she'd never become inured to death. Hardened, yah, but she hated it, hated that poverty drove her people to extremes, hated that no one else gave a damn as long as her people didn't bother the rest of the universe with their inconvenient existence.

Suppressed fury hardened her voice. "You not belong here."

"Take what we need," the man told her, but without his earlier bravado. Behind him, the woman was struggling to get up.

"Get out," Bhaaj told him. "Not come back."

The woman stood up with blood running down her face. "Hungry. Not got food."

Damn. Dice Vakaar had told Strider the same. Before the war, the cartels had plenty of resources. But now? They must be struggling, enough to goad punkers into ganger territory, seeking supplies. Bhaaj had no wish to help feed the cartels, but neither did she want people to starve, including the punkers. It drove them to violence just as much as their trade.

She held back her urge to pummel the Kajada punkers. Instead, she told them to get out and not come back. After they left, she slipped into hidden passages in the walls and followed in secret until they were good and gone from Dust Knight territory.

Angel found Strider's gang at the landing of a spiral staircase in the Aza Lan canal, part of Strider's territory. Although Angel had caught a warning in the Whisper Mill about a rich intruder, the last person she expected to see was Hyden Laj. But there he stood, with Strider's dusters, including Kiro.

Footsteps sounded behind Angel. She didn't look; she knew who approached. Sure enough, Ruzik soon caught up with her. They slowed down as they approached the stairs.

Strider turned, her hand dropping to the dagger on her belt. When she saw them, she relaxed.

"Thank the saints," Hyden muttered, his face ashen. "Are we getting out of here now?"

Angel and Ruzik joined them. "Why you here?" Ruzik asked Hyden.

Good question, Angel thought. Strider had done what no one expected, asking Kiro to be their fourth, but at least that made sense. No gangers in their right minds would recruit Hyden.

Kiro stiffened, blinking at her.

You hear me? Angel asked him.

Yah, Kiro thought.

His response came in faint and full of static, but it was enough. No wonder Strider wanted him in her gang. Angel knew almost no one else who could receive even moods that well, let alone thoughts. Just Ruzik's gang and a few people at the Kyle Division.

"Kajada go after Hyden," Strider was saying. "In Cove Canal, by the gardens."

Angel scowled. "Cove Canal belong to Oey circle. Why you there?"

"We were at the casino," Hyden said. "Coach Bhaaj was taking us home. Then some people, I don't know who, they stopped us, wanted my tech—" Taking a breath, he motioned at Strider's gang. "They joined us after Bhaaj helped me and Kiro get away."

"Yah," Lamp said. "Bhaaj send Kajada punks running home."

"Good." Angel would've pitied the punkers unfortunate enough to encounter Bhaaj, except they'd invaded dust gang territory. So much new going on, people coming who shouldn't be here. Kiro okay, but *Hyden?* Fucking hell.

Ruzik frowned at Hyden. "You shouldn't be here."

"Not worry." Strider turned to the Scorpio heir. "We take you out."

"Thanks." Hyden spoke awkwardly, his face pale in the light from their gauntlets. "Coach Bhaaj was at the casino. I don't get why. I mean, I get it now, but I never expected anyone from the team to see me there."

"She send us home." Kiro smirked. "Hyden losing. A *lot*."

"Shut up, already," Hyden muttered.

"We go with," Ruzik said. He headed up the stairs, followed by Strider and Lamp. Hyden came after them, with Kiro and Zee behind him. Angel brought up the rear, keenly aware of their surroundings, making sure no one followed. Especially not Kajada. The last thing they needed was for punkers to kill the Scorpio heir.

The staircase went around and around, its ancient steps in good condition because Strider's gang maintained them. They passed landings that accessed other canals, some large and vast, others barely more than tunnels. As they climbed, Angel pondered. What to do? Punkers kept showing up where they didn't belong.

Second time, she thought to Ruzik. *First Dice Vakaar. Now Kajada.*

Kajada came for Hyden, Ruzik thought.

Another voice reached them, dim, just at the edges of Angel's mind. *Want his tech-mech.*

Kiro? Ruzik asked.

Yah, Kiro thought.

Always want tech-mech, Angel answered. *Not need invade Knight places to pinch.*

Hyden got special mech, Kiro thought. *Punkers sell for a lot. They starving. Need buy food.*

Angel wanted to say *Tough shit if Kajada wants food,* but she couldn't. She knew some of the punkers, had grown up with them before they joined the cartel. She didn't want them to die. Maybe they could do a bargain. If they stayed out of Dust Knight territory and quit selling their shit here, she'd help them get supplies. Working at a Kyle job had its advantages. She had some byke-biz now, not a lot, but Ruzik had set up "accounts" in the city. Even if she couldn't do much, a fragile treaty with the cartels was better than killing people.

After they'd all climbed for more than five levels, the staircase ended in a spacious tunnel. Most people never came this high; they'd find nothing here but ancient statues. Tonight, they all walked along the tunnel. Up ahead, dim light trickled out from an archway. It came from the Foyer, the crystal-encrusted cave that offered access to the Concourse. Normally they left the Undercity using hidden paths instead of the Foyer, but of course they wouldn't reveal those secrets to a stranger.

Said stranger, Hyden, stayed quiet. He pretended to be an asshole during practices—well, yah, it wasn't all pretend. The dude had entitlement issues. But underneath it all, Angel sensed his commitment to his sport. He loved running. At first he'd ignored the Undercity recruits, obviously assuming they'd wash out. When they didn't, he stayed aloof, watching from the distance of his privilege. Gradually, over time, she felt his grudging respect. She suspected he no longer cared if they stayed on the team, not like his friends who came to watch him practice and afterward went drinking with him. They looked to him as a leader, and he played the part.

Angel felt mostly confusion from him now. The Undercity didn't fit what he'd expected. Well, not all of it. He *had* gambled in the infamous Top Mark, and almost had the shit beaten out of him by drug punkers. He didn't know what to think. Mostly he wanted to get home.

From Kiro, she felt a sense of peace. Around Strider's gang, he often seemed that way. Like knew like.

The path ended at a sculpted archway bordered by tessellated mosaics that Angel loved. The archaeology texts she read on the university mesh said the style came from thousands of years ago. Cries had nothing so lovely, certainly not the upscale, modern Concourse.

They walked under the arch and into the Foyer, a small cave with stone lacework for its high ceiling, as if an artist had woven the rock up there into filaments. Sculpted rock stumps down here allowed someone to sit, though people rarely did. Tourists almost never came here. Signs posted by authorities from Cries warned them to stay away.

Across the Foyer, another archway opened onto the Concourse. This far down, it just formed a narrow lane with stalls tended by bored vendors. A haze hung in the air, a mixture of smoke from braziers, and mist that formed when cooler air from the Undercity met the warmer Concourse air. Yah, sure, the Cries tourist bureau claimed the Concourse belonged to the Undercity, but anyone who knew anything realized it had no connection. Far, far up the lane, it turned into a boulevard with fancy shops, savory-scented cafés, boutiques with impractical clothes that cost too much, and anything else city vendors thought they could sell to tourists.

Strider stopped by the exit arch and turned to Hyden. "You can go alone from here?"

"Uh, yeah. Sure." He squinted at the market stalls, and their vendors looked him over, sizing him up as a potential customer. With his glitz-trousers, metallic shirt and the high-end tech, his appearance practically shouted *I'm money!*

"I'll go with you," Kiro told him. "The Concourse is safe for us."

"This is the Concourse?" He blinked at Kiro. "I go there all the time. It doesn't look like this." Then he amended, "We hang near the top, clubbing at the Blue Light Dance Palace."

"I've never been," Kiro said. "I've heard it's ultra, though."

Hyden glanced at the others. "Thanks for taking us out. Let me know if Bhaaj is okay."

"I'm sure she's fine," Angel said.

He gave an awkward wave and set off with Kiro, headed down the lane between the stalls. The vendors called out about their wares, spice-sticks and scented candles and mats supposedly woven by Undercity artists. Hyden kept going, striding as if he couldn't escape fast enough, with Kiro at his side. The Concourse stretched for several kilometers, always with a gradual upward slope. The areas Hyden knew would be near the end where wealthy slicks and tourists enjoyed the night life or daytime shopping.

Angel watched them go, brooding on what these changes boded for the Undercity.

PART TWO
Metropoli

CHAPTER XIII
New Beginnings

Even having seen the Cries Starport before, Angel still found it intense. They'd all gathered in the main concourse, an apt word given how it resembled the much bigger Concourse above the Undercity. Cafés were everywhere here, too, along with shops where you could buy useless things, like shirts with *The City of Cries* emblazoned across the chest however you wanted the smart cloth to display the words, or overpriced liquor that cost ten times what you'd pay in the aqueducts.

The Undercity athletes stood with her and stared around the place, silent. Ruzik had gone with Bhaaj and Mason to a nearby counter, talking to a woman in one of those perky white and blue outfits all the staff here wore. Too much white cloth. Didn't they know it would turn red from the dust? Then again, Cries didn't have a sensible amount of dust anywhere. Hell, they had tiny, invisible "smart bots" floating in the air that got rid of anything they didn't like.

The only other time Angel had visited this starport, two years ago for her trip to Parthonia, she'd gone into overload. Kiosks, displays, moving walkways, gleaming cool-carts: it was too much. Round daises had holo-vids running above them with entertainment programs no one seemed to watch. You could call up your own private holo, and it would hang in the air, showing whatever you wanted, including flight times and gates. Everywhere EIs talked, talked, talked. People strolled, strode, or ambled down the concourse, browsing shops or eating on the go. Others sat in bars or cafés. Holos above the concourse directed you to *Physical baggage claim, Digital baggage claim,* or *Virtual baggage claim.* Angel half-expected to see one for emotional baggage claim.

Kiro stayed here with Strider's gang, but the other Cries athletes had clumped together by the floor-to-ceiling windows that made up one wall of the concourse. Outside, shuttles trundled across the casecrete, ferrying people to the stardocks out in the desert where the noise of take-offs and landings didn't blast this building.

Bhaaj, Ruzik, and Mason finished at the counter and headed back to the team, Mason to the Cries members and Bhaaj and Ruzik to Angel's group.

"We ready?" Lamp asked Ruzik.

"Yah." He tilted his head at the Cries athletes. "Go with them."

Bhaaj spoke in the Cries dialect. "Listen, everyone. From now on, most everything you hear will be in above-city speech. Most people have never even heard our dialect. They'll find it hard to understand. But Cries speak, it's called Skolian Flag, and it's everywhere. You should start using it if you know it, and if you don't, now is a good time to learn."

"Not want," Rockjan growled, her rough voice unmistakable. In almost perfect Flag, she added, "They use too many fucking words, until your head hurts from the jabber, jabber, jabber."

"Yah," Bhaaj agreed. "You get used to it, though. Eventually."

A few people said, "Eee-ven-chew-ah-lee," followed by laughter.

Rockjan seemed mollified, or at least her glare eased. She slung on her backpack as if it weighed nothing. Dark red like the color of the desert sands, it had their team logo on its back, a soaring gold hawk. Angel doubted it was a coincidence that it looked so much like the Majda insignia, though this bird had a bigger wingspan and gold feathers instead of black.

Mason had given a pack to every team member, each with a smart-bottle that filtered water, a red and gold track suit with *Raylicon* emblazoned on the top, power bars to eat, and other useful sports biz. At first, the Undercity athletes refused the packs. Then Bhaaj pointed out the bargain, that Mason gave the packs in return for the hassle of going to Metropoli. Put that way, the exchange favored Mason, which pissed off people. So Bhaaj brought out the clincher, new running shoes, top-of-the-line, so splendid that just looking at them seemed to make you run faster. Yah, so, then they took the bargain.

Angel no longer cared about this charity biz. They should wear the outfit, shoes and all, because it promoted team unity. Every other team had a uniform, and Raylicon would look stupid without them. And of course they needed enough food and good water to do their best. Besides, if this North-Metro City was anything like Selei City on the world Parthonia, they'd have all the filtered water they wanted. Priceless, yah. It had no price because it came for free.

Angel had read about the worlds where humans lived. Having enough water, good air, and a good climate came from "terraforming" or the less extreme "biosculpting," which had worked better on other planets than on Raylicon. Metropoli had ten billion people, the most heavily settled world, more even than Earth. It turned out Earth had killed a substantial portion of its population during its Virus Wars, leaving "only" five billion. It boggled her mind to imagine so many people on one world—and it horrified her to read how many had died in the wars and the resulting collapse of civilization. No wonder they'd ventured farther into space looking for new worlds—until they discovered their lost siblings already out here, building empires.

The Olympics would be on the Skolian world called Foreshires Hold, apparently another of the beautiful ones, but first they had to qualify. So here they stood, twenty-eight Undercity kids, including two juniors, and fifteen Cries athletes, plus Bhaaj and Mason, the team doctor, the security chief, and two assistant coaches.

They soon boarded a shuttle, headed to their first interstellar tournament.

"Nahya!" Rockjan knocked the cup from Angel's hand, sending it spinning across the hotel room with water flying everywhere. "Not kill me!"

Angel scowled at her. "Water fine. Not kill."

Across the hotel room, Dice was peering at the smart-faucet, telling it to turn on and off. "Eh," he informed it. More water poured into the sink.

Angel sighed. This room, which she shared with Ruzik, currently hosted too many people, including Rockjan, all of Strider's gang, Tam Wiens, their best runner, and Dice Vakaar, who acted as if it were perfectly normal for a cartel heir to hang out with Dust Knights. The two twelve-year-olds, Crinkles and Full-up, had tagged along, as nosy as always. Angel didn't see why they had to compete in a junior competition. They'd qualified for the adult team. It irked her that above-city types tried to make being a kid last forever. They even considered *Hyden* a child, though he acted, looked, spoke, and carried on like a man well into adulthood.

At least she had a nice place to get annoyed in. The spacious room had windows with their blue curtains pulled open, letting in sunlight. The floor rugs felt softer than fluff. One counter had an oven-fridge that took orders, delivered them, and cooked the food or kept it cold if needed. The only reason Angel knew the coaches considered this place "cheap" was because when she and Ruzik had gone to Parthonia, they'd stayed with Bhaaj in a cabin owned by the Majdas that truly had qualified as luxurious.

Right now, everyone seemed subdued by the newness, which she suspected was why they'd followed her here instead of going to their own rooms. Mason had set them up as four to a room, with separate suites for coaches, and a room for Ruzik and Angel.

"Water fine," Kiro said. He filled a cup and drank it before anyone could stop him.

Strider crossed her arms and glared at him. "Now you die. Then we got no relay team."

"Am fine," Kiro told her.

"Metal bug," Crinkles announced. She pointed to the room-bot, a small drone humming along the floor as it cleaned up the spilled water. "It thirsty too."

"Kiro still alive," Tam commented. "Not dead yet."

Strider stalked over to Kiro. "Why you not dead?"

He smiled, more relaxed than the rest of them. "Not feel like doing that."

"Water good." Angel motioned at the food set up on a long table by the window. "Food, too. Eat. Stay strong."

"Not hungry." Zee sank into a blue chair by the table, then stiffened as it readjusted, trying to ease her tension. Miserably, she said, "Feel sick. Too much to see."

Tam spoke gently, a tone she never revealed to the slicks. "Take care, yah? We help."

"Will get better," Angel offered to Zee. She'd felt exhilarated the first time she went offworld. Of course, she and Ruzik had been together, which eased the shocks. It had pissed her off, though, the way people acted, as if she and Ruzik would go berserk and beat up everyone in sight.

"Too much air," Lamp said. "And too little feet. Make dizzy."

Angel knew what he meant by the air. The higher concentration of oxygen made her feel strong, as if she could run and run and run. But feet? She pointed at his. "You still just got two."

Lamp jumped. "Go too high."

"Oh. Yah. Gravity less here." Hardly any difference, but enough to notice.

"Grah-vah-tee," Lamp said, and they all laughed.

Tam bounced on the balls of her feet. "Let's go run."

"Got team meeting." Angel would've rather run, too, but she'd promised Bhaaj to look after the others.

"Got to lie down." Zee slowly rose to her feet, then went to the bed and lay on her side, closing her eyes.

"Stop being sick," Strider told her. "Have even less relay team if Kiro die and you in bed."

"Give her time," Angel said. "Will feel better."

"We go to meet." Tam said. "*Then* go run."

"And choose a partner," Mason continued, speaking to the forty-one athletes who'd crammed into his suite. His rooms resembled the others, except larger with nicer holo-paintings and a better welcome buffet. "You and your partner can look out for each other," he added.

Bhaaj stood to the side, listening. It relieved her to see Captain Duane Ebersole at the back of the room, their head of security. Tall and well-built, with an aura of confidence, he kept watch on the athletes. He came from the Majda police force, sent by them to help support the team.

As much as Bhaaj had hoped they'd send Duane, she'd had no guarantees. The House of Majda still hewed to ancient sexist customs from the age when men were property and barbarian warrior queens ruled Raylicon, though those days were long past for the rest of humanity. The Majdas didn't care. They kept their princes robed and in seclusion. Except General Vaj Majda always hired the best, and if they happened to be male, so be it. That mattered here even more than usual. Duane was one of the few cops the Undercity kids trusted, at least enough not to try whacking him if he came into any place they considered their territory.

The Majdas had also sent one of their private physicians, Doctor Izaka, as the team medic. Bhaaj had never worked with Izaka before, but she knew people held her in high regard. Although no one on the team had sought out her services yet, a few looked sick, particularly Zee.

I hope their health can manage this, Bhaaj thought.

Are you talking to me? Max asked.

Yah, I guess so.

Why are you worried? Your runners seem healthy.

They've barely even left the Undercity before. Coming to another world might be too much. The practices in Cries had helped them adapt to sunlight. Some even loved it. But this sunshine had a different quality, more golden, less harsh. *Light here peaks more in the yellow than back home.*

I doubt they notice.

Maybe not consciously. But all these little differences add up.

They have a full tenday to acclimate.

It's not enough. We should have come earlier. We needed those Scorpio funds.

He sent her a mental icon of a hawk logo. **I thought the Majdas helped.**

Even with that, we can only cover this meet and the Olympics. And Azarina is embarrassed.

You mean the Majda woman on the team?

Yah. She doesn't want this team to look like her vanity project.

His icon morphed into Azarina. **Your athletes aren't the only ones uncomfortable with Majda charity.**

Yah, well, I'd take the charity. Most teams go to the Olympics four to five tendays early, to help acclimate. No way can we manage that with our current funding.

Raise more funds.

I wish it were that easy. She sent a mental image of an exhausted runner. *We've tried everyone, including the city government. Both*

Mason and I have also invested a substantial amount of our own savings. We're still short.

"All right!" Mason was saying. "You all have an hour to settle into your rooms. Then we'll head out to the track. After practice, you'll have time to get washed up, all that." He beamed at them. "The hotel organized a get-together tonight, a dinner followed by a party where you can meet athletes from other teams." He tried to look stern, but Bhaaj knew he didn't fool anyone. He loved all this. "Don't overdo the party! You need a good night's sleep."

Crinkles, one of the twelve-year-olds, spoke up. "Not ken 'night' and 'day.' It go too fast."

Cries dialect, Bhaaj thought at her. She doubted Crinkles would get her words, but the girl might pick up a sense of them. Crinkles and Full-up were competing in the North-Metrop Juniors meet with kids from all over the Imperialate, and it would go better if people understood them. Though maybe she worried too much. A murmur of agreement to Crinkles' words rolled around the room, and it wasn't only from the Undercity athletes.

"Good point," Mason said. "Yes, the day is much shorter here. Everyone, make sure you study the files on this planet." When Crinkles started to protest, he put his hands on his hips and tried to glare. "I know Coach Bhaaj sent it to you all. Read it! Or have a hotel EI read it to you. A day here is thirty hours, a lot closer to the human standard than our eighty-hour day on Raylicon. You only sleep once per day here, at night."

"Can't do squat at midday but sleep," someone said.

"You can go outside at any time of day here," Mason enthused. "It never gets too hot."

Tayz Wilder spoke up. "Are we the only ones who will be out there practicing?"

"Not at all." Mason flicked his fingers through the holicons above the holoboard he always carried now. "Let's see... today, they've scheduled us with two other teams, Metropoli A and Metropoli B." When no one spoke, he glanced up at his audience. The Undercity kids looked impassive, but Bhaaj suspected that hid confusion. This all went so far outside their experience, they probably had no idea how to respond.

"Metropoli has a lot of people," Mason added. "Ten billion. That's why they send three teams, from three different continents." When his audience still didn't react, he said, "Well, anyway, you'll be using the track together."

Helyne Tallmount said, "Can we try the marathon routes through the city?"

"Yes, absolutely," Mason said. "You can walk or run the route. But here's the thing." He looked around at everyone. "Don't overdo your workout today. Right now, we're just getting used to this world. In a few days, we can train harder."

Murmurs rolled through the group as the runners relaxed. One interaction worried Bhaaj. Something was up with Dice Vakaar and Shiv Kajada. When they'd joined the team, she'd considered it promising, maybe a way out of the cartels for them. So far they'd avoided each other. Today, though, something felt off, their stiffer body language, a tensing when they glanced at each other, their moods. They seemed on edge.

It's probably the new world, Max thought.

Stop eavesdropping, Bhaaj grumbled.

I can't help it. Your thoughts are intense, enough to make the bioelectrodes fire your neurons, which transmits signals to me even when you don't intend to.

Sorry. I don't mean to be cranky.

"One thing you distance runners should be aware of," Mason was saying. "The longer races take too much time to do heats. They just have the one final, and you all start together. They put the top-ranked people in front, and the rest of you start behind them."

"That isn't fair," someone said. "It will make the times longer for people in the back."

"You'll have vid-timers on your shoes," Mason told her. "They activate when you cross the starting line and stop when you cross the finish."

"Yah," Angel said. "But it can slow you down if you get caught in the crowd."

Bhaaj remembered reacting the same way when she'd run the classic marathon for the army team. She stepped forward. "It isn't enough to matter, especially not in events that take hours. For this meet, they have fewer than two hundred runners in each marathon. It's different than with huge meets, like the Boston Marathon on Earth, with its thirty thousand entrants."

"Ho!" Tam said. "Thirty *thousand?*" Her face lit up. "Goddess, that's ultra!"

Bhaaj blinked at the usually taciturn woman. She'd never heard an outburst like that from Tam. "Well, uh, yah, it is."

Doctor Izaka was also watching Tam. "I'll be at the track. If any of you feel dizzy or giddy from the air, talk to me. Your bodies are still adapting to the higher oxygen content here."

"Ox-ee-jen-cahn-tent," Lamp said, evoking laughter from Strider and Kiro. Zee looked too green to laugh.

"All right!" Mason grinned. "Come on team! Let's go!"

Bhaaj walked out of the stadium tunnel to the outdoor track, beneath the vibrant blue sky. Beyond the stadium walls, the silver towers of North-Metro City rose high into the sky, all agleam in the copious sunlight. Gold and black flyers soared over the city, and media drones whirred closer by, above the track, seeking views of the athletes. It relieved her that the weather remained clear. Their team had enough to handle without the additional shock of a storm, which none of them, Cries or Undercity, had ever experienced.

The hum of the city came to her even here, and the air had a tang to it, an antiseptic quality from the smart dust that kept the atmosphere as clean as stripped bones. The place thrummed with life and energy.

Angel fell into step with her. "Eh."

"Eh," Bhaaj said. Angel seemed less stressed than the others. She was one of the few who'd taken advantage of the army's offer to use their military training center on Raylicon to help acclimate runners to lower gravity worlds.

"Got an ask," Angel said.

"Go ahead." Bhaaj had trouble focusing. It wasn't only the kids who got sick in this new biosphere; she felt lousy, too.

Angel spoke in the Cries dialect, which she did more and more often since she'd started her job. "Can you get me access to the Kyle mesh? I'd like to do some work in my free time, so I don't get behind in my telop training."

"I'll check with the army rep in the city," Bhaaj said. "They can grant the hotel permission to set up a psibernet console for you. Just give them your credentials from your job."

She scowled. "I tried. The army wouldn't do it. Their EI says my Undercity accent makes me suspect."

"Damn it," Bhaaj muttered. Remembering her intention to clean up her language, she added, "I'll take care of it."

"Thanks." Angel took off, headed to where her teammates were jogging on the track. As Bhaaj watched, Shiv stumbled and collided with Tallmount and Dice. Tallmount took no offense, but Dice said something, his face strained. Before Shiv could respond, Angel joined the group, "happening" to put herself between Dice and Shiv. Crisis averted, at least for now.

"Well, so, we've got tons of administrative stuff," a man said.

Startled, Bhaaj turned to find Mason walking with her, reading a holoboard. Far too many of its floating holicons flashed red, demanding attention.

"Lovely," Bhaaj grumbled. "My favorite part."

"It's not so bad." He flicked his finger through a blinking dot, and it morphed into a list of athletes with headshots floating by their names. "We only have one hurdler entered, Tanzia Harjan in the 100 meters. We don't have anyone on the 400-meter. Do you think Ruzik might? He's one of our strongest jumpers. We still have a few days to make changes for athletes already in the meet."

"At *this* late date? Ruzik hasn't trained for hurdles." True, he jumped over debris all the time during his Undercity runs, so much so that Bhaaj suspected he sought out routes with blockage on purpose because he enjoyed it. But still. "Besides, he loves the marathon."

"I didn't mean not do the marathon!" Mason said. "He can do both. The 400-meter hurdle is on the morning of the first day and its finals are that evening. The royal marathon isn't until day five. That gives him plenty of time to recover."

Bhaaj considered the idea. "How about the steeplechase? The longer 3000-meter distance suits him better." She smiled. "And he loves jumping over water. He thinks it's funny."

Mason's face lit up. "We've never entered *anyone* in the steeplechase." He flicked the holicons, moving them around or replacing them with new ones. "Okay, problem. The steeplechase is only two days before the royal marathon. That doesn't give him a lot of time to recover."

"I'll talk to him," Bhaaj said. "But if he has doubts, I'd counsel against it."

Mason sighed. "We don't have enough athletes. Rockjan is the only one of yours doing either the javelin or discus."

"She likes throwing things." What Rockjan liked was using weapons, but Bhaaj left that unsaid. "I thought Jon Casestar did the discus." He'd started on the Army Olympic team, but after they stationed him on Raylicon, he'd received permission to join Mason's group. "He's a powerhouse."

"Yes!" Excitement suffused Mason's face. "He's on both javelin and discus, like Rockjan. It's the first time we've ever had two athletes in both events."

"Good." The more they got Rockjan involved in training the less likely she was to get in trouble. Speaking of which, she asked, "What's with Shiv and Dice?"

Mason looked confused. "Something happened to them?"

"Not at all." She hoped it stayed that way. "You have Dice on the cliff climb, right? And Shiv is doing mid-length runs." Those events not only came on different days, but the rock climbing took place in a large park outside the city. It would keep the two of them apart.

"That's right." Mason sounded preoccupied as he looked over his data. "And Angel? You're all right with putting her in both the 200 and 400-meter sprints?"

"That's fine." Although Angel ran long distances all the time, as a ganger looking after the largest circle in the Undercity, the sprints suited her better given her muscular legs and explosive take-off. Bhaaj worried more that Angel would overextend herself with a high-powered city job, Olympic training, and her duties as a leader among the Knights. "Mason, I wonder if it's a good idea to have them on multiple events. They're all so new to all this."

"I know." He pushed his hand through his already mussed hair. "But they can't go to the Olympics without qualifying, and this is the only IOC-accredited tournament we can afford before then that doesn't require its own qualification."

Bhaaj's frustration swelled. "If Scorpio hadn't withdrawn support, we could've taken at least some of them to other meets before the Olympics."

"We'll work up to it over the next years." He sighed. "For this year?

We may have to accept that not all our qualified athletes will make the Olympics."

Bhaaj looked out at their runners on the track. Most had stopped jogging and were doing weight-lifting exercises designed to improve skills specific to their events. "We'll see."

He stopped as his board beeped. "What the hell? Someone registered a complaint about us."

"How?" She squinted at the holos floating above his board. "The meet hasn't even started."

"It's from Earth's Olympic Track and Field committee. They say Tam is supposed to be in the men's division."

"What men's division?"

"It says here she's a man."

"She transitioned years ago." Bhaaj motioned at where Tam was running around the track again. "She's obviously female. But who cares? Why would they want her disqualified?"

"They don't. They just say she should compete as a man."

"What for? Everyone competes together, female, male, or however else they identify."

"Yeah, but we messed up." He motioned at his board. "We were supposed to fill out some form. I never did because I didn't know Tam was trans."

Bhaaj crossed her arms. "When I trained for the Olympics, I knew athletes who considered themselves different sexes than what the doctors recorded at their birth. No one gave a shit."

"The Allieds do."

Exasperated, she said, "They know we don't separate events by sex. It's not our fault they bred their women to be weaker than their men."

Mason spoke dryly. "They claim we engineered our women to be stronger. And you know perfectly well that we claim they engineered their men for greater upper body strength."

"Well, that's bull, too," she grumbled, then fell silent as Mason concentrated on the messages from the athletic committee. She never knew what to make of Earth policies. After Earth realized the Imperialate Athletics Committee wouldn't change their rules about all sexes competing together, they'd focused on improving the performance of their female athletes. It had already been happening anyway, especially in endurance events like the marathons where women had already closed the gap. However, Earth had driven a hard bargain.

Separating events by sex allowed Earthers to enter more athletes in the Olympics. If you could have, say, three in an event, that meant a total of nine: three men, three women, and three non-binary. In the Imperialate, they also allowed three, but given that an event included all sexes, that meant three total. At first Earth demanded the IAC change the limit to nine for all events. Since no meet had the resources to triple in size, the IAC offered a compromise: four in each. Earth countered by saying it was still too few, but they'd go with it if everyone used their metric system for measurements. The IAC quickly agreed to the apparent capitulation: four entrants in each event, any sex, with all meets using the metric system.

Earth had the last laugh.

Of course, their metric system spilled into other parts of life. It came with no connection to either Skolia or Eube, so both civilizations were willing to use it—until now *everyone* in human-settled space had adopted Earth measures for everything. Not only metric, either; a standard day became equal to the day on Earth, a standard year became equal to Earth's year. Those last two felt right somehow, with human bodies naturally tuned to diurnal cycles on the planet of their ancestors.

"It looks like Tam should be fine." Mason was reading more holos above his board. "We just need to file an extra document. When we submitted the forms letting the committee test our athletes for cybernetic enhancements, drugs, genetic manipulation, all that, we were supposed to include one for Tam verifying she didn't have augmentation during her transition."

Bhaaj just grunted. It seemed like busy work. Any illegal enhancement would come out in the test process regardless of how many forms they submitted. She rubbed her eyes, exhausted, trying not to remember the people she'd seen dying from carnelian rash.

Mason watched her with his too-perceptive gaze. "Are you all right?"

"Yah. Fine." She wasn't; she felt even worse now than on Raylicon.

He motioned to where Doctor Izaka was talking to Zee across the stadium. "Go see the Doc." In the no-nonsense voice he used with the kids, he added, "I need you at your best."

She pretended to give him a military salute. "Yes sir, Coach."

He laughed, then waved her away. Bhaaj took off, jogging along the wall. In the distance, Doctor Izaka and Zee were sitting in chairs, doing tests it looked like. Zee had slumped back, barely nodding as the doctor spoke.

She sent a thought to Max. *Do you have any new data from my health meds?*

Not much, he answered. **Just that you have a higher-than-normal concentration of some chemicals in your body. Your meds haven't tried to remove them, though.**

That's vague. What chemicals?

That's all I got. On the positive side, the lack of data means nothing registered as a problem.

Max, that's not positive. I didn't get carnelian rash before because of proteins my body already produces. It's a genetic thing, like eye color or whatever. Those proteins prevented the carnelian virus from entering my cells and using them to replicate. So even though I had the virus in my body, it couldn't produce enough of itself to make me sick. But if I still carry the virus—and it's mutated enough to enter my cells—then it won't register as new, just as a greater concentration of chemicals already present.

I see your point. Max sounded worried now. **I will continue checking.**

When Bhaaj reached Izaka and Zee, the doctor looked up and spoke with no preamble. "She's got carnelian rash."

Damn! Bhaaj watched Zee with concern, and the sprinter regarded her with a worn-out look. No sign of the telltale rash showed on her arms or shoulders. But then, it didn't on Bhaaj, either.

"You not know?" Bhaaj asked her.

"Had it before. Doc Karal treated. It went away." Tiredly Zee added, "Except now worse."

"It's the long-term version," Izaka said. "I've given her additional treatments. She'll feel better soon." To Zee, she added, "Get plenty of rest and drink a lot of water."

Zee scowled at her. "Not got water."

"Got plenty of water," Bhaaj assured her. "Turn on faucet like Angel show."

"Faucet thing not got filter," Zee said.

"All faucets got filters." Bhaaj motioned as if to encompass the entire planet. "Water not bad here. And they *still* filter it. So double pure." She regarded Zee sternly. "Go to hotel. Sleep. Take care of self. After that, you come run."

Zee sighed, but nodded, her easy acquiescence a sign of her illness more than anything else. With that done, she took her leave and slowly headed on her way.

Izaka stood up next to Bhaaj. "She'll be fine."

"I hope so." Bhaaj regarded her uneasily. "I'm pretty sure I have it, too."

"Did you get vaccinated?"

"Yah. I was in Deep last season when the new variant swept their population." She'd never forget the wrenching experience, with so many people dying. "I carry the k-protein that blocks the virus, so I didn't get sick."

Izaka seemed baffled. "Then why would you get it now?"

Bhaaj grimaced. "That blasted virus mutates fast, doesn't it?"

Concern creased the doctor's face. "Yes, it does." She flicked through the icons above her holopad. Soon, Bhaaj holos were floating in the air. Focused on them, Izaka said, "I need to scan your body. Is that all right?"

"Go ahead." She waited while Izaka used a hand scanner on her.

The doctor took a sample of her blood and loaded it into the unit. Soon she went back to her holopad, bringing up numbers and chemical symbols. "Hmmm—yes. I see. Interesting. Have you gone through menopause yet?"

"Of course not. I'm too young."

"You're fifty. That's not too young." Izaka studied the stats above her holopad. "You look much younger and have the health to match, but that's no guarantee. Your hormone balance is off."

"My meds do cellular repairs that delay my aging," Bhaaj said. "I won't see menopause until my seventies." It didn't really affect her, given that she never had visible signs of her period. Her meds took care of matters, absorbing the blood and tissue back into her body and finding a use for it, a much more sensible process than what nature had inflicted on women.

"Hah!" Izaka suddenly said. "That's not it. Here we go."

"My meds need an upgrade, don't they?"

"Your meds are fine." Izaka flicked through the holos. "We'll put you on new vitamins. And you don't eat enough." She frowned at Bhaaj. "Don't you check your health app? You're worn out."

"So that's it? I'm tired and need vitamins?" Granted, she often forgot to check the app, but Max would have let her know if he detected a problem. "My meds haven't sent any alert."

"I'm checking... ah. Here's the problem. You didn't set your meds for this alert."

Bhaaj scowled at her. She always kept her health system current. "What alert?"

The normally hardnosed doctor smiled at her. "Pregnancy."

What? The word hung in the air. Bhaaj couldn't absorb it.

After a moment, Izaka said, "Coach?"

Bhaaj took a breath. "You've made a mistake. I'm not pregnant. If my meds are operating as well as you say, their birth control functions should also be working."

"Well, they aren't." The doctor grinned. "Congratulations. You're almost four months along by the Earth standard." Her smile turned into a frown. "You should have started to show. You're not eating enough. You need to take better care of yourself."

Bhaaj stared at her. "I *can't* be pregnant. I have top-line meds. They don't just fail."

"No birth control method is one hundred percent effective."

"Yah, well, mine is damn close. This can't be true."

Izaka spoke carefully. "I take it this isn't good news?"

Bhaaj stopped, flustered. "Well, uh, it's just, I never expected to have children." She and Jak had never discussed it, except for the rare joke about what a disaster they'd be as parents.

The doctor gentled her usually gruff voice. "Why don't you talk this over with your husband and your usual doctor. You have some tough decisions to make."

"Yes. Of course." Bhaaj needed to get away from her, from everyone. Somehow she needed to absorb this. Pregnancy was impossible.

Except her body didn't know that and had let the impossible happen.

CHAPTER XIV
Revelations

Bhaaj and Angel walked together through the lobby. Plants thrived in North-Metro's lush climate, including here in the hotel, where small trees in earthenware planters stood near walls that had water sheeting down them. Hanging pots bloomed with flowers in pink, purple, and blue. The many windows let in sunshine, laying golden light across the tiled floors, and blue sofas set around tables invited people to sit and talk. Overhead, globes with swirling opalescent colors shed yet more light.

"Pretty," Angel commented.

"Yah." Bhaaj glanced at her. "I got you an access code for the Kyle system." She hesitated. "Can you work now as a telop?"

"Some," Angel said. "I can link to the Kyle mesh, but I don't have the best control. Yet."

"I need to talk with Jak private," Bhaaj confided. Although both the law and the extensive security protocols on the Kyle mesh prohibited telops from listening in on conversations, a skilled operator could evade those restrictions. At a meet as prestigious as this one, coaches and athletes never stopped trying to spy on other teams.

"I could probably get you to the Top Mark," Angel said. "Does it have Kyle tech?"

"Yah. Jak can link from his office."

Angel thought for a moment. "I'll need some time to figure out the system here. How about you come by my room at nine. Ruzik's going to the hotel gym to work out, so we'll have privacy."

Good. That gave her time to figure out what to say to Jak. "I'll see you then."

The grid of Kyle space rippled as if a tremor had gone through the system. Startled, Angel paused her spy survey of the hotel mesh. Although she didn't need anything from the hotel system, she'd decided that the more she knew about accessing networks, the better. She took care, though. If anyone caught her sneaking around, she could have trouble.

A chime pinged in the air.

Eh? She hadn't heard this chime before.

The pleasant voice of the EI in her hotel room came to her in the Kyle. **You have a visitor. I've identified her as Major Bhaajan, retired.**

Oh. Yah. Take me out of psiberspace.

Done.

The grid faded until Angel became aware of the room. With an exhale, she removed the skullcap, giving it time to withdraw its threads from her scalp. Still holding it, she went to the door, which had an arched shape that reminded her of the Undercity. Those arches had existed for millennia, though, and this one, all in blue and white, looked as modern as they got.

"Eh," Angel told the door.

"Would you like me to open?" it inquired.

"Yah."

The door slid open, revealing Bhaaj. She had a gaunt look, with dark circles under her eyes.

"You okay?" Angel asked as she invited her mentor into her room.

"Fine." After Bhaaj entered, the door closed with no fuss. Moving slower than usual, Bhaaj pulled over a chair and sat by the console. "You sent link to Jak?"

"Yah." Angel settled in her own seat and put on the neural cap. The more she practiced, the faster it all went. Today the Kyle gate only appeared for an instant before she reached the grid. It spread all around her like the desert, its colors vivid, some areas forming a flat surface and others showing symmetrical peaks.

Top Mark, Angel thought, imagining the casino in her mind to access the link she'd worked on earlier this evening.

A peak rose from the grid, a black mountain with silver lines. **What want?** a voice rumbled. It sounded like Royal Flush, Jak's EI.

Bhaaj need talk to Jak, Angel told him. *Private.*

I check, Royal said.

In only a moment, Jak's thought growled through the Kyle. *Eh.*

Eh, Angel answered. She refocused on her hotel room. As her awareness of real space increased, the Kyle grid faded until it became only a haze overlaid on her view of Bhaaj.

"Jak here," Angel told her.

"Thanks." Leaning over the console, Bhaaj tapped a panel with the letter ψ. "Jak?"

"Eh, Bhaaj." His voice came through a comm on the console.

Angel spoke to Bhaaj. "I not know how to keep link active unless I here. That okay?"

"Yah, fine," Bhaaj said. "But what you hear, it private."

"I ken."

"Good." Bhaaj spoke in the comm. "Jak, got news."

"What?" He sounded wary.

"Need Cries talk."

"Why?"

Bhaaj switched into the above-city dialect. "Because Undercity talk is too damn constrained for what we need to discuss."

"All right." Now he sounded puzzled. "What do we need to discuss?"

"Do you remember when Doctor Rajindia told us that some of the people who had carnelian rash were suffering long-term effects?"

Concern tinged his voice. "Is that why you've felt sick?"

"Yah and nahya."

"If you want Cries dialect," he said dryly, "then use it."

She took a breath. "I meant no, that's not why. But the virus did, um, affect me."

"Bhaaj, you need to take care of yourself. Do you want me to come out there?"

Angel expected Bhaaj to tell him what she always said, that she felt fine.

"Uh, no," Bhaaj said. "I, um... Jak, I don't know."

His voice gentled, something Angel had *never* heard from the notorious casino boss. "What is it you're having so much trouble telling me?"

Bhaaj took a deep breath and let it out slowly. Then she said, "You're going to be a father."

Ho! Angel gaped at her. Bhaaj *pregnant?* No wonder she wanted this private.

Angel's sense of the Kyle changed. The peak that represented Jak flashed with jagged lines as it fragmented, then reformed, darker now and glinting. "Not funny," he said.

"Yah. It's not." Bhaaj took a breath. "But it's true. The Deepers outlive the epidemics that decimate their population because the survivors have a specific response to the viruses. It interferes with their birth control. I was down there helping Doctor Rajindia during the last outbreak, so it affected me too, even with my more advanced meds." Her words came with an awkwardness that made Angel wish she could fade like the Kyle grid.

"You remember how glad we were to see each other when I got out of quarantine?" Bhaaj asked. "When we knew I wasn't going to die."

Jak's voice deepened. "Yah. I remember."

"It happened then." Her voice cracked, one of the only times Angel had heard her defenses crumble. "I'm four months pregnant. It's why I haven't felt well."

Silence.

Finally Jak said, "Holy shit."

"I don't know how sanctified it is," Bhaaj said. "But yah."

"We can't be parents," Jak said. "At least, I'd be terrible at it. You'd be a goddess."

"How?" Bhaaj said. "I don't know squat. Who'd we have to look up to? Dig's mother, Jadix Kajada? Yah, great role model, one of the most murderous cartel bosses in history."

Jak spoke quietly. "We had Dig. She was more like a mother to us than anyone. She didn't change until she took over the cartel."

Bhaaj spoke with pain. "Dig could have been a great leader if her life had gone differently. But it didn't." Although she sounded calm, her grief filled the room. "I'll always love the Dig I knew in our youth, Jak, and I'll always mourn what she became later. But she wasn't our mother."

"Then think of her own children." Jak spoke intently. "Dig never let her kids follow in her footsteps. Look at her oldest daughter. Digjan is the first person from the Undercity ever to become a Jagernaut starfighter pilot. That happened because of Dig."

Angel didn't know which shocked her more, Bhaaj's announcement or the length of Jak's response. She'd never heard him speak more than five words at one time.

"Even so," Bhaaj said. "I don't know how to deal with this."

Jak spoke carefully. "Do you want to end the pregnancy?"

Silence.

Then Bhaaj said, "No. It's our child, Jak. I couldn't."

"Well. So." He didn't try to hide his relief.

"That doesn't mean I have any clue what to do."

"We'll meet with Doctor Rajindia when you get back here. See what she says."

"All right. Doctor Izaka gave me vitamins and sent Max a menu she wants me to follow." Bhaaj spoke wryly. "And she told me to sleep more. Like I have time for luxuries."

"Find the time." Given Jak's tone, Angel could almost see his worried scowl.

"I'll be all right," Bhaaj said.

"You take care of yourself," he told her.

"I will."

With those swooning declarations of love, they cut the link.

Bhaaj regarded Angel. "So."

"Good news?" Angel offered.

"Eh." Bhaaj seemed at a loss for how to respond.

After the silence became long, Angel tried again. "Someday Ruzik and I do same." Right now, they had too much going on, but they'd talked about it. An unsettling thought came to her. "I went to Deep to bring vaccine. Rash affect me too?"

Bhaaj looked her over. "You look same as always. Run same."

"Am same," Angel realized. "Doc Izaka always check us. Not say I have baby."

Bhaaj relaxed. "So."

They sat in silence. Eventually Angel said, "Dice and Shiv argue about Hyden."

Bhaaj tensed. "What for?"

"Kajada punkers want beat him up. Cuz you beat them up."

"Could've beat them a lot worse," Bhaaj growled. Then she added, "They talk about Abyss?"

The question startled Angel. "You mean chasm?"

"Nahya. Abyss is corp."

"Oh. Yah. Talk about execs." Angel wished she could store files in her memory like other telops. Apparently getting a "node" in her spine would help. Someday maybe she'd try it out, since it would also let her link to Kyle space without a cap, but for now she disliked the thought of putting biomech inside her body. Besides, she couldn't do it and still compete. "They say Abyss and Scorp fight. Kajada like Abyss, Vakaar like Scorp."

"Why they take sides?" Bhaaj seemed baffled. "Cartels not got deals with corps."

"Kajada like Abyss cuz Vakaar like Scorp. Not know why Vakaar like Scorp."

Bhaaj stood up. "Got to go."

Angel stood as well. In a gentler voice, she added, "Congrats on beybee." She used the word that implied a wanted child.

Bhaaj nodded, her tense posture easing. "My thanks." She left then, off to do whatever took her time when she wasn't coaching the team.

Kiro didn't know what to think. Normally the Metropoli runners watched them from a distance. Their only interaction had been on the first day the Raylicon team showed up to the track. A Metropoli runner asked if they came from the Undercity. When Ruzik said many of them did, she'd laughed and sauntered back to her team. After that, the other athletes using the stadium ignored them, except for a few curious glances.

Until today.

Kiro was warming up on the lawn inside the track when Andi Jinda, a woman from the Metropoli team, walked over to Tam. Kiro concentrated, listening. Maybe it was true, what Zee claimed, that they could hear better because they read people's moods as well as their words.

"I hear you're doing the royal marathon," Andi said to Tam.

"Eh?" Tam asked, wary.

Andi spoke slowly, exaggerating her syllables. "You think you've got what it takes, hmm?"

"What mean, 'takes'?" Tam asked.

"What did you say?" Andi looked her up and down. "I can't understand your accent."

Tam seemed unimpressed. "Not know what you mean by 'What it takes.'"

"You think you can run." Andi motioned at the athletes around the track, most of whom were watching now. "You dust rats think you can beat us."

Tam stiffened. "I beat all your crappy runners."

Tam, careful, Kiro thought. Tam had earned the respect of her teammates not only because she treated everyone well, but also because she would stand up to any outsider who gave them grief. Like now. Except for Tam's sake, Kiro didn't want her to piss off the top-ranked track and field team in the entire Imperialate.

"Prove it." Andi said. She thought *You stupid Undercity bitch* with such intensity that Kiro picked it up. Nor did he think he was the only one. Ruzik was walking over to Tam and Andi.

Tam didn't rise to the bait. Instead she spoke with her usual calm. "Easy to prove." She motioned at the track. "We do now." In Flag, she added, "I'll run with as many of you who want to try, one 800-meter race."

Andi laughed. "Sure." She waved to her avidly watching teammates. "Anyone want to do a practice 800?"

Ruzik reached them. "You want to compete?" he asked Andi.

She looked him up and down. "So you're the Raylicon captain, hmmm?"

Hyden Laj also joined them. He spoke to Andi with a perfect Iotic accent, the speech of royalty and nobility. He was neither, but he'd mastered the accent so well, he sounded like the real deal. He even looked the part. "Ruzik is the Undercity team captain." He nodded toward Ruzik with a respect he never showed when it was just the Raylicon team. Apparently outsiders ranked even lower in his worldview. Or maybe that view was changing. He'd seemed subdued ever since that night the Kajada punkers had almost beat the shit out of him. "We all support him."

Andi squinted at his perfectly straight black hair, his aristocratic features, the extravagant tech-mech bands on his wrists. "I thought you all came from the Undercity."

"About two-thirds of us," Ruzik said in Flag. "The rest are from the City of Cries."

"Interesting." Andi looked as if she didn't know whether to be intrigued, offended, or confused. "Anyway. We'll do a run." She motioned around the field, her gesture taking in everyone. "Whoever wants to."

Kiro relaxed. This could be fun, especially with nothing at stake. It would give him a sense of how competing here felt. Although he was becoming more used to the differences, he still didn't know how the biosphere would affect him in actual competition.

After they all agreed on rules and checked out a starter orb, ten athletes lined up at a makeshift starting line, including Kiro. Although he preferred the 400-meter race, he liked the 800. Tam would run of course, also Wild, Rockjan, and Hyden. For Metropoli, five runners joined them, including Andi. Kiro didn't recognize most of them, but of course he knew Baytornia Mesonet, the sprinter everyone called Bayonet for the way she knifed through her competition. She currently ranked first on Metropoli and third in the entire Imperialate for the 800-meter.

We all do well, he reminded himself. Coach Mason brought them here because he believed they could qualify for the Olympics. Sure, most of them wouldn't win medals or break interstellar records like Bayonet, but just being included exhilarated him. All his life, he'd wanted this. He'd ached with his failures, so many of them. Now, incredibly, that had changed. Strider, Lamp, and especially Zee made it even better. He felt proud to be with the Undercity athletes.

And they could *run.* Angel had won the Selei City Open in the classic marathon last season, but now she trained for the 400-meter and 800-meter sprints. Although Ruzik preferred marathons, he ran any distance he needed in the Undercity. As for Tam—who knew. At practices, she trained for the marathon, but she liked it all. She raced like no one else, which was probably why Metropoli had singled her out. No one could best Bayonet at the 800-meter, but Raylicon could make a reasonable showing.

They took their starting positions, the orb called out, "Ready!"—and bam! They were off!

The pack immediately sorted itself out. They didn't have to run in lanes, so they all crowded toward the inner edge. As Tam pulled ahead, Kiro sensed disdain from the Metropoli runners. They let her stay in front as a pacer. Kiro had seen it often, where a runner took an early lead and then dropped back toward the end of the race. He hadn't understood until he started training with Mason. Having a pacer allowed the other runners to conserve energy because the pacer protected them from wind resistance and helped them maintain a consistent speed.

To Kiro, the 800-meter felt like an endurance sprint, using bursts of speed that demanded more oxygen than his muscles could store, which meant he drew on his energy reserves. Although it meant his muscles tired faster, he didn't need them for long. Mason said it worked for him because he had a lot of fast-twitch muscles that helped with those energy bursts.

The Metropoli runners obviously thought Tam had made a rookie mistake. As a marathoner, she excelled at aerobic endurance, developing a steady supply of oxygen she needed for longer distances. Marathoners had more slow-twitch muscles, ideal for long, sustained efforts but not great for short bursts of energy. She'd have to slow down when she used up her energy reserves.

Kiro wondered about that, though. Mason called the Undercity kids hybrid runners because they needed to excel at both short and long distances to survive, so they developed both types of muscles more than most people. Raylicon runners also tended to use oxygen better, and the slightly lower gravity could also favor them, assuming they'd learned to retime their steps. Yah, they'd do fine.

Kiro's smug mood faded. Sure, Tam did some dual training, but she stayed focused on the marathon. She *had* started too fast today, trying to outshine the Metropoli runners, who had the advantage of competing in their native environment.

As the runners finished the first of two laps, Kiro stayed with the pack. Last year, he couldn't have kept up, but after training with Mason and running in the Undercity with Zee, his speed had increased. He'd never excel at longer distances, but this combination of sprinting and endurance felt good.

Tam remained in the lead, with Bayonet close behind—*there!* In a burst of energy, Bayonet surged ahead, overtaking Tam—

Ho! Tam lunged into the sprint that Undercity runners had made famous on Raylicon. She battled Bayonet for first place, the two of them running hard. They were coming up on the finish, together, together—with a shout, Bayonet crossed ahead of Tam.

"Hah!" One of the Metropoli runners yelled. "Good job, Bayo!"

As the other runners came in, with Kiro in sixth, Tam and Bayonet slowed to a walk. Kiro could tell it bothered Tam to lose. That never happened on Raylicon. But seriously? She'd come in a close second to the top sprinter on Metropoli. Bayonet obviously hadn't run full out, whereas Tam had given it her all, but still. Tam ought to be proud of her showing.

Kiro felt good. He'd held his own with Olympic athletes. wonderful!

Calm down, he told himself. *It was just practice. You've a lot more work to do.*

"Eh." Zee came alongside him. "Good run."

Kiro grinned at her—and suddenly realized what he'd done. That reaction in the Undercity could be a sexual invitation. His face burned with embarrassment.

"Is fine," Zee said. Then, shyly, she added, "Me too."

She liked him too? He felt it simmering under her thoughts. They didn't need words. When Zee smiled, Kiro touched her arm.

Coach Bhaaj's irate voice interrupted their moment. "You want to what?"

Looking up, he saw Tam and Bhaaj talking. Curious, he inched closer. Ruzik and Angel had positioned themselves to keep away people who felt inclined to eavesdrop, but Kiro managed to catch the words anyway.

"Nahya," Bhaaj told Tam. She had a take-no-prisoners look. "Absolutely not."

"Ab-so-lute-lee yah." Tam stood resolute. "Came in second now. Come in first at meet."

Bhaaj motioned at the track scoreboard. "See time? Bayonet not even run hard. You run your most. You lucky not hurt self."

"Feel fine," Tam told her.

"Too late to sign up for 800," Bhaaj said. "Meet in six days."

"Not too late." Tam lifted her arm, showing Bhaaj the gauntlet she'd bought on the shadow-market. "Just looked up. Got two days to add."

Bhaaj's voice quieted as she switched into Cries speak. "It isn't a good idea to run the 800-meter in a meet where you're already doing the royal marathon *and* the ten-kilometer race. And you aren't a sprinter." When Tam started to protest, Bhaaj held up her hand. "Yah, I know, you *can* sprint. But the more you sprint, the more you tire your body. You don't want all that lactic acid in your muscles. The 800-meter has preliminary heats and then a final. Could you make the final? You might, actually. But that means even more muscle fatigue. And it's only two days before the royal. You'll be too tired when you get to the marathon."

Tam crossed her arms. "Never too tired to run."

"Tam, listen. You have a chance to medal in the royal. Don't blow it."

Tam spoke in a less stubborn voice, using the Cries language with a strong Undercity accent. "I don't need my best time here. If I can qualify for the Olympics in all three, I want to try."

Bhaaj met her gaze. "The 800 is a long shot for you. What you just ran wasn't an Olympic qualifying time. Yah, Bayonet underestimated you. That won't happen again." She took a breath. "It'd be different if the 800 was your main event and you tried a marathon afterward. It wouldn't matter if you tired yourself in the 800-meter, since you wouldn't be going for an Olympic time in the royal. But Tam, you *are* the royal marathon. You have the potential to be great in that event. If you wear yourself out in sprints, you could end up not qualifying in anything."

"Eh." Tam frowned.

"Think about it," Bhaaj said. "If you absolutely want to run the 800, I'll sign you up. But before you make that decision, go read about it on the mesh. Talk to Coach Mason. Talk to Doctor Izaka. You need to understand the risks."

Tam nodded. "I think on it."

Bhaaj returned her nod. "Good."

Kiro had to admit he felt exhausted, and he hadn't even given that practice his all. He started walking again, letting his body cool down. Most athletes were leaving the field. Time to let teams from Foreshires Hold and Earth use the stadium. As he and Zee entered the stadium tunnel, two Metropoli runners jogged past them, Andi Jinda and another woman.

"Hey dust rats," Andi called. "You think that was fast? Bayonet wasn't even trying."

As Kiro stiffened, Zee laid her hand on his arm. He wanted to tell Andi exactly what he thought, but he held back, remembering the speeches Bhaaj and Mason had given them about good sportsmanship.

The other Metropoli woman spoke to Andi. "Would you shut up?" Glancing at Kiro and Zee, she added, "Sorry."

Zee nodded to the second woman. After the Metropoli athletes moved on, Zee spoke in a low voice. "Ass-byte woman—she run royal marathon. Not 800."

"You mean Andi?"

"Yah. The 800 not her event. Maybe she just want to wear out Tam."

A voice interrupted them from nearby. "Yah, well, screw you," a girl said.

"You fuck with team," a guy answered. *That* sounded like Dice.

Up ahead, Shiv Kajada and Dice Vakaar were standing in an alcove, a place of privacy, except Kiro and Zee had come close enough to overhear.

"You fuck with planet," Shiv told him.

"Entire planet?" For an instant Dice looked like he would laugh. Then he said, "Nahya!" and shoved her against the shoulder.

"Ass-byte!" Shiv shoved him back.

"Stop it!" a man said.

Swinging around, Kiro saw Ruzik and Angel reach the alcove. As Shiv and Dice lunged at each other, Ruzik caught Shiv and Angel grabbed Dice.

"Damn it," Kiro muttered. If Shiv and Dice got into a fight, they could get disqualified from the meet. He didn't sense hostility from them so much as... what? Confusion and agitation. They were arguing because they didn't know any other way to interact. Fortunately, no one else saw the dustup. Everyone had gone on ahead, and athletes from Foreshires Hold and Earth used a different tunnel to enter the stadium.

"Not fight," Ruzik told the two cartel heirs.

Shiv pulled her arm away from him. "Vakaar ass-byte. Diss my family."

"You diss Vakaar," Dice told her.

"You both stop," Angel said. "Not bring cartel shit here."

"Eh." Dice's voice lost its edge. Looking at Shiv, he added, "Not fight?"

"Not fight." She scowled at Dice. "*You* not rumble with Strider and them."

"Not rumble! We stop." Dice glared at her. "*Kajada* attack. Try beat on Hyden."

Shiv said only, "Scorp," but if a single word could be a condemnation, hers would have sent the entire Scorpio Corporation to hell.

Ruzik frowned at them. "What about Scorp?"

"Hyden heir to Scorp cartel," Shiv said. "Dice heir to Vakaar cartel."

"What are you talking about?" a woman said.

Kiro spun around. Coach Bhaaj stood only a few paces away. "Why you say Scorp a cartel?" she asked.

Dice and Shiv stared at her, silent.

"Want see you both at my suite," Bhaaj said in her take-no-prisoners voice. "Come when I comm you. Or you not run in meet. Ken?"

"Yah," Shiv growled in the same moment Dice grumbled, "Ken."

Bhaaj motioned at them all. "Now get out of here. All of you. Back to hotel."

They all made fast work, getting out of there pronto.

"I don't understand." Mason stood by the window in his suite, bathed in sunlight. "Kids argue all the time. I agree, we should help them get along. Build team spirit. But we can't force them to like each other." He hesitated. "Unless you think they might get violent? I don't want to seem like I'm stereotyping. I've seen the garbage people heap on your athletes. But you look so worried."

Bhaaj sighed. This was going to be difficult. "You better sit down."

"Uh, all right." Watching her warily, he settled onto one of the sofas. Bhaaj sat on the other end, leaving plenty of space between the two of them, both physical and psychological.

"What's up?" he asked.

"The two runners, Shiv and Dice—they have last names."

"*That's* the problem?" He squinted at her. "I mean, I know a lot of your people only have one name. Bhaaj. Angel. Ruzik. But what's wrong with having two?"

"Nothing. Except Shiv is Shiv Kajada. Dice is Dice Vakaar."

"Yes, I recall their registration." He hesitated. "Do your people dislike second names?"

"It depends on the name." Bhaaj watched him closely. "You don't recognize theirs?"

"I hadn't thought about it. Should I?"

"Kajada. Vakaar."

"And?"

"Those are the two drug cartels in the Undercity."

"*What?*"

Bhaaj spoke flatly. "Shiv Kajada is a cousin of the Kajada boss. Dice is the son and heir of the Vakaar boss."

Mason stared at her, stunned into silence for one of the few times in his life.

Bhaaj waited.

"You must be joking," he said.

If only. "No. I'm serious."

"Are you telling me I have two drug runners on my team?"

"I didn't say they were punkers. As far as I know, they aren't involved in cartel business."

"Punkers?"

"Drug runners."

"But they live with people in the drug trade." His voice hardened. "Those cartels cause hundreds of deaths in Cries every year, many more injuries, mental problems, and addictions, not just on Raylicon, but offworld as well."

"Dice and Shiv have nothing to do with that."

"Even so." Mason raked his hand through his hair. "We have to drop them from the team."

Bhaaj wished this had gone a different way. "It's impossible to avoid the cartels in the Undercity. And lately the punkers have come into Dust Knight territory. If you drop every person who ever associated in any way with any cartel, then you'd have to drop all the Undercity runners and probably some from Cries. Hell, Mason, you'd have to drop me."

"What? You've nothing to do with the cartels."

Her gaze never wavered. "Dig Kajada was my sister."

"Your *sister* was the most notorious crime boss on Raylicon?" Mason looked as if he'd slammed into a wall. "That can't be true. *It can't.*"

"It's true."

"But—no. You aren't Bhaaj Kajada." He stopped. "Is that why you don't have a second name? You dropped Kajada?"

"No. I don't have a second name because I never knew my parents. My mother died giving me birth and my father disappeared." Before he could ask more, she said, "In my youth, before I enlisted, I ran with a dust gang. Dig Kajada led us. She and I were like sisters. She was a good person, Mason. And she hated the drug trade. She swore never to take over the cartel."

"It didn't work out that way, did it?" Anger edged his voice. "The entire Imperialate knows the name Dig Kajada."

Bhaaj didn't want to talk about it, not now, not ever, but Mason deserved to know. She forced out the words. "The previous Vakaar boss murdered Dig's mother. Dig took over the cartel to get vengeance." Quietly she added, "And she did. She and the Vakaar boss both died in the war that erupted between the two cartels."

"Gods." His dismay saturated her. "How much do your athletes interact with the cartels?"

"Not a lot. Most probably know a few punkers, though."

"But their tests never show any hint of drugs. They come out better even than some of the Cries kids." He sounded as if he were willing her to say this was all just a story. "They're clean."

"Yes. They are." Bhaaj spoke firmly. "I require the Dust Knights to swear by a Code. It includes no drugs. If they break the Code, I kick them out. Dice and Shiv aren't Knights, but they keep the rules." She willed him to understand. "Both cartels agreed to let their kids join your team. This is a chance for at least two of their children to escape the violence that's saturated their families for centuries." She turned her hands palms up, as if to show him she had no weapons. "Please, Mason. Don't take it away. Being part of your team makes a huge difference to them." It was one of the longest speeches she'd ever made to him, but it needed saying.

"I don't want to, I really don't." He looked as if he were breaking inside. "But what if it hits the press that I've got heirs of the drug cartels on my team?"

"You say what I've told you. They have no link to the trade. They're as clean as any athlete on any team." Her voice lightened. "It's a great redemption story, how your team gave these young people struggling with such a harsh future the chance for a better life."

"It's inspiring, yes." He spoke awkwardly. "People think everyone in the Undercity is a drug addict. I've no patience with the naysayers, but this plays right into that stereotype."

"Yah, life can suck," she said. "You think the downside of the Undercity will disappear because it has this athletic upside no one knew about? I can hardly begin to tell you how much it means to me that you've welcomed my athletes. But the problems won't go away. If you're going to help, it means acknowledging both the good *and* the bad."

Mason sat there, healthy and handsome in the golden sunlight with no clue about how privileged a life he led. As much as Bhaaj wished she could have kept quiet, she knew it would have undermined the team. If some newshounds got wind of the truth, she didn't want them springing it on an unaware Mason. She also needed to know if he'd kick out the Undercity kids. The fallout would be bitter, inflaming their relations with Cries, but better it happen now than at the Olympics.

His face took an inwardly directed look. Bhaaj continued to sit, schooling herself to calm even though she wanted to burst with impatience.

He focused on her again. "Thank you for telling me all this."

"You're welcome." *Come on,* she thought. *What are you going to do?*

Give him time, Max thought. **He's a good man. Trust in that.**

Stop eavesdropping.

I can't help it when you yell your thoughts.

"I'd be a hypocrite to drop your athletes when they've done nothing wrong." He spoke dryly. "If Olympic athletes couldn't have any family, friends, or acquaintances who'd ever broken the law, probably every team in existence would lose a significant portion of their members."

Relief trickled over Bhaaj, but they weren't in the clear yet. "They just need a chance."

"You're sure they won't bring cartel business into our team?"

"It's unlikely." As much as she wanted to promise they wouldn't, she couldn't go that far. "If you want me to give you an absolute guarantee, I can't. But they want to stay on your team, and they know it means no drugs. Mason, they genuinely care about what you're creating here."

He sat thinking, his expressive face going through a gauntlet of emotions: concern, sadness, hope, frustration, pride, determination. Finally he said, "I stand by our athletes. All of them. But you must do your part. Don't let them give anyone a chance to say *I told you so*."

Bhaaj exhaled, her relief turning into a flood. "I'll make sure they understand."

"Good." His voice turned resolute. "Because if they give me reason to believe otherwise, I'll have to take this to the Raylicon Athletic Committee."

"I understand." She started to continue, then closed her mouth.

He watched her warily. "I hope that's all."

"Um... You need to know something about me, too."

"There's more?"

"I'm married to Jak."

He blinked. "You're married to someone named Jak? So what?"

"He's the proprietor of the Top Mark."

"For flaming sake!" He thumped his hands on his legs. "What will you tell me next? You take the team on field trips to his casino?"

"Well..."

"*Bhaaj!*"

"No, I don't take them to the casino. But Hyden Laj went there." She winced. "He was losing big-time. I got pissed, went out to the floor, and sent him home." With a wry smile, she added, "You should've seen his face when I showed up. I thought he'd have heart failure."

"Blast it, if he gets arrested, I may have to drop *him* from the team."

Her voice turned bland. "No one gets arrested for going to the casino."

"Why not? It's massively illegal."

"Because some of Jak's patrons pay the salaries of the people who would arrest them." She shrugged. "City cops never come to the Undercity. We don't bother them, they don't bother us."

"Who enforces the laws, then?"

"We have our own laws. And we enforce them." Particularly since she'd founded the Knights. They'd become the guardians of the Undercity.

"Well, enforce this. *Anyone* who shows up at the casino gets kicked off the team."

"You have my word." Undercity kids didn't have the money to gamble there, and Bhaaj sure as hell didn't need Jak cheating the city athletes she coached.

Mason spoke more calmly. "Gambling isn't illegal here. Or pretty much anywhere except Raylicon. Casinos are part of the recreation sector in most places."

Which was why Jak called them *fluff-pup playgrounds*. That was better left unsaid, though.

"You've got that look again," Mason said. "Like you have more to tell me."

"No. That's it." She hesitated. "Sort of."

"Ah, Goddess," he muttered. "How much more can I take?"

"This is different."

"*What* is different?"

"I'm, uh, pregnant. I'm due not long after the Olympics."

He gaped at her. "You? You're kidding! *You're* going to have a *baby?*"

"For fuck's sake," she growled. "You don't have to act so surprised."

He grinned at her. "You'll have to clean up your language if you're going to be a mother."

Of all the thoughts that had circled in her mind since she learned the news, cussing hadn't come into it. Everyone in the Undercity talked like her. In fact, she swore less than most. She had to sound civilized for her elite clients.

But...

Just as the cartels wanted a better life for their children, so hers would have a better life than the crushing poverty she and Jak had lived as children. Would Jak see their kid as his heir like Dice's mother saw Dice as her successor? Or would he want their child as far from his crime empire as their circle-sister Dig had wanted for her children?

"Ah, Mason." She sighed. "It's complicated."

"What about the team?" Now he looked worried. "We need you."

"I can still coach." She'd already thought through her options. "Most things I can do fine. I shouldn't act as your pacer anymore, though. You need someone who can run at the speeds elite athletes need for their training."

"All right. Keep me updated." With a dour look, he added, "Unless you have more surprises to tell me now."

"No more, I promise."

He smiled. "One thing I'll say. You're never boring."

She couldn't help but laugh. "Thanks. I think."

Bhaaj just hoped life didn't get any more interesting in the three months to the Olympics.

CHAPTER XV
Secrets

It relieved Bhaaj to have Captain Duane Ebersole as security chief. He knew his biz. In his youth, he'd served in the Imperial Fleet, working as an engineer and optic-electrician. He'd helped develop some of their most versatile spacecraft, and the J-Forces had often borrowed him to work with new models of the Jag starfighters. He retired from the military after fifteen years and worked as a security contractor with various shadow agencies, until Vaj Majda noticed his record and hired him. He worked his way up the ranks in her police force, outlasted his Majda critics, and finally earned the prestigious position of Security Chief for Raylicon's Olympic track and field team.

Right now, he looked royally pissed.

"I've seen them arguing." Duane paced across Bhaaj's hotel room. "First Shiv is angry, then Dice, then Shiv, then Dice. If they come to blows, I'll have to arrest them." He stopped, regarding her. "They're taking too many risks. Don't they understand what's at stake?"

Bhaaj felt just as wound up, unable to sit. "I'll talk to them. Let me know if you hear anything that sounds strange."

He spoke dryly. "A lot of what your kids say sounds strange."

She couldn't help but smile. "Yah. But something more is going on with them." She paused. "It might connect to Scorpio and Abyss Associates. I just don't see why they'd care about two Cries corporations. What's the link?"

"Something with the cartels?"

"I can't figure why either company would risk getting involved with the drug trade. It's a big gamble without much payoff compared to their legal businesses. They already make billions."

"I'll let you know if I find anything."

"Thanks." He could offer valuable help in her investigation. Before she read him in, though, she had to clear it with the Majdas. To do that from here meant using the Kyle, which she didn't trust. She did trust Angel, but her protégée didn't have enough experience to ensure her privacy.

"Shiv and Dice are coming to talk to me," she said. "Can you secure my suite while they're here? I've checked it for monitors and it's clean, but I don't want to risk anyone disturbing us."

"Sure. No problem."

She smiled slightly. "Give them that impassive stare of yours. It's the Undercity equivalent of saying, 'Don't fuck up.'"

He chuckled. "I'll give them the full treatment."

Not long after Duane stepped outside her door, the room EI said, "You have a visitor."

"Who?" Bhaaj asked.

"According to my records, the person at your door is Shiv Kajada. She looks uneasy."

It sounded like Duane was doing his job. "Let her in."

The door whisked open, and Shiv stalked into the room. As the door closed, she stopped and crossed her arms, glowering.

Bhaaj motioned toward the two couches. "Sit."

Watching her warily, Shiv went to sit on the edge of the sofa. When its smart cushions shifted under her, trying to ease her muscle tension, she glared even more.

Bhaaj sat on the couch across from her. "You and Dice."

"Screw Dice." Shiv almost sounded convincing.

Almost.

"You fight, we all get sent home," Bhaaj said.

"Not like Dice."

"Tough. You on team. He on team. Not want? Go home."

"Nahya!" Shiv jumped to her feet.

"Sit!" Bhaaj said, exasperated.

Shiv sat. "Not go home. Run." She smirked. "I stay. Beat city slicks."

Bhaaj wasn't having any Undercity bravado today. "Why mad at Dice?"

"Dice is, um, ass-byte."

"Is that so. Why?"

The teen spoke as if she stated the obvious. "Vakaar."

"Yah. And you Kajada." Puzzled, Bhaaj added, "At first, you and Dice, you avoid each other. Not fight. What happen?"

Shiv shrugged, avoiding her gaze.

"Kajada try beat on Hyden Laj," Bhaaj said.

Shiv looked at her. "Not me! I not there."

"But you not like Scorp Corp?"

"Ass-bytes," Shiv stated, far more convincing this time.

"Like Kiro?"

Her face creased with confusion. "What? Kiro not Scorp. Kiro Abyss."

Ho! Kiro never mentioned his mother's job to his teammates. Bhaaj had watched him avoid anything that might sound arrogant, boastful, or otherwise annoying. He was so discreet, even she'd never have suspected he came from such great wealth if she hadn't seen his house.

She decided to probe, using reverse psychology. "Kiro not Abyss."

"Yah, is Abyss," Shiv informed her. "We know."

"You not know."

"Do know. His hoshma make numbers for Abyss."

Bhaaj snorted. "What, he tell you that? Not think so."

"Kiro not say," Shiv admitted. "Dice tell."

Dice Vakaar had told Shiv Kajada? That made no sense. "Dice not know."

"Yah. He know."

"I not believe. Even if he know, he never tell you."

Shiv smirked. "I eavesdrop."

Bhaaj pretended to look unimpressed. "Bullshit."

Shiv spoke with teenaged certainty. "Kajada spy on Vakaar."

Disappointment washed over Bhaaj. "That why you join this team? To spy?"

"Nahya! Join to run. Like to run. *Just* run. Never want to punk." Her voice lightened, "Even like to run in circles. Silly, not to go any place, but fun. Beat rivals. And no one dies."

And no one dies. It was an apt, if horrifying, comment on life in the Undercity, that their children would value doing something simply for the fun of it, without the prospect of injury or death. Just as mind-boggling, Shiv implied she didn't want to run drugs for the cartel, an admission that could get her killed if the Kajada enforcers found out. Bhaaj hadn't expected that trust.

She spoke quietly. "No one dies. Is good."

"Yah." Shiv looked less annoyed.

"So why fight with Dice?"

"Not fight. Only words."

"You shove. He shove."

"Well, um." Shiv squinted at her. "Some days he make me mad. But it goes away."

Huh. That sounded more like teens bickering, Undercity style, than anything cartel related. "Why you get mad?"

"He say not hurt Hyden." Shiv shrugged. "I say wasn't me."

"Kajada punkers invade duster canals." Bhaaj didn't believe for one moment they'd just happened to show up. They'd heard about Hyden.

"I never beat on team circle," Shiv stated. "Not even slick."

"No one beat on Hyden." Bhaaj frowned at her. "I beat on Kajada punkers. That what you want? For your coach to fight your family?"

The girl stared at Bhaaj, her face contorting as she tried to stay impassive. "Not say more."

"Shiv, what's wrong?" Bhaaj put just enough concern into her voice to reassure without sounding above-city soft. "Help me help you."

For a long moment Shiv said nothing. Just when Bhaaj thought she'd have to find another way to reach her, the girl spoke. "Vakaar likes Scorp. So Kajada likes Abyss."

Bhaaj squinted, not sure what she meant. "Abyss got no part of Scorp."

"Scorp want Abyss."

Feigning indifference, Bhaaj said, "Scorp not care about Abyss."

"Does care," Shiv informed her. "Scorp need Abyss. Need Vakaar, too."

Bhaaj continued her show of indifferent disbelief. "Not care about Vakaar, either."

Shiv glared at her. "You not know."

"Nothing to know."

"Is too. I know."

Bhaaj snorted. "Not believe."

Anger sparked in her voice. "Scorp want weapons. Vakaar got them."

Ho! Did Shiv mean the Vakaar cartel was acting as a weapons dealer for Scorpio? That made even less sense than Scorpio getting into the drug trade. They dealt in utilities like water and optic-electronics contracts, which for worlds with large populations offered a far more lucrative business than any drugs or arms dealing. Their control of the utilities on Metropoli gave them a monopoly over ten billion people, and that was only one of their contracts.

Tread carefully, Max thought. **If you seem too eager for information, she'll close up.**

Yah. Bhaaj said only, "Vakaar not got weapons. Only shit that make you high."

"I not know what Vakaar got," Shiv admitted.

"But you think they smuggle guns?" It wouldn't be the first time.

"Not guns!" Alarm sparked in Shiv's voice. "Not after war."

Her reaction didn't surprise Bhaaj. The cartel war had exploded because stolen weapons saturated the Undercity, and it had destroyed two of the largest canals. Rebuilding those ancient ruins was one of the only cooperative ventures ever undertaken by the Undercity and Cries, with Bhaaj as liaison. It had helped lay the groundwork for their second cooperative venture, this team.

"If not guns, then what?" Bhaaj asked.

"Not sure," Shiv admitted. "I not ken Scorp cartel."

"Scorp not cartel." She couldn't imagine Zaic Laj, who despised the Undercity, going into business with the Vakaars. Far better ways existed to expand his empire, like taking over Abyss.

"Yah, but corps act like cartels," Shiv said.

Although Bhaaj had no doubt that comment would outrage many an exec, Shiv had a point. "Even so. Why Dice care that Kajada try to beat on Hyden?"

"Cuz, um, Dice ass-byte." Then she amended, "He not like cartel, either."

"Dice run Vakaar cartel someday," Bhaaj said.

"He not want that," Shiv said.

Goddess almighty. Did Shiv realize what she'd just revealed? Dice was Hammerjan Vakaar's heir. She expected him to take over the cartel in the same way Dig's mother had expected Dig to run the Kajada cartel. And just as Dig had never wanted that role, now Shiv claimed Dice didn't either. Even if Shiv and Dice liked each other, rather than the hostility people expected them to feel, why would they risk sharing such potentially fatal knowledge?

Something seemed to have loosened in Shiv. "Dice want to run," she said. "Have fun. Go to—to—what is word? Yoon? Space place. He pinch time there."

Did she mean Dice stole things from the starport? It seemed odd, given how hard it was to reach the port compared to the Concourse. "You mean at starport?"

"Nahya," Shiv told her. "He read all time. Study stuff. He want go to place with books. In Cries. Yoon—universe—"

Holy shit. "He wants to go to *college?* To Cries University?"

"Yah!" Shiv gave her an approving look. "Like Kiro."

Ah, gods. Such a wonderful dream—except Dice didn't have transcripts or anything else he'd need to apply. That didn't mean he'd never studied. Decades ago, Bhaaj had become the first Undercity kid to steal time on school meshes in Cries so she could study for her army exams. Since then, it had become more common, until now apparently even drug punkers did it. She could help Dice verify his education. If he became an Olympic track and field participant, a college might offer him an athletic scholarship. Except the cartels could shatter that dream.

And what about Shiv? Bhaaj considered her. "Not hate Dice, eh? Maybe like too much."

"Nahya!" Shiv looked ready either to fight Bhaaj or bolt from the room. "He *Vakaar*."

"I not tell. You have my oath."

Shiv's impassive look was crumbling. "Vakaar and Kajada never join in Undercity. But here, this other place, yah? Dice, he want learn astro—astronomy. About other worlds." In a careful voice, she added, "Maybe on a world where it okay for Kajada and Vakaar to join."

"Maybe," Bhaaj said softly.

Shiv sighed. "I done, Coach." She looked exhausted.

"I ken." Bhaaj nodded with respect. "My thanks for your words."

Shiv returned her nod, then stood up. "I go now."

"Yah." Bhaaj also felt tired. Ready to collapse.

But she still had another interview.

Dice arrived late.

Bhaaj felt ready to throttle him by the time he showed up, an hour after the time they'd set. She tried contacting him, but either he'd turned off his gauntlet comm or else he ignored her. Duane had other duties to attend, so he left.

When Dice finally showed up, he stalked into her living room, watching her with the Undercity impassive face. Bhaaj wasn't fooled. It didn't take an empath to see how nervous he felt.

She motioned at the sofa. "Sit."

He remained standing and crossed his arms.

"What, you want fight me, too?" She scowled at him. "Not got time for this."

"You asked us to speak in Skolian Flag," Dice said, his above-city accent almost perfect.

"Yes. I did." Bhaaj said, startled but glad that he'd learned. She indicated the couch again. "Have a seat, Dice. We've a lot to talk about."

He stayed on his feet. "I have nothing to say to the woman whose sister murdered my grandmother."

Ho! *That* she hadn't expected. Bhaaj and Dig had gone their separate ways long before the war where Dig and Hammer Vakaar killed each other. Dice knew she had nothing to do with his grandmother's death. After everything Shiv had told her, she suspected he used his anger to hide a deeper fear, one rooted in his wish to escape what could seem like an impossible situation.

He wanted college. *Like Kiro.* Dice had seen that someone could live both lives, be from Cries and the Undercity at the same time. Sure, he saw it with Bhaaj too, but she came from a different generation. And then some. In the Undercity where kids became handfasted and had children young, so they might live long enough to raise their families, Bhaaj was old enough to be his great-grandmother. And here she was, only months away from giving birth herself. What a mess.

In a more accepting voice, she said, "Dice, talk to me. As long as we can work out a way for you and Shiv to manage without fighting, you can both stay on the team."

Although he still made no move to sit, he lowered his arms. "Shiv is an ass-byte."

Bhaaj almost laughed. His supposed dislike was even less convincing than hers. "Shiv is a lovely girl, Dice. Now sit down."

"A 'lovely girl'?" He gave a startled laugh. "Who the fuck talks that way?"

"Cries," Bhaaj admitted. "The two of you need to stop fighting. It just feeds into stereotypes about the Undercity."

He shifted his feet, then went over and sat on the other couch. "We're done arguing."

"Good. Does that mean Vakaar is done dealing with Scorpio?"

He jerked. "Who told you that? Don't say Shiv! She'd never betray me."

Damn. She'd hoped she was wrong. "You just told me."

"What?" His fists clenched the couch. "You fucking tricked me."

"Dice, you can't be involved."

"I have nothing to do with it." His grip on the couch loosened.

"But your family does."

He just looked at her.

Her voice tightened. "You can't bring that into our team."

"I haven't brought anything into our team." Then he added, "Except me."

"Do you swear you're here only as an athlete, not as an agent for the Vakaar cartel?"

He met her gaze steadily and spoke in their dialect. "Yah. I swear."

Bhaaj nodded. For her people, using Undercity speech carried an even heavier burden than the oath alone. He meant what he said. "I ken."

"I like it here, Coach." He hesitated, then said, "I love it. All the sunshine. I feel so light. So alive."

"It is a beautiful world. Crowded though."

"I like that, too." He exhaled. "Back home, it's all darkness and people hurting people."

"Dice, did someone hurt you?"

He turned impassive. Maybe he didn't like the life his family mapped out for him, but he'd never betray them. She didn't push.

Bhaaj also had another concern, one more in line with her

coaching duties. "You and Shiv can't fight," she said. "You need to make a good impression. Recruiters will be at this meet, including from university teams."

"Recruiters?" He squinted at her. "What does that mean?"

"People looking for runners to join their team." She met his gaze. "Teams at universities. If they like what they see, Dice, they might offer you a scholarship."

"Not ken." He laughed and added, "Skol-are-ship?" Then remembering himself, he switched back into the Cries dialect. "What is a scholarship?"

"It's a proposal for a bargain," she said. "Colleges have their own sports teams. They want the best athletes they can get. If they think you're among the best, they'll pay for you to attend their school. In return, you agree to run with their team."

"That's all I'd have to do?" He grinned. "Run in circles and they send me to school? It's a joke, yah?"

"No. It's true." She told him what an army recruiter had said to her so long ago. "It's a way out, Dice. A new life." Given the wealth of most citizens in Cries, their university didn't offer many scholarships, besides which, their sports teams weren't any better than Mason's had been before her runners joined. This world offered a far different story, though. "Recruiters from Metropoli universities will be at this meet. If you and Shiv don't get in trouble and give this your absolute best, they might take an interest in you. You both have a shot at it."

He spoke in a low voice. "And we could live here? Away from the Undercity?"

"Yah." Bhaaj knew what he meant. Away from the cartels.

Dice sat thinking. Bhaaj waited. She'd given him a lot to digest. In the Undercity, he and Shiv could never live together. But if they left Raylicon, the cartels were unlikely to go after them.

"It's a lot to think about," Dice said.

"Yah." She thought about the hurdles they faced. "We need to formalize your schooling with records they understand. Most colleges have avenues for homeschooled students to apply."

"Homeschooled?" His forehead creased. "What?"

"It means you learned on your own. Or with your circle."

"Oh. Yah. I ken." He rose to his feet. "Got to go. Got practice."

Bhaaj stood up. "Of course. Stay out of trouble, Dice. Both of you."

He headed for the door, but he paused there and turned back to her. "Coach—"

"Yah?"

"Hyden not know. About Scorpio and Vakaar."

"Hyden is Scorp heir."

"He and his father not speak. They angry." For a moment he just looked at her. Then he added, "Scorpio has holdings on Foreshires Hold."

"Yah. It's a subsidiary called Scorpio Foreshires." Why bring that up?

"Vakaar got a link there too."

Her breath caught. "How?"

"Enough." With that, he left the room, leaving her alone with this new, potentially explosive secret, that Scorpio and Vakaar had connections, possibly on the world hosting the Olympic Games.

"All right, everyone." Mason stood in front of the windows in his hotel room, his back to the predawn sky. "Just to recap. Today we start with the preliminary heats for the shorter sprints. I've sent you the schedule."

Kiro stood with Strider's gang in a clump to one side. He wished Coach Bhaaj had come to this meeting; seeing her helped his confidence. But she had to finish whatever tasks coaches did on the first day of a meet.

"Got it," some athletes said, including Strider who sounded confident. She didn't fool Kiro. They all felt like a string pulled too tight. Today was the day! The sprinters would be the first Raylicon athletes to compete. Kiro didn't know if he liked it that way. It meant they didn't have as much time to get nervous, but it also meant less time to prepare.

Tam remained serene. She'd made her decision days ago: she wouldn't run the 800-meter. It relieved Kiro. The more he knew Tam, the more he liked her. Everyone wanted to see her crush the royal marathon.

Mason glanced at Ruzik, who stood across the room, his dark hair a contrast to the pale wall. "The steeplechase is tomorrow. They aren't doing heats, just a final." The coach didn't look pleased. "For sixteen entrants. If it were my choice, I'd do two heats. But they've decided not to."

"It's fine," Ruzik said.

"Just remember," Mason told him. "You don't have running lanes. Don't get boxed in. It's only 3000 meters, but you've got both hurdles and water jumps. Resist that thing where you kick too early. And don't forget! Those barriers are solid. Hitting one or landing wrong in the water is going to slow, slow, slow you down."

"No worries," Ruzik told him. "I'm good."

"That was tactful," Helyne Tallmount said amiably. "Better than, 'Yes, Coach, you've said it a million times.'"

Mason smiled. "Sorry. I know I keep repeating stuff. It's a coach thing."

"Is good," Angel told him. She and Ruzik stood together, not touching, but with that sense they always had, as if they were two parts of a whole.

"All right, let's see." Mason continued to flick holicons above his board. "Marathoners, you don't compete until the last day, but you can check out the course more today if you want. The royal goes through the countryside, exactly 80 kilometers." He made a face as if he'd bitten a sour fruit. "The classic is that bizarre distance of, yes folks, 42.195 kilometers. Don't ask me why!"

"Isn't it historical?" Azarina Majda asked in her elegant Iotic accent, sounding every bit the aristocrat. It didn't bother Kiro. She never projected that lofty arrogance he had picked up from other Majdas he'd met at galas he attended with his parents.

"I think so," Mason said. "It has something to do with some war on Earth."

"I like that distance," Hyden Laj said. "It's unique."

Mason squinted his holopad. "Hyden, you, Tam and Wild have five days between the ten kilometer and marathons. No heats for the ten kay, but *a lot* of runners. You'll have a staggered start. Don't forget to make sure your timing chips are working." He gave the whole group a stern look. "Always check your tech. And don't forget! Spectators are watching feeds about you and doing interactive sims. They like to experience what you experience. Some even do events virtually with their favorite athletes. And media techs are making reels about you all the time, everywhere. Be careful what you say! It all goes out there."

After they all responded with a dutiful *Yes, Coach,* he motioned at the window, which showed the sun peeking above the city skyline.

"Azarina, you're in heat two for the 1500-meter after the sprints this morning. You should get there early."

"All set," Azarina told him. "We looked at the schedules last night. This morning, too."

"Excellent!" Mason said. "Team Raylicon, let me hear who rules!"

"Raylicon," they all said.

"Who?" Mason shouted.

"RAYLICON!"

Mason grinned at them. "All right! Crinkles and Full-up, you stay here so we can talk about the juniors. Everyone else, off you go!"

A murmur ran through the team as they dispersed and the twelve-year-olds went over to Mason. Kiro left with Zee, walking behind Strider and Lamplight.

Today they competed in their first interstellar meet.

Kiro lined up with seven other runners for his heat of the 800-meter. They each had their own lane, with runners in the outer lanes farther ahead to compensate for the curve of the track. Unlike with shorter sprints, here they could all move to the inside lane after they started. It unsettled Kiro that the officials put him in lane one, the innermost lane; it meant everyone would converge on him. On Raylicon, he'd practiced starts in every lane, though, to learn how each felt.

As announcers introduced each runner, holovids of their past races ran in the air above them. In the stands, holos floated everywhere as people watched feeds, listened to interviews, or learned more about an athlete. VR techs were recording the sprinters to get material for spectators who wanted to immerse themselves in the experience, even "run" with their favorite athlete in a virtual feed of the race. Kiro had heard of people designing entire movie-shorts about the runners. Officials kept the techs away from the real competitors, however, so nothing interfered with the actual run.

The official Starter, a spinning orb with opalescent colors, floated down their line. A voice came out of the glowing sphere. "On your marks!"

Kiro took his position, standing instead of crouching as he did for shorter sprints. The Starter called out a correction to the runner in lane seven, saying her foot was over some line. As soon as she fixed her position, the Starter hummed on its way.

"Set!" the Starter called.

Kiro leaned forward, poised—

The noise of a pistol cracked—and bam! Kiro exploded into his run. Although he controlled his urge to hit his maximum speed right off, he still went wicked fast. And sure enough, here everyone came into his lane, crowding him. He picked up his pace, breaking out of the box before they pushed him to the back. He managed to stay in fourth—he so much wanted to *push* into third, knowing only the top three finishers were guaranteed the finals, but he controlled his urge to go too hard too soon. Even so, when he saw their split times on the check-point holo after the first lap, it was faster than he'd ever done in practice. He didn't even feel tired!

Relax, pax, sax, wax, he sang in his mind, a mantra he'd come up with to stay calm. Before he learned that technique, he'd used up too much energy tensing his muscles during his runs. But still! The tight turn of the inner lane made it harder to maintain speed and gauge the positions of the other runners. Almost time to move forward—

As Kiro came down the last stretch to the finish, he sped up. For several moments he ran with a woman from the Imperial Fleet team. Then she started to flag, barely slowing, but enough for him to move into third. Time to *GO!* He lunged into the "Undercity kick" Zee had insisted he learn. *Got to go fast,* she'd told him. *Outrun bad-biz.*

Kiro broke ahead of the person in second, but then someone else surged past him. He battled them for third, pushing, pushing, *pushing*. He felt ready to "hit the wall," his energy reserves used up, but he was close, so close—

Kiro rocketed across the finish in third place, then lifted his arms and shouted. He'd done it! He'd made the finals! The holos floating at the scoreboard showed his best time ever—

Except.

It wasn't good enough for the Olympics. He'd come close, but not enough. As he slowed to a walk, gulping in air, someone handed him a water bottle. Grabbing it, he took a swallow.

"Eh," his benefactor said. "Good run."

He turned and grinned. "Zee!" His smile faded. "Not good enough for Olympics."

"Still got finals." Her smile lit her face, making her large eyes seem like the proverbial velvety black pools. How a pool of water could be velvety, who the hell knew, but that's how they looked to him. She had a jaunty cap on her head with the logo of the Raylicon team on it, a Majda hawk even though no one called it that. If Scorpio hadn't pulled their support, they'd probably have wanted their logo there as well. He didn't care. She could wear anything, and she'd look beautiful. Pulling her close, he hugged her. Then Strider and Lamp were there, talking and walking with Kiro.

So far, life looked good. They'd all made at least one final in their chosen events.

"It's appalling," Bhaaj told Mason. The couch in his hotel living room shifted, trying to ease her tension, but it didn't work any better for her than for her athletes. "They put our runners in the worst possible lane in every race."

"Well, not *every* one," Mason hedged. "Wild, Azarina and Hyden got better placements."

"Yah, right," Bhaaj said. "Azarina is a Majda. Hyden is the son of a billionaire, and Wild gets his placement based on his past performance in the Olympics."

"I have to admit," Mason said. "It isn't usually this bad when I only bring Cries athletes. Sure, they don't all get the lanes they want, but they don't *all* get their last choice."

"We should complain."

"For what?" he asked. "They haven't violated any rules. Even if our athletes had interstellar rankings, the officials could put them wherever they want. No one on this team except Wild has even competed at an elite level before."

"Angel won the damn Selei Open." Bhaaj glared at him. "But in this meet, they gave her the worst choice in every race, including her heats, the semi-finals, and the finals."

"Yes. But she was sprinting this time. The Selei Open was a marathon." With satisfaction, he added, "Besides, she still won the silver in the 200-meter and came in fourth in the 400. What an ace!"

"Well, yah, that felt good," Bhaaj admitted. "You know, I'd pegged her as a marathoner last year, maybe more muscular than ideal, but still a distance runner. I understand now why she wanted to do sprints. She's freaking *fast*."

"She's trained hard." Then he scowled. "What the hell is going on with your sprinters, that they all signed up for the royal?"

"What are you talking about?"

"Before the meet." He squinted at her. "I thought you knew."

"I had no idea." Why the blazes would her sprinters do an ultra-marathon?

"They said you told them they could sign up."

"I most certainly did not."

"That's not what Tam said."

Tam? "Oh, shit."

"Bhaaj?"

She squinted at him. "Tam wanted to do the 800 meter. I was trying to talk her out of it."

"That 800-meter *sprint*? What for?"

"It irked her to lose that practice against Bayonet. She wanted another chance." Thinking back, she added, "I told her it would be different if, as a sprinter, she wanted to try a marathon, that it wouldn't matter if it tired her out because the marathons came last at the meet."

"Why the blazes would you tell a sprinter to run a marathon?"

"I didn't! I told Tam if she tried the 800, she could risk her results in the marathon."

"Well, that did work," Mason acknowledged. "She never mentioned the 800 to me."

Bhaaj saw all too clearly what had happened. "The Undercity kids don't know enough about track and field to realize they shouldn't do sprints and marathons in the same meet."

"Well, they've signed up." His expression brightened. "It's true, though, that it doesn't matter if they don't finish the marathon or come in last. What they're doing in everything else is amazing. I've never had such a strong showing at this meet. Usually we come in close to the bottom. But last I looked, we were fourteenth out of over eighty teams. Fourteenth!"

"Mason, that's great." The ranking system extended beyond Metropoli. The Skolian leagues had always ranked teams, but the Olympics on Earth were a different story. Only the medal count mattered. As Earth combined sports events with Skolia, though, that had expanded. Although the Olympic focus remained on medals, they also now ranked teams. The standings came from cumulative results for the top twenty athletes in each event, with weights for higher placements or events considered more demanding, always a controversial choice, including multiple points for multipart events like the decathlon. The process was complex and lengthy and had taken decades to evolve, but it had become a respected measure of where teams stood on the interstellar stage.

Mason was going over his roster. "So far Ruzik has qualified for the Olympics in the steeplechase, and Angel in both the 400 and 800. Tam, Wild and Hyden made the ten kay. Goddess, Bhaaj, I'm gobsmacked that Tam won the bronze! Our first ever in that event at any major meet."

Bhaaj smiled. "Yah."

"Let's see..." He continued perusing his holicons. "Azarina and Shiv are both good for the Olympics in the 1500 and 5000-meter, and Dice for the cliff climb. It was close for Dice, given the way he had trouble figuring out the safety harness on the cliffs, but he made it. Tanzia Harjan just barely qualified in the 100-meter hurdles, but that's all it takes. Strider made it in both the 400 and 800, Lamp for the 100 and 200, Zee on the 400 and Kiro in the 800. Their team qualified for the 4×400 relay." He looked up at Bhaaj. "Kiro almost made it in the 400 meter. If we could get these kids to another meet, I'm sure they'd qualify in more events."

"Probably." She thought of how Metropoli had overwhelmed the Undercity athletes. "But let's not overdo it. The more experience they get, the more they can consider multiple events in the future."

"I forget sometimes how new this is to your runners." Mason brought up another display. "I love how well Crinkles and Full-up are doing in the juniors. Gold for Crinkles and silver for Full-up in the 3000-meter. Hah!" He grinned at Bhaaj. "Goddess, how could I have never known the incredible talent you have down there in the Undercity? It's like I found a platinum mine."

She'd hesitated to make predictions, superstitious enough to believe she'd jinx the results, but she felt more relaxed now. "It doesn't surprise me, given they qualified for your adult team."

"Indeed." He sounded preoccupied again. "The marathons tomorrow are the last events, so even if it exhausts your sprinters, they can sleep it off on the flight home."

Bhaaj wished they could stay longer, but she'd agreed with Mason that if they didn't have enough funds for an extended stay, it was better to have as much time as possible before the meet, helping the athletes adapt to the new world. "Thanks for letting them try. They won't get Olympic-qualifying times, but they'll enjoy it."

His expression changed with its usual lightning speed, turning into satisfaction. "The marathons are heavily weighted in the overall standings. If Tam, Ruzik, Wild and Hyden do as well as we hope, who knows? Tam might even medal. Maybe our entire team could medal at this meet."

"Well, hmmm, maybe." As a team, they had no chance of medaling, which he well knew. The Metropoli A and B teams were powerhouses, as were the teams from Parthonia, the seat of the Imperialate government, and Foreshires Hold, home to the upcoming Olympics. Some of the larger universities had strong teams as well, and this meet allowed them to enter. She doubted Raylicon would move higher in the rankings than they'd already achieved. Even so, Fourteenth still gave them a far better result than they'd ever before seen.

"Mason." She spoke carefully. "Have you noticed anything odd about Hyden?"

"Not really." He thought about it. "He has seemed a bit subdued since this mess with his father. He's running well, though, enough to get him into the Olympics on the ten kay even if he doesn't qualify tomorrow for the classic."

"He prefers the marathon." Bhaaj had no doubt on that score.

"Well, he and Tallmount are the only ones doing it to qualify, so if he gets a good time, he'll make it." Mason glowered at her. "Assuming none of your Dust Knights beat him. *Angel* is going to run the classic. It's nuts! And Rockjan is doing the freaking royal? She's not fast, but she's got endurance like I can't believe."

Bhaaj shrugged. "She and Angel are only doing it for fun, because you go somewhere instead of in circles on a track."

"That's not the point. If any of them beat Hyden, it will bother him." He stopped, then said, "Okay, yes, I see what you mean about him having changed. In the past, I'd never have thought he cared. He was always so cocky. But you're right, he seems less confident lately."

"He's not comfortable enough with me to open up," Bhaaj said.

"But he likes you. Why don't you talk to him, see if you can figure out what's up?"

"All right. I'll let you know." He snapped off his holoboard. "Come on, let's go down to the buffet and celebrate with the kids. I'm starved!"

As they rode down to the lobby, Bhaaj stood lost in thought. She feared Hyden's unease might have nothing to do with the team. What had Dice meant that Hyden didn't know? They'd better not have a link to secret weapons deals with Scorpio.

CHAPTER XVI
Distance Begun

They put Tam and Ruzik at the back for the royal marathon.

Everyone gathered on a road in a park beyond the extensive sprawl of North-Metro City. The starting line stretched across the smooth pavement, and vine-birches lined the road, genetically altered trees adapted for Metropoli with leaves that resembled vines. The sun hadn't yet risen, but dawn lightened the sky. In the east, the clouds had turned red and gold.

Thirty-eight runners had signed up for the race, not only Tam, Ruzik and Wild, but also Strider's gang and Rockjan. Bhaaj had made it clear to the meet officials that Tam, Ruzik and Wild hoped to qualify for the Olympics. She'd pointed out how well Ruzik had done in the steeplechase, and Tam and Wild in the ten kay. The officials hadn't seemed to care. Only Wild got a position closer to the front, in the second line.

Blast it all, Bhaaj thought.

What's up? Max asked.

They start everyone together. You know that puts anyone at the back at a disadvantage.

No it doesn't, Max thought. **It takes at least six hours for elite athletes to run the eighty kilometers of this course. A few moments of delay at the start won't matter. Besides, they don't start timing runners until they cross the start line.**

As much as Bhaaj knew he was right, it still irked her. She had no doubt Tam and Ruzik could qualify for the Olympics regardless of where they started, but she also wanted to ensure they achieved the best possible ranking. It would be their first on the interstellar stage.

None of her runners seemed to care. Tam and Ruzik stood together at the back, relaxed and silent. Strider's gang had gathered to one side, laughing and chatting in the predawn light. Rockjan waited across the road, her arms crossed, basking in the coolness of the day.

An official walked through the crowd, arranging the runners in lines, giving them plenty of room on the spacious road. He then withdrew to a kiosk by the road and activated the Starter orb, which rose into the air and whirred above the runners. His voice boomed out from the sphere as he reminded them of the rules and the rest stations along the route. Although Bhaaj had already gone over it all with her runners, they needed to hear about the stations as much as possible, letting it sink in that here, unlike in the Undercity, they could stop for water or food without risk to their lives.

"On your mark!" the Starter orb called out.

Most of the runners in the front lines, including Wild, leaned forward. Those in the back also prepared, though with less of a forward tilt. They had room; their holding back seemed more psychological than an actual need for space.

"Set!" the Starter called.

With a boom, the orb started the race. No one exploded into motion, they just ran, and not particularly fast. Tam and Ruzik added a bit to their usual speed, making their way through the crowd. When they reached Wild, the three of them fell into a run together, keeping a steady pace.

"They're off," a man said next to her.

Bhaaj turned to find Mason. "Eh," she told him.

He smiled. "What does that mean anyway?"

"What does what mean?"

"'Eh.' You all say it, all of you from the Undercity, all the time."

"Oh." She blinked, bemused. "It varies. Sometimes it means, 'hello, how are you today, I hope you're feeling well.' Or it could be, 'Go away, I'm too busy to talk to you.' Or 'That was interesting' or 'That was boring.' It depends on the context and your tone."

He laughed good-naturedly. "Well, that clears it up."

Bhaaj couldn't help but smile. "I guess so. Did you get everyone set for the classic?"

"Yep. They'll start in about an hour, inside the city. Sixty-four entrants, including Hyden, Tallmount and Angel."

She spoke warily. "And their starting positions?"

"Um, yes, well—" Mason squinted at her.

"They put Angel at the back, didn't they?"

"I'm sorry," Mason said. "I reminded them that Angel medaled in the 200, but they said it's a sprint. They didn't think she should even run the classic. They don't have a valid reason to disqualify her, so they didn't, but she'll be in the last line."

Bhaaj couldn't believe they'd wanted to disqualify the woman who'd won the Selei Open. "What about Hyden and Tallmount?"

"They're closer to the front. Tallmount has run interstellar marathons before, and she does have a ranking. It's not that high, but it was enough to get her in the third line. They put Hyden there, too, even though this is his first marathon." He looked out at the marathoners. "They've reached the turn."

Following his gaze, Bhaaj saw the leaders rounding a corner in the road. Orbs whirred above them, recording the race, one for about every four people.

"Let's go to the coach's lobby," she said. "We can get breakfast and watch from there."

As soon as Bhaaj pulled down her helmet, the virtual reality system plunged her into a lively space with athletes, spectators, and media personalities. The sim turned the route of the classic marathon into a marketplace of excitement, with avatars popping up everywhere, even on the track where the athletes were running. Virtual breezes caressed her cheeks, soft and pleasant. Vendor signs glowed in the air, offering food, sports clothing, and mementos, all which they promised to deliver as real products within minutes no matter what your location. Tantalizing smells wafted in the air, from spice-sticks to buzz-brew to that scrumptious Earth delicacy called pizza.

The view picked up where she'd specified, moving with Angel and several other athletes along a city street, passing spectators crowded behind barricades. When Bhaaj had looked at Wild and Hyden earlier, using a feed of the real event, the crowds had been sparser, mostly family and friends calling out encouragement. She had no idea how many of these virtual spectators were real, but given that people couldn't stand along the route unless they signed a form allowing the media to use their images, she suspected at least some were avatars created by this sim.

A man and a woman floated above the marketplace in the basket of a balloon striped in red, yellow, and blue. They hovered to the side of the path at about twice the height of the runners, drinking from cups that glowed with ads for an energy drink. As official media commentators, they looked beautiful and charming, so much so that Bhaaj suspected the sim enhanced their appearance.

"Angel has moved into tenth!" the woman exclaimed. "The silver medalist in the 200-meter *sprint* has reached the top ten in the classic marathon!" She spoke straight to the viewer as if she needed no tech at all. She had to be sitting somewhere in a media-booth, though; no way could a hot-air balloon that small carry a basket with two people, a table, and two chairs, especially given how it moved along with the race without any sign of tech to keep it going. Bhaaj liked the way it looked, though, crisp and bright.

"But can Angel hold the pace?" the man asked. "My bet? She won't finish the race."

"I'm not so sure." The woman took a swig of her drink, making its ad, a red logo of two triangles, flash. "She won the Selei City Open last year. Her speed now is about what she averaged there."

Bhaaj's ear-buds, what people called subs, gave a low beep and asked, "Would you like to see a holo of Angel in the Selei City marathon? We don't yet have stories about this athlete at this meet, but you can make your own reel if you wish."

Bhaaj sighed. She and Mason needed to get promo-reels out for the team. They'd been so swamped with preparing everyone for this meet, they'd had no time for extras.

No thanks, she mouthed. Her subs used muscle and bone-conduction tech to register her words.

"These Undercity runners must be hybrid athletes, training for short and long distances," the male commentator was saying. "It could be risky, making them good at both and great at nothing."

"And yet Angel medaled in the 200-meter sprint." The woman's voice hardened. "Of course, some athletes try to get away with doping or hidden cybernetic augmentation."

"For fuck's sake," Bhaaj muttered.

Mason appeared next to her, also standing behind the barricades, he and Bhaaj moving with Angel as if an invisible scooter transported them along the path. In reality, he was sitting on the other end of the couch where they'd settled in the coach's lounge, chowing down on a sandwich.

"Angel *is* amazing, though," Mason said. "If she keeps this up, she'll qualify for the classic, too. I've never heard of that!" He smirked. "Teach them to underestimate your runners. And it's all natural, the way survival selected for good runners over the millennia."

"Yah." Bhaaj relaxed some. "All that training we do helps, too."

"You could say 'Eh,'" Mason told her. When she laughed, he grinned.

Their view abruptly shifted to the lead pack of the race, four runners led by a leanly muscled woman. A new pair of commentators in another balloon morphed into view. Bhaaj suspected it was the same duo as before, except with new avatars. It looked good to have different commentators assigned to each part of the race, but it probably cost too much to hire more than two actual people.

An ad scrolled above the balloon, inviting Bhaaj to buy *Sleep-Deep! Insurance,* which would pay her if an EI-controlled device disturbed her sleep. Of course, you had to prove you hadn't wanted to wake up, but the ad neglected to mention that fact. It just showed holos of sexy people looking happy and well-rested.

Oblivious to the ads above their balloon, the commentators continued their coverage. "Xi Aio from Metropoli, last year's gold medalist here, is in second place," the woman said. The view focused on one of the men, a dark-haired fellow with black eyes. "He's just behind Fina Caster, who took bronze at the Olympics four years ago."

"No surprises there," the male commentator said. "The lead pack started with fifteen runners, but it has thinned to four, with a chase pack of three not far behind. Behind those, the three Raylicon entrants are running together like clockwork."

"It looks like they're pacing each other," the woman said. "These Undercity types seem to do that a lot."

"Two of them aren't Undercity," the man said, as if reassuring her.

"Hyden Laj is the heir to Scorpio Corporation, and Helyne Tallmount has a history of doing well in lesser-known meets. The other one, Angel, is an Undercity gang member."

Bhaaj swore. "Hyden is a corporate heir and Helyne has a history of doing well but Angel—who came in first in Selei City with a better time than either Hyden or Helene have ever managed—is a 'gang member.'" She scanned the menu at the bottom of the sim, looking for the reel that went to the commentators. She wrote a protest about the phrasing, then made herself pause to make sure it sounded polite. Yah, good. She sent it off using the generic Raylicon account. It didn't identify anyone, only their team affiliation, but those accounts did go straight to the commentators.

The commentators continued to chat. A moment later, the woman said, "We've had protests from the Raylicon team. They object to the portrayal of their athletes." An image flashed, showing a reel some spectator had made that superimposed a rat's ears and tail on a view of Rockjan throwing her spear in the javelin finals.

"Seriously?" Bhaaj said. "That's how they respond, by showing something that reinforces the insults?"

"They should know better," Mason said. "In what universe is calling people 'rats' okay?"

When the image of Rockjan morphed back to the view of Hyden, Tallmount, and Angel running the marathon, the man said. "These Undercity athletes make no secret of their gang affiliations. I'm surprised the other members of the team feel safe with them."

"According to Coach Mason Qazik," the woman said, "The Dust Knights aren't a gang, they're a martial arts club founded by Coach Bhaajan, a retired army major."

"Whatever they are, these runners are shattering expectations," the man said. "This is almost the first time Raylicon has won *anything* here. Their only other athlete who medaled competed over thirty years ago, when Garnet Jizarian won the classic marathon."

"Jizarian didn't actually come from Raylicon, though," the woman said.

"Garnet was too from Raylicon," Mason grumbled.

"I thought you recruited her from Parthonia," Bhaaj said.

"Well, yes," he admitted. "But she lived on Raylicon while she ran for us." He sighed. "It just feels like they keep trying to put down our team. No one ever called us winners before, but they never treated us this way."

Bhaaj turned down her subs so she didn't have to hear the commentators. "Two-thirds of the team comes from the Undercity. No one likes it."

"Yeah, I noticed. Do you put up with this stuff all the time?"

"Actually, this is mild." Bhaaj didn't want to dwell on the past. "I think sports is a good way to ease my people into the public view."

It went much further than Undercity athletes. Even before the Skolian Imperialate and Eubian Concord had combined their Interstellar Games with Earth's Olympics, sports had offered a peaceful way of bringing people together. Interstellar meets were the only way Skolia and Eube could interact without war. Skolians called the Eubians "Traders" because their economy depended on the sale of human beings. Their leaders, the Trader Aristos, wanted to conquer everyone. Period. They looked upon the rest of humanity with more contempt than even the worst Skolian critics viewed the Undercity. Aristos considered *everyone* except themselves less than human.

As an army officer, Bhaaj had heard the Aristo claims. Yes, many of their slave populations had a good standard of living. And what that left unsaid? Those populations had no freedom, no choices, no self-determination. Obey their owners, and the Aristos allowed them relatively normal lives. But nothing changed the one crushing fact that a few thousand Aristos owned over two trillion people spread across thousands of worlds and habitats. They called their empire a Concord because supposedly everyone got along. Right. Anyone who stepped outside the lines paid a severe price, anything from a reduced standard of living to prison sentences.

And if they rebelled? Genocide.

The Aristos "removed" any population that challenged their domination. They coveted the Skolian Imperialate of Bhaaj's people and the Allied Worlds of Earth, and they never let up in their inexorable drive to control humanity. A "muted war" had existed between Skolia and Eube for centuries, fought in propaganda or with combat on less settled worlds. Interstellar sports offered the only way their peoples could meet in peace.

Mason was watching her face. "Bhaaj, what haunts you?"

Startled, she refocused on him. "What?"

"Sometimes you go somewhere else."

"I was just thinking about my years in the military." She spoke uneasily. "The Traders don't come to this tournament, but they will be at the Olympics."

"Can you handle that?"

"I'll be fine. It just catches me sometimes." She felt as if she'd bitten into a sour fruit. "For the Aristo officers, fighting us is like squashing bugs. Their slaves can never be officers, but they fight if their owners tell them to. Some of them hated us, but most were just doing their jobs. They were in awe of the Aristos. Or in terror." She exhaled. "At least with the prejudice my people get from Skolians, ways exist to protest. Like you and I requesting they not call our athletes rats or criminals. It takes a while to make change, but it can happen."

He spoke firmly. "Your athletes have as much right to be here as anyone else. I don't care who withdraws their support. No one can force me to drop Undercity members."

Bhaaj smiled. "Anyone ever tell you you're a good person?"

He laughed. "Not enough. But you can all you want." He motioned at the balloon, which was morphing out of existence. "I think they're going somewhere else in the race."

"Let's go watch the royal, see what's up."

"Sure." Mason winced. "But can we get out of this sim? The ads drive me nuts."

"No kidding." Bhaaj thought, *Max, cut my VR link.*

The world went dark until Bhaaj pushed back her helmet and found herself in the lounge. The dais closest to the couch where she and Mason sat was still showing the classic. In the center of the lounge, the main dais showed the royal, the holos high enough in the air that she could see them above the watchers. They showed a woman jogging at a steady pace well ahead of several other athletes in the background.

Bhaaj vocalized a command to her subs. *Pick up the feed for the royal marathon.*

A new voice came into her ears. "—the runners still have several hours until they reach the stadium," a woman was saying. She sounded different than the commentator for the classic, calmer and less urgent. "The lead pack has stretched out over hundreds of meters."

"So far no surprises," a man said, someone with a deeper voice than the fellow on the classic. "The leader is Vanya Longbow from Metropoli A, last year's gold medalist in this meet. She's won the royal here for several years now, with no real competition."

"Oh, she's got a competitor," the woman said. "The Aristo runner Kryx Quaelen isn't here, but he'll be at the Olympics. He's triumphed in every meet he's attended."

"True. But we have a lot of special interest stories right here," the man said. "This is our largest field ever for the royal, and more than one fifth of them come from the Raylicon team."

"Yes, I noticed." Unlike the woman covering the classic, this one sounded more bemused than irate. "Their team is one of the smallest here. They don't even have entrants in some events, like the pole vault or long jump. But eight of them wanted to do the royal, including four sprinters and a javelin thrower."

"The sprinters are close to last," the man said. The view shifted to show Strider and Lamp running together, with Kiro and Zee a few meters behind. Although Kiro looked more worn out than the others, they all seemed relaxed, as if they were jogging along an Undercity midwalk. Every now and then one would comment to another, and once they all laughed as if someone made a joke.

"They don't seem to be taking the event seriously," the woman said.

"Some people just love to run," the man said. "The more interesting story is their teammates. Look at Tam Wiens." The view switched to show Tam loping up a hill. "She started at the back, but she's kept a good pace, and she's in fourth now, behind Manuel Rodriguez from Earth, last year's bronze winner." The view morphed into a dark-haired man walking up a steep incline.

"Most ultra-marathoners walk the steepest part of this course," the woman said. "So far Wiens has kept up a steady jog. If Rodriguez doesn't start running again, she could pass him."

"That's only if Wiens maintains her pace," the man cautioned. "And that's a huge 'If.' It's unlikely *anyone* could keep that pace for much longer, let alone a runner new to the sport."

"Still, she's making a name for herself here at North-Metro," the woman said. "She took the bronze in the ten-kilometer race."

"It's unprecedented," the man said. "Every athlete on the Raylicon team has qualified for at least one Olympic event, most of them from the Dust Knight family."

"Apparently Dust Knight isn't their name," the woman said. "According to a reel posted this morning, these Knights guard the Undercity."

"Whatever you call them, it looks like four here could make Olympic qualifying times."

"Four?" Mason glanced at Bhaaj. "Tam, Ruzik, and Wild are three. And Wild isn't a Knight."

She shook her head. "I don't know what they mean."

The scene shifted, showing Ruzik running in an easy lope. The woman said, "Ruzik of the Dust Knights is currently in eleventh. He could move into the top ten if he doesn't slow down too much later in the race."

"And Tayz Wilder," the man said. The holos morphed to show Wild and two other runners going downhill at a faster pace. "He's currently in twelfth. At the last Olympics, he came in thirty-eighth in a field of one hundred and ninety." The view shifted again, showing another familiar face. "Rockjan of the Dust Knights is in fifteenth."

"Ho!" Mason said. "You didn't tell me that Rockjan could do marathons."

"I didn't realize." Given Rockjan's preference for throwing stuff, it hadn't occurred to Bhaaj to suggest the royal. "But you know, every time I see her in the Undercity, she's running."

The scene shifted, this time showing the Metropoli runners in fifth, sixth, and seventh, with holos of their current rankings glowing in the air. Bhaaj recognized one of them, Andi Jinda, the Metropoli woman who'd challenged Tam in the 800-meter practice.

"I didn't realize Andi Jinda was a marathoner," Bhaaj said. "Isn't the 800 her event?"

"Nah, she's always been distance," Mason told her. "In that practice, I think she just wanted to pit Tam against Bayonet, someone they knew could beat her. They seem to have targeted Tam."

"I suppose." Bhaaj smiled. "Tam almost beat Bayonet."

"Bayo wasn't running her best," Mason said. "You saw the 800 finals, right? She pulverized the interstellar record."

"It was impressive." Far more gratifying to Bhaaj was that Kiro had qualified for the Olympics in the same finals. "If Jinda keeps up this pace, she could catch Tam."

"It's odd, actually." Mason squinted at the scene. "Jinda isn't considered a top contender, barely top twenty at best."

Bhaaj stood up and stretched. "I need to go walk a bit. I'll be back."

With that, she set off to find out more about Jinda.

CHAPTER XVII
Persistence

Bhaaj slunk through the back alleys and hidden grottos of the shadow mesh, searching, searching...

I've a lead on Jinda talking about Raylicon, Max thought.

The scene changed, morphing into a digital club full of young people, discordant music, and bizarre tech. One machine with daggers for hands kept digging up pieces of the glittering mesh beneath its feet, after which another flat machine would repair the grid, designing it in new patterns. Bhaaj could see through the grid to the level below, a darker space, as if the players down there preferred to keep their activities even more secret than usual in the shadow mesh.

You think Andi Jinda hangs out here? So far, Bhaaj had found only the usual sports reels, sites, and holo-vids where Jinda enthused about her races or posed with friends. It was all boringly normal. Bhaaj didn't buy it. She'd met above-city types like Andi before, glossy on the outside, but with a venomous edge they tried to hide.

I found a record from yesterday, when she visited a proscribed chat room, Max said.

Proscribed? That described everything in the shadow mesh.

Here. The view changed, dumping Bhaaj into a murky café with no horizontal surfaces. The floor tilted, the walls tilted, the tables tilted. It didn't matter; the virtual drinks stayed wherever people put them. The lights had a dusky red color, leaving half the place in shadow.

Bhaaj hid within her shroud, one she'd fine-tuned for decades until she could cloak herself anywhere.

How is this proscribed? she asked.

The shadow mesh has its own laws and enforcers, Max said. **Just like the Undercity.**

Yah, well, who decided to make this place more forbidden than the rest of the shadow mesh? It looked strange but otherwise innocuous.

Actually, the people who come here to hang out.

And are they? Proscribed, I mean.

Not really. He shifted her view to a slanted table with four people slouched in tilted chairs around it, including a hollow-eyed version of Andi Jinda with her hair spiked up, giant leather-and-chain gauntlets, dark trousers and a ripped muscle-shirt.

She's trying too hard, Bhaaj decided.

I'd say that's true for most people here. Those I can identify come from well-placed families on Metropoli. They're 'slumming it,' you might say.

Like Hyden in the casino.

Yes. But with far less glamor than the Top Mark.

Bhaaj studied the people at the table. Although she didn't recognize anyone but Jinda, that didn't say much, given that you could look however you wanted here. *Can you get closer without tripping any alarms?*

Easily. Their attempts at secrecy were clumsy.

The view shifted until Bhaaj stood next to the table where she could hear the two women and two men talking.

"—teams from all over," Jinda was saying. "Most aren't that good, not compared to ours."

Bhaaj smiled. *That sounds too mundane given how hard they're trying to be thugs.*

"I heard about the Raylicon team," one of the men said. "Can you believe it? They brought stinking dust rats! They ought to be disqualified."

"We'll get rid of them," Jinda said. "We can't allow them to compete with decent people."

Bhaaj stopped smiling. *Yah, well, then you need to get rid of your crap selves.*

You should take the high road, Max thought.

Why? I'll just fall down a cliff.

"Get rid of them how?" the other woman asked.

"We haven't figured that out yet," Jinda said. "We'll come up with something."

We? Bhaaj asked. *It sounds like she means more than one person. But not the people here.*

I'm searching to see if she has links to groups that act against the Undercity. So far nothing. Her public links go to her team, family, and friends.

This meet has to abide by the rules of the IOC if they want to serve as an Olympic qualifier. That includes letting anyone compete. Even the Traders could have if they'd wanted.

Maybe Jandi is just boasting, Max suggested. **Trying to impress her friends in a place where no one else knows.**

Yah, well, she should be more careful. No place on the mesh is completely hidden.

True, but you can't use anything you learn here. You'd have to reveal you were slinking around where you shouldn't be, and with a lot more expertise than these kids.

He had a point. *Even so. It helps to know where Jinda is coming from. I don't trust her.*

I'll keep looking into her, Max said. **We should go, though. Duane Ebersole wants to talk with you.**

All right. Pull us out.

The slanted, nausea-inducing room vanished in the haze of the shadow mesh.

"Dice and Shiv haven't had more arguments," Duane said as he walked into the living room of Bhaaj's suite. He waited until the door closed, then added. "But each of them, on their own, has gone into the city to meet with someone outside of the tournament."

Bhaaj didn't like the sound of it. "Who did they talk to?"

Duane leaned against the room's console and crossed his arms. "I couldn't tell. Whoever it was knew how to evade a tail. Either they figured out I was following them, or they always take precautions. But they aren't the kids that Shiv and Dice normally hang out with, they aren't athletes, they aren't sports officials, and they aren't recruiters. It doesn't look good."

No kidding. "Did you a record the meetings? Visual? Audio?"

"I couldn't get close enough for audio. When I sent in a palm-drone, its systems got fried."

"So they've got security." Bhaaj thought about what she'd overheard in the shadow mesh café. "Do you think they're trying to affect the Raylicon team?"

"I didn't get that impression." He started to pace. "My gut instinct? I don't think this has anything to do with the tournament beyond the fact that it brought Dice and Shiv here."

Bhaaj had learned to trust his instincts. "Something between Scorpio and the cartels? Abyss Associates? Weapons deals?"

He stopped and stood with that inwardly directed look people got when they talked to their EIs. "My EI can get some of their words by reading their lips." He focused on Bhaaj. "It's about people balking. Or... Balkers?"

"Balking at what?"

"I'm not getting anything else."

"What about when Shiv talked to them?"

He accessed his EI again. "Something about weapons, it looks like."

"Guns? Bombs?"

"Actually no. Something else, I'm not sure what. I'll have my EI send Max the records."

"Good idea—" Bhaaj stopped as her comm buzzed.

"Mason wants to talk to you," Max said. "It's urgent."

Bhaaj tapped the comm panel on her gauntlet. "Hey, Mason. What's up?"

"It's Angel! She's almost at the finish line."

"Already?" Bhaaj turned back to Duane. "Let's talk later, yah?"

He waved his hand at her. "You go. I'll let you know if anything else comes up."

"Thanks!" With that, she strode from the room.

The male commentator was practically yelling when Bhaaj ran into the coach's lounge. "—she never faded! She's entering the stadium now!"

The holovids evolving on every dais showed Angel leaving the tunnel that exited into the stadium. She loped along, steady and calm, looking tired, but not spent. People filled the lounge, coaches from almost every team, and assistants from those where the main coach had gone to meet a finisher. Bhaaj and Mason would've been at the finish line too, except they hadn't thought they'd need to yet.

"She's in sixth place!" the female commentator said. "Who'd ever have expected this from a sprinter! Saints almighty, I can't believe it."

Bhaaj watched as Angel ran her final lap around the track. Both Xi Aio from Metropoli and Karanja Kiptanui Njoro from Earth had already finished, as well as Fina Caster and a woman from the space habitat called Docker's Haven. It looked like Angel was too far behind the fifth-place runner to pass him before the finish—

And then Angel kicked.

"Ho!" someone said in the lounge, in the same instant the male commentator shouted, "And there it is, what they're calling the Undercity kick! How could she do that at the finish of a marathon? This is unbelievable."

"Absolutely unbelievable!" The female commentator sounded more angry than excited.

"Look at that," Mason said, for once calmer than everyone else. He'd seen that kick often.

With a final surge, Angel caught up with the fifth-place runner. They jockeyed for position, but he'd obviously hit his limit. Angel sprinted past him and finished in fifth.

"Holy shit," Mason said in a voice that carried only to Bhaaj given all the exclamations from everyone else. "I've never heard of anyone who qualified for the Olympics in both sprints and a marathon at one meet. Never!"

Bhaaj hadn't either. "Come on. Let's go down to the finish."

After Angel cooled down and drank more water, she joined Bhaaj and Mason in the area set off for coaches and runners. They didn't have long to wait. Hyden came in a few minutes later, in ninth, with Tallmount not far behind in tenth, both with qualifying times for the Olympics, just barely for Tallmount, but it was enough.

The holo-reporters couldn't come into the coach's area, but as soon as the athletes stepped out of it, broadcasters converged on them, calling out questions.

"Angel, how did you do it?" someone called. Someone else shouted, "What techniques do you use?" while yet another called, "What's your secret?"

Angel looked around, clearly frazzled. To no one in particular, she said, "I run."

"How can you medal in the sprint and qualify for an Olympic level marathon?" a man asked.

"I run a lot." Angel looked like she wanted to escape.

"What's your training regime?" a woman asked while a man said, "Shouldn't your focus be on one type of event?" As they yelled more questions, Angel's face creased with confusion.

When someone shoved a holo-cam in her face, Angel said, "Undercity. Run fast, you live. Run slow, you die."

"All right." Bhaaj tugged her away from the reporters. "We'll do a press conference later." She had no idea if any of them were interested enough to come, but they were shouting at Hyden and Tallmount, too, questions about Scorpio. Hyden tried to ignore them, and Tallmount stayed as taciturn as always.

Bhaaj and Mason managed to get the three of them into the stadium tunnel where the reporters couldn't come. As Mason exhaled with relief, Hyden said, "Goddess, they're loud."

Angel chuckled, which said more about how she viewed Hyden now than any comments. "Yah. Too much noise."

Helyne Tallmount grinned at them. "We did it!"

"We did." Hyden sounded happy again, which he hadn't since his father pulled his support of the team. "How are our runners doing in the royal?"

Mason was squinting at small holicons above his sports band. "It looks like the leaders are a couple hours from the finish." Looking up, he added, "Tam is in fourth and Andi Jinda is in fifth."

"Let's find a place to watch them," Tallmount said. "Where do you go?"

"The coach's lounge," he told her. "Athletes can't go in there, though."

"We can go to one of the athlete's lounges," Bhaaj said. "Some allow coaches."

Mason beamed. "Let's do it!"

"Look at that." Hyden leaned forward on the sofa as he stared at a holoscreen on the wall with a three-dimensional holo in front of it. "Andi Jinda has almost caught up with Tam."

"I've never heard of Jinda doing this well," Mason said.

"Interesting," Bhaaj mused. "Maybe she wants to provoke Tam into wearing herself out."

"It isn't working," Tallmount said.

Bhaaj turned up her subs to hear the feed from the commentators.

"—Vanya Longbow has moved into first, ahead of Manuel Rodriguez and Canda Azi," a woman was saying. "Tam Wiens from the Raylicon team and Andi Jinda of Metropoli A are battling it out for fourth."

"Not much of a battle," the male commentator said. "Look at Jinda. She can't maintain that pace for even a few more minutes. I doubt Wiens can, either. And they haven't even reached the cliff. It isn't unusual for inexperienced runners to push too hard and then run out of energy."

"Something doesn't look right with Jandi," Bhaaj said.

Mason glanced at her. "What do you mean?"

"She keeps stumbling."

"She's going to fall," Angel said.

"No!" Bhaaj stood up, realizing what Jandi intended. Her mind, misinterpreting the intensity of her reaction, flipped her into combat mode, and the scene seemed to unfold in slow motion. Jinda stumbled again—and toppled into Tam. Both athletes went down in a crash that left them sprawled on the dirt path. As Jinda groaned, Tam's face contorted with pain.

"Damn it!" Bhaaj said. "Jinda tripped her on purpose!"

"Bhaaj." Mason stood up next to her. "It looked like an accident."

She lowered her voice so the others couldn't hear her. "It was deliberate. Trust me, I know." Bhaaj could still hear Jinda's voice in the shadow-mesh café: *We'll get rid of them.*

They watched as Tam and Andi sat up. Medics converged on them, but both athletes waved them away. The commentators were going bonkers, delighted to have something happen in the hours-long event.

"Both runners went down!" the man was saying. "It's bad!"

"They fell into each other when Jinda tried to pass Wiens."

"You think Wiens tripped her on purpose?"

Bhaaj swore under her breath. "Why do they assume it's the Undercity runner?" Tam was obviously in pain, holding her ankle.

"It looked like Jinda did it on purpose," Tallmount said, coming to stand with Bhaaj.

"Wait—Jinda is on her feet!" the man said. "She's telling the medic she doesn't need help."

"Wiens is moving more slowly," the woman said. "Both runners are losing time. They may have to say goodbye to the Olympics."

Angel came over to them. "Tam, get up. Come on. Not let them stop you."

"We need to go out there." Bhaaj turned down the feed, unable to listen to them go on about how this would destroy Tam's dreams. *Max, take me out of freaking combat mode.*

Done.

"You know we can't go to her," Mason said. "If we break the rules, it could disqualify her."

"I know." Bhaaj made herself stand still. Tam was struggling to her feet, clearly in trouble, but when a medic tried to help her, she waved her away.

"Why won't she take help?" That question came from someone else in the room, a young man on another team. Looking around, Bhaaj realized everyone was riveted to the holo-feed.

"She's probably afraid it will disqualify her," someone else said.

Tam finally regained her feet, her face strained. Three runners passed her and Andi, leaving them tied for seventh. When Tam spoke to the medic, the orbs recording the scene picked up her voice and sent it to everyone watching the feed. "Can I take a bandage and use it on myself? Would that disqualify me?"

"I can give you the bandage," the medic said. "You're allowed to accept it the same way you accept food and water at the support stations. You can get more medical help at those, too."

Andi was listening. With a grunt, she started walking, then fell into a slow jog. Another runner passed her, putting Andi in eighth and Tam in ninth.

"I'll take a bandage then," Tam said.

The medic was already going through her bag. She handed Tam a support bandage. "Use it to brace your ankle. I can't tell without a more thorough exam, but it looks like it's sprained. Did you hear anything snap, or have your health meds warned you it broke?"

"Not hear snap," Tam told her. "Meds not good enough to say more."

"What?" Mason demanded. "I thought they all took the regulation meds."

"So did I," Bhaaj said. "They don't like to, though. It's like pulling teeth with no anesthetic to get them to agree." Dryly she added, "Some of them would rather have their teeth pulled."

Tam sat down and slowly wrapped the bandage around her ankle, arranging it for support the way that Doctor Izaka had taught them during the team's first aid classes. When the medic tried to talk to her, Tam motioned her off. Agitated, Bhaaj turned up the commentator's feed.

"—doing her own medical treatment," the woman was saying.

"She's obviously in pain," the man said. "Her coaches should pull her out."

"No, they shouldn't," Bhaaj said.

"He has a point." Mason said. "You know Tam. She'll finish even if she has to crawl. She could make the injury worse, maybe enough that it won't recover in time for the Olympics. She may have lost her shot at the royal, but she still has the ten kay."

"She knows how to judge her condition," Bhaaj said. "My people learn at a young age not to push more than they can give. Until a few of years ago, we had no formal medical care." She hated seeing Tam in pain, not only from her ankle, but also from the knowledge of what she'd lost. Although Tam liked the ten-kilometer, the royal had been her dream. Had Jinda taken that from her? If Bhaaj hadn't heard Andi swear she'd get Undercity athletes disqualified, she might have accepted it as an accident. But now? She wanted an investigation.

Finished with her bandaging, Tam stood up and took a few steps. Wincing, she tried several more. Although she looked uncomfortable, the next steps came more easily. Walking with care, she limped along the path, resuming the race.

"Tam Wiens is staying in the marathon," the male commentator said. "She's in ninth now and moving slowly. She'll drop back in the rankings as other runners pass her."

"This is a death knell to any hopes she had for a strong finish here," the woman said. "She won't make the Olympic cutoff."

"That's true," the man said. "Though remember, for an ultra-marathon, you have a wider range of qualifying times."

"She'd still have to speed up. If her injury is as bad as it looks, that won't work."

Miserable on Tam's behalf, Bhaaj watched her limp along the path. "She's hurting."

"I wish we could do something," Mason said.

"I know we can't afford to take the entire team to another meet," Bhaaj said. "But surely we could manage one for Tam, give her another chance to qualify for the royal."

Mason thought about it. "Not many royal qualifying meets are left before the Olympics. The one on Deisha is in a month and anyone can sign up, but I think that's it. If Tam tries another ultra too soon, she could make her injury worse. It's not worth the risk." With regret, he said, "She can compete in other Olympics. She'll have plenty more opportunities."

"Yah." He had a point. She doubted Tam would see it that way, though.

Bhaaj turned up her subs in time to hear the female commentator say, "—it's heartbreaking. Until now the Raylicon team has done an amazing job. This set back is going to hurt."

On the screen, Tam picked up her pace, walking with more confidence. Bhaaj hoped it was because the bandage gave her good support, not because her ankle had gone numb. A man appeared, jogging up behind her—

"Eh," Angel commented in the same moment that Mason said, "Ho! Good job."

"The Raylicon team may still place a competitor in the royal," the male commentator said. "The man who just caught up with Wiens is Ruzik, the Undercity team captain."

As Ruzik fell into step with Tam, talking in a voice that didn't carry to the broadcast, the women commentator said, "Tayz Wilder from Raylicon isn't far behind. Wiens and Ruzik are in ninth, but if they continue to walk, Wilder will pass them."

Tam gestured at Ruzik, waving him forward. After a few more words of what looked like support, he took off, running in that easy lope of his, leaving Tam behind.

Bhaaj and Mason continued to watch, and over the next hour, more of the Raylicon team joined them in the lounge. When the display showed Wild catching up with Tam, a murmur went around their group. Wild slowed down to walk with Tam, clearly offering support. After she waved him on, he took off, and she kept going on her own.

When nothing else interesting happened, the commentators went back to their usual chitchat, until Bhaaj tuned them out. Although the view switched back to the leaders, she'd cleared it with the meet officials to let her beetle drones follow her runners at a distance. Her blue beetle provided a steady stream of Tam's progress, which Max showed above her gauntlet.

Mason eventually spoke. "Tam keeps looking at her wrist timer."

"She always does that when she's running," Bhaaj said.

"Not this much, though," he mused. "Maybe she's still trying to qualify."

"Max," Bhaaj said. "At Tam's current speed, could she qualify for the Olympics?"

"No," Max said, "She'd need to go faster. Not a lot, though."

They all waited, watching. Eventually they sat down, chatting, eating, watching.

Watching.

Watching.

Andi Jinda stayed in the race, but she soon fell behind. As Tam passed the Metropoli runner, Jinda shot her a glance that looked like pure hatred.

"Whoa," Mason said.

"You saw it too," Bhaaj said.

"Yeah. But one hostile look doesn't prove Jinda tripped her on purpose."

"I know." Bhaaj wanted to say more, but she held back, aware of the people around them.

When Tam reached the cliff, she made a choice Bhaaj had never seen before: she agreed to a safety harness. It was a rough ascent, a good three stories high, and Tam took it much slower than she climbed in the Undercity. At the top, she removed the harness and set off again, jogging in a slow but steady pace. She soon reached the last section of the course, leaving the countryside behind as she headed down a city street toward the stadium.

"She's going too fast," Mason protested. "Look at her face. She's in pain."

"It's enough, though," Max said.

"Enough what?" Bhaaj asked, aware of people turning to look.

"If Tam can maintain this pace for twenty more minutes," Max said. "She could beat the cutoff time to qualify for the Olympics."

"Yeah, and she may injure herself beyond her ability to recover in time." Mason swung around to Bhaaj. "Maybe we should insist she pull out of the race."

"Hell, no," Bhaaj said. "She'd never forgive us."

"She's hurting!" He looked even more distressed than Tam.

"Mason, this is our way of life. It's not the first time she's suffered an injury. If she thinks she can finish, I trust her judgment."

He spoke intently. "All right. But let's get down to the finish line. I want to be there when Ruzik, Wild and Tam come in."

"And Rockjan," someone said.

Looking around, Bhaaj saw Crinkles and Full-up sitting cross-legged on the floor. Crinkles motioned at the screen, which showed Rockjan scaling the cliff without a harness. The meet strongly cautioned against such a choice, but Undercity runners hated the harness. They had no safety anything when they scaled Undercity cave-ins or walls. Rockjan scrambled up the cliff and vaulted over the top, easily landing on her feet, then resumed running at an even pace.

"What about Strider's group?" Bhaaj asked.

"Here," Max said. The view from her gauntlet switched to the feed from her green drone and showed Strider and Lamp jogging at a slow pace. "They're tied for twenty-eighth." The scene changing again, zooming in on Kiro and Zee walking together. Kiro seemed exhausted. "It looked like Kiro would have to drop out a while back," Max added. "Zee stayed with him at the support station. After he rested, they started up again. My guess? They'll finish. Last, but I don't think they'll quit. Three other competitors have already dropped out."

"Huh." Mason shook his head. "Amazing."

"He's stronger than we gave him credit for," Bhaaj said. At first she'd worried about the way Strider's group pushed Kiro. He'd improved dramatically since he'd joined them, though, both in running and in tykado. He'd just needed teammates who believed in him.

She and Mason went to the coach's area at the track, leaving their athletes in the lounge. By the time they arrived, warm in the late afternoon of the Metropoli spring day, the fourth and fifth-place finishers were coming in, a man and woman from Metropoli B. Vanya Longbow had already finished in first, winning the gold for the second year in a row. Manuel Rodriuez took the silver and Canda Azi the bronze.

A dull roar rose from the stadium crowd, a packed audience that had also gathered for the final ceremonies that would take place after the marathons. The sixth-place runner had entered the stadium, and she waved to the crowd as she did her final lap. When she crossed the finish, she slowed down, heaving in air while her team clustered around her.

Another shout went up with the crowd, and Bhaaj turned to see Ruzik enter the stadium. He did his final lap with the same steady pace he'd used throughout the race. Although he'd stopped a few times at stations along the way, he'd never flagged. He cruised into seventh place, then grinned as the Raylicon support team gathered around him. Not long after, Wild came in eighth, to another appreciative if dutiful roar from the crowd, and the same for the ninth-place finisher.

When Tam jogged into the stadium in tenth place, the crowd rose to their feet with thundering applause. Startled, Bhaaj flicked her on audio.

"—she can still make it in time to qualify!" the woman was saying. "An incredible showing by this runner who took an injury that nearly dropped her out of the race!"

"She never gave up!" the man said. "She never faltered. Yet she only has seconds left."

"She's so depleted," the woman said. "Can she make it?"

Indeed, Tam came down the final stretch with her face contorted in pain, her stride jagged and unsteady. An orb spun above her, lit up with how much time Tam had left to finish the race and still qualify for the Olympics. It showed less than ten seconds.

"Saints almighty," Mason whispered. Then he bellowed. "Come on, Tam! You can do it!"

Bhaaj heard herself shouting, heard Ruzik and Wild yelling. Tam put on a final surge, her pace so ragged now that she was almost falling. The orb counted down the seconds, three, two—

With a cry of pain, Tam lurched across the finish line and collapsed on the ground, her entire body shaking. As Bhaaj ran with Mason and

Doctor Izaka over to her, other medics gathered as well. The commentators were yelling and the crowd roared. Ignoring it all, Bhaaj knelt by Tam.

"You all right?" she asked, her voice low and urgent. "You okay?"

Tam rolled onto her back, gasping, her face drawn. "I—make it?"

"Yah." Bhaaj's voice shook. "You make Olympics."

"Good." Tam closed her eyes. "Done," she added. "For today."

"—get her on an air-stretcher," Doctor Izaka was saying. "Get her to the medical center!"

Within moments the medics were ferrying Tam away from the track, headed for the stadium hospital with Bhaaj and Mason running at their side.

CHAPTER XVIII
Challengers

Bhaaj paced the waiting room of the med center. She couldn't sit. Mason wasn't doing any better. He kept walking over to a holopodium to talk to the EI nurse. It gave him the same answer every time: A medic would come soon to talk to them.

At first almost the entire team crowded into the waiting room, Undercity and Cries athletes alike, even Rockjan who'd finished only a few minutes after Tam. Mason sent most of them back to the hotel, but he let the captains stay, both Ruzik and Wild. They stood together, too tense to talk. The blue walls of the room did their job, which was to look calming, like the holoart of landscapes that floated in front of them. Bhaaj didn't feel the least bit soothed.

A door across the room slid open, and a woman in the blue scrubs of a doctor walked out. She headed to where Mason was talking again to the holographic EI nurse.

"Coach Qazik?" the doctor asked.

Mason swung around with a start. "Ah! Yes. Yes, that's me. Do you have news on Tam?"

As Bhaaj, Ruzik, and Wild joined them, the doctor said, "She's resting. She'll be fine."

Bhaaj spoke tensely. "And her ankle?"

"A sprain," the doctor said. "A bad one. She made it worse by running on it for so long. But it will heal." She gave Mason and Bhaaj stern looks. "You must make sure she stays off it for at least five days. It's vital if she is going to race again this year. I gave her repair meds allowed by the IAC, and those will help her heal faster, but she needs to let her body rest."

"We'll take care of it," Mason said in the same moment Bhaaj said, "Understood." She'd make sure Tam rested that ankle if she had to hold her down herself.

"I'm going to keep her here for a couple more hours," the doctor said. "You can pick her up this evening. I'll comm you. She'll be ready to walk by then as long as she uses motor-crutches."

Relief flowed over Bhaaj. "Doctor, thank you. That's good news."

Mason nodded, preoccupied, for some reason staring at the holicons above his gauntlet. Glancing at the doctor, he said, "Thank you. We appreciate all you've done."

Not good, Bhaaj thought. Mason sounded even more tense now than before.

As soon as the doctor left, Mason turned to Bhaaj. "I need to talk to you. In private."

"*Disqualified?*" Bhaaj stared at him in disbelief. "The *entire* Undercity contingent?"

Mason was angrier than Bhaaj had ever seen him. "It's bullshit. How could Undercity runners be genetically engineered? Most of your kids don't even have full nanomed series." They were back in Mason's suite with their tech turned off, private for now. "Who the blazes did this supposed engineering? It takes years. You've had one doctor for your entire population, and she's only been there for a few years."

"It'll never hold up," Bhaaj said. "The medics here tested everyone before we competed. They didn't find anything remotely illegal."

Mason heaved in a breath, then spoke in a more even voice. "We need to stay calm when we respond." He sounded as if he were talking to himself more than her. "They're fast-tracking the investigation, but we probably can't leave tomorrow."

Yet another blow to their struggling finances. "We can't afford to put the team up for another night in the hotel, or the charges for changing so many tickets."

Mason nodded. "I'll ask the meet officials to get the team re-tested tomorrow in time for their flights. That way, we can send most of them home. You and I can stay, along with the team captains, Ruzik and Wild. Also Hyden."

"I'll stay, absolutely. But why Hyden?" Her fury was big enough now that it extended to anyone above-city, especially the privileged kids of billionaires.

Mason spoke tightly. "Because they also disqualified him."

Bhaaj felt as if she'd run into a wall. "What?"

"His father contacted the tournament and said Hyden didn't have permission to compete."

Bhaaj scowled. "Hyden is twenty-freaking-four years old. He's an adult."

"Not by Imperialate law." Mason looked ready to punch holes in the sky. "If his father wants to play the 'legal minor' card, the committee must honor his decision."

"Why did he wait until *after* Hyden competed?"

"I've no idea." More quietly, Mason said, "I think he was hoping Hyden wouldn't qualify for the Olympics. Then he wouldn't have had to worry."

"That's inexcusable." Bhaaj couldn't believe it. "And this claim by the Metropoli teams that we have an unfair advantage because living on Raylicon is like training at high altitudes—so what? Anyone can train at high altitudes. If we start penalizing teams because they come from different biospheres, then home teams should be penalized because they *don't* have to adapt. We should demand they disqualify the Metropoli teams." She knew it was ridiculous, but that just underlined the absurdity of these protests.

To her surprise, Mason said, "I've already registered that complaint."

"You're kidding."

"No." With a bitter smile, he added, "Apparently you and I think alike. Great minds and all."

She took a breath, calming her pulse. "They included Kiro with the Undercity athletes."

"I corrected that. But the House of Kaaj still want him and Ruzik disqualified."

Kaaj? It was one of the most conservative noble Houses. "Whatever for?"

"Because," Mason stated. "They claim Kiro and Ruzik used inappropriate sexual behaviors to distract Kaaj runners during the royal marathon and so affect their times."

"I didn't think this could get any stupider," Bhaaj said. "What are they talking about?"

"At one point in the marathon, Ruzik took off his shirt. Kaaj claims he did it as a distraction, because it's well known the House of Kaaj requires their men to wear robes in public. Here, look." Mason tapped his gauntlet and a holoscreen activated on the wall. Its display showed Ruzik running in the marathon, sweating profusely in the midday heat. He pulled off his tank top and wiped his face, then tied it to a loop on his shorts, never once breaking his stride.

"I don't see the problem," Bhaaj said. "A lot of men take off their shirt when it gets hot."

"Watch again. Not Ruzik, but the woman about ten meters behind him." Mason tapped his band, and the scene replayed, showing Ruzik well ahead of a woman with the Kaaj insignia on her clothes. As he took off his shirt, she did a double take, then stumbled and fell. For a moment she just sat, looking stunned. Then she got up and continued running.

"Ruzik didn't break any rules." Bhaaj snorted. "It isn't his fault Kaaj women can't deal with handsome men who don't live like we're a thousand years in the past."

"They claim our athletes targeted their runners deliberately. They think that's why Kiro did the royal even though he's a sprinter." Mason brought up a new display that showed Kiro jogging through the countryside with Zee at his side. When they passed a Kaaj runner standing by a wall, resting, Kiro smiled absently at her and continued on his way.

"I don't get it," Bhaaj said. "Your people always smile, everywhere."

Mason spoke dryly. "Kaaj men don't smile at women except those of their family."

Bhaaj was so baffled, it even blunted her anger. "They can't expect everyone to follow their customs. Besides, Kiro and Zee came in last. That Kaaj runner beat them by nearly an hour."

"Kaaj is trying to establish a pattern of behavior to support their claim against Ruzik." Mason sighed. "If he's disqualified, their runner gets a nudge up in her interstellar ranking, enough to qualify for the Olympics that way."

"We need to challenge this," Bhaaj said. "Female athletes wear just as skimpy clothing, and no one accuses them of inappropriate behavior. Hell, Azarina is a Majda and they're even more conservative than Kaaj." She snorted. "We better watch out. Azarina might lose control if Ruzik runs by her in tight shorts and no shirt."

Mason gave a wan smile, but it immediately faded. "Two officials on the committee come from stricter backgrounds, enough that they might see merit in the accusations." He spoke dryly. "I don't know if you've noticed, but Azarina *does* look uncomfortable when she's surrounded by men wearing only running shorts."

"You're kidding." It didn't fit the forward-thinking young woman Bhaaj had come to know.

"I'm not saying she'd protest or even comment on it," Mason added. "But she's from one of the most socially conservative families in the Imperialate."

"Yah. Except her own brother talked the family into letting him go to college."

"Even so," Mason said. "Her father lives in seclusion and never leaves the palace unless he's robed from head to toe. Even if she doesn't agree with more senior members of her household, she grew up saturated with those views. We just better hope no one on the panel feels the same."

Bhaaj wished she had someplace to put her anger. "At least they can't disqualify Tam. We filled out that form for her."

"Yeah, but guess what?" Mason gestured as if throwing away papers. "Metropoli wants her disqualified for accepting too much medical aid after her fall."

"The medic gave her the go-ahead!" Bhaaj spoke firmly. "We need to register our own protest. Andi Jinda deliberately tripped Tam."

"Done already. Unfortunately, that fall looks like an accident."

"Yah, well, you haven't heard Jandi talk down the Undercity on the shadow mesh."

Mason raised his eyebrows. "And you have?"

She met his gaze. "That's right. I made a recording of it."

"You can't submit it as legal evidence."

"These investigations aren't legal proceedings."

"Even so, they'll probably refuse to see it." Mason inhaled, then slowly let out his breath. "I do think we have a good chance of winning these cases. Except for Hyden." He lifted his hands, then dropped them. "Zaic knew his son planned to compete long before we left Raylicon. He never said no. And I forget that legally Hyden *isn't* an adult. Neither of us realized his parents hadn't signed the form until his father lodged his complaint. No way will the committee here go against someone as powerful as the CEO of Scorpio Corporation."

Although Bhaaj doubted she'd ever feel comfortable with Hyden, she'd discovered she rather liked him when he wasn't swaggering. "I don't see how his father could do this to him." How could their wonderful meet turn into such a disaster?

Mason looked miserable. "We need to call a team meeting."

Only twelve Undercity athletes remained in the waiting room of the med center, but they looked as annoyed now as when everyone had arrived earlier today for their tests. The medics were working quickly, but it had still taken several hours.

Rockjan looked ready to knife someone, leaning against the wall with her arms crossed, her scarred biceps bulging. Bhaaj walked over and spoke in a low voice. "Not hurt medics."

"Screw medics," Rockjan muttered.

"Not medics' fault," Bhaaj said.

Rockjan gave her a withering gaze. "Then screw Metrop."

"Not by fighting." Bhaaj met her gaze. "They *want* you to get mad. Make you attack. Make you break rules. Then they say you out and we can't argue." She tapped the gauntlet on Rockjan's wrist. "Keep record. Not say shit. Not make rumble. Do tests. Prove them wrong."

"Maybe let them live," Rockjan allowed.

Bhaaj just nodded. Rockjan was joking—she hoped. Even a slight deviation from "perfect" behavior by Undercity athletes, particularly now, would ruin their chances for participating in the interstellar sports community. Too many people wanted them to fail, just waiting for a misstep, and if they didn't make one, apparently those who wanted them gone would fabricate one.

The doctor opened the door and looked around the room. "Rockjan?"

"Eh." Rockjan pushed away from the wall and stalked over to her.

"Uh, yes, um, please come with me." The woman indicated the doorway and Rockjan strode through it, followed by the flustered doctor. In the room beyond, Bhaaj could see another doctor talking to

Shiv Kajada. At least no one had complained that two of the Undercity athletes had the same names as the drug cartels.

After the medic closed the door, Bhaaj looked around. Although she'd talked to most of the kids here, she still had Strider's team. She went over and pulled up a chair to sit with them.

"Hate this," Strider said.

"They really take it all from us?" Lamp asked.

"Nahya," Bhaaj assured him. "Tests show you not cheat." She regarded them steadily. "You be calm during test, yah? Polite."

Strider snorted. "Po-fuck-them-lite."

"Eh." Bhaaj had no disagreement there. She turned to Kiro. "They not ask to test you."

He shrugged. "I stay."

She hesitated, worried. "Kiro, listen. You have some of the highest quality, most expensive meds a person can carry in their body. The Metropoli doctors okayed them as within the athletic standard, but I can't guarantee they won't change their minds, given the current situation. You could be risking everything if you let them test you."

He met her gaze. "They test my team. I part of team. We together."

Bhaaj nodded, noting that he used the Undercity dialect with the three-syllable word *together* to give honor instead of ridicule.

Strider also noticed. "Kiro our fourth." She spoke firmly. "We not let them pull us apart."

"I ken." It was breaking Bhaaj's heart, seeing them go through this, knowing all they'd done to get here, and now it could collapse beneath them.

Kiro sat on the edge of the exam-bed with machines and holoscreens arrayed around his seat. The man standing in front of him looked exhausted.

"My greetings," he told Kiro. "I'm Doctor Oxard." He sounded as if he'd said the words a million times. "This won't take long." He was already scanning Kiro. One of the machines snicked out a needle and took a blood sample with barely a prick on Kiro's skin.

In the next exam-bed over, the female doctor was talking to Strider, who sat with her long legs dangling off the bed. After a moment, Strider's doctor looked over at Oxard. "It's the same for this one. No doping or engineering of any form. She doesn't even have *meds* in her body."

Kiro glanced at Strider. *Should take meds,* he thought.
Not like, she told him.
Even so. They help.
Will think about, she allowed.

"I've got everything I need," the woman told Strider. "You can go."
That was fast, Kiro thought as Strider slid off the bed.
Not for you. She sounded worried.

Kiro focused on his doctor, who was squinting at holos above his pad. "Is anything wrong?"

The fellow looked up with a start. "You have Abyss Series-A nanomeds in your body."

"That's right." Kiro tensed, feeling as if he would fold into a knot.

"How?" Oxard seemed more confused than anything else. "No other athletes on your team have such expensive meds, not even those from the City of Cries."

"My meds were cleared when we first got tested, before the meet." This was the same doctor, in fact, who'd tested him then.

"What? Oh, yes, I know. They're fine. I just don't understand how an Undercity native got such high-end medical treatment. We didn't think that was possible."

And there it goes, Kiro thought with bitter triumph. He wondered if Oxard realized he'd just admitted no one considered it possible that someone from the Undercity could even have high-end meds, which meant no way could they have the more expensive and lengthy genetic engineering needed to design their bodies so they could run better than other humans. Good thing he'd set his wristband on record. It could prove useful if Raylicon moved ahead with a discrimination case against the Metropoli Athletic Committee.

"I'm not from the Undercity," Kiro said. "I live in Cries. My mother is an Abyss exec." He regarded the doctor with the implacable gaze he'd learned from Zee. "I attend Cries University."

Oxard gaped at him. "I'd never have guessed that! You look Undercity."

So everyone tells me. Except Doctor Rajindia had found no trace that he had any relatives in the Undercity, let alone a father. Although her DNA database didn't include every person in the aqueducts, she had a good portion of them. If he had an Undercity family, something should have come up. However, his DNA probably wasn't unique to the Undercity; they all had the same ancestors. As far as he knew, his biological father piloted star-yachts for wealthy people with too little to do in their lives.

He didn't want to offend the doctor and risk making him change his mind about the meds, so he forced a smile. "We all come from the same world. It only has a population of a few million. With such a small gene pool, we tend to look more alike."

"Ah. Yes." Oxard's surprise faded. "Anyway, you're fine." He sighed. "All you kids are fine. This genetic challenge is stupid, and this investigation is a waste of everyone's time."

Ho! Kiro beamed, knowing his wristband had recorded that priceless comment. Since he hadn't asked for the doctor's consent, they couldn't use the record in a formal proceeding, but Coach Bhaaj would find a way to get it in front of any panel that needed to hear it.

After Strider and the others finished, the four of them left the med center with higher spirits. Perhaps it would be okay—if he didn't get kicked out for freaking *smiling* at another runner. It would have flattered him to know the Kaaj women considered him so good-looking that he distracted their runners, except they'd turned it into a weapon to wield against his dreams.

"The Boston Marathon," Bhaaj told Hyden. "You must have heard of it."

"Well, sure, yeah." He stood in the living room of her suite, his face tired, his gaze hollowed. "Everyone runner knows that race. But what does it matter? My father would get me disqualified from that one, too."

"He can't," Bhaaj made herself stop pacing. "On Earth, you legally became an adult at eighteen. They aren't going to disqualify you. If anything, given how much our IAC annoys them for requiring men and women to compete together, they'll probably be happy to help. And Boston is an Olympic-qualifying event."

"It's too late for me to sign up."

"You still have a few days," she assured him. "We know people we can talk to there, and your time from this meet qualifies you. The Earthers already think Skolians are idiots for making twenty-five our age of legal majority." Especially since Imperialate law allowed minors to enlist at eighteen. The Allieds didn't buy the Skolian claim that modern civilization required greater maturity than most eighteen-year-olds exhibited, whereas the military offered them structure and guidance. Bhaaj didn't care. The Undercity had no official age of maturity. In a culture where until recently most people didn't live past their twenties, adulthood came early.

Hope flickered on Hyden's face, then died. "It won't work, Coach. I mean, I appreciate what you're doing, and I'd love to run in the Boston Marathon, but even if I get an Olympic qualifying time there, my father won't let me compete at the Olympics and my mother supports him."

Bhaaj felt his anger burning, that his own parents had crushed his dreams. She spoke with care. "When I first tried to enlist, I was fifteen. They wouldn't take me. I came back at sixteen and they took me, but they put me in school instead of letting me fight. Said I had to wait two years." She shrugged. "I didn't want to wait. So I applied to become an emancipated minor. The process took a while, but I became a legal adult at seventeen and shipped out with the troops." Her gaze never wavered. "You're in a far better position to get emancipated status. You've completed college. You've held high-powered jobs. You've years of showing you operate fine as an adult."

Hope battled with resignation in his expression. "My father will try to stop me."

"Yah. It won't work."

He spoke bitterly. "He'll pay the judge to rule against me."

"It's not as easy to corrupt the system as you think." At least, she hoped.

"I suppose it's worth a try." Hyden stood up straighter. "How do I register for Boston?"

"We'll take care of it." She thought for a moment. "We can't afford to stay long on Earth or put you up at more than a low-quality motel, but we can get you there."

"I can help. I've money saved." He winced. "You stopped me in the casino before I lost it all."

Bhaaj scowled at him. "You shouldn't gamble there. You'll never win. Jak rigs everything."

"You shouldn't say that. He might retaliate—" He stopped, then said, "Oh. Yeah. I forgot. You're married to him."

She smiled slightly. "I put up with him."

Hyden hesitated. "When are you having the baby?"

What the blazes? "How did you know?"

"We've all figured it out." He spoke awkwardly. "You're starting to show, Coach."

"Oh." Bhaaj instinctively put her hand on her stomach. Since she learned about the baby, she'd been careful to eat well, and she'd put on a few pounds. Her bump barely felt noticeable, but apparently it was enough. "It won't be long after the Olympics."

Alarm flashed over his face. "Does that mean you aren't coming?"

"I'll be there. My husband, too." Jak had insisted.

"But is it safe to travel that late in a pregnancy?"

His concern touched Bhaaj. "It's all right. I'll be seven months when we leave for Foreshires Hold. Nowadays starships are better protected against radiation even than some planets with thick atmospheres. And I'll take extra precautions." Although in earlier centuries, space travel for a pregnant woman had carried risks, nowadays it had become safe and common.

He still looked worried. "By the time the Games finish, won't you be too far along to travel?"

"I plan to have the baby there." She and Jak had already contacted a clinic on Foreshires. "No worries, I'll be at the Olympics." In a firm voice, she added, "And so will you."

"I hope so." He grinned, some of his confidence returning. "I'll blast it out in Boston."

"I'll bet you do."

When he left, his step seemed lighter. Bhaaj hoped it worked out, for Hyden and for the rest of the team.

They had a lot to do in just a few days.

CHAPTER XIX
Resolutions

"We have gone over the medical reports in detail," Director Myr said, seated behind the judge's bench in one of the hotel's conference rooms. He glanced at the other three people at the bench, two women and another man. Together, the four of them made up the panel hearing the protests against Raylicon. When the others nodded, the director turned back to the people gathered in the room.

Bhaaj sat with Mason at a table to the right of a cleared area before the bench. Six coaches, two each from the three Metropoli teams, sat at a longer table to the left. The onlookers were in a makeshift gallery with folding chairs that the hotel staff had set up this morning, the area separated from the panel by a railing at waist height. Bhaaj appreciated how fast the committee had moved to address the protests. This morning session left the team time to reach the starport and catch their evening flight to Raylicon.

"We haven't found a single case of illegal enhancement in any Raylicon athlete," Myr said. "Nor have we found any indication of genetic engineering."

A murmur ran through the people crammed into the room, relief from some and hostility from others. Bhaaj glanced at Mason, and he gave her a shaky smile. They'd overcome one hurdle.

The director wasn't done, however. "In fact," he said, his voice stern as he spoke to Mason and Bhaaj. "Some of your athletes don't have the basic nanomed series expected to ensure they maintain their health." He frowned at them. "Your Undercity team members look like they haven't had proper healthcare most of their lives. Signs of broken and improperly set bones, scars from knives, bullet wounds—it's appalling."

Bhaaj stared at him in disbelief. He had *no* freaking idea. It had taken huge steps just getting Cries to recognize that her people *existed*. Prior to a few years ago, no doctor would see anyone from the Undercity. That had only begun to change in recent years since Bhaaj began serving as a liaison, especially after the military discovered her people had something they desperately needed.

Myr added, "I hope you can provide the healthcare for your team that they've lacked."

Like we aren't already trying? Even as Bhaaj tensed, Mason kicked her foot under the table. Forcing herself to stay put, she just nodded to Director Myr.

"In any case," Myr continued. "We're dismissing the case against the Undercity athletes on genetic engineering and reinstating their results, including their medals and Olympic qualifications."

A subdued cheer went up from the gallery. The Undercity athletes didn't say much, but they indicated their approval with that thumbs-up gesture from Earth that had become universal among athletes. The Cries runners made more noise, all of it approving, which seemed to startle the other people listening, mostly members of the teams that lodged the protests. A few athletes from those teams seemed angry, but most looked relieved. Apparently they hadn't liked the protests, either.

"Now to the Metropoli claim that Raylicon athletes should be disqualified for the advantage of living on a world with a lower concentration of oxygen in the air," Myr said. "And the Raylicon claim that Metropoli athletes should be disqualified for living on the world where the meet took place." He gave them incredulous looks, both the Metropoli coaches and Bhaaj and Mason. "These protests are ridiculous, and you all know it. No panel has ever disqualified anyone because we all come from different colonies. We couldn't hold the Olympics otherwise. So deal with it."

"Good for him," Mason said under his breath.

"Yah." Bhaaj hadn't expected either protest to go anywhere.

The director then said, "In regard to the claim that Tam Wiens accepted illegal help, we find that she did not. As to the claim that Andi Jinda tripped her on purpose, we find no evidence of that, either. Both cases are dismissed."

"Damn it," Bhaaj muttered.

Mason spoke in a barely audible voice. "They didn't disqualify Tam. That's what matters."

The panel officials conferred among themselves, and then one of them spoke, a woman named Dean Claymore. "Regarding the claim that Ruzik and Kiro Caballo deliberately tried to disrupt the performance of the Kaaj runners, we are split; two of us have voted to uphold the disqualification and two have voted against it."

"What the hell?" someone said in the audience.

Bhaaj had no idea who spoke, but they expressed her sentiments exactly. As she stood up to protest the protest, Dean Claymore held up her hand. "Given the deadlock, we will allow reps from both teams to make a statement before we reach a final decision. We will break for an hour to give you time to prepare." With that, she banged her gavel on the bench, a habit they'd picked up from the Earthers, and declared the hearing closed for lunch.

Bhaaj sat down again. "It's ridiculous. I can't believe half that panel agreed."

Mason looked miserable. "I was afraid this might happen."

"I'll do whatever I can to help prepare a statement." She wasn't comfortable with public speaking, but she'd learned to manage over the years.

"I already put something together, just in case." He smiled dryly. "I figured I'd better make sure they didn't get a certain coach from the Raylicon team telling them to go eff themselves."

Bhaaj winced. "I'm on my best behavior, I promise. But yah, you should speak."

A commotion came from the gallery, and Bhaaj turned to see some of the athletes trying to get past the guard keeping the audience contained. She got up and went over to them.

"You can't come in," the guard was saying, his voice tense.

Rockjan regarded him with an impassive stare. "We talk to coach."

"It's all right," Bhaaj told the guard. "I'll go out there."

As he moved aside, watching Bhaaj with suspicion, she went into the gallery, leaving Mason at the table to work on his statement. The

Raylicon athletes gathered around her, Undercity and Cries alike. Even Tam had come to offer her support, leaning on robotic crutches that supported her weight. Kiro stayed back, his expression crestfallen. He was obviously tired from the royal. It would have been fine, given how happy he'd been to finish, but now he looked as if he had nothing left. Ruzik didn't seem worn out, not even after his marathon yesterday. He stood to one side, his face cold and his arms crossed, his tattooed muscles bulging. Angel stood with him, her expression and posture just as formidable. All the Undercity kids looked angry, now on behalf of Ruzik and Kiro.

"I don't understand," Wild was saying. "How can they do this? I mean, hell, I took my shirt off too during the marathon."

"Yeah, but you didn't do it while passing some entitled Kaaj girly," Tanzia Harjan said.

"We'll deal with it." Bhaaj wished she could assure them that she and Mason would make it go away, but it didn't matter how outrageous they considered the protest if the panel ruled it valid. "For now, you all need to get to the starport. Coach Tena will get you set for the flight to Raylicon."

Kiro stepped forward, edging past Rockjan. "Coach, can I stay?" Although he kept his face neutral, she couldn't miss his reaction. He felt as if he'd attained his heart's desire and then had it yanked away, destroying his work, dreams, efforts, and joy."

Strider came to stand with him. "We all stay, yah?" She put her hand on Kiro's shoulder. "It affects us all."

Bhaaj knew they couldn't afford to have all four of them stay; the penalties for changing their flights at this late date would kill their already decimated budget. But she couldn't say no. She'd liquidate more of her retirement funds to cover their costs. "All right. You can all stay."

She spent the hour helping Tena get the team off to the starport. Other audience members also left, a few grumbling, but most just going on their way. Three Kaaj reps stayed in their seats working, regal and aloof in their aristocratic assumption of privilege. In some ways, they were worse than the Majdas. Yah, sure, the Majdas intimidated just about everyone alive and ranked at the top of Imperialate social hierarchies even in this modern time when an elected Assembly formed the government. It didn't matter that the age had long passed when their barbaric warrior queens dominated civilization with their rampaging armies. Now they wielded their power through their financial empire.

The Kaaj noblewomen held less sway than the Majdas, but that only increased their intent to establish superiority. Bhaaj felt their response in every glance they deigned to send her Undercity athletes. The House of Kaaj considered them little more than detritus to sweep away.

As the three Kaaj reps took their places at the table on the left, Bhaaj returned to the table where Mason had stayed. When she sat down, he said, "I think I'm ready."

"Good." To herself she added, "Diplomacy."

More than an hour had passed, but the judges still hadn't reconvened. Instead, they were conferring again, discussing some tiny holos floating above Director Myr's armband.

"I wonder what's up," Mason said.

"I've no clue." Bhaaj wished they'd get this done. She could feel Kiro aching and Ruzik simmering.

Director Myr looked up. "We've had a request from one of the Raylicon team members."

Mason got to his feet. "I'm not aware of any request."

"It just came through." Myr glanced at the holos, then up at Mason. "Azarina Majda would like to make a statement."

"What?" Bhaaj stood up. "That's not appropriate." The last thing they needed was a Majda weighing in on this issue, besides which, Azarina couldn't speak without an okay from her coaches.

She can if the panel allows it, Max thought.

We are royally screwed, Bhaaj answered. *Both literally and figuratively.*

"We will include your protest in the record," Director Myr told her. Turning to the Kaaj reps, he asked, "Do you protest?"

One of the women spoke. "We would be honored to hear from the House of Majda."

"Not good," Mason muttered. "What the blazes is Azarina doing?"

"I don't know." Bhaaj had no clue.

The panel continued to sit, silent, so after an awkward moment, Bhaaj and Mason sat down.

They all waited.

After about ten minutes, Director Myr said, "I apologize for the delay. Apparently Lady Azarina needed some time to get here."

Lady Azarina. Great. Just great. By acknowledging Azarina's title, which she never used with the team, they gave their tacit support to the privilege she enjoyed with her royal heritage.

"I don't get it," Mason said in a low voice. "I thought Azarina was here in the hotel."

"She wasn't in the gallery." It had surprised Bhaaj. That didn't seem like Azarina, not to show up in support of the team.

They all sat, waiting.

Waiting.

Just as Bhaaj was about to stand again, Director Myr got another message. After reading it, he looked up and said, "She's arrived in the hotel. It should just be a moment."

Bhaaj looked at Mason and he looked back at her.

They waited.

Voices suddenly came from outside the double doors of the room. They swung inward, leaving Azarina framed in the entrance. She appeared every inch the aristocrat, from her straight black hair, high cheekbones, classic nose, and dark skin. For a moment she looked at them all.

Then she stepped aside—and an older woman strode into the room.

Azarina might be a civilized, toned-down version of the barbarian queens who had ruled Raylicon in ages past, but this woman could have been the genuine article. Well over six feet tall, she walked with the assurance of a sovereign. Steel grey streaked the black hair she wore pulled back, just like steel seemed to permeate the aura of power that surrounded her. The medals and gold braid on her army uniform glinted, and her austere features spoke to a career lived at the highest levels in an interstellar empire, not only as the Majda Matriarch but also as General of the Pharaoh's Army, a joint commander for one of the most massive military machines in human history.

Vaj Majda had arrived.

Everyone in the room jumped to their feet, the judges included. In an almost inaudible voice, Mason said, "That's it. We've lost."

As far as Bhaaj knew, Vaj hadn't already been on Metropoli, which meant Azarina must have personally asked her to make the trip, probably yesterday after they knew about the protest. No wonder

Azarina had been late this morning. She must have gone to meet Vaj's ship at the port. But why would Vaj agree? That was no small ask by her niece. Besides, the general *knew* Ruzik. She'd met both him and Angel, and she'd agreed with recruiting Angel as a telop.

She doesn't know them well, though, Max thought. **Also, given the Majda support of the team, the behavior of your athletes affects their reputation. The last thing they'd want is for the public to think they encouraged inappropriate sexual behavior among men.**

He had a point. A damn good one. But still. *When have you ever known the Majdas to give a flying fuck about what people think? They do what they want.*

Yes. Exactly. Including treating their princes like we're still in the dark ages.

As much as Vaj frustrated Bhaaj, both in her lack of understanding about the Undercity and her ingrained assumption of privilege, the general also impressed her. Besides, Vaj served a male Imperator, the man who commanded the entire military, and nearly half the people in the army Vaj commanded were men. The general had adapted.

That doesn't mean she wanted to adapt, Max said.

True. But she hired Randall Miyashiro as her tykado master and promoted Duane Ebersole to a captain on her security forces. She didn't have to do either.

And she often doesn't see it when she passes them over for assignments they deserve.

Bhaaj hated that he had a point. She hoped he was wrong.

The general came to a stop in the open area before the bench, between the tables where the coaches all now stood. The Kaaj reps looked stunned but pleased.

"We are greatly honored by your esteemed presence, your Royal Highness." Director Myr was practically stuttering. He left out some honorifics, and he should have said General instead of using a civilian title given that Vaj was in uniform, but Bhaaj doubted Vaj cared. She couldn't fathom why a joint commander of the Imperialate military would take time from her demanding schedule for this, or why Azarina had asked it of her. Did the young Majda woman really feel that uncomfortable about the men on the team?

"My thanks," Vaj said curtly. "If it pleases the bench, I would like to make a statement in regards to this case."

"Yes, yes, certainly, go ahead," Myr said. "You're welcome to."

"Thank you." Vaj looked around at everyone. "Please sit. It isn't necessary to stand."

Oh. Yah. Of course. Embarrassed, Bhaaj sat down, along with everyone else. Having known the Majdas for over four years didn't stop her from getting intimidated by Vaj.

The general wasted no time. "The House of Kaaj has protested the behavior of two young men on the Raylicon team, Ruzik, the Undercity captain, and Kiro Caballo from the City of Cries."

"That is correct," Director Myr said.

In her side vision, Bhaaj saw the Kaaj reps exchange glances. They looked relieved.

And indeed, Vaj continued with, "I have great respect for the House of Kaaj. I honor their line and I honor their customs. The House of Majda wishes that to be clear in the record."

"Thank you," Myr said. "We will do so. Are you asking that we honor their protest?"

Vaj regarded him with the formidable stare that had been the undoing of many a powerful foe. "I also know both Ruzik and Kiro Caballo. They are principled young men of good character, and neither would seek to cheat in any form, certainly not by deliberately acting in a disruptive manner. I ask that you dismiss this case against them and reinstate their results."

"Holy shit," Mason said, then turned red as everyone except Vaj turned to stare at him.

Myr cleared his throat, looking confused. The other members of the panel seemed too shocked to move.

After a moment, Myr spoke to the Kaaj reps. "Based on the character reference given by General Majda, would you be willing to drop your claims against the Raylicon athletes?"

The reps didn't even confer, they just looked stunned. The woman in the center said, "Of course. We honor the House of Majda and have great respect for their character reference. We hereby withdraw our claims against Ruzik and Kiro Caballo."

Ho! Just like that. No careful, lengthy arguments, no back and forth, no contentious debates. Nothing. Zilch. General Vaj Majda walked in, said *Drop it* and boom! The case vanished.

"Very well." Myr glanced at the panel, and they all nodded.

Turning to Vaj, he said, "Thank you for your statement, General Majda. We are honored that you took the time to speak here. We hereby drop all charges against Ruzik and Kiro Caballo and reinstate their results in the meet."

Vaj inclined her head to him. She glanced at Bhaaj and Mason with a look that clearly said, *Make your athletes behave,* then turned on her heel and strode from the room, sparing a nod for Azarina as she blew past her niece.

In the silence after the doors closed behind the general, Bhaaj turned to Mason. He met her gaze and spoke in a low voice only she could hear. "Azarina came through for us."

"Yah." She had no idea how Azarina convinced her aunt to come, but they owed her a debt.

Director Myr spoke, his voice subdued. "You have strong supporters, Coach Qazik."

"Apparently so." Mason looked as caught off guard as the Kaaj reps. Glancing at Ruzik and Kiro, Bhaaj saw their relief. Something deeper was going on with Ruzik, she wasn't sure what, but she suspected he knew what it meant for one of the most powerful authorities in the Imperialate to speak on behalf of an Undercity man.

"I guess we're finished." Director Myr banged his gavel. "We reinstate the results for all Raylicon athletes." He spoke to Mason and Bhaaj. "With one exception, unfortunately. I'm sorry I can't do anything for Hyden Laj. His disqualification must stand."

"We understand," Mason said.

With that, they headed out of the conference room. When Ruzik, Wild, and Strider's gang joined them, Kiro smiled at Bhaaj, making no effort to hide his joy. Although Ruzik kept a more neutral expression, Bhaaj felt his relief.

The hotel was quiet as they left the conference room, but voices came from somewhere distant. As they turned a corner, coming into view of the lobby entrance, a flood of sound swept over them. Holo-reporters clustered around the entrance, held back by Duane Ebersole, who stood firm in his uniform with his hand resting on the pulse revolver holstered at his hip.

Bhaaj stopped next to Duane while holocams blinked and hummed, and people called out questions. The athletes on the team stayed behind them, but they'd soon have to brave the walk across the lobby. The only other way out was to backtrack and leave via a rear entrance of the hotel, where she had no doubt reporters also waited, just in case.

Besides, she *wanted* to make a comment. Everyone seemed to have an opinion about the Undercity despite knowing almost nothing about it. The time had come for that to change.

Holding up his hand, Mason spoke to the gathered reporters. "The Metropoli Track and Field Committee has found no basis for any of the charges against any members of our team and has dismissed them all."

"It just came through the holo-feed," a woman said. Other reporters were reading glyphs scrolling above their armbands or gauntlets.

A man said, "Coach Bhaajan, do you have any comment about the accusations made against your Undercity athletes?"

Bhaaj regarded him steadily. "The accusations were baseless, unfounded, and prejudicial. None of our athletes cheated in any way, nor would they do so."

Another woman said, "Rumors say your athletes have *less* health treatments than they need. Is it true that the Undercity has no medical care, and your athletes have no health meds?"

Bhaaj wondered where she'd heard that. Officially, the panel couldn't release details of the hearing, only the results. Still, it bore a comment. "It is true that in the past, for most of our history, no doctors were willing to treat us, and we weren't eligible for healthcare." Which put that ugly policy in far nicer terms than it deserved. "However, we now have a clinic and are getting health meds for all our athletes."

The reporters kept asking questions, most of which Mason could answer. Finally a man said, "Coach Bhaajan, what do you say about the Undercity motto that's been all over the meshes?"

"Motto?" Bhaaj had no idea what he meant.

Another reporter repeated the words Angel had told reporters after the classic marathon. "Run fast, you live. Run slow, you die."

"Running is a way of life among my people," Bhaaj said. "It always has been. Even if we could afford mechanized transportation, we wouldn't use it because it damages ancient ruins in the Undercity. Some are thousands of years old."

More questions flooded them, until Bhaaj had difficulty making out who said what. She'd never expected they'd attract this attention. Before this meet, people knew only the ugly rep of the Undercity in the popular media. Her people made excellent villains because, except for the cartels, they'd never interacted with the rest of humanity. They kept off the grids that permeated civilization, only using them through shadowy backdoors. Anyone could say anything, and her people almost never even knew. Now, when they finally showed up in public, they shattered expectations.

The onslaught of questions was too much. Even as a mild empath, one trained to protect her mind, Bhaaj couldn't take the flood of moods. If she had so much difficulty, she could only imagine how it affected her runners.

"Duane," she said. "We need to get the kids out of here."

Stepping forward, he raised his voice. "All right. That's enough. Let the team through." With that, he moved into the throng like a steady, unstoppable train, deftly putting the reporters aside. Startled, they stepped back enough for Bhaaj and Mason to usher their athletes through the crowd. Ruzik brought up the rear. With Duane and Ruzik on the job, they made it to the lift and escaped the holo-casters. As the doors slid closed, Bhaaj heaved a sigh of relief.

"Noisy," Strider commented.

"Yah," Lamp said. "Talk too much."

"Glad pan fin," Ruzik said.

Mason squinted at him. "Sorry. I didn't get that."

"I'm glad the hearing panel finished and we're okay," Ruzik said.

"I *never* expected that," Kiro said.

Zee smiled at him. "We interest them."

"Yah." Strider laughed, her relief spilling into her voice. "We make good whispers, eh?"

"Metrop got no Whisper Mill to spread news," Lamp said.

"Sure they do," Ruzik told him. "They call it social media meshes."

The lift stopped and the doors snapped open. The empty foyer outside was a relief.

"Listen," Bhaaj said. "Go get ready to leave. If we hurry, we can still make our flights."

Bhaaj had company.

She knew someone waited in her hotel room even before she

opened the door. During her time in the army, they'd classified her ability to sense others as exceptional situational awareness. She realized now it came at least in part from her Kyle abilities, that at a low level she sensed their moods, not much, but enough that sometimes she'd detect a presence she couldn't see.

The mind of whoever waited inside came through with a strength that made her wary. *Max, put me in combat mode.*

Done, he answered.

Her senses sharpened, letting her hear, see, and smell better. Her body felt primed to fight.

"Open," she told the door.

It flashed a light across her face, then slid open. Bhaaj walked into the living room—

And stopped.

"General Majda." She blinked at the woman standing by the window, looking out at the spectacular panorama, not only the stadium but the city beyond, with its silver-and-mirrored towers.

The general turned to her. "My greetings, Major."

Bhaaj felt like she ought to salute. She'd been out of the army for many years, but with Vaj she tended to revert to a military mindset. Still, she just said, "My greetings, General. Thank you for speaking for Kiro and Ruzik at the hearing." To Max, she thought, *Combat mode off.*

"Azarina was upset," Vaj said.

Bhaaj went over to her. "I didn't realize she'd contacted you."

"She didn't, actually." Vaj studied her with that probing look that seemed to see straight into her. Although the general had even less Kyle ability than Bhaaj, she had a preternatural ability to put people off their guard. "She contacted her mother, my sister Corejida, and asked for help. My sister thought I'd be a more effective person to speak. I was traveling anyway, so I stopped here."

"We appreciate it." Bhaaj was the queen of understatement today. The General of the Pharaoh's Army didn't just make a "stop." Coming here had to have inconvenienced her—and she'd done it anyway. That support of their team meant just as much if not more than the financial backing that House of Majda provided.

Vaj remained focused on her. "I've also wanted to find out about your investigation into Scorpio and Abyss. From those noncommittal messages you've been sending, I gather you didn't want to talk over the mesh."

"That's right." Bhaaj reoriented to the new subject. "The more I find, the odder it gets."

"Odd? That's an unusual term for a corporate takeover attempt."

"Scorpio might have some sort of weapons deal with the Vakaar cartel. Abyss comes into it somehow, I'm not sure how."

Vaj frowned at her. "That makes no sense."

Bhaaj lifted her hands, then let them drop, the Undercity gesture for a shrug. "It gets even stranger. For some reason, the Vakaar and the Kajada heirs on the track and field team met with people here on Metropoli, something about balking—"

"Bloody hell." Vaj looked even less happy. "Who did you just say was on this team?"

Don't get rattled, Bhaaj told herself. "Shiv Kajada and Dice Vakaar. Both qualified for the Olympics. Shiv is related to the Kajada cartel boss. Dice is heir to the Vakaar boss."

"These athletes of yours are a problem and a half." Vaj looked as if she didn't know whether to be angry or frustrated. "We don't need a war between cartel members. You better not tell me they're fighting, Major."

"It's even worse," Bhaaj said dryly. "They're in love."

"Great," Vaj said. "Just great. A forbidden teenage love affair between the rival heirs to the most vicious criminal enterprises on Raylicon. Just what we need."

No kidding. "Duane is monitoring their activities. He's invaluable. I'd like to bring him into the loop on the Scorpio investigation, if that's all right."

"Yes, of course." Vaj's face took on that *I'm-talking-to-my-EI* look. "Make sure he knows it's confidential."

"I understand."

Vaj focused on her again. "You said balking. What did you mean?"

"I'm not sure. It had some connection to the people Shiv and Dice talked to."

"Find out." Vaj frowned. "You think these cartel kids are carrying messages for the cartels?"

"It seems unlikely." She couldn't be certain, though. "I can say this much. They want out of the cartels. If either of their families gets wind of their relationship, their lives could be in danger."

"And you think they know something about the Scorpio takeover attempt of Abyss?"

"They know Abyss and Scorpio are fighting." Bhaaj thought back to her talks with Shiv and Dice. "This seems to be about weapons, but not guns, bombs, that sort of thing."

"Economic battles, maybe," Vaj mused. "My sister Corejida runs our financial holdings. She's on the Scorpio Board of Directors."

Bhaaj had already ferreted out that link, and also less obvious factoids, like that the Majdas had supported Zaic Laj when he took over as CEO during a shake-up of the Scorpio board a few years ago. But Abyss? She'd found a lot less. Well, what the hell. She might as well be blunt.

"Are any Majdas on the Abyss Board of Directors?" Bhaaj asked.

Vaj went silent and her face turned bland.

Okay. Bhaaj knew that look. She'd learned a lot about Vaj over the years, probably more than the general realized. Vaj's husband lived in seclusion, invisible to the rest of humanity. He came from another noble house, one with a more current outlook; before his wedding, he'd enjoyed the freedoms men took for granted in this modern age. Their Houses had arranged the marriage, however, and on his wedding day, he gave up his freedom to become a Majda prince. The Majdas had no doubt chosen him for his noble blood and the connections he brought to the marriage.

What no one revealed, indeed never hinted at, was that he was also a financial genius. Vaj's husband lived in a seclusion more constraining than most people could imagine, but he also operated as an invisible wizard in the world of finance. Given the general's suddenly deadpan expression, Bhaaj had little doubt that her husband served on the Abyss Board of Directors as a shadow member who never appeared in person. Scorpio had to publicly list their Board of Directors, but she had no doubt the Majdas found ways to disguise his influence.

Bhaaj spoke carefully. "Let's hypothesize that the House of Majda has links to both Abyss and Scorpio." She paused, waiting. When Vaj didn't object, she continued. "If a corporation as powerful as Scorpio acquires another mammoth like Abyss, it will make Scorpio the biggest player in the Raylicon economy. Its stock value will soar. If the takeover fails, then Abyss stock goes up. Either way, Majda wins."

"Perhaps." Vaj's look remained noncommittal.

"The question," Bhaaj continued, "is which benefits your house more, Scorpio getting Abyss or Abyss holding them off?" Vaj hadn't put it that directly, but they both knew what she wanted to know. "Normally, I'd say Scorpio."

"You just need to get us information," Vaj said.

Bhaaj stood thinking about the political ramifications of the takeover. Although the Imperialate had an elected government, its culture still harkened to the age when the Ruby Dynasty had ruled. The Skolian population had even democratically voted to retain the word "Imperialate" in the name of their civilization, oblivious to the cognitive dissonance of that choice. Although Vaj would never openly admit it, Bhaaj suspected that as General of the Pharaoh's Army, she put the Ruby Pharaoh before the elected Assembly, walking a fine line in her loyalties, both political and financial. She didn't need Scorpio souring things by brokering weapons deals with drug cartels.

"If it came out that Scorpio dealt with the Vakaars," Bhaaj said, "its stock could plummet."

"You said Kiro Caballo's mother does predictive models," Vaj said. "Did you get a sense of what those models forecast for any of this?"

"Nothing specific. She seems too savvy to reveal anything to her son's coach."

Vaj scowled at her. "Yes, well, you should tell her son to keep his clothes on." When Bhaaj bristled, the general held up her hand. "I realize men smile at women and run without shirts all the time nowadays. But the behavior of the men on your team will get greater scrutiny." Before Bhaaj could respond, Vaj added, "And don't bother telling me it's wrong or sexist or whatever. Trust me, I already get an earful on that from younger members of my family." She regarded Bhaaj steadily. "Your team gets one pass from me, Major. And you've used it, for Ruzik and Kiro."

Bhaaj squashed her protest. "Understood, ma'am." She thought of Gwen Caballo. "I don't think it's only the takeover attempt that worries Kiro's mother."

"What else?"

"I'm not sure—"

"Make a damn guess."

Ho! The general was prickly today, not surprising given her

unscheduled stop on Metropoli. "I'd say Abyss isn't supposed to know Scorpio has a link to the cartel, but Kiro's mother figured out at least some of what's going on."

"I don't get it," Vaj said. "Why would either Scorpio or Abyss bother with the cartels? Any weapons deal would be insignificant compared to the billions those corporations handle daily."

"Maybe the cartels approached them." It would be a desperate move, but from what Bhaaj had seen, neither cartel even had enough to eat. At least, they hadn't before she and Mason worked out a discreet bargain where Shiv and Dice got even more food and filtered water in return for their staying after practice for extra training. It meant that they left after everyone else, so no one saw them taking additional supplies. It also left them no time to punk for the cartels, which Bhaaj suspected played a larger role than she'd initially realized in their quick agreement to the bargain.

A new idea came to Bhaaj. "General, our greatest line of defense isn't bombs, lasers or antimatter annihilators. It's our telops."

Vaj didn't look convinced. "That doesn't seem likely to involve the cartels. Maybe Abyss, but they deal in architecture, not Kyle production."

Bhaaj thought of Abber Isles, the Abyss exec from offworld who'd spoken with Zaic Laj. "On Raylicon, yes. But Abyss subsidiaries on other planets deal with Kyle research and development. If Scorpio gains a monopoly on Kyle production, they've cornered the market on a vital resource. On an interstellar scale, Abyss is one of the largest companies involved with Kyle research. Scorpio ranks sixth, but if they acquire Abyss, they become first."

"Interesting," Vaj mused. "Their stock could skyrocket after the waves from such a large acquisition settled down."

Bhaaj scowled, even though no one did that to the general unless their power rivaled hers, which limited the scowlers to a small pool indeed, one that didn't include her. She spoke anyway. "Yes, which benefits Majda. But is it in the best interest of the Imperialate for one corporation to build a monopoly on one of our most valuable resources? If they drive up prices, the military pays a huge price. *Everyone* pays, anyone who ever, for any reason, needs the Kyle mesh."

Vaj's tone cooled. "You know, Major, I've fired people for using that tone with me."

Well, shit. "My apologies, ma'am."

Vaj considered her. After a moment, she said, "One could argue that the well-being of the civilization we protect takes precedence. We are the Pharaoh's Army. Our loyalty to the Pharaoh is paramount." She had an odd tone, as if forcing herself to admit the takeover she favored wasn't in the best interest of the Skolian Imperialate she had sworn to protect.

However, Bhaaj didn't miss that Vaj specified the *Pharaoh* rather than the Imperialate. For many, the Pharaoh's well-being was indistinguishable from the Imperialate, not due to any titular throne, but because only she created the Kyle mesh. If it ever came to a showdown between the Pharaoh and the Assembly, though, Bhaaj had no doubt that Vaj and her army would side with the Pharaoh. Either way, Scorpio came in as a distant contender.

She said only, "I agree," and let Vaj take it however she wanted.

"I will discuss it with my sisters," Vaj said. "You keep looking into Gwen Caballo." She gave a wry smile. "Normally I'd say, 'I'll have my people look into it,' but in this case, that's you."

Bhaaj returned that slight smile, but didn't overdo it, in keeping with the Majda restraint. As in the Undercity, where a smile indicated trust, so it did with the Majdas. She had her own thoughts on what that said about the origins of the Undercity, just as she did about the way that her people, with their high cheekbones and large eyes, resembled nobles from the Houses, but she kept them to herself. She'd already annoyed Vaj enough.

She still didn't know what linked Vakaar and Scorpio. Time to find out what Hammerjan Vakaar had cooked up with Zaic Laj.

A small crowd waited in the arrivals area of the Cries starport. When Bhaaj and Mason appeared around the bend in the walkway, headed to the lobby, a cheer went up from the crowd. It swelled as the team appeared, including Tam on her motorized crutches. Happy voices rolled out as the athletes called to everyone who'd come to meet them.

Within moments, they'd reached the crowd and people surrounded them, hugging, laughing, offering congratulations. The port-bots carrying their luggage beeped with confusion in the chaos. Conversations swirled, *Best ever... so proud of you... can't believe that genetics claim!... you did so well...*

No one from the Undercity came, but Bhaaj hadn't expected otherwise. They'd celebrate with their circles when they got home. However, people from Cries also surrounded the Undercity athletes, their congratulations spilling onto the entire team. They loved Tam, who seemed flustered but pleasantly surprised by the attention. Everyone had witnessed her fall, her struggle back into the race, and her dramatic finish.

Kiro and Zee were another two that everyone wanted to greet, perhaps because when they finished the royal, it had also ended the final event of the meet, just before the Closing Ceremonies in a packed stadium. When Kiro stumbled across the finish with Zee, the media loved it, cheering the two young lovers struggling to finish the most demanding event.

People surrounded Ruzik, too, despite his intimidating, tattooed self. No one missed what the Kaaj nobles had noticed, that he was an extraordinarily handsome man. He seemed disconcerted, and Angel frowned, but they were savvy enough to let it happen. Although it annoyed Bhaaj to see people react more to Ruzik's looks than to the amazing feats he'd accomplished, she had to admit it worked as PR, the gorgeous Undercity prince guarded by his equally gorgeous and intimidating queen.

Bhaaj relaxed, enjoying the exuberance of their welcoming committee. Interstellar media had already picked up their story, and for once Bhaaj had felt happy to give her opinion. Mason had done the same, dealing far better with the reporters. When the news went viral that the Majda Matriarch had shown up to speak on behalf of *male* athletes, the media crowed with delight.

The Metropoli athletics committee didn't want Raylicon to name them in a discrimination case, especially now that the Majdas had taken notice, so they did their best to shine a positive light on the Undercity athletes. In return for the good press, Bhaaj and Mason declined to take further action against them. So the team returned home to a great reception. Although Bhaaj knew a debate would soon start in the media about the implications, pro and con, of Undercity athletes doing interstellar athletics, for now the kids could celebrate.

Bhaaj didn't expect anyone to come greet her—so at first she missed Jak. Then he appeared, stalking through the crowd, dressed in

Undercity black with million-credit gauntlets on his arms. People stepped aside fast to let him pass.

Bhaaj waited at the fringes until he reached her, watching her with his dark gaze. If he could have designed an app to give people that smoldering look of brooding sensuality, he'd have made a fortune. Not that he needed more wealth. He did even better than she did, not only from his ill-gotten gains but also because they shared the same compulsion to save their money, one bred from growing up with a poverty so crushing, they'd expected to die before age thirty.

"Eh, Jak," she said. He deserved both words of the greeting.

"Eh, Bhaajo." The hint of a smile played around his lips.

With their passionate greeting done, Bhaaj said, "Not expect you here." She'd intended to meet him at the Top Mark after she got all the kids off to their homes.

He looked at her stomach and its subtle curve. "Yah. Not expect. But you are."

"Ah, Jak," she murmured. "What are we doing?"

He shook his head and Bhaaj felt his intensity. Other people kept shooting glances their way. It wasn't often that one of the most notorious criminals on the planet just walked into the starport. Of course no one would arrest Jak, in keeping with their unwritten bargain: the city officials ignored the Undercity, and in return, the Undercity stayed in its hidden world.

Except that had all changed. The Undercity had gone public. Big-time.

PART THREE
Foreshires Hold

CHAPTER XX
Maze

Angel prowled the hidden byways of the Kyle universe.

Her first impression of a grid with hills had changed over time, as she concentrated on forming images that fit her activities. Today she stalked through dark alleys that wound behind hidden walls of the mesh. She'd spent a good amount of time with Hack learning the shadow web. It intrigued her how he veered into such different directions than her tutors in the Kyle training center. By now, she could find backdoors or submerged entrances that none of them knew existed.

Angel stopped at a recessed archway filled with shadows. *Maze, you got record of this arch?*

Shadow mesh place, her EI answered. **Near Scorp Corp.**

Angel stood to one side of the entrance and poked its shadows. She couldn't be certain about Maze's insights. She'd created it by copying the *can't-do-shit* EI provided to telop-trainees and then modifying her copy. Her first step: make it invisible, not only to the training staff, but also in the Kyle. Hack had offered useful ideas to help her design.

What's inside this doorway? Angel asked.

It goes into a psiber-den created by hackers at Scorpio, Maze said. **They veiled it because such shadow mesh hideouts violate company policy.**

What they do with it?

Porn. Gambling. Buying drugs.

Boring.
I will note your response in my files.
Why?
So I can continue to evolve with you and better form our association.
Yah. You do that. Only with me.
Understood. We are partners.
Not partner. You my aide.
Understood.

She trusted only one person as a partner. Ruzik. Of course those Kaaj girlies got all hot and bothered when he took off his shirt. Ruzik was way out of their league, too much of a man for them. She'd never known much about General Majda beyond her being the hard-line authority who employed Bhaaj, but after that hearing, which had gone viral when it leaked to the media, Angel liked the General, not only for her support of Ruzik, but also her *don't-fuck-with-me* attitude. Come in, take care of biz, and leave. No extra talky-talky. Angel approved.

You want to see more of this den? Maze asked. **Or find a less boring place.**

Maze sounded different today. Usually the EI used talky questions like, *Do you care to investigate this location further? Or perhaps you would like to find a different Kyle location that you consider of greater interest.* It sounded better tonight. All the time, Maze improved.

Less boring, Angel said. *Find place Scorp execs use for secrets.*

Searching, Maze said.

Angel slipped down the alley, scanning not only the walls and ground, but also the shadows above her. One thing she'd discovered: people didn't look up as much when they searched a new place. Looking "up" in the Kyle tended to reveal more hidden doorways. It wasn't in those places, though, where she found the mother lode of data. It hung in plain sight, a shimmering oval about two meters tall in the murky alley.

Eh, Angel thought. *Maze, what is that?*

I'm not sure. After a pause, Maze said, **This hidden portal came up in my search for hidden Scorpio places you'd find less boring. Except its security didn't hide it from you.**

Why not?

Another pause. **A Kyle lock protects it. That means you need to be a stronger Kyle than whoever created it to find the portal. Its creator is stronger than 98% of all telops. You are stronger than 99.5%. So you can see it.**

More than see. Lock open. The door glistened like the molecular air locks on starships.

You turned the key, so to speak. You're using invasion methods unknown to security experts in Cries, maybe unknown to anyone except Hack.

What on other side?

I don't know. You need to go through the doorway to find out.

Not smart just walk through. Need probe.

We can extend a tendril of my code through the doorway.

Not want door to see your code.

I can apply a Kyle lock. Given your 99.5% rating, it will be stronger than whoever created this portal.

Intrigued, Angel said, *I stronger than they think in Kyle Division, eh?*

Yes. By a long shot.

Good. Give me probe.

Look in your hand.

A small ball appeared in her palm. Tendrils waved on it, delicate streamers, pale colors, green, blue, pink. *Pretty,* she thought. *You can use it?*

Yes. Send it through the portal.

Angel tossed the ball at the shimmering oval. When it hit the membrane, the oval sucked it away and then smoothed back into its shimmer.

You get stuff from probe? Angel asked.

Yes, Maze answered. **The probe is still hidden. If I use the same code for you, then you also can go through the portal and remain hidden.**

What in there?

A storage space.

For Scorpio?

Let me see ... it's for Zaic Laj.

It didn't surprise Angel that she'd found a link to Hyden's father in Kyle space, given how many thoughts she'd had about him lately, none of them good. Hyden could be an ass-byte sometimes, but not like Zaic. What a bastard, to kill his son's dreams.

Zaic Laj is gang leader of all Scorp, yah?

If you mean is he in charge, then yes, he is the CEO and majority share-holder.

This got more interesting by the moment. *Good work, Maze.*

Thank you. What would you like to do?

Want to see what scares Zaic Laj so much, he hides it with a lock that keeps out 98% of all telops. An unpleasant thought came to her. *That mean Zaic Laj is stronger Kyle than 98% of the human race?*

From what I've found, he isn't a Kyle at all. He must've hired someone to create this lock.

So some psibit-wiz also knows Zaic Laj's shit.

They know it's hidden. Maybe they know its location, maybe not. Someone else may have hidden the data. Doing it with two people would provide extra security.

Yah. Or he might just whack the tech-wiz who made it. Then no one knows but him.

I suspect not.

Why?

My profile of Zaic Laj doesn't suggest he would commit murder. Although many consider his ethics compromised in financial dealings, he hews to what most people consider moral behavior in physical dealings.

Angel tensed. *You saying Undercity not moral?*

What do you mean?

I kill fighter in cartel war when I protect circle. I am murderer, then?

You were a soldier protecting your people during combat. What's surprising isn't that you had to kill someone to save your dependents, but that you managed to protect them without more deaths. My profile of you indicates a strong moral and ethical base, more so than Zaic Laj. It is particularly notable given that you come from a more difficult background, one with brutal poverty, violence, and hunger that he's never known.

Angel had no idea how to answer. *Eh.*

I'm sorry, I don't understand your comment.

Maybe Zaic Laj think he fight war too. Financial war. Not with knives or guns. With numbers and mesh codes.

An intriguing analogy. Maze went silent. Then: **I still don't think he'd murder anyone to protect this place.**

Good. We take look. Angel stepped through the oval—into an office filled with light, air and what she'd heard called "old-fashioned filing cabinets." Except they didn't look old-fashioned, they seemed surreal, made from clouds and sky. The closest one reached her height but was only two handspans wide. A vertical line of handles ran down its front, each also composed of blue sky with clouds. Whoever designed it either didn't live on Raylicon or knew far more about other worlds than most people here, because Raylicon had no clouds. The atmosphere couldn't form them, except underground when the evaporating lakes exuded a poisonous vapor.

Strange, Angel thought. All the air, sunlight, and sky made her feel lighter. She pulled the handle on the cabinet and its drawer slid open, revealing slices of clouds and sky hanging in neat rows within the interior.

Intrigued, Angel slid her hand between two slices of sky. They felt smooth. *Why sky?*

I don't know, Maze said.

Guess.

I don't know how to guess.

Tell me things about these sky slices that could be true. You know, do math and give me high probability possibilities. With a wince, she added, *If you evolve to fit my speech, include this in your code. That last sentence had words with an in-sul-ting number of syllables.*

Insulting?

Yah. More than two is either an insult or means great honor. The more syllables, the bigger the effect. Only when you talk, though. Use more syllables when think, if need to.

Undercity has four syllables.

Yah. Great honor.

Understood. I've put that into my code.

You can use "ken" for "understood."

I ken.

Good. Now talk about these sky slices.

They may represent files. In ancient cabinets such as these, folders hung in the drawers like these sky slices hang here.

Angel wondered why the designer chose this motif. *The clouds— they like sky on other planet?* Maybe the coder came from offworld.

They resemble the sky on the world called Parthonia. After a pause, Maze thought, **Am I insulting the world Parthonia by using so many syllables?**

Nahya. It's a slick world. Slicks think more syl-a-bull-shit make you smart.

Ah. I will add that to my code. Does nahya mean no?

Yah. And yah means yes.

Got it. Then it added, **Why do people of the Undercity think speaking many syllables is ridicule? I would not consider my speech in this comment as ridiculous despite its many multisyllabic words. And you seem to think in sophisticated, multisyllabic speech.**

Angel paused, considering his question. *Slicks talk so much. They use more words than they need. More syllables.* Then she allowed, *Since I've come to work at the Kyle center, I've realized all those words and syllables do have a use when you need to express yourself accurately, especially about technical aspects of the work. Like I just did with that sentence.*

You seem to switch back and forth from Undercity to Cries speech at will.

I suppose. I don't think about it, or at least not always. Since I started my job, I think my mind chooses whatever mode seems best for what I'm trying to say.

Why do you feel like slicks talk too much?

Not need all those words. Angel almost left it at that, then realized that stating the obvious might not be obvious to an EI still learning to be an EI. *We sense what people mean. Feel moods. Even thoughts. Not need a lot of words. Too many hurts. Got to protect your mind. Build walls.*

Ah! Because you are Kyle operators.

We not call it that. She shifted her feet, which apparently was how the Kyle showed her agitation with this conversation. *I need look at these files before I get caught.*

Try pulling out a slice of sky.

Angel pulled out the first one. It opened like a paper folder in her hand, the kind that almost no one used anymore. Documents lay inside with glyphs floating above them like white clouds.

Huh. Angel scanned the glyphs. *This is a record of payments.*

Payments? You mean someone's bank statement?

Not sure. Looks private.

Angel, do you remember our discussion about your ethics?

Eh? Distracted by the great wealth listed on the document, she barely noticed his words.

Reading someone's private financial files could be termed unethical.

Angel raised her virtual head. *Yah. But Maze, this is a list of payments Zaic Laj made to the Vakaar cartel. Someone here is screwing around bigtime, and it isn't me.*

Then you're in trouble big-time, because what you just told me could get you killed. I retract what I said about Zaic Laj not being capable of murder. The deeper you go into this, the more it appears he has a vested interest in making sure no one finds out what he is hiding. You need to get out of here. NOW!

Angel put back the file and sprinted from the room, withdrawing from the Kyle as fast as she could manage, all the while erasing her virtual, digital, and whatever-the-hell-else footprint.

"Hyden's lawyer thinks they can get a hearing before the Olympics," Max continued.

Bhaaj relaxed on the living room couch in her penthouse. Although she'd never felt at ease in this luxurious place the Majdas provided as part of her retainer, she adored the view, so unlike anything she'd known in her youth. The window-wall opposite her looked out over the desert all the way to the mountains edging the horizon. The sun had reached its high point, which meant the heat had become close to unbearable outside. Here in the climate-controlled penthouse, with the window tinting itself enough to make the sunlight beautiful instead of searing, she felt almost content. She never truly felt settled unless she was running, but given her fatigue, right now sitting was good.

"I hope the lawyer thinks Hyden can win," she said. Zaic had already tried telling Hyden to quit with the legal business. Given that his son was no longer speaking to him, that hadn't led anywhere. Zaic had other weapons, though. "Or is he under pressure to refuse Hyden's case?"

"Not his lawyer," Max said. "It's the judge he'll need to worry about. Would Zaic threaten or bribe a judge to stop his son? Someone with his resources might get away with it, but if the trial goes public, which it will if Hyden has to appeal, the media will vilify his father."

"Yah, true." Unfortunately, it didn't matter. "Hyden wouldn't have time to appeal before the Olympics. And he turns twenty-five just afterward. It makes emancipation moot."

"I don't think he cares," Max said. "He'd appeal anyway. If he misses the Olympics, he wants his father to suffer. He's furious."

"He hides it well."

"With you, yes. Not in his messages to his lawyer."

Bhaaj scowled. "Max, you know what client-lawyer privilege means, right? Hyden's correspondence with his lawyer is confidential."

"Understood. Sorry."

The EI didn't sound the least bit remorseful. He'd taught himself covert methods too well. Given that he'd evolved with her for over two decades, Bhaaj wasn't sure she liked what that said about her. If she needed things done that she wouldn't do, he sometimes stepped in without her knowledge. Some would argue that he acted as an extension of her own mind, an idea that led to ethical complications she had yet to resolve. For now, she didn't ask for details she shouldn't know.

"Any news on the Boston Marathon?" she asked.

"Mason's contact in the Boston Athletic Association arranged a spot for Hyden. They'll use his time from Metropoli as his qualifier."

Relief washed over Bhaaj. They could have refused, given the disqualification. Hyden still had a lot to do, though. Boston was in ten days, and he needed to get to Earth as soon as possible to start acclimating to the birthplace of humanity, so unlike the world of his actual birth.

"Also," Max said. "Angel sent a message. She wants to meet with you."

"Okay. Tell her I'll get back to her soon." Bhaaj scanned the holos above the table in front of her, a list of the tasks she had waiting. "We need to get Hyden on the next flight to Earth."

"I'll look into it with him." Then Max added, "Angel says it's urgent."

Huh. Angel was the queen of stoic patience. She wouldn't say urgent without good reason.

"All right," Bhaaj said. "Tell her I'll meet her in the Concourse Café in fifteen minutes."

The round table where Bhaaj and Angel sat was on the outdoor balcony of the café, overlooking the Concourse. This close to its top end, the street formed a large boulevard bordered by upscale shops, restaurants, and boutiques. Tributary lanes wound away from the main avenue, back to posh clubs and glitzy bars that served the trendy elite. This supposedly dangerous Undercity thoroughfare was a high-priced tourist trap. Bhaaj had always liked this café, though. At two stories above the Concourse, it offered a good view of the street.

Across the boulevard, the sole canal in the Concourse ran parallel to the avenue. Water burbled in it, coming from an underground spring in the desert that the city planners redirected here. A graceful bridge arched over the canal with curling vine patterns carved into its white stone posts.

"Not ken," Bhaaj told Angel, who sat across from her. "What 'sneak under Scorp' mean?"

"Eh." Angel shifted in the chair.

Bhaaj waited. Angel looked uncomfortable in this place, so unlike the café where she and Ruzik dined in the Undercity, the one in Jak's casino. They paid for their food, but most Undercity natives couldn't afford to eat there. Jak made a bargain with anyone desperate for food: a meal in return for a work shift. He otherwise financed his Undercity café with the wealth spent by the Cries slicks as they lost, lost, and lost in his casino.

"I was thinking about Hyden's father," Angel said. "Piss me off."

"Yah." Bhaaj had no arguments there.

"Maybe I think too much about him in Kyle place."

"You work in Kyle mesh today?"

"Yah." Angel continued to look evasive.

Oh. Of course. She knew what Angel meant by *under* Scorp. "Easy to find shadows, eh?"

Angel regarded her with a guilty look. "Eh."

It didn't surprise Bhaaj that Angel accessed the shadow mesh. She'd find it far more stimulating than the pasteurized areas where the Kyle Division sent novices to practice. What startled her was how freaking *fast* Angel learned.

"You dig into Scorp shadows?" Bhaaj asked.

Angel regarded her with an impassive look. It didn't fool Bhaaj. Something had majorly thrown off her protégée's usual composure.

Bhaaj tried again. "Scorp Corp play in shadow mesh?"

"Same old stuff." Now Angel sounded bored.

"But?"

"Found Zaic Laj den." Angel stopped looking bored. "Vakaar got Scorp bad."

"What that mean?"

"Vakaar make Laj pay to keep secret. Pay a lot."

Bhaaj stared at her. "For *what* secret?"

"Not know. Maze say get out. Fast."

"Maze?"

"My EI."

"Where you get EI?" It wasn't standard issue at the novice level.

"I copy silly practice EI. Then remake."

Saints almighty. That couldn't be what Bhaaj thought she meant. "On your own?"

"Yah." She looked guilty. "Mostly on own time. Hack help some."

Bhaaj didn't care whether she used her own time or did it during work. If Angel was already designing her own EI, she'd gone light-years ahead of where anyone expected. Add Hack to the mix, and gods only knew what she'd come up with. If she pushed too hard, though, her protégée would back off. So she put on a standard Bhaaj-frown and said, "Not pinch EI from Kyle school."

"Not steal," Angel said. "Just copy."

"Same thing, with code." To duplicate the EI, she'd have to crack its security.

Angel was watching her intently. "You more upset than you say, yah?"

So much for subtlety. Angel read her too well. Bhaaj had known her for years, enough that their mental barriers tended to fade with each other.

"Got to be more careful," Bhaaj said. "You want to spy? Need to learn risks."

Angel grimaced. "I get out fast. And hide. Not think any other spy notice me."

"Hope not." If Angel had stumbled on a record of Vakaar squeezing the Scorpio CEO for money, she'd launched herself into a whole new realm of danger, something she had no idea how to deal with. Hell, neither did Bhaaj.

But she knew who could.

"Extortion?" Colonel Lavinda Majda stood in her office, bathed in the harsh Raylicon sunlight flooding through the windows. "For what?"

"Angel doesn't know," Bhaaj admitted, standing across the desk from her.

"Then why does she think Vakaar is extorting Zaic Laj?" Lavinda asked.

"That's how her sim defined it."

"That doesn't mean this simulation she created is accurate. Angel is a novice."

"She learns fast. I swear, Lavinda, it's surreal." Bhaaj regarded her steadily. "Angel needs better mentors. Security experts who know how to train a genius and convince her to stop taking so many risks." Dryly she added, "Like spying on CEOs." Even most financial crackers involved in high-level corporate espionage couldn't have managed what Angel had done.

"I'll assign someone qualified to work with her," Lavinda said. "They'll make sure she doesn't find trouble." Her gaze turned flinty. "Or cause it."

"Angel is dedicated to her work for the army," Bhaaj said, because she had to give Lavinda that assurance. She had no doubt Angel would learn to protect herself and then dig up more secrets. Lavinda knew the danger. The army could ensure Angel's dedication by giving her an outlet for her insatiable intellect. "Make her feel like part of the team, at a level equal to her ability."

"Believe me, we want to." Lavinda paused. "Have you found anything more about this Abyss exec who was talking with Zaic Laj at that reception in Selei Tower?"

"Her name is Abber Isles. She's the CFO of an Abyss subsidiary on the world Parthonia." Bhaaj thought over her research. "I did find something odd. A detective in Abyss security here on Raylicon is named Patrik Laj."

Lavinda stiffened. "Any connection to Zaic Laj?"

"Not that I've found. But it's not a common name."

"Keep looking. That's too much of a coincidence."

"I thought so, too." It could offer a way for someone connected to Scorpio to approach Abber Isles, the Abyss exec, without drawing too much attention.

"My psiber intelligence team will contact Angel," Lavinda said.

"Good." Bhaaj had already warned Angel to expect the experts. Given how people underestimated Angel, though, Bhaaj suspected the mesh wizards were the ones who needed to worry.

CHAPTER XXI
Boston and Beyond

With their metaphorical middle finger raised to the Imperialate for disqualifying an Olympic-level athlete because they considered a twenty-four-year-old man a minor, the officials at the Boston Marathon gave Hyden a position in the first group of runners, along with the other top-ranked athletes. They would start the race ahead of everyone else, only a slight advantage, but for Hyden, a huge mental boost after Metropoli.

Bhaaj had never seen so many athletes gather for *any* track and field event. They clogged the streets for kilometers. Crowds lined the route, people come to witness one of the most famous marathons in three interstellar civilizations. She and Mason went to the starting line located in Hopkinton, Massachusetts on "Main Street," which seemed to be the name of about half the streets on the planet. They couldn't assist Hyden during the race of course, but they checked and double-checked for any logistical issues that might arise. Nothing did: it all looked good.

The officials started the race in four waves, each with about 7500 runners, each separated by twenty-five minutes. The waves and the corrals within them used rolling starts, which meant the runners didn't go all at once, but rather in a steady flow. The elite runners went ahead of the waves, as did the wheelchair division, the handcycles and duos, the over-ninety-years-old division, and the Military March that honored fallen service members and first responders. Everyone wore a mesh-linked vid-chip that initiated when they crossed the starting line and stopped at the finish.

When the crowd behind the barricades suddenly cheered, their exuberance burbled past the mental barriers Bhaaj had raised to protect her mind against so many people. Turning, she saw about fifty runners gathering at the starting line. Hyden was on the far side or the group, looking around. When he caught sight of her and Mason, he waved, and they waved back. He grinned, then nodded to the people on either side of him, a courtesy he'd never shown in the early days. Back then, he'd been more likely to smirk or trash-talk his competitors.

"He's matured," Bhaaj said.

Mason glanced at her. "You mean Hyden?"

"Yah. He's all right, you know."

"The good was always in him," Mason said. "I think having his parents withdraw support, both financial and emotional, sobered him up."

"Financial?" That didn't make sense. "I thought Hyden supported himself. Doesn't he have some ultra-high-paying job?"

"Had. At Scorpio." Anger edged Mason's voice. "When Hyden's case for emancipation got the go-ahead, his father fired him."

Did it never end? "That's a lousy way to treat his kid."

"Hyden found another job. Nothing as prestigious as his Scorpio position, but enough to support himself."

The race officials near the starting line used a Starter orb to give instructions. Commentators described the athletes at the head of the elite pack, including Hyden, while holo-vids about them played in the air and on various feeds and apps. The noise of the crowd swelled as one of the race officials theatrically raised a starter pistol.

And bang! The race was off.

It will work, Bhaaj told herself. *It will.* Hyden had trained well, and he looked ready. The rich air of Earth and its clear blue sky were like gifts. They felt *right*, as if she'd known this place all her life, though she'd only made a few brief visits here.

She and Mason headed out to watch Hyden along the route, anywhere they could find a break in the crowd.

"And there it is!" the male announcer cried. "Karanja Njoro from Kenya is first in the Boston Marathon. That's only weeks after he took the bronze in the royal marathon on Metropoli. What an athlete! Even before this race, he already ranked first in classic marathon on Earth and eighth on the interstellar stage. This will move him even higher."

Bhaaj waited with Mason, only half-watching as Njoro finished. She kept her attention on the holos of Hyden above her gauntlet, the feed sent by her red drone. He looked tired, but he'd maintained a steady pace similar to his marathon on Metropoli. That had earned him an Olympic qualifying time, but it had been close. Too close.

Mason clapped dutifully for the winners from Earth. Everyone cheered when a woman came in second. The crowd seemed delighted that she'd done so well.

"I don't get it," Bhaaj said. "The Earthers act like they don't know their female runners have caught up with the male runners."

Mason shrugged. "The difference in times was ingrained in their culture." He glanced at the holos produced by her gauntlet. "How is Hyden doing?"

"It's too close to call." Bhaaj shifted back and forth, unable to stay still. It would be heartbreaking if Hyden went to all this trouble and didn't qualify. Even with his help and the funds she and Mason donated, they hadn't had enough to get him to Earth more than a few days ahead of the race. If he made the Olympics here, they could still afford the Games, though, including going a full two tendays ahead of time. She just hoped the shorter prep here didn't hurt Hyden's chances.

At about the same time that the fourth-place runner finished, Bhaaj caught sight of Hyden far back on Boylston Street, the last stretch of road, running behind the woman in fifth place.

"No, no," Maron muttered, studying his own tech-mech band. "He's not going to make it."

"Come on, Hyden!" Bhaaj shouted. "You can do it."

"Go, Hyden!" Mason yelled. "You've got this!"

Hyden glanced their way, then at his own sports band, and his face twisted with frustration.

"Come on," Bhaaj said. The moments were going by too fast as he came down the final stretch. He would miss it by seconds—

And then he kicked.

"Ho!" Bhaaj shouted. It was the *Undercity* kick, that surge of energy her athletes used at the end of the race. It wasn't typical in a marathon, at least not with the energy Undercity runners managed, but it didn't matter. Hyden had enough left to surge across the finish line, gasping for breath—and two seconds under the Olympic qualifying time.

"Hyden!" Bhaaj shouted, at the same time Mason called, "Hyden, over here!"

Gulping in air, he came toward them, dousing his head with water from a bottle someone handed him. When he reached the barricade, Mason reached across and pumped his hand up and down like an Earther while Bhaaj jubilantly wrapped the Raylicon flag around his shoulders. Grinning, Hyden stepped back and raised his arms high, letting the flag ripple in the breeze.

"You did it!" Mason exulted. "You're going to the Olympics."

"You bet!" Hyden said.

Even as Bhaaj congratulated him, she hoped they weren't offering false hope. They still had to deal with his obscenely powerful father and the lawsuit.

Skulking around the actual City of Cries didn't seem much different to Angel than skulking around Kyle space. At night, the back alleys of Cries looked as shadowy as the back alleys of the Scorpio mesh. Except even the high-level security in the city wasn't as good as what the Kyle Division used to protect its telops.

Angel had searched for a shroud like the one Bhaaj used to hide from the Majdas or anyone else who wanted to keep track of her. Soon, Angel had Bhaaj-like tech that hid her from sensors, including optical, ultra-violet, infrared, radar, microwave, and neutrino. The scavenged parts in the shroud were military grade or pinched from a tech-corp. It worked like a dream. Even Hack couldn't find her when he did tests. She used her telop salary with its invisible credits to buy pico-hawk drones, little fliers that would warn her if anyone in real space tried to spy on her.

Angel slid the telop cap over her head and felt the now familiar tingle as it inserted nanomed filaments into her skull and beyond, to her brain. She didn't like it any more now than she had the first time, but it would serve its purpose until she finished competing as an unaugmented athlete.

The tournaments for augmented athletes made no sense to Angel.

You could add *anything* to your body or genetically engineer it to any extreme. Some of the enhanced "athletes" didn't even look human. The meets became a battle to see who could engineer the most enhanced cybernauts. She preferred the Olympics, which supposedly allowed no enhancement. It did, given that the rules accepted, even required health meds, but that didn't bother her since everyone had them. The doctors at Metropoli had even wanted to upgrade hers. She turned down their offer; she knew nothing about them. She'd work it out with Doctor Izaka.

When the tingling from the neural cap stopped, Angel thought, *Maze?*

I'm here, her EI answered.

Where is Vakaar punker meeting with Scorp agent?

About fifty meters down the lane to your right. Then Maze added, **This place isn't safe.**

Safer than mesh. With her back against the ceramix-brick wall, she listened, using skills sharpened by a lifetime of spying on rival gangs.

Nothing.

You hear anyone? she asked.

I don't have tech that lets me hear, Maze said.

Huh. She'd have to ask Bhaaj how Max always knew what was up.

After a few moments, she caught words from someone nearby. In low tones, a woman said, "—or we'll tell Hammerjan that Laj didn't pay shit."

"I've got it," a man said. "There. I sent ten thousand bykes to the Vakaar city account."

Ho! It was true then, that the cartels had Cries bank accounts. Few people in the Undercity used byte-bucks. You couldn't see or touch bykes, so in the Undercity they meant nothing. Except of course the cartels needed bank accounts, or whatever shady version of those they'd worked out. You couldn't trade drugs worth millions for Undercity bargains.

"This is the last payment," the Scorp man said. Angel didn't recognize his voice, so it couldn't be Zaic Laj. She'd often heard him talking to Hyden at practices, back before Zaic stopped acting human. That Zaic sent someone in his place meant that another person knew about the payments. Not good, at least for anyone who had the misfortune of being Zaic's go-between.

"We let you know when it's enough," the woman said.

Come ON, Angel thought. *Say why you make payment.*

I'm not making payments, Maze informed her.

Not you. I listen to people talk.

"I'm serious," the man said. "You tell Hammerjan. Why the hell is she trying to raise the price now, after all these years? Laj won't pay more. If Vakaar tries to force it, she'll be sorry."

"Crap-sucking Laj will be sorry," the woman said. "When his wife learns truth."

Angel blinked. Surely this wasn't about something as mundane as an affair, not for the huge amounts Laj had paid. Nor could it be because of his wife's overdose all those years ago. Everyone already knew.

"Don't even try it," the Scorp man said. "Or Zaic will talk to Abyss."

Abyss? Where did that come from? Angel concentrated, willing the speakers to say more, but she heard only the whisper of boots against cobblestones, as if they were walking away.

Eventually, after a while, Angel thought, *I think they gone.*

I not know, Maze answered.

I need to get you sensors.

That would be useful.

Moving with care, she slipped away into the night.

"You're doing well," Doctor Karal Rajindia told Bhaaj. "Healthy and fit. The baby is thriving."

"Good." Bhaaj relaxed on the recliner in Karal's clinic. "I still feel tired all the time."

"Of course you're tired. You're living for two people now."

Footsteps came from the waiting room, and then the beaded curtain for the room parted as a man entered. "Not mean to be late," Jak said. "Fight happen in Top Mark. Had to kick out a drunk."

Bhaaj didn't envy whoever he'd banished. "Babe is fine," she assured him.

He came over to the recliner, his face creased with concern. "You look like shit."

"Good to see you too," Bhaaj said. Romance wasn't one of her husband's strong suits.

He touched her cheek. "You okay?"

"Yah, fine."

"For once when she's saying that," Karal added, "it's actually true."

Jak smiled, not his killer grin this time, but a warm look of relief.

More footsteps sounded outside, and the beads clinked again as Angel burst into the room.

"Enough already," Bhaaj said. This was turning into Grand Central Station.

"Got to talk," Angel told her.

"How you find me?" Bhaaj kept her appointments with Karal private.

"Maze make guess," Angel said.

"Why need me so fast?" Bhaaj growled. She'd looked forward to a few moments with Jak.

Angel glanced at Karal and said nothing.

"You can go," Karal told Bhaaj. "Just get more sleep."

"I will." Bhaaj slid off the recliner and stood up next to Jak, the two of them watching Angel. With no further ado, they all headed out of the room.

"You spy in Cries?" Jak asked Angel. He sounded approving. "Good."

"Not good," Bhaaj growled. They were walking along a path hidden within the wall of a canal. "You spy on Zaic for this, you get whacked."

"I not whacked," Angel pointed out.

"What you find?" Jak asked.

"Zaic's wife not know some secret." Angel switched into the Cries dialect. "Vakaar is threatening to tell her if Zaic doesn't pay up, but Zaic is threatening to tell Abyss something if Vakaar doesn't back off."

"Tell Abyss what?" Bhaaj asked.

"They not say," Angel told her.

"Zaic was talking to Abber Isles at that reception," Bhaaj mused. "Isles works for an Abyss subsidiary on Parthonia. Max, see what else you can find about her. Look up Gwen Caballo, too."

"Maze need to learn how to do that stuff," Angel told her. "Hack help."

Goddess, what a combination, Hack and Angel. If they combined his genius for physics and invention with her genius in the Kyle, the universe wouldn't know what hit it. Bhaaj frowned at her. "Not take ad-van-tage of Hack."

"Yah." Angel nodded. "Good point. We find bargain."

"Fine," Jak growled. "Angel and Hack take over universe. We get back to Isles now?"

"Max, you got more about Abber Isles?" Bhaaj asked.

"So far, nothing," he said.

Jak's EI, Royal Flush, spoke in his deep voice. "Shall I help?"

Bhaaj glanced at Jak. He was notorious for letting no one access Royal except himself.

"Yah," Jak said. "Go ahead."

A thought came to Bhaaj. "Zaic probably hates that Dice Vakaar is on Mason's team."

"If he were our kid," Jak said, "I'd want him off the team."

If he were our kid. It sobered Bhaaj to realize they'd be thinking that way for the rest of their lives. "You think Zaic is protecting Hyden?"

"It'd make him seem less of an asshole for trying to crush his son's dreams," Jak said.

"Still asshole," Angel said. "Call us dust rats." A gleam came into her eyes. "We bring him here. Let him live like dust rat."

"Uh, nahya," Bhaaj said. They absolutely didn't need dust gangers hauling Zaic Laj here for whatever fun they thought they could have with the CEO. "Not touch Scorp execs."

Jak focused on Angel. "You hear any biz about Mason's team in your spy trip?"

"Nahya. They not care about Olympics."

"How you know?" Bhaaj asked.

"Feel their minds." Angel tapped her temple. "I let down shields. Learn how at job."

"Good." Bhaaj wished more of their people would learn. Otherwise, they struggled when they ventured into Cries, trying to endure the pressure of so many minds. About a thousand people lived in the sparsely settled Undercity. Millions lived in Cries.

"Here's the thing," Bhaaj said. "If Hyden's father wanted to protect him, he'd have taken his son off the team as soon as he learned about Dice. He got the list of athletes along with everyone else. He still let Hyden participate, even go to Metropoli. He didn't forbid it until Hyden qualified for the Olympics."

"Maybe it's not the Olympics," Jak said. "Maybe Zaic doesn't want him going to the world Foreshires Hold."

"But why?" Bhaaj asked. "How is that different from anywhere else?"

"Abber Isles, maybe?" Angel said. "She born on Foreshires."

"Yah. But now she live on Parthonia," Bhaaj said. "Not see problem."

"Maybe Zaic is doing some power thing," Angel mused. "Show Hyden who's boss."

"Might think Hyden give up on Olympics," Bhaaj said. "Like folding a poker hand."

Jak snorted. "That kid never folds his hand. Including when he should."

She glared at him. "Your damn casino took money he needs, now that his father disowned him."

"I don't think Zaic disowned him," Jak said. "At least, that's not the word on the Whisper Mill. Hyden just lost his job." Then he added, "Either way, he hasn't come back to the casino."

Bhaaj thought through the possibilities. "Maybe Vakaar is squeezing Zaic because they know he's trying to get a monopoly on Kyle production. That's a huge market, one that would make Scorpio one of the most powerful corporations anywhere. So Zaic pays Vakaar to keep them quiet. His spy on the inside at Abyss, Abber Isles, originally came from Foreshires Hold. He doesn't want Hyden to know, so he's trying to keep him away from Foreshires."

"That sounds too convoluted," Jak said. "Abber Isles doesn't even live on Foreshires anymore. Besides, why would he care if Hyden knows? The guy is his heir."

"He not trust Hyden," Angel said.

Bhaaj blinked. "What?"

"Him and Hyden argue a lot," Angel said. "Hyden not like how father does Scorp biz."

Interesting twist. "But how would Vakaar know that?"

"Vakaar got deals in Cries," Jak said. "Even offworld. Same for Kajada."

"Same for you," Bhaaj growled at him.

"Top Mark would be legal on other worlds," Angel pointed out.

"Top Mark not on other worlds," Bhaaj said.

"Still." Jak was watching her intently. "I know what goes on in places beyond Raylicon. It's my business to know. The same would be true of the cartels."

He had a point. "But you aren't privy to inside details of Scorpio's attempt to grab Abyss," Bhaaj said. "And you have more reason to know than the cartels. Execs are always going to your casino. That's not true for the cartels. So how would they know more about Scorpio than you?"

"Not know. I got no biz with the cartels." Dryly he added, "They don't like me because I'm married to you. And they *really* don't like you."

"Kajada like her," Angel said. "She cousin."

"Kajada tolerates me, just barely, as long as I don't bother them," Bhaaj said.

"And the cartels tolerate me," Jak said, "If Hammerjan gambles at the Top Mark, I forgive her debts, and in return she doesn't try to whack me. Bargain works. But that doesn't mean I know what Vakaar knows. Maybe they found a backdoor into Scorpio."

"I suppose." The cartels were obviously looking for new revenue streams. "Of course, this all assumes Abber Isles is a Scorpio spy."

"I found more about her," Max said. "Isles has a niece who married one of Patrik Laj's maternal cousins. Patrik Laj works in Abyss Security here on Raylicon. He's also Zaic Laj's second cousin once removed through his father's side."

Jak gave a dry laugh. "I suppose you could call that a link, if you're generous."

"It does connect Abber Isles to Zaic," Bhaaj said. "Or at least to his relatives."

"Abber Isles also has family on Foreshires Hold," Max said. "She was born there, and she visits all the time. She recently purchased a ticket to attend the Olympics."

"So Zaic Laj has got his spy skulking around the Olympics," Angel said. "No wonder he doesn't want Hyden there."

"You think so?" Bhaaj didn't find it credible. "I mean, I can see why Zaic might want to distance his son from all this. But killing Hyden's life-long dream just to make sure he doesn't run into Abber Isles? That seems over the top."

"Maybe." Angel shrugged. "They slicks. Never make sense."

"Oh, they make sense," Bhaaj said. "Just in their own convoluted ways."

"Screwed up ways," Angel said. "Hyden's father break his heart."

"What about his mother?" Jak said. "Did his father cheat on her?"

"So what?" Bhaaj said. "I mean, yah, it could mean he's an ass-byte to his wife, too, but people cheat all the time. Why would he pay millions over so many years to hide it?"

"Hyden's mother used to come watch his practices," Angel said. "Smiles a lot."

"She's big on the Cries socialite scene," Bhaaj said. It hadn't always been that way. Hyden's mother had dealt with some rough problems in her youth, those brought on by addiction. The cartels extended their tendrils everywhere, even to the highest levels of Cries society. But his mother had stayed clean for over twenty years since then, becoming a spokesperson for drug rehabilitation programs. "She seems happy now."

"What about Gwen Caballo?" Jak asked. "Is she going to the Olympics?"

"Yes, indeed," Max said. "Both Kiro's parents are attending."

Although Bhaaj had expected Gwen, his father was another story. Nial Caballo seemed less interested in his family than his glamorous career. Did he suspect Kiro might not be his son? It could be moot. Doctor Rajindia had compared Kiro's DNA with her entire database and found no one related to him in the Undercity.

It wasn't impossible Kiro's DNA came from his star-yacht father. Everyone on Raylicon had the same ancestors. If you went back far enough, so did everyone in the Imperialate, even the Traders. On most planets, the colonists engineered themselves to adapt to their new world and compensate for their small gene pool. It made the accusation of genetic engineering against the Undercity even more absurd. They were probably the only population *without* altered DNA. They'd lived in isolation for millennia, interbreeding until they suffered the highest rate of birth defects anywhere. With all that, Kiro could have DNA similar to the Undercity and still have a Cries father.

She said only, "I'm glad his father is going. Kiro will like that."

"You find anything else on his mother?" Jak asked.

"Gwen Caballo seems ordinary," Royal commented. "Just an analyst."

"What about her wealth?" Bhaaj asked. "Isn't it out of proportion to her income?"

"It's true, she's only in the middle pay range for her job," Max said.

"That's odd, too," Bhaaj mused. "I mean, she's had that job for decades, and from what I understand, she's brilliant with it. That should've put her on the high end of the range."

"Maybe she pissed off someone at Abyss," Royal said.

"Or maybe she has family money," Max added. "Her husband had a large dowry."

"Dowry?" Jak asked. "What does that mean?"

Angel smirked. "She buy rich husband."

"For flaming sake," Bhaaj said. "That isn't what it means."

"A dowry is the wealth, goods, or estate a man brings to a marriage," Max said.

"Or a woman," Royal added. "They used it that way on Earth."

Bhaaj grinned at Jak. "Where's your dowry, eh?"

"What," he said. "You think I give you the Top Mark?"

She squinted at him. "What the blazes would I do with a casino?"

Jak laughed. "You'd let everyone win. It'd go bankrupt. Sorry, no dice, Bhaaj. Literally."

"Dowries went out of style long ago," Max said. "Except for the wealthy or aristocrats."

"So Kiro's mother married his father for his money?" Bhaaj asked.

"Possibly," Max said. "It isn't enough to explain their standard of living, though."

"Maybe she loved him," Royal said. "They were an item, sort of, before their marriage."

"Why sort of?" Bhaaj asked.

"A lot of rumors swirled about the merger of their families, but they didn't date much."

"Sounds like an arranged marriage," Jak said.

"Ho, look at this!" Royal suddenly said. "Gwen Caballo had Kiro tested for Kyle DNA not long after his birth. She did it anonymously, sending the inquiry offworld."

"It makes sense," Bhaaj said. "If she wasn't sure about his parentage, she'd want the tests done in secret, away from her life here."

"That's true," Max said. "But get this. She used a clinic on Foreshires Hold. Want to guess who ran that clinic?"

"No," Bhaaj said, irked at his dramatics. EIs weren't supposed to do that.

"Abber Isles," Max announced.

"Hah!" Jak said. "I knew it."

"Did Isles figure out who she tested?" Bhaaj asked.

"It doesn't look like it," Max said. "Not that she didn't try. Gwen Caballo, however, had the savvy to keep it secret. From what I found in, um, messages someone thought they deleted—"

"Max is misbehaving again," Angel said. "I need him to teach Maze."

"Like hell," Bhaaj growled. Just what she needed, having her EI teach her protégée's EI how to break the law.

"It doesn't look like Isles managed to uncover anything about Kiro," Max said. "She just got his anonymous test results. Kiro is an eight on the Kyle scale."

"Like Strider's gang," Bhaaj said. "Isles was a lab tech then. How'd she became an exec?"

"Training programs," Max answered. "She worked her way up the corporate ladder."

"Now she works for Abyss and might spy for Scorpio." Bhaaj never liked coincidences. "Maybe she eventually figured out Kiro's identity and told Scorpio."

"What for?" Jak asked. "You think Zaic Laj is Kiro's father? Goddess, that'd be a hoot."

"Yah. But it's not true." Bhaaj thought of the team files for Hyden and Kiro. "The athletes let us look at their genetic profiles. It helps us hone their training, to capitalize on their strengths and compensate for weaknesses. Hyden has nothing resembling an Undercity DNA profile. He's pure high-level Cries. Also, he and Kiro have no relation."

"Oh, well." Jak sounded disappointed. "Would've been a great reveal."

Bhaaj smirked at him. "You like gossip, eh?"

"Not gossip," he informed her. "Tools of my trade."

"Okay." Bhaaj knew he'd never admit how much he enjoyed the Whisper Mill. "Max and Royal, let us know if you can find anything else."

"Will do," Max said at the same time Royal purred, "Anytime, Bhaajo."

For flaming sake. "You got to stop this biz with your EI," she told Jak. "Make him behave."

He grinned. "My EI can't do for you. Only me."

She tried not to smile. "Cocky one, aren't you?"

"You two done playing?" Angel asked. "I got to get back to work."

"Yah. You go." Bhaaj didn't bother telling her to quit skulking around the shadow mesh. It wouldn't stop her. "Just be careful, eh?"

"Will do." Angel took off, jogging down a side tunnel that would take her back to Cries. Bhaaj headed in a different direction with Jak.

Time to investigate Vakaar.

"A Majda!" Mason exulted. "The judge is a freaking *Majda*."

Bhaaj peered at the holo-slate he'd handed her the moment she walked into his office. "It says her name is the Honorable Del Ama Rase. I don't see anything Majda." She waved the slate at him. "This just says she's going to hear Hyden's case."

"You bet. Tomorrow. She let his lawyer fast-track it." He seemed ready to jump up and down with glee. "I looked her up. She's married to Lavinda Majda's son!" He danced a few steps, which was hilarious given his complete inability to do the moves. "No way will Zaic Laj bribe or coerce a Majda to do what he wants, especially to hurt a team that includes a Majda runner."

"Oh!" No wonder he wanted to shout. "That's great news."

"I've added Hyden to the Olympic team," Mason announced, his good cheer burbling in his voice. "We're going to Foreshires Hold!"

CHAPTER XXII
Legacy

The Olympic Village on Foreshires Hold clustered on the edge of Eos City. Jacob's Shire spread out beyond it for many kilometers, a paradise of gentle hills carpeted by cloud grass which, true to its name, rippled as if clouds tipped by golden sunshine were flowing across the land.

Kiro walked with Zee in silence, immersed in the beauty. Metropoli had been exciting, full of urban marvels and gleaming skyscrapers. Here on Foreshires, countryside rolled everywhere, a testament to how ecosculpting could make a world more habitable for humans than Raylicon, where the failure of even the more extensive terraforming became worse every century.

The amber sun shone more benignly here than the harsh white orb that punctured Raylicon's sky. It looked bigger even than Kiro's palm when he held up his hand to block the golden rays. Foreshires was the second planet of an orangish star called Ruth, named for the scout who had rediscovered it after Raylicon regained star travel and went searching for colonies that had survived the fall of the ancient Ruby Empire.

The sun had just reached its zenith when their ship landed this afternoon. Only a few hours had passed since then, but already the orb had descended more than halfway to the horizon, bearing witness to a day of a mere twenty-two hours. The small tilt of the rotation axis for the planet meant less variation in weather. Winter might be a few degrees cooler, and its night a bit longer, but nothing drastic. Kiro couldn't imagine living in a place like this, so kind to its human settlers.

The gravity, however, was another story. He felt heavier, only a bit, but even a slight difference could affect his performance. At least they had twenty days to adapt before the Olympics.

He looked forward to spending time here. From what he'd read, this continent had twenty-three cities. It amused him that the original colonists named them with numbers. Eos City started with the exciting designation of Seventeen. When the Imperialate discovered Earth and its Allied Worlds, however, the people here renamed this city Eos for a dawn goddess in Allied mythology. They honored the dawn of a new era, now that they—Earth's lost children—had found their home of origin after believing for thousands of years that Earth was no more than a myth. It seemed impossible they'd left that home six millennia ago. No culture on Earth from that age bore any resemblance to those of her lost children. Yet no doubt existed; they all came from the same stock. Earth had given birth to Kiro's ancestors.

Nothing on Foreshires awed Kiro as much, however, as its rings. At this latitude, they spanned the sky in a glorious arch with its high point about halfway to the zenith. The arch looked mostly white, but as it curved to the ground, it shaded into gold, pink, and then red. The rings had formed a few centuries ago when a tiny asteroid glanced off the surface of the planet. Given that the impact happened on the other side of the world, the colonists hadn't realized it occurred until the sky dimmed and the rings formed. They survived the worst of the fallout as the planet recovered, but bits of material still sometimes showered the planet like falling stars.

Kiro took a deep breath. The air felt fine, not gritty. Although the fog from the impact had long ago cleared, an almost invisible suspension of ash still floated in the air. His nanomeds handled it fine, keeping his lungs healthy, but he didn't know yet if it would affect his athletic performance. He liked the visual effect, though. Foreshires Hold had a golden sky instead of the bluer hues humans had come to expect on worlds where they could breathe.

"Not like home," Zee commented.

"Pretty," Kiro said.

"Yah. Heavy, too." She glanced at him. "You see okay?"

"Fine. You?"

"Is good."

With that lengthy exchange done, they entered the lobby of a one-story building where the team was gathering. He could see the grounds of the Olympic complex through the many windows, its cabins set in the bucolic landscape. This place had more trees than buildings, with paths shaded by graceful arches of branches.

Mason motioned everyone over to him. "Coach Bhaajan is checking us in. You can go get settled in your cabins now. At hour sixteen this evening, we'll meet for dinner in the Skylark Room of this building. Make sure you get the time right; the day here is a *lot* shorter than on Raylicon."

As a murmur went through the group, with people asking questions, Kiro looked around the lobby. It had wicker furniture and many plants in large vases. On the far side, Coach Bhaaj and her husband were talking to a server-drone. When Kiro traveled with his parents, they always stayed at luxury hotels with human employees. Even knowing such hotels meant their staff as an amenity for their wealthy clientele, Kiro preferred the drones. He could always tell what the human staff felt, despite their outward courtesy. Many disliked their rich customers. Robots didn't care.

Now that he spent so much time in the Undercity, the luxury of his life bothered him deeply. He had no right to such privilege, living in that huge house with almost no people. His mother had agreed to donate anonymously to Mason's athletic fund when Kiro asked, which helped fund the banquets that fed the Undercity athletes and their families. His main regret about spending less time at home nowadays was that it left his mother alone. He appreciated her even more after seeing how Hyden's parents had tried to destroy his dreams. At least the judge had ruled in Hyden's favor, giving him emancipated status so he could come here.

It didn't take long to get their cabin assignments in the Olympic Village. At their request, Kiro, Zee, Strider, and Lamp shared one with four beds in two bedrooms. No problem there. Circles of kith and kin in the Undercity often shared living accommodations, with rooms partitioned off by handmade screens painted in bright colors or rock formations that resembled delicate stone curtains.

After they got settled, Kiro stood at the large picture window in the living room and looked out at Jacob's Shire. Close by, several dirt paths meandered through the meadows, and farther out a single country road stretched across the fields. A few groves of vine-willows cast double shadows, one from the sun and a more diffuse silhouette from the rings. As he watched, three animals with purple fur and big ears leapt out of the grass, playing. In here, he smelled the clean scent of the cabin and heard Lamp grumbling in the other room about his shoes, but he remembered the subtle perfume of the cloud-grass outside and the whisper of shimmerflies in the air.

Yah, this was good. He looked forward to the Games. He'd reached for his dream—and caught that elusive ribbon of hope.

"The point," Jak repeated as he unpacked his duffle bag, "is that we aren't actually married."

"Yah we are, by common law," Bhaaj set her duffle on the bed, intending to unpack, but instead she sunk into a well-cushioned wicker chair. She just wanted to sleep. Goddess, she felt so *heavy*. Yah, she was in her seventh month of pregnancy, but she hadn't felt like this on Raylicon. At least she could still get around fine.

"The problem is, we have no proof," Jak said. "We're lucky the port authority took our word." He'd dressed in his usual black, lean and mean, along with his gauntlets, all tech-mech and black leather. The smart-buckle on his belt contained its own mesh system, able to communicate with his gauntlets and anything else he wanted. The cognitive dissonance of that exorbitantly priced tech with his Undercity style hadn't pleased port security, who'd wanted to hold him despite his documents being in order. When Mason stressed that Jak came with their Olympic contingent, the husband of Raylicon's pregnant coach, the reluctant authorities had relented and let him through.

"I'm not sure we can even claim we're married by common law," Bhaaj admitted. "We don't live together."

He went back to unpacking, which consisted of tossing his clothes on a chair. "Sure we do."

"Not officially." She shifted, trying to get comfortable. The smart-chair did its best to help. "My legal address is that penthouse the Majdas gave me in Cries."

"Yah, but you stay at the Top Mark more than you sleep there." He took out his shaving kit with its top-line meds that he sometimes let clean stubble off his face.

"Yah, that's really going to convince the authorities we're married," Bhaaj said dryly. "I'm living in your illegal den of iniquity."

He sat on the edge of the bed, facing her. "All the more reason for us to make it legal by Imperialate law. I don't want any question about our child being legitimate. Or for travel. If port security had checked me out more, they could've found out I'm considered a criminal on Raylicon. Better we avoid searches like that by having documents ready to show them."

Good point. "We can do it here. But where? And when?"

"I'll look into it." He watched her intently. "You sure you're okay?"

"I'm good." When he started to speak, she lifted her hand. "Really. The ship's doctor said I'm fine, and the baby's fine." Tiredly, she added, "It's just this gravity."

"Really? I can't tell any difference."

"You're not hefting around a kid." Although she hadn't gained as much weight as Karal Rajindia wanted, she'd managed enough that the doctor had okayed this trip to Foreshires.

He laid his hand on the swell of her abdomen. "Still not believe it."

Bhaaj felt her face doing embarrassing things, like softening. "Not real, eh?" Except it was real. They were becoming parents. Along with that terrifying truth, she felt an emotion so strong, she struggled to define it, a mixture of love and a fierce protectiveness.

"Not know how to be parent," Jak said.

"No idea," she agreed.

"We need learn."

Bhaaj grinned. "Got great way to learn. You get me dinner. Good start."

He laughed. "You're perfectly capable of getting your own dinner, my non-wife wife. Besides, we've got that team meeting in twenty minutes."

Bhaaj sighed. She had too much to do, with only two tendays for it all. "I need to check on Dice and Shiv too." Although both had behaved since Metropoli, they all needed to be extra careful. Sure, the media had come out on their side lately, but it didn't stop haters from saying Undercity athletes didn't deserve success. She'd interested recruiters in Dice and Shiv on Metropoli, but that had fallen through after the cheating allegations. Now, with the Undercity resoundingly cleared, she hoped to pursue those inquiries again. Which meant Shiv and Dice had better be on their best conduct.

"I've checked both cartel boys," Doctor Izaka said. The mild breeze in the Foreshires stadium lifted her hair, then gently released the strands. "They're fine. No sign of drugs."

Bhaaj scowled at her. Bad enough that many Cries citizens couldn't tell people from the Undercity apart. Izaka couldn't even get their sex right? She was a doctor, for flaming sake. She ought to know better.

"Shiv is a girl," Bhaaj said shortly. "Not a boy."

"Shiv Kajada?" Izaka squinted at her. "Yes, she's clean too. When you said the cartel pair, I thought you meant the Vakaar boys."

Boys in plural? Bhaaj didn't know whether to be confused or angry. Although she knew most of the Undercity athletes, she hadn't met a few of them before they joined Mason's team. Had the Vakaars hidden the identity of a second family member? Hammerjan better not be using these kids to carry secret cartel biz to other worlds.

"Which two boys?" Bhaaj asked.

"You know," Izaka said. "Dice and his cousin."

"Dice doesn't have a cousin. Someone lied to you."

The doctor scowled at her. "I'm talking about genetic results, not what anyone told me."

"He can't have a cousin." She might not recognize all the Vakaars, but she'd know about a relation that close to Hammerjan. The cartel boss only had one child; if this supposed cousin existed, he'd be second in line as her heir.

"Of course he has a cousin," Izaka said. "Kiro Caballo."

CHAPTER XXIII
The Opening

"Then why the blazing hell didn't anyone tell me!" Mason's voice boomed in the living room of his cabin. "You didn't think this was important enough even to *mention?*"

"Your athletes are my patients!" Izaka, who normally never raised her voice, sounded furious. "Their records are confidential!"

"I *needed* to know," Mason said.

"I'm the team doctor, not your spy!" Izaka barked.

"Enough!" The single word thundered from Duane Ebersole, with a military snap that made Bhaaj raise her head. She'd been sitting at a table with her forehead in her hands, but now she looked up at Duane. Everyone stared at the usually silent security chief standing by the door. No one else had sat down; they'd all faced off like combatants in a boxing ring.

In a quieter voice, Duane said, "Yelling at each other solves nothing." Turning to Bhaaj, he said, "I gather you had no idea about Kiro."

She rose to her feet. "No one does. I doubt even he knows."

"Why wouldn't he?" Izaka asked. "Don't all these Undercity kids know each other?"

"He's not Undercity," Bhaaj said. "He lives in the Cries Willow District." Izaka would recognize that name as the most affluent area in an already wealthy city. "His mother is an exec."

"Goddess," Izaka murmured.

Mason spoke uncomfortably. "Someone has to tell him."

"I will." Bhaaj wasn't sure how yet, but Kiro needed to know.

"We should wait until after the Olympics," Izaka said. "It might affect his performance."

"He'd never forgive us," Bhaaj said. "He wants the truth. Not knowing is tearing him apart. Yah, he hides it. But imagine realizing at his age that your father might not have sired you, except no one can say for certain, and you dread asking your mother. Talk about stress."

"I don't see how he can be Dice's cousin," Jak said. "Hammerjan only had the one brother, and he died years ago."

"Twenty years." As the realization hit Bhaaj, she added, "Kiro is twenty years old."

"Shit." Jak summed it up in one word.

"Do you think the Vakaar cartel boss knows?" Duane asked. He had that look Bhaaj recognized, the one that meant he'd discovered a problem that needed investigation, and fast.

"I doubt it," Bhaaj said. "Kiro was born long before Hammerjan took over the cartel."

"What about Gwen Caballo?" Mason asked. "Is she actually his mother?"

"Yes," Izaka said. "Her genetic profile was in the documents she provided. Not his father's profile, though."

"No wonder Doctor Rajindia didn't find a genetic match for his father in her Undercity DNA database," Bhaaj said. "The Vakaars won't let her treat them."

Jak's look darkened. "These doctors have no business keeping DNA profiles on us."

"The athletes ask us to." Bhaaj motioned at Doctor Izaka. "Our medic has records for the kids on this team. For the rest of the Undercity, Doctor Rajindia talks it over with her patients. It's their choice whether to let her keep their genetic data."

He gave her an incredulous look. "And people actually agree?"

Her voice gentled. "Jak, yah. It can identify people at risk for diseases, and it helps Doc Rajindia find the best medical treatments." Softly she added, "It's also how I found my only living relative. My cousin."

"That was good," he acknowledged.

"Your athletes know I'm keeping records," Doctor Izaka said.

"Do they understand the ramifications?" Jak asked. "Without their written permission, it's illegal to create genetic profiles for them."

Mason spoke. "Actually, that was part of the docs they signed for the team." He glanced at Bhaaj. "They understand what those forms meant, yes?"

"Yah. I went through it with them in detail." Bhaaj saw Jak's point, though. He'd never met Izaka before this trip and had no reason to trust her, not like they had with Doctor Rajindia, who'd spent years running the Undercity clinic. To Izaka, she said, "Just to be sure, any DNA records you make don't go beyond this team, right?"

"Absolutely." Izaka looked apologetic. "I genuinely thought you knew about Kiro."

Jak spoke in a rumble. "If Bhaaj believes it's acceptable for you to have DNA profiles for the athletes, I trust her judgment. But understand me, Doctor. You have no permission to keep genetic data on either myself or our daughter, either before or after she's born."

"I don't intend to." Although Izaka met his gaze, Bhaaj recognized her tells. Even this hard-nosed Majda doctor feared Jak.

"Ho!" Mason exclaimed, suddenly delighted. "It's a girl, then?"

"Ah, fuck," Jak said.

Bhaaj smiled at him. "It's all right." They'd intended to keep that private, but she didn't mind his unintentional reveal.

"Well," Mason said, reading the room. "We need to decide how to move forward."

"Decide what?" Izaka asked. "Knowing this about Kiro changes nothing."

"Yah," Bhaaj said. "It does change one thing." One huge thing.

She had to tell him.

"I don't understand." Kiro stood with Bhaaj in the shadow of the stadium wall. The golden day, with its gentle sunshine and perfect temperature, did nothing to ease his strained look. "You're saying my biological father ran drugs for a cartel?"

"I'm sorry." Bhaaj wished she had better news. "He was the brother of the current Vakaar boss. Dice is your cousin."

"*Dice?* That can't be. My cousin?" Then he added, "Except he's an empath. You know, right? A strong one. It's why he wants out of the cartel. He can't bear it."

It didn't surprise her that Kiro had figured it out. Nor did it surprise her to realize the two of them resembled each other. She hadn't seen it before, not consciously, probably because to some extent Kiro looked like all the Undercity kids.

"But my mother," he said. "I saw the forms. She's absolutely my mother." His voice caught. "You're telling me that she had an affair with one of the worst criminals on Raylicon."

"I'm sorry," Bhaaj said, knowing he needed to hear the Cries words.

Dismay surged in his voice. "Zee! Strider and Lamp! They'll shun me. Cartel members can't be Dust Knights."

"You aren't a cartel member." Bhaaj's gaze never wavered. "Anyone can be a Knight if they do the training, which you've kept up despite your other commitments, and if they agree to the Code, which you did that day you told Strider's gang you would become their fourth in full, with all that it meant." Since then, he'd spent most of his limited free time in the aqueducts, helping look after their circle. "That oath against drugs is why we have no cartel members, and why they hate us. But it isn't unheard of for a punker to join the Knights. One did, years ago."

"What happened to him?"

"Her." The memory still troubled Bhaaj. "Her name was Dark Singer."

"The Vakaar assassin?" He squinted at her. "I thought the police caught her after she killed all those Kajada punkers."

"Not exactly. Singer became a Dust Knight after the war. She had a husband and a child, and she wanted out of the cartel. She was an empath. But we couldn't do enough for her." That failure haunted Bhaaj. In the end, though, some good had come from it. "She asked for my help in going to the authorities, and I arranged a deal. In return for them giving her family witness protection offworld and sparing her from execution, she gave them everything she knew on both cartels. It's one reason the cartels have lost so much power."

"Witness protection." He watched her with unease. "Will I need that now?"

"No, you won't." She spoke firmly. "It's your choice who to tell. Even if Hammerjan learns the truth, you're an adult now, not someone she can mold from birth." Bhaaj hesitated. "I can't be sure what would happen, though. You're second in line to run the cartel, after Dice."

"I'm *what?*"

Goddess, she hated this. "You're the spare for the heir."

His voice turned harsh. "Cartels aren't royalty. I would *never* join them."

"I'm sure Hammerjan would realize that. But I'd advise against telling anyone. It's safer."

"I can't lie to Zee, Strider, or Lamp."

"I know. But Kiro, they don't want to lose you." On that, she had no doubt. "They won't tell anyone without your okay. If people ask if you come from the Undercity, give a limited truth. Tell them Doctor Rajindia never found a genetic relation for you with anyone in the Undercity."

"That's because she doesn't have DNA records for the Vakaars."

"You don't have to say that."

"Zee and them will know." He sounded miserable. "What if they reject me?"

"They won't. You're part of them." She spoke dryly. "Given how closely related we all are in the Undercity, I wouldn't be surprised if they have relatives in the cartels, too. I think Zee is second cousin to a Kajada. Strider and Lamplight probably have some relation they don't know about just like you didn't know about yours."

He looked out over the stadium, where athletes were doing exercises to adapt to the heavier gravity. Strider, Lamp, and Zee were jogging together around the track. As soon as he focused on them, they looked in his direction, almost as one. Zee waved.

"You four are a unit now," Bhaaj said. "It happens that way with strong empaths."

He turned back to her. "Like my mother with my father."

"Yes, probably. He offered her something no one from Cries could give her."

"What happened to him?"

That was more difficult to answer. "Kiro—he died. Twenty years ago."

His face paled. "I was born twenty years ago."

"Yah." With regret, she added, "I don't know much. Back then, I was in the army."

"Do you think his death—did it have anything to do with—with how he lived?"

She gave him the difficult truth. "Yes, I think so."

"Why?" Anguish creased his face. "Didn't he care about his family in Cries? It takes nine months to have a baby. If he died twenty years ago, my mother was already pregnant."

"I think it meant everything to him." She'd heard his father wanted to stop punking, and she could guess the rest. He must have intended to start a new life with his new family. Except back then, Hammer Vakaar had run the cartel, and she made her violent daughter, Hammerjan, look like a saint. Hammer had left a swath of bodies in her wake, her violence reaching into Cries and even offworld. Legend claimed she had her son murdered for trying to leave the cartel. In her psychotic view of the universe, she'd rather see him dead than free to live his own life. If she'd known she had a grandson, she'd have stopped at nothing, including killing Gwen Caballo, to kidnap Kiro, replacing her son with her grandson.

Bhaaj spoke as gently as she knew how. "Your father tried to leave the cartel before your birth. Hammer Vakaar would have seen that as the ultimate betrayal. She'd have tried everything she knew to find out why. But he didn't tell her. If he had, she'd have come for you." Softly she said, "Kiro, he gave his life to protect you and your mother."

His voice caught. "Because he was a cartel heir, next after his sister?"

Bhaaj stared at him as the full import hit her. "Kiro! Your father was born first. And you're older than Dice. It's *you*. You're the firstborn Vakaar heir." No wonder his father died to protect him. Kiro's life could have been so much crueler had the Vakaars known he existed.

"Coach." Kiro sounded as if something broke within him. "This is—I can't—It's too much."

She so much wished she could take away the pain. "If it helps any to know, I've no doubt your parents loved each other. It's the way with empaths." She didn't add the bitterest truth for the cartel, that it destroyed an empath to be so close to that violence and brutality.

"But what about Dice?" Confusion furrowed his forehead. "They let him come here."

"My guess? Hammerjan doesn't want her son to go through what her brother suffered." She suspected similar held true for the Kajadas. Dice and Shiv were empaths—and they had to get Kyle DNA from *both* parents for the traits to manifest. Which meant both cartel bosses carried at least some of the DNA. Life had warped Cutter Kajada, the Kajada leader, twisting the inquisitive child Bhaaj had known into a sociopath. And Hammerjan? She was harsh, yes, but not with the horrific edge of violence wielded by her psychotic mother.

Kiro glanced beyond her and nodded. Turning, she saw Zee, Strider, and Lamp a few meters away, watching them, their faces concerned. She didn't doubt that they'd picked up his pain.

She looked back at Kiro. "Go with them. Let them help."

He just nodded, his face strained.

"I wish I had better news," she murmured.

"At least you told me. Everyone else lied."

With that, he went to the others. As they gathered around him, Bhaaj turned away, giving them privacy. She could see Duane loping toward her along the stadium wall. Normally she'd have jogged to meet him, but she felt too heavy today, worn out from carrying the heir for yet another criminal boss. No, damn it. They'd find a better way for their child.

She met Duane by the stadium wall. "What's wrong?"

"It's the Trader teams." He spoke grimly. "They've arrived, all four of them."

Bhaaj forced herself to use a neutral voice. "They have a right to be here."

"They've asked about the Undercity athletes."

She froze. Did the Traders *know* the Undercity had a wealth of the one resource they valued above all others? Kyle operators served two and only two purposes for them: to counter the advantage the Kyle mesh gave to the Imperialate, and to act as providers, the slaves that Aristos craved beyond all reason.

"Why the hell are they asking about our athletes?" she said.

Anger edged his voice. "They consider us all less than human, but that goes twice for the Undercity. They're offended the officials here expect them to compete against our team."

Bhaaj stared at him. "They actually said that?"

"The exact words of the Quaelen coach were, 'The Olympic

Athletic Committee should be ashamed for asking us to run against worthless animals.'"

"Well, fuck them." Memories of her decades fighting the Traders rushed back to Bhaaj. Their brutality made the cartel bosses look mild. The Aristo assumptions of superiority had become so ingrained in their worldview that it grated just to hear their voices as they spread their narcissistic views throughout humanity.

"You have to talk with your athletes," Duane said. "Warn them."

"I have, believe me."

"Still. Warn them again." Dryly he added, "Patience and turning the other cheek are not, shall we say, the Undercity way."

She gave him a wry look. "Yah, true."

"Let's just hope the Traders don't realize so many of your athletes are empaths."

"We can't hide it. They know when they come near one of us. They feel it." She shuddered. "Torturing Kyle operators is pure ecstasy for them. And we can sense them. Their minds are like a hellwind waiting to destroy us."

He grimaced. "Why would anyone breed an entire race designed to prey on empaths?"

"They didn't." Bhaaj had studied the histories during her time in strategic ops, looking for ways to counteract the Aristos. The army did their best to hide the worst of the ugly truth. However, the Majdas had told her that she could read in Duane, and she took a wide-ranging interpretation of that permission. The history wasn't confidential, just downplayed. "The Skolian scientists meant to *protect* empaths, to shield us from negative emotions. They called it the Rhon project, after the head geneticist. And the project worked—but in a twisted way. It created the Aristos." With the best of intentions, the Rhon scientists had created the monster themselves.

"I've heard bits and pieces," Duane said. "Never the full story."

"Aristos are anti-empaths." Bhaaj took a moment to collect herself. "When they detect pain from someone's mind, their brain reroutes the signal to their pleasure centers. It doesn't happen with normal humans, but empaths project moods as well as feeling them. The stronger the empath, the greater the effect." She grimaced. "They use the word transcendence for what they experience from Kyle operators."

He was watching her closely. "You're an empath."

"Only mid-level." She thought of Strider's gang, of Dust and Shiv, of Tam, Angel, and Ruzik. "We've a lot of strong empaths on the team, Duane. Keep watch over them."

"I will, no doubt there." He regarded her with concern. "And you keep away from the Aristo teams, Bhaaj. I mean it."

She somehow managed a wry smile. "Trust me, I will."

As long as they didn't bother her athletes.

Kiro lifted his face into the breezes and sunshine, struggling to savor the day. He stood with the rest of the team outside the stadium, all of them decked out in their Raylicon uniforms, waiting for what he'd always considered one of the best parts of the Games, the Opening Ceremonies.

Soon they'd enter the stadium, where a celebratory holographic light show would bathe them in radiance while they walked around the track carrying the red and gold Raylicon flag. Every Olympics had a different way of showcasing the teams: arrivals on giant air-balloons, in boats on a river, runs down a mountain, or what Foreshires did today, the traditional parade around the stadium while the crowds roared. It was exciting, full of energy, and he loved it all.

A shadow loomed over his joy, though. He understood why his mother never told him the truth about his father, but it still hurt more than he could say.

Zee laid her hand on his arm, watching him.

"Am okay," he murmured.

"Yah. Beautiful Kiro," she said.

Lamp and Strider put their palms over Zee's on Kiro's arm.

"We one," Strider said.

"Four made into one," Lamp told him.

"Always," Zee said.

Kiro laid his palm on top of their hands. "Always."

Music swelled in the stadium, loud enough to hear even out here where they stood waiting their turn. Excitement bubbled among the athletes until the enthusiasm became contagious. Their moods flooded Kiro, filling him with happiness instead of the pain he'd felt these past days.

Only two more teams to go before Raylicon. Athletes from the world Qabi were gathering at the tunnel entrance, ready for their turn to wave at the crowds, not only the one hundred thousand people who crammed the stadium, but also the trillions watching throughout settled space. Holo-casters predicted this would be one of the largest audiences in history for the Games.

"Goddess," Lamp murmured. "I never—so many people. In *one* place. And so happy!"

"They cheer for us, too?" Strider seemed stunned that such an experience could exist, let alone that they were *part* of it.

The Qabi team poured into the tunnel. When they finished, the next team approached, one that had kept their distance from everyone but now streamed forward. The Quaelen team.

Traders.

The burble of voices among the Raylicon athletes quieted as the Quaelen athletes gathered at the tunnel entrance and spilled everywhere, hundreds and hundreds of them. Kiro froze, realizing he was about to see Aristos in person for the first time. He felt an odd pressure on his mind, one that dampened his joy. The Quaelen track and field team looked magnificent, every athlete with the perfect build for their choice of events, long-legged distance runners, muscular arms for the throwers, powerful legs for sprinters.

Seeing them, Kiro couldn't believe Metropoli had accused Raylicon of genetic engineering. The Trader Aristos had entire programs dedicated to creating super-athletes, finding every means possible to get around the prohibition against genetic engineering. He'd always wondered if they paraded their athletic heroes through the media because it gave their people icons to worship, distracting them from their constrained lives. Given that a few thousand Aristos owned two trillion people, they had to keep their populations content enough that they didn't rebel.

The Traders never sent more than four teams to an Olympics held outside their empire, but those four were huge, each over a thousand strong, with the maximum allowed in *every* event. In contrast, Raylicon could have brought many, many more athletes; in some sports, like skiing and surfing, they had no one at all. Kiro didn't even know what "surfing" meant. No such paucity ailed the Traders. They sent their best from across an empire of two trillion people, finding every possible way to get around the restriction that prevented teams from representing populations larger than three billion. Even with only four teams, they always came in first or second in the medal count.

Despite the intent of the Games to stay free of politics, it never failed to rear its powerful head. According to treaty agreements between Skolia and Eube, any Trader slave who entered Skolian territory and asked for asylum became free. The Eubians balanced the risk of losing their best athletes to freedom with their determination to prove their athletic superiority over the rest of humanity. They took fewer teams so they had fewer people to control.

Similarly, when the Traders hosted the Olympics, far fewer Skolian or Allied athletes attended. Trader law classified them all as slaves. Aristos couldn't enforce that in Skolian or Allied territory, but they had no qualms in their own realm. Yes, the IOC had worked out a treaty that guaranteed the freedom of any Skolian or Allied citizen who attended Games run by the Traders. But every now and then the Traders claimed certain athletic superstars requested asylum to stay in their empire. Asylum from what? Kiro couldn't imagine giving up his freedom forever, not even for the Olympics.

Whatever the politics, the Eubians had arrived today. The Quaelen team gathered at the stadium entrance and spread out everywhere. The pressure on his mind increased, becoming almost unbearable. Why? He'd heard that being near an Aristo, or even a Trader with partial Aristo blood, could affect empaths. Although the Quaelen Aristo Line owned the team—literally, including all the athletes on it—he saw no one who looked Aristo—

And then Kryx Quaelen walked past the Raylicon team.

Oh yes, Kiro knew him; Quaelen ranked as the undisputed interstellar leader in the royal marathon despite his youth, only twenty-two. Tall and perfectly proportioned, he had the lean muscles and long legs of a distance runner. His face resembled the sculpture of a god too handsome to be human, with his high cheekbones, straight nose, and skin like alabaster. His black hair shimmered as if a lunatic deity had spun it out of black diamonds. His eyes truly were *red*. Kiro had always thought the media exaggerated that feature of Aristos, that they probably had brown eyes with a red tinge. But no, Kryx Quaelen's were pure red, as hard and as brilliant as rubies.

The young Aristo stopped only a few meters from the Raylicon team and stared at them. In perfectly cultured Skolian Flag, with a Highton accent, he said, "Goddess, you're all *providers*."

Kiro couldn't tear away his gaze. His mind felt caught on the edge of a mental sandstorm, frantically struggling to pull free before it destroyed him. He sensed agony from Zee, Lamp, Strider, from all the Kyles among the Undercity athletes, as if they were suffocating, gasping for a mental breath. He would die if it didn't stop, but he couldn't die, he could only live the misery—

Quaelen let out a long, slow breath as if he'd taken a drug that provided the ultimate ecstasy. "So many of you," he murmured. His thoughts oozed like an eel slithering toward them. *Suffer for me, little providers. Let your pain elevate you to a higher existence. You are mine, mine, mine...*

"Enough!" Suddenly Coach Bhaaj was in front of the team, facing Quaelen. Her next words came with a courtesy Kiro *knew* she didn't feel. Every word dragged out from her, but she managed them with what sounded like respect. "My greetings, Lord Quaelen. Thank you for your notice."

Quaelen's voice turned hard. "Is this how Foreshires Hold shows esteem to its Olympic guests? By letting people address a Highton with such massive discourtesy?"

Kiro didn't know which flabbergasted him more, that Quaelen described her greeting as rude or what he picked up from Quaelen's mind, that the youth expected honorifics such as *Your most esteemed, radiant Highness*. Quaelen's contempt blazed, that someone from the Undercity dared speak to him instead of groveling at his feet. His reaction went beyond narcissism; it stunned him that Coach Bhaaj could even look at him, let alone talk.

The storm of the Aristo's presence pounded Kiro's mind. Quaelen didn't do it on purpose; his mere existence created the agony. But the Aristo *knew* the misery he caused them, and he accepted it, coveted it, considered it right, proper, and decent, indeed, that it was his due. He believed it elevated the Raylicon team to suffer from his existence.

You can go to hell, Kiro thought, wondering if the Aristo could pick up thoughts. Given Quaelen's lack of response, he suspected that no, he detected only the pain.

Bhaaj met Quaelen's gaze straight on. Kiro felt her anger and revulsion so strongly, he wondered that it didn't scorch the Aristo

Lord. If Quaelen picked it up, he showed no sign. And he did affect Bhaaj, less than with stronger empaths, but enough to wrench her mind.

She said only, "My apology if I caused offense."

Her apology failed to impress the Aristo. He no longer cared, though, caught in his fascination with Bhaaj. "Ah, Coach," he murmured. "Or should I say Major, hmmm? I understand you fought against my people during your military service."

Bhaaj remained calm, not letting him provoke her into behavior that might get the Raylicon team penalized. It was, Kiro realized, what the Aristo wanted. The moment he'd realized they were Kyles, he knew that if he provoked them into violence, he could be rid of them before the Games even started.

"But you bring life, too, don't you?" he continued, his voice oozing disdain, so low that Kiro wouldn't have heard if he hadn't been standing right behind the coach. "Making little dust vermin. How nice of you, to create more providers to come under the umbrella of our glorious empire."

Bhaaj stared at him with no outward response, but Kiro felt the firestorm in her mind. She wanted to crush the Highton lord. As a sixth-degree black-belt in tykado, she could have pulverized even him, a highly trained athlete. Instead she chose diplomacy, besides which, she was eight months pregnant even if she didn't show as much as most women. Her fierceness burned with an intensity born of her Undercity background and a mother's drive to protect her child.

The Aristo waited for Bhaaj to explode. When nothing happened, he frowned. "You do know your spawn is an empath, right? I feel it. That little dust rat inside of you has a stronger mind than your own."

A wisp of surprise came from Bhaaj. She hadn't known her child had that much Kyle strength. Again, she just stood in front of her athletes like a wall barricading the Aristo. And she had done exactly that, Kiro realized, using her decades of experience to create a mental wall that not only protected her baby, but all of them, Undercity and Cries athletes alike. She didn't have enough strength to give them all barriers as powerful as she raised for her child, but she managed enough that Kiro no longer felt overwhelmed by the Aristo.

A woman came to stand with Quaelen. She wore the Quaelen colors, white with ruby accents, and her badge identified her as the

Quaelen head coach. Given the rusty red of her eyes and her elegant face, Kiro thought she probably had Aristo heredity. She looked around Coach Bhaaj's age, though it was hard to tell with the age-delaying processes high-end meds could provide. Kiro could also tell she desperately wanted to get the Aristo lord away from the Raylicon team before it started a diplomatic incident.

"Most Esteemed Lord Quaelen, your splendid Highness," she was saying. "My greatest apologies for disturbing you. We are ready to enter the stadium now, but we absolutely cannot go without your magnificent presence."

Seriously? Kiro thought. Her overdone honorifics so amazed him, the distraction helped him regain his equilibrium and strengthen his mental shields the way Bhaaj had taught them: *Imagine a fortress around your mind, one with every protection you can envision. It will spur your brain to alter your neural processes enough to interfere with the way an Aristo's mind affects you.*

As Kiro envisioned the walls and locks he'd practiced, Quaelen's effect receded. It cleared his mind enough to pick up more from the Quaelen coach. If she didn't speak to the Aristo with those platitudes, Quaelen could dismiss her, demote her in the slave castes, even send her to prison, whatever he wanted to do as punishment.

Quaelen, however, just gave her a wry look and spoke in his perfect voice. "You are tactful, Coach. I understand." With that, he nodded to Bhaaj and went on his way, joining his team. They were watching with fascination, their reactions varying from avid enjoyment to unease.

Kiro exhaled. As the huge number of Trader athletes poured into the tunnel and disappeared, so did the storm hammering at his mental barriers. He took a deep, shaky breath.

"Holy shit," Strider muttered.

Bhaaj turned to the Raylicon group. "How are you all?"

Ruzik took a breath. "Good."

"Not let them bother us," Tam stated, her gaze burning with defiance.

"Damn Aristos." Hyden looked as shaken as Kiro felt. "They act like we're nothing."

Kiro wondered if Hyden had any idea that the way he treated the Undercity athletes didn't feel that different from the way Quaelen had treated him. But no, that comparison didn't work. Hyden had changed, becoming less overbearing, even showing respect to his Undercity teammates.

The voice of an official boomed in the air, the fellow directing what the organizers called *The Parade of Humanity*, the entrance of each team into the stadium. "Raylicon, please gather your athletes at the tunnel. We'll be ready for you in about twenty-five minutes."

"Twenty-five?" Tallmount said. "It didn't take that long for the other teams."

"Trader team big," Shiv said. "Too big. We send some home, eh?"

Amused rumbles came from the Raylicon athletes, Cries and Undercity both. They headed toward the tunnel, not just track and field, but the other Raylicon athletes, too, including gymnasts, cyclists, sword fighters, and the soccer team. They had no water sports given that Raylicon had no surface water. Well, none if you didn't count the human-created lake at the Majda palace, which probably cost more to maintain than the entire economy of a space habitat. Regardless, they only allowed family to use the lake.

Bhaaj moved among the team, chatting with them. When she reached Strider's dust gang, she said, "You all handled yourself well."

Strider grimaced. "Not like boy with red eyes."

No kidding, Kiro thought. "Are Aristos all like that? I mean, in the way they affect Kyles."

"Yah," Bhaaj said. "Not many full Aristos come with their teams, though. They probably only have one for every fifty of their taskmaker athletes."

"Taskmaker?" Zee said. "What mean?"

Bhaaj spoke quietly. "Slave."

"Why he call us 'pro-vi-ders'?" Lamp asked, making the word an insult.

"Means empath," Bhaaj said. "Like you four."

"They bring empaths here?" Strider asked.

"Nahya. Lock them up. Not risk their empaths run away." Bhaaj switched to the Cries dialect. "I doubt he'd ever seen so many Kyle operators in one place."

More of the team had gathered around them. Hyden said, "I don't think anyone here has."

Jon Casestar, the army lieutenant, said, "Competing against Aristos can rattle empaths, shake them up, disturb their confidence."

A murmur of agreement rumbled among the athletes. Kiro didn't want to imagine how it would feel, running neck and neck with someone who affected him like Quaelen.

"Is true," Ruzik said. "But we can use being empath to help us."

Everyone blinked at him. "What you mean?" Rockjan asked in her gravelly voice.

"Sense how other runners feel," he said.

"Help us judge how to react," Angel added.

"It can help." Bhaaj spoke thoughtfully. "I never did it consciously when I competed, but I think I did react on a subconscious level, judging the behavior of other runners by their moods. It also helped with my situational awareness, especially in martial arts or ball sports."

"*Ball* sports?" Dice asked, trying to keep a straight face.

"Soccer, baseball, volleyball, that sort of thing," Bhaaj said.

Shiv smirked. "Lot of wicked balling, eh. Slicks give you medal, you do it well?" Laughter rolled around the athletes and their posture relaxed.

"For flaming sake." Although Bhaaj glared, Kiro could tell she wanted to laugh.

As the tension eased, they gathered into the groups the Raylicon officials had practiced with them. It seemed only moments passed before the orb floating above their team boomed with an official's voice. "All right, Raylicon. Start walking! Welcome to the Games!"

Together, they entered the tunnel, about sixty athletes total, a small team, but the largest ever brought by Raylicon. Kiro heard the haunting sounds of the Eubian anthem playing in the stadium, a work of incredible beauty in a minor key that seemed to weep. The end of the tunnel loomed, a wide arch with sunshine streaming into it. As if to join that optimistic vision, the Trader music faded away and the more joyous Raylicon anthem swelled.

In that moment, the first Raylicon athletes walked out of the tunnel and into the stadium. The crowd had given loud applause to the Trader team, especially their kin and friends who'd managed to wangle tickets from their government to come. The Eubian officials apparently kept tight control over who they allowed to attend. They wanted to make sure no one tried to stay on Foreshires Hold, but they also just as obviously wanted people to cheer for their athletes, to show that humanity celebrated Eube even in the territory of their enemies.

What astounded Kiro far more was how that applause swelled into a roar when Raylicon entered the stadium. People cheered everywhere for the world that represented the birthplace of both the Skolian Imperialate and the Eubian Concord, not just their friends and family but everyone, even the Allieds. Kiro raised his hand, grinning, waving at the crowd like the rest of his teammates. A flood of joy swept over him, the perfect antidote for Kryx Quaelen. Yes! They'd made it. Despite everything, the pitfalls, crises, barriers, and disappointments, they'd reached the Games.

CHAPTER XXIV
Semis

Four hundred meters.

It never ceased to amaze Angel that slicks spent so much time, effort, and expense to run that short distance faster than anyone else, not because they needed to escape, but just to go around a track one time, ending up where they started. Even more incredible, some of them had become so good at it, they beat even her. Slicks fast enough to survive in the Undercity. Amazing.

For the semi-final, she and the other runners left the waiting area inside the stadium and walked into the Foreshires sunshine. Bhaaj stayed in the coach's section inside. Just Bhaaj: Angel had needed it that way today. She hadn't wanted to tell Mason not to come because she didn't want to hurt his feelings. She liked him, even considered him part of her circle. He just talked too damn much, and it disrupted her concentration before a race. Somehow he seemed to understand. He stayed back, leaving her alone with Bhaaj before the race, and in that, he earned Angel's respect.

Regardless, they allowed no one on the track except the sprinters. Bhaaj and Mason would watch from their coach's seats in the first row of the stadium, near enough to the finish that Angel could go over for a knuckle-bump after the race. Some athletes even hugged their coaches. That seemed extreme to Angel, but she secretly liked seeing it happen.

Taking time to center herself, she bent over to stretch her leg muscles. She'd done well in the prelims, first in her heat and third overall. It earned her a better lane than on Metropoli. Apparently at the Olympics they didn't care as much about where you came from. Even the Traders had come, including that arrogant Aristo everyone knew would win the royal marathon.

Angel grimaced, trying to shut Kryx Quaelen out of her mind. She'd read about how Aristos affected Kyle operators. Bhaaj had also told her, more terrifying in her taciturn statement of *yah, they monsters,* than if she'd gone on at length about the horrors she'd faced in combat. But nothing had prepared Angel for Kryx Quaelen. Even now, far away from him, the memory of his malignant thoughts preyed on her mind.

Not think about, she told herself. She took a deep breath, then let it out. Yah, she felt good. She hadn't yet beat her personal best here, the time she'd earned in the finals on Metropoli, but given the heavier gravity on Foreshires, that seemed okay. She wouldn't have noticed the difference if she hadn't been competing; it only mattered when everyone ran so fast that the gap between winning and losing could be fractions of a second.

Angel shifted position, which did nothing except make her feel more prepared. She had on the Olympic-approved band Mason had provided in their sports kits. It said what she already knew, that she was ready to race. Her pulse, respiration, oxygen, and everything else looked good. In this afternoon warmth, she'd worn racing briefs and a crop-top. It astonished her that slicks designed clothes so well for running, right to the edge of illegal augmentation but never over that line, using cloth they called "lightweight and breathable, with maximum aerodynamic efficiency," which seemed far too many syllables to say, "Fast digs." It shaved fractions of a second off her time.

Everyone dressed that way. The men wore muscle shirts, not only because the super-cloth helped their times, but also because no one wanted to risk what happened to Ruzik and Kiro on Metropoli. From what Angel had seen, the House of Kaaj hadn't succeeded in doing anything except piss off the advertisers who showcased their products during the Olympics. Apparently the skimpier the clothes worn by the athletes, the better their sales. Whatever. Angel would have found it funny if the Kaaj nobles hadn't targeted her husband and Kiro.

Media orbs spun everywhere, including above the starting line. As more cheers went up from the crowd, a holo-vid ran above one of the other runners in this semi-final heat, showing her in a previous race. Ho! That footage came from the Metropoli meet. And yah, that was Bayonet, who'd crushed the field that day with her interstellar record in the 800-meter. Like Angel, she also ran the 400-meter, and today Angel had the misfortune to be in her heat.

The crowd had no such qualms, shouting their approval for the champion. Holographic reels of Bayo running appeared everywhere, the images floating high in the air, and anywhere else with a holoscreen, not only people's wrist bands, but bleacher seats, poles, food wrappers and water bottles. The crowd continued to cheer as the orbs announced the other runners in the heat.

When the intros reached Angel, the crowd also applauded her, which she'd never expected, given that almost no one knew her here. Their excitement flooded her mind, washing away her memory of Quaelen.

The Starter's voice came out of an orb, calling them to their assigned lanes. Angel was in lane six. She'd have preferred four or five, but this would do. It let her avoid the curve of the inner lanes, which she'd discovered helped her maintain a good rhythm during the race, but it wasn't so far out that she had trouble seeing the sprinters ahead and behind her. They used a staggered start, with sprinters in the outermost lanes farther ahead on the track.

As Angel took her place at the starting block, it beeped at her. "Your foot is over the line. Please adjust your starting position."

"Am doing," Angel grumbled. Holos glowed on other blocks, too, letting people know who needed to fix what.

The Starter called, "On your marks!"

Angel crouched down.

"Set!" the Starter called.

Lifting her hips, she balanced—

Boom! Angel exploded off the block—damn! She took the barest misstep, almost nothing, but it cost valuable time. Already she'd fallen into sixth. Pushing harder, she passed the person in fifth as she navigated the track's curve. They'd already finished half the race!

With a burst of speed, she kicked hard, passing the fourth-place runner. They were in the final stretch! Setting her sights on the person in second, only a few meters—about to pass—she leaned forward, shaving off milliseconds, but even as she crossed the line, she knew it wasn't enough. The final result would come from the laser beam across the finish and the holo-record, but Angel already knew. She'd placed third, which meant she'd failed to qualify for the finals.

The disappointment hit hard. Slowing to a walk, she tried to calm her raging adrenaline. She nodded to the sprinters who'd beaten her and won a place in the finals. Someone gave her water and a smart-towel that could judge the temperature she needed, so she nodded to them too. Although she drank some of the water, she dumped most of it on her head, trying to cool down. Her body had gone into fight-or-flight mode, and her instincts wanted her to *fight*. She had to calm down; otherwise, if someone startled her, she might sock them.

Angel stopped and closed her eyes, motionless. When she felt more centered, she opened her eyes and realized she'd halted by the coach's area. Mason was standing on the other side of the barricade, only a few steps away from her.

"—holo-finish record verified you came in third," he was saying.

"Not tell me that," she growled. Normally she liked it when he talked *after* a race because his voice soothed her adrenaline. Right now, though, she didn't need to hear about her failure.

"Angel, listen," he said. "The finals need eight people. We have three semi-final heats. Taking the top two from each heat only gives six."

"I know—oh!" Of course. After taking the top two runners from each heat, they'd still need two more for the finals. In these Games, they took the top two times from the runners who didn't qualify. "How my time go with other runners?"

He looked tentatively pleased. "So far, only one other person has a better time than you. If none of the non-qualifiers in this next heat best your time, you go to the finals."

"What you think?" she asked. "I make it?"

"This was the fastest heat so far." He thought for a moment. "The next heat has good runners, but they aren't as strong overall as in this one. So yes. I think you have a chance." Then he added, "But it's going to be close."

"I ken." Angel smiled her thanks, then realized what she'd done. Eh. It seemed she trusted him more than she'd realized. She resumed walking, regaining her equilibrium.

More runners nodded to her, so she did the same for them. It felt right. A code had existed among dust gangs even before Bhaaj formalized it for the Knights. If you won a challenge, you kept the spoils and let the losers go; if you lost, you gave up what you'd fought for and left. Of course, if vengeance, hatred, or cartels got involved, you ran like hell because what you gave up could be your life. It didn't work that way with slicks. You could nod to opponents without risking your life.

After a few moments, Angel left the finish area and went to join Bhaaj and Mason. As she came up to them, Mason said, "The next heat starts in about ten minutes." He sounded as worked up as she'd felt after her run.

"Still a chance," Angel offered, feeling verbose. Her adrenaline hadn't completely settled.

Bhaaj nodded. "And for Strider."

Good point. Angel didn't want to make the finals by excluding Strider. Zee was already out of the 400-meter after failing to qualify for the semis.

"What happened at the start?" Mason asked her. "It looked like you stumbled."

"Bad timing." Then Angel admitted, "Maybe I am too wound up."

"Not problem," Bhaaj said. "Gives way to learn for next race."

"Still got semis for the 200-meter," Angel said. "And classic on last day."

Mason beamed at her. "This thing with the classic, the holo-casters love it. You're the first person in Olympic history to run a sprint and a marathon at the same Games." He waved his hands with enthusiasm. "Have you heard the coverage? The media are going crazy."

Angel shrugged. She'd trained for sprints. She ran long distances because she'd done it all her life and enjoyed it. Mason liked to say how she had "all those slow-twitch fibers" as well as her "multitude of fast-twitch fibers," making her the "most amazing hybrid runner" he'd ever seen. Usually he added something like, "Not that I've seen that many hybrid runners." She didn't know what to make of all this twitching. Yah, sure, she'd looked it up, and she knew what it meant, but she enjoyed the way Mason glared when she told him she never jerked while she ran.

"I maybe come in last on marathon," she admitted. No one disputed her comment.

Beyond the coaches, in the stands, Ruzik was striding along. As Bhaaj turned, following Angel's gaze, Ruzik reached them. "Good run," he told Angel.

"Wish that true," she said.

Other members of the team joined them, talking and talking. It seemed only moments when the distant roar of the crowd in the stadium swelled again. Startled, Angel tapped her sports band.

"—crushed his previous record with his fastest time yet for these 400-meter semi-finals," a commentator crowed. "It's an amazing feat."

The male commentator said, "Strider from Raylicon is in second, and third goes to—"

"Yes!" Mason shouted.

Even as Mason grinned, the commentator added, "Had Strider of the Raylicon team run in the other heats, she'd have failed to qualify. However, this was a slightly slower semi. And we do have another first for the Raylicon team. This is the only time they've ever placed two sprinters in the finals, both Angel and Strider. Normally they don't place any."

Mason's happy face turned into a scowl. "For flaming sake. Did they have to add all that?"

Bhaaj laughed, making no attempt to hide her relief. To Angel, she said, "Nice work."

Ruzik beamed at his wife. "We go party."

"Angel still got 200-meter semi," Bhaaj said. "And you got steeplechase tomorrow." Giving them a stern look, she added, "*Not* party."

"Not go out," Angel promised.

She and Ruzik could stay in for their own private party.

Duane found Bhaaj as she was walking through the Olympic Village. He caught up to her so fast, it startled the purple-furred hoppers out of their hiding places among the flowers. Shimmerflies rose in a cloud, sparkling in the sunshine. Duane looked nowhere near as sanguine as the scenery.

"What is it?" Bhaaj asked.

"Dice and Shiv," he growled. "They're doing it again."

Again? She'd thought they knew they had to be on their best behavior. "What happened?"

"They went into Eos City to meet someone, same as on Metropoli." Surprise leaked into his voice. "Except this time they went together."

That made no sense. If Dice and Shiv were carrying messages so secret that the cartels didn't trust the Kyle mesh, they'd never go together. "Did you get any of what they talked about?"

"A lot more this time. I brought better equipment." He took a breath. "Bhaaj, it's *not* the cartels. They're asking for asylum. They want to stay here, on Foreshires Hold."

"But they know recruiters have asked about them." Several universities were looking at the two teens, especially since Shiv had reached both the 1500 and 5000-meter finals. Dice's climbing event would take place in a few days in a mountainous area north of Eos City, a ten-kilometer course over grueling terrain with several cliffs. Given his ability, honed over years of scrambling up rock falls, Bhaaj had no doubt he'd do well. "Why risk that to talk to—well, who?"

"It isn't any recruiter you've mentioned," he answered. "And something else. This time I distinctly heard Dice say they weren't balking."

"Balking at what?"

"At first I thought he meant they wouldn't balk at whatever they had to do to stay here. But I don't think that's it." Duane paused. "On Metropoli, they used Balker as if it referred to a person. Have you heard of that?"

"Max?" she said. "That ring any bells?"

"It could refer to several things," Max said. "Most generally, it means someone who refuses to comply. It's also used for a holo-art movement that challenges traditions, a native plant on the world Diesha, and a criminal syndicate on Metropoli."

That last didn't bode well. "Dice and Shiv met these people the first time on Metropoli."

Duane spoke grimly. "When Dice said 'balking' here, it sounded like he was saying he and Shiv didn't want involvement with something, and I doubt he meant that hideous art form or a twig-bug on Diesha." His face took on that *I'm-talking-to-my-EI* look. Then he said, "I wouldn't be surprised if the Vakaars reached out to the Metropoli syndicate years ago, when the cartel was more active in building offworld contacts. That seems to have stopped since the cartel war."

This sounded worse and worse. "You think these Balkers are trying to rebuild those links?"

"Possibly." Duane considered the thought. "If I had to guess, I'd say Dice and Shiv turned them down, but in the process, they revealed they wanted to stay on Foreshires. Whoever they're talking to might use that as leverage, to coerce Dice and Shiv to do what they want, or as an incentive, promising to help them stay here in return for their help."

Damn. "I need to talk to them again," Bhaaj said.

Duane nodded. "I'll let you know if I find out anything else."

After they parted, Bhaaj continued along the blue-stone path. Goddess, she felt heavy. The gravity didn't affect just her; the whole team was having trouble, including stumbles from both Angel and Zee in their sprints, and Azarina, who hadn't finaled in the 5000-meter race, only in the 1500-meter. Clearly thrown off in his timing, Jon Casestar didn't make the javelin finals. He compensated better with the discus, enough to reach that final, but Rockjan didn't get past the discus semis. She made the javelin finals because only ten people achieved the qualifying distance. To fill out the top twelve, they'd taken the athletes with the next best distances, including Rockjan. Mason had asked Bhaaj to work with both Rockjan and Jon today.

Before she did anything else, though, she had one other stop to make, something small compared to the big events here. It wouldn't take long, no fanfare, nothing of great interest.

For Bhaaj, it would be one of the most important events in her life.

Jak was waiting outside the county building. "You're late," he growled.

She smiled. "Such a ro-man-tic greet."

Although Jak returned her smile, it didn't take away the concern in his gaze. "You look tired."

"Baby kick too much." She motioned at the building. "We go, yah?"

"Okay." He still looked worried.

As they entered the building, her mood lightened. "Big day."

"Yah." Rolling his shoulders to ease muscle kinks, he added,

"Never thought do this, eh?"

"You never ask me," she said.

"You not ask me, either."

She pretended to glare. "You tell slick at the Top Mark first, before tell me."

His laugh rumbled. "He try pick you up. I just scare him a little."

A *little?* She'd never forget that time when a rich kid in the casino had hit on her while she waited by the bar. Jak had appeared and told the kid to quit bothering his wife. Ho! *Wife?* Where'd that come from? It startled Bhaaj, but it terrified the kid. He'd stared at the infamous Mean Jak with his mouth open and then stumbled over himself to apologize.

Today, she and Jak found the justice of the peace pacing her office, looking at the timer on her wrist. Even as they entered, she stopped and started to gather up her belongings.

"My greetings," Jak rumbled, his attempt to sound pleasant.

The woman looked up with a start. "Oh! You're here. I thought you weren't coming."

"We're terribly sorry," Bhaaj said. She'd long ago learned that apologies, no matter how strange they felt to her, went a long way with slicks. Setting her hand on her bulging stomach, she added, "I'm slower lately."

"Goodness." The woman smiled at them. "Congratulations."

"Thanks." Jak tilted his head toward Bhaaj. "We need to finish this soon, if we can. She's a coach for a team at the Games."

"Hey, that's exciting!" Now that they'd provided a good reason for the delay, she seemed all smiles and welcome. "Take a seat. I've got the forms ready."

So they sat. And signed the forms. It took all of five minutes.

In a sense, today was their semi-final. Except their final would have only two people and two winners. Someday, in the Undercity, they'd do a full ceremony with kith and kin. Today, this was enough. According to any law in any human civilization, she and Jak were now married.

CHAPTER XXV
Highton Privilege

Too tense to sit, Bhaaj stood with Mason in the coach's lounge where they planned to watch the steeplechase, clenching her VR helmet in her hand. *He'll do fine. He will.*

He has trained well, Max thought.

She hadn't meant to activate the EI, but he helped calm her down. *Hey, Max.*

The steeplechase offers Ruzik a chance to showcase his combined abilities in endurance, speed and technical skill, Max said, sounding like an advertisement.

Yah, but more comes into it. Like Ruzik's state of mind and how well he'd adapted to Foreshires. At 3000 meters, this event suited him better than shorter hurdle races, but he had to navigate water too, seven and a half laps around the track with twenty-eight fixed hurdles and seven water jumps.

The largest holo-display in the lounge showed the entrants prepping to run. Ruzik was pacing the way he did when he visualized a race, planning his strategy. Last night, he'd come to the track with several other athletes during their scheduled time to check out the course.

She pulled on her helmet, plunging into darkness. *Max, link me to the virtual feed for Ruzik.*

Done.

A display formed, the Olympic "marketplace," which showed the runners getting ready—and a lot more. Numerous avatars populated the track, available to provide whatever a viewer wanted to know about the Games. They could also let you place bets on a dizzying variety of options or create sims where people could "participate" in the steeplechase with the actual runners. Real and created spectators jammed the bright stadium, and commentators in striped balloons floated in the sky, telling the life-stories of the athletes.

When the announcers got to Ruzik, virtual replays of his Metropoli race ran as they talked about his performance. Although they said he came from the Undercity and belonged to a fighting group called the Dust Knights, they didn't have much to add, given that the Undercity was one of the few places that existed off the grids. They seemed to like focusing Ruzik, though, the young man who'd succeeded despite overwhelming odds—

And the advertisers loved him.

Behind Ruzik, displayed in huge letters, an ad for *Power-Run-Bar!* blazed like a visual shout. The advertisers designed the placement so well, Ruzik's image fit exactly into the ad, his handsome face and beautifully toned body acting as the perfect selling point for Power-Run. They'd even deep-faked an inset showing him holding one of their power-bars with a wide smile that he'd *never* do in public.

"I don't *believe* it!" Bhaaj yanked off her helmet.

Mason swung around to her. "What happened?"

"Power-fucking-Run is using Ruzik to sell their bars without his consent and without paying him." She felt ready to throttle someone. "We need a lawyer."

Scowling, Mason hit the EI panel on his gauntlet, then put on his helmet. "Show me the main feed—yes, that's it—the steeplechase—yes, Ruzik—holy shit." He pulled off the helmet. "I can't believe it. A sponsorship like that is worth millions. And they expected to get away with it?"

"They can't." She felt ready to punch someone. "Can't!"

Mason tapped at his gauntlet, flicking holos back and forth so fast they blurred. "Okay—there. I've set up the complaint—also commed the team lawyer—good. Yes! Sent."

Bhaaj blinked. "We already have a lawyer?"

He looked up at her. "Of course we do."

Her pulse started to calm. "Has this happened before? You did that so fast."

"It's my EI. As soon as I told it the problem, it knew who to contact and how. Spend enough years at this, and you learn how to get things done." When his gauntlet buzzed, he looked down, reading glyphs as they appeared. "Okay, my EI got the complaint filed—*seriously?* Someone has rocks in their brain."

"What?" Bhaaj asked.

He squinted at her, his face red. "On behalf of all of us who are mortified by the garbage the universe inflicts on the Undercity, please accept my apologies." Before she could respond, he added, "The EI representing Power-Run claims they didn't realize they needed sponsorship agreements with Undercity athletes."

Bhaaj stared at him in disbelief. "Are you kidding?"

Max held up his hand. "Don't explode."

"Why the hell not?" She felt ready to power-blast holes in someone.

Mason showed her his gauntlet. "Our EIs work much faster than us."

Bhaaj read the glyphs scrolling across his screen. *IOC Marketing and Legal Affairs has verified the illegal placement of Ruzik in the Power-Run advertising campaign and extends their apologies to him and to the Raylicon team. We have withdrawn the ad. The advertiser will be penalized and also required to pay the athlete for use of his image.*

"Hey," Bhaaj said. "How'd you get that done so fast?"

"The system is set up to deal with situations like this." He spoke dryly. "The IOC doesn't want their Games marred by scandals. They primed their EIs to catch problems before people make holo-reels about them that could go viral to the public."

She took a steadying breath. "You think Power-Run will actually pay him?"

"They better. Our lawyer will make sure of it." His voice lightened. "Maybe Power-Run will offer him a genuine deal. They obviously think he helps sell their product."

"We'll see." Bhaaj still wanted to throttle someone, but less than before.

On the dais across the room, a voice suddenly boomed out. "Runners, take your positions."

Startled, she turned toward the holo-display, which showed the steeplechase runners lined up in a waterfall formation, a curved line that ensured they all covered the same distance. Ruzik was roughly in the middle. It worried her. He tended to hold back at the start, which worked fine against weaker athletes, but his advantages faded here. In his current position, he could get boxed-in when everyone converged on the inside lane, pushing him to the back of the group.

"He'll be fine," Mason was saying. "He looks good." He turned to Bhaaj. "He looks good, right? Calm, composed."

"Yah. He does." Of course, Ruzik always looked calm and composed regardless of whether he felt happy, furious, in love, confused, determined, irate or bored, but she left that unsaid.

With a bang, the digital starter rang out. The athletes set off, and yah, they immediately crowded Ruzik, pushing him back. Then he notched up his speed, not a full kick, but enough to maneuver his way forward.

"Not too much," Mason said as if Ruzik could hear him. "Don't push too early."

When Ruzik reached third place, he fell into pace with the runners ahead of him. It didn't last, though; with everyone jockeying for position, another runner soon passed him. Although he showed no reaction, Bhaaj recognized his look. He wanted to *run*, fast and hard. Yet he held back, pacing himself within the front pack, but not in the lead.

Already they were approaching the first hurdle, a medium-height barrier. Unlike in the other hurdle races, these were solid, unable to fall over.

"Don't hit it," Mason said. "Come on, Ruzik. Get over—yes!"

In almost perfect form, Ruzik adjusted his stride and launched over the first hurdle.

"Only twenty-seven more," Bhaaj said. Watching, watching, if he could keep his form—there! He went over the next hurdle, not as smoothly, but not hitting it either. Although some athletes planted one foot on the barrier to get over it, Ruzik's height made it easier to clear the hurdles. He conquered them with smooth, practiced motions. When he arrived at the first water jump, he didn't judge his stride quite right and needed an extra step. This time he put his foot on the hurdle and launched himself forward enough to clear most of the water beyond the barrier.

So the first lap went, the second, then the third, until they were halfway through the race.

Bhaaj's ear subs suddenly activated, without her request, which meant Max wanted to let her know something had come up about the Raylicon team.

"—and the runner currently in fourth is Ruzik of the Undercity Dust Knights," the female announcer was saying. "He's the first Raylicon runner ever to do the steeplechase."

"It's been a good meet for their track and field contingent," the man said. "They've never had so many athletes in the finals. They rarely even reach the semis, as evidenced this year in gymnastics and fencing. Raylicon may be the most revered of all our worlds, but with its dying biosphere and tiny population, they just don't have enough people to compete on this level."

"That may be changing," the woman said. "This track and field team has four times as many athletes as their usual. And they're young. With one exception, the marathoner Tayz Wilder, these kids just recently qualified for the Olympics, all of them at the North-Metro tournament."

"It's a real shocker," the man said. "They blasted through that meet, doing so well that accusations of doping and genetic engineering abounded."

"And were proved false," the woman said. "In fact, the IAC issued a warning that their athletes needed better nanomeds to meet the health regulations."

"Ah, yes, the Undercity effect," the man said. "Apparently this huge influx of stars comes exclusively from the Undercity, a population that scholars describe as one of the most underserved in the Imperialate. Until a few years ago, they had no medical care at all."

"Indeed," the woman said. "Apparently they didn't have much available in the crime-ridden slums where you can't escape disease or violence."

"We've all heard the Undercity motto," the man said. "Run fast and live. Run slow and die."

"We don't have a motto," Bhaaj growled. "If we did, it wouldn't be that."

"That isn't even exactly what Angel said," Mason added. "But it's true, isn't it?"

"I suppose." It bothered her to hear their lives reduced to crime, disease, and violence. The problems they endured didn't define them, and they sure as hell didn't live in a slum.

"The leaders are still jockeying for position," the woman was saying. "Nancy Wilson from the Alpha Centauri team of Earth's Allied Worlds has moved into the lead."

"That's a triumph for Earth," the man said. "Having male and female athletes compete together has always provoked controversy with them. They almost refused to combine their Olympics with our Interstellar Games over it."

"The gap between their female and male athletes had already been closing, though," the woman said. "And more since then. In endurance events, their women can match any of ours. Their men have always been at the forefront in events that require greater upper body strength."

The man spoke dryly. "Along with our claims that they genetically engineer that advantage into their male athletes."

"Well, they claim we do it with our women," she said. "The truth is this: The officials here tested *every* athlete. They've so far had no violations."

"Enough already," Bhaaj muttered. She'd heard the arguments ever since she'd run for the army team and had the Earthers insist she was too tall, too strong, and too fast for a woman. She was only six feet tall, using the odd measuring unit that often cropped up in Earther measurements. It put her a bit on the tall side for a Skolian marathoner, but not so much that her longer stride didn't compensate for the extra weight, especially given that she'd been leaner back then.

Annoyed with the commentators, Bhaaj turned off her comm and focused on Ruzik. He'd reached the sixth lap, still in fourth despite the fight ahead of him for the three medal positions.

Mason studied the stats above his sports band. "He's running faster now."

Bhaaj could see it too. "He looks good. Not tired."

As Ruzik reached the final lap, the fifth-place runner behind him sped up, trying to move into fourth. Ruzik matched his speed, running in a steady lope. It moved him closer to the three leaders, but too gradually to pass—

And then he kicked.

With a sudden burst, as if he were running for his life, Ruzik surged into his final lap, gaining on the leaders. One glanced back, an

Aristo from the Traders, and then sped up. Ruzik ignored him, pushing hard, hard, *hard*.

"Come on," Mason muttered. "Remember what we talked about. You need speed, yes, but you need to maintain it for this entire lap."

"Mason, he's fine." Bhaaj's pulse leapt. "Look at him! He's going to pass that Aristo."

Her comm suddenly reactivated. "—and the Undercity runner, Ruzik of the Dust Knights, has moved into third place!" the man cried. "He wants that bronze medal!"

"It's what everyone is calling the Undercity kick!" the woman enthused. "Run fast, you live; run slow, you die."

"I really wish they'd quit saying that," Bhaaj grumbled.

"No Undercity runner has ever medaled at the Olympics," the man enthused.

"Wait!" the woman cried. "Barthol Iquar from the Iquar team of the Eubians just sprinted—good gods, look how close he is to Ruzik—they could collide on this last hurdle."

"An historic race!" the man said. "Look at Ruzik's face—he looks like he's in *pain*—

Iquar and Ruzik went over the hurdle at the same time, flying through the air. Iquar didn't need to attack Ruzik's concentration; his mere existence did it for him. And he *knew*. Bhaaj saw it in his face. Ruzik's mental pain was making the Aristo transcend, an edge no rule could even codify let alone forbid. What did you say, *my opponent cheated by causing me mental anguish that gave him pleasure, because I'm an empath and he's a sadist?* Yah, right, they'd be a laughingstock.

The two men came out of the hurdle with Iquar in third, moving fast, destroying Ruzik's hopes for a medal—and then Ruzik's face transformed. Yah, Bhaaj knew that look, his refusal to give in to anyone. Iquar's mental attack infuriated him even more than it rattled him. He kicked *again*—

"It's incredible!" the male announcer enthused. "Ruzik is fighting for third—he's even with Iquar—gaining on Wilson. Oma Ziel from Parthonia is still in first!"

"Ziel wins the gold!" the woman shouted. "Ruzik looks possessed— *HO!* It's Ruzik for the silver and Wilson for the bronze."

"Gods all freaking mighty!" Bhaaj yelled, in the same instant that Mason shouted. "He did it! He really did it! Bhaaj, look what he did!"

"Ziel is happy, that's for sure!" the female announcer enthused. "And right she should be. This is her second steeplechase gold; she's the defending champion from four years ago."

"She gives reality to the reputation of the steeplechase as an enthralling blend of athleticism, strategy, and grit," the man exclaimed. "This race is as much a mental battle as physical."

"That's certainly true for Ruzik," the woman added. "If ever anyone looked stunned to win a medal, there it is. Wilson seems pleased with her bronze. She came in eighth at the last Olympics, so this is a substantial improvement, her first medal in the event."

"Barthol Iquar is *not* happy with fourth," the man said. "It looks like he's motioning over his coach—I'm not sure what's going on—"

"Fuck, no." Bhaaj spun around and strode for the exit.

Mason caught up with her. "We need to get out there fast."

"Not to the track." She broke into a run. "The Aristos are going to hit the roof, having one of their stars lose a medal to an Undercity runner."

In moments, they reached a tunnel that led to the finish area. As they flashed their badges, an official directed them into a corridor usually off-limits to coaches. A man was running down it toward them, a fellow in the blue uniform of Olympic officials, with the five-ring logo of the Olympics and the arching rings from the Foreshires flag on his chest. He motioned for them to follow, then took off with them back the way he'd come.

"What is it?" Bhaaj asked as she and Mason ran with him. "What happened?"

"Barthol Iquar claims Ruzik deliberately shoved him on the last hurdle," the official said.

"Like hell," Bhaaj said. "We saw the footage. They didn't touch."

"Iquar claims otherwise." The man ushered them into a control center where people stood gathered around a holo-dais that displayed, again and again, the moment when Ruzik and Iquar hurdled together over the barrier.

Bhaaj strode to the dais. "They didn't touch! You can see it right there."

As the officials turned to them, Mason said, "I don't understand the protest. No contact took place. Even if it did, athletes in a closely packed steeplechase often touch each other. They can't help it. Accidents happen."

"Except nothing happened here, damn it." Bhaaj scowled at the officials. "Barthol Iquar doesn't want to lose to an Undercity runner. Period. He's lying."

"Bhaaj." Mason laid a warning hand on her arm.

She took a breath, then let it out. "My apology. I don't mean to be discourteous."

None of the officials looked offended. "I don't see it, either," one man said, watching the holos. "If they didn't touch, how could Ruzik have committed a foul against Iquar?"

A voice came from behind them, supremely arrogant—and familiar. The woman spoke Flag with a Highton Aristo accent. "If Barthol said this Undercity boy committed the foul, then it happened."

Combat mode toggled, Max thought.

No! Turn it off! The last thing Bhaaj needed right now was for her body to initiate combat. She recognized the woman who'd just arrived, someone she'd seen many times on holo-broadcasts. Vizara Iquar served as Trade Minister to the Highton Emperor of the Eubian Concord, one of the most powerful positions within that empire.

Iquar came to the dais, watching them with disdain, the epitome of an Aristo, with her classically perfect features, skin as smooth and cold as snow marble, glittering black hair, and ruby eyes. She wore the badge of head coach for the Iquar Track and Field team. Bhaaj had no doubt that her decision to coach had nothing to do with sports expertise. Her son and heir, Barthol Iquar, ran on that team, and among Aristos nepotism reigned.

Bhaaj felt as if a mental hurricane raged against her Kyle defenses. *Max, have my combat systems strengthen my barriers. Protect the baby.*

Done, he answered.

The Trade Minister studied Bhaaj. "So," she said. "They put providers in charge of sports teams now. And from the Undercity no less."

"What the hell?" That came from a man to Bhaaj's right, one of the Olympic officials. He was watching Iquar with a hunted look that matched how Bhaaj felt. *Another empath?*

Iquar turned away from him as if dismissing a bug that scuttled on the ground. She spoke to the official with the highest rank, a woman with the word *Referee* on her blue shirt and a holo-badge with the name Lyra Mollin. "My son says the Undercity boy hit him. If he says it happened, then it happened." She waved her hand at the display, which continued to show, over and over, that "it" had never happened. "Whatever you have there is irrelevant."

Everyone stared at her, stunned into silence. Bhaaj knew if she spoke, her anger would explode. *Max, get my nanomeds to control my adrenaline.*

I'm working on it.

The referee finally found her voice. "Minister Iquar, you honor us with your appearance at these Games." She spoke with respect, albeit probably not the obsequious fawning Iquar expected. "However, we must go with the evidence." She tapped her sports band, and the display on the dais cycled through different views of the moment when Barthol and Ruzik went over the hurdle. Every recording showed the same result: no touch. "As you can see, no contact occurred."

Iquar seemed genuinely puzzled. "What difference does that make?"

That evoked another silence. Obviously no one wanted to offend the Eubian Trade Minister, one of the most powerful humans alive, but just as obvious, her claim had no basis.

Bhaaj finally felt calm enough to respond. To everyone, she said, "Highton privilege."

Lyra Mollin, the referee, turned to her. "What?"

"Goodwoman Mollin," Bhaaj said. "Have you read *The Ascendence of Eube*?"

"Well, no." Lyra seemed baffled. "I've never heard of it."

"I've read it." That came from the official who had responded to Iquar's presence as an empath. His badge read *Tarj Hawkson*. "I studied political science and interstellar relations in college. That book was part of the curriculum."

Iquar nodded as if he had said the only intelligent thing she'd so far heard. If she sensed the horror emanating from his mind, she gave no indication. No, that wasn't true. The Minister *liked* Tarj. She sensed how uncomfortable, even injurious, her presence felt to him, and it pleased her.

"I don't understand," another official said.

"It's a treatise about how Aristos view their place in the universe." Tarj said, leaving out the meat of the text, its thesis that slavery offered the only humane treatment for the rest of humanity, that genocide would be preferable—except it would leave the Aristos without the vast infrastructure to build the empire they deserved as godlike beings. Yah, Bhaaj knew that treatise. Few regular citizens read political texts that dense, but every Skolian officer had to study it thoroughly, to understand what they faced with the massive Eubian military.

Bhaaj spoke in a flat voice. "*The Ascendence of Eube* defines the Aristo view of human life. Hightons rank at the top. If they make a statement, it becomes true. Period."

One of the other officials said, "Is this a joke?"

Minster Iquar's voice could have chilled ice. "You will not talk to me with that tone."

Bhaaj, this could get out of hand, Max said.

I won't let her steal Ruzik's medal because of their sick view of humanity. I don't care how exalted she considers herself. She doesn't have the final word here.

Technically, you're right. However, she could cause grief for these people.

Lyra Mollin's face tightened, and Bhaaj could tell she was about to tell the Minister to go screw herself, maybe with more tactful language, maybe not. Bhaaj spoke quickly. "Exalted Minister Iquar, please know that no one here would ever wish to show disrespect to your supreme self or your most esteemed son." How she got the words out, she'd never know; what she *wanted* to say would have burned the ears of a hardened criminal. "You honor us beyond measure with your presence. Please understand that in the lesser universe of our existence, we require rules and structure to operate. Your glorious son of course has no such limitations, and all here see the great honor he bestows on us by his participation, now and forever."

Everyone else, Mason included, gaped at her. In their view, she'd just groveled miserably to the Minister. It didn't matter. In the convoluted double talk of Aristos, she'd just told Iquar that if she got her son a medal by Highton-sanctioned cheating, everyone who watched the Games now or ever—which included a substantial portion of humanity—would know he succeeded only because his mother used Highton privilege to steal it for him.

Bhaaj chose their style of speech, despite her lack of skill at it, because it was the only way she knew that wouldn't violate Highton protocols. To be any blunter would have meant someone they considered the lowest of the low, an Undercity native, openly spoke ill of the Trade Minister's heir, in front of other people the Aristos considered almost as low. It would antagonize the Traders, possibly enough to damage the Games, for Aristos would never let such a slight go unpunished.

The Minister watched her with an appraising gaze. "Interesting, that a former Skolian military officer—a woman responsible for many deaths of my soldiers—speaks with eloquence." She made Bhaaj's rank sound like an insult. "The military, however, does not belong at the Games."

Bhaaj fought her instinct to clench her fists. Iquar knew perfectly well that a third of the Trader athletes here served in various branches of their military. She wanted to deflect attention from what Bhaaj had just said about her son. Well, two could play that game. She spoke coldly. "It is my understanding that many Trader soldiers compete with your teams."

The Minister waved her hand in dismissal. "It isn't the same."

"I don't understand," Lyra Mollin said, obviously thrown by the change of subject. "Do you mean it's all right for members of your military to participate in the Games, but not for a retired Imperialate officer to coach?"

Iquar considered Lyra as if she were a bug. "This is not about who coaches your teams."

Forcing out her words, as much as she hated them, Bhaaj said, "Please most Esteemed Minister, my people do not have your great intelligence. If you might, I entreat you to honor us with an explanation of why it doesn't matter that many of your athletes serve in your military, but it does with our lesser selves."

In other words, *Tell them what you really think, Minister.*

Even as Lyra opened her mouth, obviously to protest Bhaaj's words, Iquar said, "Of course it is different. You are inferior beings. You don't deserve to live. We do."

Silence descended. Bhaaj had nothing more to say. Iquar had just done it for her.

In the stunned silence, as people struggled to find a response that wouldn't inflame matters, Iquar turned to Lyra. "For the sake of your ability to manage these games, I will allow your rules to stand. I would not wish to see your attempts at running the Olympics fail due to a lack of proper oversight." Her tone left no doubt as to what she considered "proper" oversight: control by Highton Aristos. "You can consider our protest withdrawn. The Undercity boy may keep his little medal." After one last appraising look at them all, she turned and left the room, her stride firm.

As the pressure on Bhaaj's mind eased, she groaned and dropped into a chair by a console. Putting her head in her hands, she muttered, "Shit and fuck it all to hell."

Mason pulled up a chair next to her. "Thank you for waiting to add that eloquent estimation until after she left."

Bhaaj gave a shaky laugh but didn't raise her head.

Someone on her other side laid a hand on her arm. "Are you all right?"

Straightening up, she saw Tarj Hawkson standing there. "You're a Kyle?" she asked.

He sat in the chair next to her. "Another reason I studied that godforsaken book."

Lyra Mollin spoke up. "What just happened?"

Looking around, Bhaaj saw the other officials staring at them. "Hightons affect Kyle operators," she said. "Their minds—they're a nightmare for us. We can sense them. It's like being suffocated. Or obliterated."

Tarj spoke bitterly. "The worse we feel, the better they feel."

"She called you a provider," Lyra said. "What does that mean?"

"It's the name they give empaths," Bhaaj said. "Our pain 'provides' them pleasure. They call it transcendence."

"I'd heard about that," another official said. "But isn't that an exaggeration?"

"No." Bhaaj took a breath, willing her adrenaline to ease. "It's real."

"What you just saw," Tarj said. "That was mild. They deliberately inflict pain on their providers. The more pain they create, the better it makes them feel."

"That's appalling," Lyra said. "I can't believe her presumption, either, assuming we would discard the evidence showing her son fairly lost the race."

"Who does she think she is?" another official said.

"The Eubian Trade Minister." Bhaaj spoke tiredly. "It's the way things work with Aristos. A slave's word means nothing no matter how obvious any evidence that supports it. The Aristos adapt to these Games because they consider it an opportunity to demonstrate their superiority over the rest of humanity. To them, those of us from the Undercity rank even lower than the rest." Dryly she added, "A lot of people see us that way, not just the Traders."

Lyra spoke firmly. "Be assured, that is *not* how we see it here."

Bhaaj leaned back in her chair, heavy with fatigue. "She's still one of the most powerful humans alive. If we'd humiliated her, she'd have found a way to make us pay."

"We appreciate your ability to defuse the situation." Lyra grimaced. "The way you spoke to her—that couldn't have been easy."

Another official looked up from his comm. "The Ceremony Coordinator wants to know our status. The DCO finished testing the medalists and verified the winners used no drugs, cybernetics, biomech, genetic enhancement, or other alterations. The medal ceremony is waiting on our report."

"Tell them they can go ahead," Lyra said.

With that, they were done with the Aristos.

For now.

Ruzik stood on the podium, the breezes stirring his hair. For a moment, as the official put the silver medal around his neck, he even smiled. When the Undercity athletes had started on Mason's team, none had realized the significance of those medals. In the year since, it had become real, perhaps even more so than for other athletes. That medal symbolized a life that no one from the Undercity had believed could come to them from the universe beyond their constrained existence.

Watching Ruzik, Bhaaj felt a hotness in her eyes. It had to come from the dust in the air. She never cried. None of them did, none of the Dust Knights or punkers or cyber-riders or their kith and kin. The wetness on her cheek, surely it came from her eyes reacting to the atmosphere. Never mind that it had never affected her that way before.

Mason unabashedly wiped his palm across his face. When Bhaaj turned to him, he gave her a shaky smile. "Who'd have thought it? An Olympic medal, only the second one for track and field in the history of Raylicon."

"Yah." Bhaaj stood straighter. He was right; they all deserved the joy of this moment.

She hoped it wasn't their last.

CHAPTER XXVI
Progeny

Dice and Shiv were waiting at Bhaaj's cabin when she got back. With all that had happened, she'd forgotten she asked them to come by after the steeplechase.

"Saw Ruzik get medal." Dice beamed at her. "Good job, eh?"

"Yah." Bhaaj ushered them into her living room. "Maybe you two next. You're doing well." Shiv had qualified for the finals in both the 5000-meter and 1500-meter races, and Dice looked forward to the climb, a grueling event that always thrilled audiences. Although he'd never admit it, she knew he'd spent much of his life exploring Undercity places where canals, walls, or caves had collapsed. The cartels wanted routes no one else knew about so they could move their product in secrecy. Bhaaj hoped that skill would offer him an escape from that life—if he and Shiv would quit getting involved where they had no business going.

As soon as they settled onto sofas, Bhaaj got more serious. "You see Balkers again, eh?"

They exchanged glances, then moved apart, putting space between themselves on the couch.

Shiv motioned at Dice. "Not go with him. He, uh, ass-byte."

"Yah." Dice offered. "Kajada ass-byte, too."

"Seriously?" Bhaaj said, exasperated. Neither of them would ever win an acting award.

Dice's shoulders sagged, and Shiv pushed her hand through her tousled curls. They looked like kids trying to deal with the mess the universe made of their lives. At seventeen, they ranked as adults in the Undercity; many couples their age had already begun families. Bhaaj would never forget the day she and Jak promised to spend their lives together. They'd been twelve. Life, the army, and his casino had intervened, but they'd always come back to each other. It didn't take an empath to see Dice and Shiv felt the same.

"Coach—" Shiv lifted her hands, then let them drop.

"I here for you," Bhaaj said. "Coach Mason, too. Why talk to Balkers? You got us."

Dice squinted at her. "How you know we talk to Balkers?"

You just told me, she thought. Aloud she said only, "Know all," which wasn't even close to true, but still. With Duane's help, she knew a lot more than they realized. "You go at same time, yah? Vakaar and Kajada together." She used the three-syllable word *together* for emphasis. "Big risk."

Shiv spoke tiredly, as if giving up their pretense. "Bigger risk if go alone."

"Why go at all?" Bhaaj said. "I find you better escape."

Shiv's look turned impassive. "Not real."

"You tell us this on Metrop," Dice said. "Re-cruit-ers. But they change mind."

She could imagine how much that had disappointed them. "Not happen here."

"How you sure?" Dice demanded.

How indeed. Given the ramped-up testing at the Games, and how the Metropoli panel had upheld the honesty of the Undercity athletes, Bhaaj doubted anyone would try that route again. With the Aristos, though, who knew what they might do? She thought over the upcoming events. Traders were competing against both Shiv and Dice, but only the 1500 finals had an Aristo, and neither Shiv nor Azarina was likely to beat her. "Not think it happen here."

"We not take risk." Dice switched into Flag. "Coach, we don't want to go home. We never wanted that life even before we knew about this team."

Shiv struggled with her halting Flag. "I can't bear it. My brain—I don't know the words. It hurts. That anger, hatred, cruelty. The— the—" Her voice cracked. "The killing."

"We feel it." Pain saturated Dice's voice. "My mother knows, even if she doesn't say. If I stayed on another world, I think she'd let it happen. She'll never say it aloud, but I know her mind."

"I'd wondered," Bhaaj said. It wasn't without precedent. Dig Kajada had kept her children away from the cartel. On her deathbed, she'd told Digjan, her oldest daughter, *not* to follow in her footsteps, that she should look to Bhaaj instead. Digjan became the first Undercity applicant accepted to the Dieshan Military Academy, and last year she'd graduated as a Jagernaut starfighter pilot.

"It is possible for heirs to leave the cartels," Bhaaj said.

"Kajada went," Shiv affirmed. "Digjan."

"That why you talk to Balkers? They say they help you be like Digjan?" As far as Bhaaj knew, neither Shiv nor Dice had ever shown an interest in the military.

"Nahya." Dice shrugged. "Balkers reach out. Hear about us from Metrop."

"On Metrop, we stop talks with them after you say schools want us." Shiv scowled. "But that not work."

"The Balkers have people here, too," Dice said. "They claim they'll help us."

Bhaaj wondered if they realized they were switching back and forth between dialects. She spoke in Flag, which could someday be their language. "You're both Olympic athletes. And you're doing well. Recruiters *are* interested. I've had inquiries."

"You said the same on Metrop," Shiv told her. "It didn't happen."

"I can't promise nothing will go wrong," Bhaaj said. "But I can tell you it's unlikely."

"Hope so." Shiv grimaced. "We not like the Balkers."

"They know we cartel," Dice said. "That why they talk to us."

"They conda," Shiv added.

"Conda?" Bhaaj asked.

"Con-de-scend-ing," Dice said. "Think we stupid." His voice changed, taking on an almost perfect Iotic accent. "They would fall over from shock if I conversed with them in this manner."

Bhaaj gave a startled laugh. She hadn't expected that out of him either.

"They not really want help us," Shiv said.

"They want we spy for them." Dice switched to Flag. "Coach, I don't trust them. They thought we'd help because they think we're criminals on Raylicon. They figured we'd happily break the law for them in return for them helping us leave the cartels."

"Break the law?" Bhaaj asked. "How?"

"I'm not sure," Dice admitted. "They want information about 'elitist CEO koyos,' whatever that means."

Bhaaj froze. "What did you tell them?"

"We pretend we not ken," Shiv said. "We act slow. Real slow."

"Yah." Dice took on a blank look. "We get real stupid."

"When they think we too stupid to help, they send us away," Shiv said.

"We'd planned to talk to you even if you hadn't asked us here," Dice added.

"You handled it well." Bhaaj stood up, her pulse spiking. "You protected yourselves and got away from them." Koyo. *That* slang she recognized. It meant the son of corporate parents with too much wealth and power. She slapped her comm. "Duane? You there?"

His voice came into the air. "What's up?"

"Can you get a security contingent on Hyden? Now. It's vital."

"On my way. Are you worried someone wants to hurt him?"

"Kidnap him." She spoke harshly. "Or kill him."

"I don't get it." Hyden was standing in the living room of the cabin he shared with Wild and two other athletes while security people swirled around the place, checking it for unwanted tech. "Why would anyone go after me?"

"Seriously?" Bhaaj asked. "You're the sole heir to one of the wealthiest families on Cries. Your father is CEO of a major corporation."

Duane came over. "We're set up here." He nodded to Hyden. "We'll also have a bodyguard with you at all times. He'll be disguised as an extra coach so we don't tip our hand."

Dice and Shiv had come with Bhaaj, but they'd stayed back while security swept the room. Now they came forward. "We got prob, too?" Shiv asked. "Balkers think we tell you, they hit back at us."

"What they say when send you away?" Bhaaj asked.

"Say we better not tell," Dice said. "Or they tell people we cartel kids. Get us kicked off team."

"What, they think we not know?" Bhaaj gave a dismissive wave of her hand. "Not worry."

Dice switched into Flag. "What if they go public? Could we lose our scholarship chances?"

"I never hide that truth when I talk with recruiters," Bhaaj said. "I also make sure they know you don't work for the cartels, that going to school offers you a way out of that life. They love the redemption story." Her voice turned steely. "You not make liar out of me, eh?"

"You not liar," Shiv said.

"You say true," Dice told her.

Duane spoke more gently. "It took courage, what you two did, telling Coach Bhaaj even after they threatened to destroy your Olympic hopes."

Dice blinked and Shiv looked confused. Bhaaj doubted they'd ever heard a positive word from a police officer. Here Duane served as the head of security for all things Team Raylicon, but in their view that made him even more of a keyclink authority, someone they'd normally avoid like a plague.

"Eh," Shiv said.

"Eh," Dice agreed.

Duane nodded to them, then went back to talking with the security team.

Hyden spoke to them both. "Thank you."

"Eh," Shiv said. Dice opened his mouth to make the same comment, then changed his mind. Instead he answered in Flag. "You've had a lot to deal with too. But you stuck it out."

With that, the cartel teens took their leave, walking together as they left the room.

Hyden looked as if he didn't know how to react. "They're different than what I expected when they joined the team."

Bhaaj regarded him curiously. "How long have you known they were from the cartels?" She'd never told anyone, and they mostly went by a single name.

Hyden shrugged. "We all figured it out pretty fast. The Undercity kids already knew. Dice and Shiv avoided each other at first." He smiled. "Then it turned into fake avoidance. They tried to pretend they didn't like each other, but we could tell." He watched the security people testing the monitors they'd installed in his room. "Will they put sensors on me, too?"

"Yes. We're clearing it with the Olympic authorities." She regretted his loss of privacy, but better that than a kidnapping or worse. "Do you think your father knew? Maybe that's why he didn't want you here."

"If he suspected, why wouldn't he tell us?" Hyden shook his head. "Better ways exist to protect me than forbidding me to come, especially without saying why."

She spoke carefully. "Could he be involved in things that, uh, he didn't want you to know?"

"Like what?"

"I don't know. His business dealings. Scorpio is at war with Abyss."

He spoke dryly. "It's a takeover attempt, not a war. Besides, Scorpio doesn't have much presence here, just a small subsidiary. I can't see how that would link to—well, to what? Balkers? What does that even mean?"

Bhaaj thought of Abber Isles, who supposedly had no link to Scorpio. "What if it's more?"

"More? I don't follow."

She couldn't reveal to Hyden that Dice's mother was extorting his father. Not only had Angel learned about it illegally, but if his father had gone to such extremes to hide his dealings with the cartel, she could open a shitload of trouble by revealing anything. Bad enough she'd had to tell Lavinda. She couldn't take any more risks, especially not with Zaic's own child. What to do?

Hyden was watching her closely. "You know something."

"Nothing useful." She needed a good answer; he was too savvy for her to get away with a phony cover story. "You know I'm on retainer for the Majdas as a PI, yes?"

"I'd heard." He sounded wary now.

"If market upheavals affect them, they hire someone like me to look into it."

"And?"

She could tell he wouldn't let her put him off, so she chose something he probably already knew. "I think your father wants a monopoly on the Kyle markets. If he manages it, he'll become one of the richest people alive. And you're his heir."

Hyden didn't look surprised. "It's always fascinated him, this business with telops and the psibernet. He even had me tested when I was a kid to see if I had any ability."

"Really?" Bhaaj hadn't expected that, mainly because any Kyle operator could sense Hyden wasn't one. "What did he find?"

"I'm not a Kyle." He shrugged. "He was so secretive. I don't know why. Neither he nor my mother are Kyles, so how could I be?" Before she could find a suitably diplomatic response to his last statement, he added, "And yes, I realize that if they weren't my parents I could be an empath. But they are. I've seen the genetic workups."

"I'd never suggest otherwise," Bhaaj said. At least, not to him.

"Both he and my mother have a few of the Kyle genes, just unpaired," Hyden mused. "Maybe he hoped some might pair up in me."

"It's possible."

"That doesn't explain why he'd care if I came here, though." Hyden spoke awkwardly. "It's the Undercity. I'm sorry, Coach. He's been an asshole, and I was too."

"It's all right, Hyden. I am glad you decided to come with the team."

"So am I." He said it calmly, but she picked up the depth of his reaction. Being here meant the world to him. "And hey, I got as far as the semi-finals in the ten kay. I still have the classic marathon."

"Coming in twelfth in the ten kay is a result to feel proud about." It bothered Bhaaj that so few of them seemed to appreciate such results. The emphasis went to athletes who won medals, as if nothing else mattered, but making it here at all was an achievement on an interstellar stage.

His tense posture eased. "Thanks, Coach."

Mason left his conversation with Duane and came over to them. "Your finish in the ten kay helped our overall team score, too." He showed them holicons above his gauntlet, a listing of teams. "That's the track and field team ranking."

"We're in fifteenth?" Bhaaj asked. "That's great." Although the IOC had codified how they calculated ranks over the past few decades, she'd never paid much attention. Teams drawing on large populations always took the top spots. Metropoli A usually vied for first with Earth and the Aristo teams. Metropoli B, Alpha Centauri and Parthonia also ranked well. It wouldn't surprise her this year if Foreshires did too, given their home advantage. Although Raylicon's fifteenth might still drop a few places, they'd have their best finish ever. Usually they came in last or close to it.

"Anyway, it's time for the javelin final," Mason said. "Let's see how Rockjan does."

Bhaaj laid her hand on her abdomen. "I'll meet you in the lounge. I need to rest a bit first."

"See you there," Mason said, already headed for the door.

After everyone left, Bhaaj sat on the couch and leaned back, closing her eyes. How had humans managed to create so many of themselves when having even just one took so much energy?

Bhaaj, Max thought. **Hyden's comments about his parents secretly testing him got me looking in some new places.**

New places? What do you mean?

Abber Isles. Apparently twenty years ago she had a private business venture. She provided a secret Kyle testing service for wealthy execs from places like Raylicon.

Is she the one who tested Hyden?

That's right. Zaic Laj went to Foreshires to get the results.

It makes sense. If he'd wanted to hide the tests, going in person avoided the Kyle mesh.

I've been running probability scenarios. I think Zaic and Abber Isles were having an affair. It could explain why she's willing to spy on Abyss for Scorpio.

Interesting. Maybe that also explained why Hammerjan had put the squeeze on Zaic. It still seemed odd, though. Sure, no one wanted their spouse to learn about an affair, but given how much Zaic had paid the cartel and for how many years, a garden-variety affair seemed an overreach. It also didn't explain how Hammerjan could know about the affair.

Keep looking, she thought.

Bhaaj found Mason and Hyden already in the lounge, along with other team members and Hyden's bodyguard. The display on the main holo-dais showed the javelin finals.

"You made it!" Mason beamed at her.

"Hey Coach Bhaaj," Tanzia Harjan said. "Look. The 100-meter

finals are about to start, too." She indicated a small inset at the bottom of the javelin display that showed a field crew preparing the track for the sprint finals.

"Where Lamp?" Strider said. "He in sprint final."

"He come soon," Bhaaj said. "Sprint final after jav throw."

"Rockjan is up!" Mason spoke to the holo-image of Rockjan as she walked to the throwing area on the track. "Remember what we talked about. Don't let your angle get too high."

"Coach, she not hear you," Tam Wiens said.

Mason gave a rueful smile. "I know. I just can't stop."

A ripple of amusement rolled among the athletes. Bhaaj wondered if Mason had any idea of the import in that small moment. In the beginning, no Undercity athlete had trusted him enough to crack the slightest smile, yet now they laughed with ease. It stirred an odd sense within her, as if she wanted to cry. Except of course she never cried. Must be the pregnancy hormones.

Bhaaj wished she and Mason could go to an area in the stands near the javelin finals. That event had breaks where an athlete could have a brief word with their coach. Some meets allowed it, but the Games this year had chosen otherwise.

As Rockjan gripped the long handle of her javelin, someone tapped on the audio-feed and a man's voice rose into the air. "—from the Raylicon team. This is Rockjan's first Olympics, her debut on the interstellar stage of track and field."

"She's one of only two women in this final," the female announcer said. "Men from the Allied Worlds of Earth dominate the list, six of them. The other woman is from the Iquar team."

"Eh," Shiv said. "Earth men got big arms."

"Not that big," Dice growled.

"Have you seen images of Imperator Skolia?" Azarina Majda asked them. "He's *huge*. He makes those Earth men look puny."

"His grandfather came from a low-gravity world," Tanzia said. "All their people got big. They genetically engineered themselves to adapt to the world."

Shiv snorted. "Ge-ne-ti-cal-y-en-geh-nerd." Laughter burst from the Undercity kids while the Cries athletes looked confused, the hilarity of creating a word with eight syllables lost on them.

"Rockjan is about to go," Mason said, as if the rest of them couldn't see her life-sized holo facing the wide lane where she'd run to build momentum for her throw.

"Keep your run smooth," Mason said to her holo. "Don't overdo it. Time yourself."

"Yah," Shiv told Rockjan's holo. "Beat the shit out of those other crap javers."

"Shiv!" Mason glared at her. "Language!"

"Look at Rockjan's intensity," the female commentator was saying. "She's ready to attack."

"She said it in one of her interviews," the man responded. "The better you throw a weapon, the more likely you are to, as she put it, 'whack' your rivals."

"Throwing weapons isn't just a sport for Undercity athletes," the woman said. "It's life."

Bhaaj wanted to groan. She'd warned her kids to watch their words. It didn't help their reputation if they sounded like they were threatening people.

"And there she goes," the man said in the same instant that Rockjan took off running, pulling her arm back to throw. With a yell, she hurled the javelin at an almost perfect angle—

And the field judge raised her red flag.

"What happen?" Tam asked. "Why they not show where her jav land?"

"That had to be a great throw," Azarina was saying. "Her form looked perfect—oh. Damn."

"What?" Dice asked. "They cheat on Rockjan?"

"Nahya," Bhaaj said. "They fair." It had been an almost perfect throw. *Almost.* "Throw not good. Her foot touch line." Rockjan's toes had just scraped the foul line at the end of the lane, but that was all it took to disqualify the attempt. The broadcast hadn't shown where her javelin landed on the grass field, but Bhaaj's beetle-bot recorded the result. The throw went well over ninety meters, an effort that could have ranked Rockjan among the leaders anywhere. It would have been her best throw ever—and it didn't count.

"She out?" Tam asked.

"Nahya," Bhaaj said. "Get two more tries. If she in top eight then, she get three more."

So it went, each thrower taking a turn. On her next attempt,

Rockjan's throw was valid but nowhere near as good as the previous, affected by a problem that had long plagued her, throwing at too high an angle. The other athletes also seemed dogged by red flags, as they grappled with the unfamiliar gravity. Rockjan dropped to eleventh place, but she managed enough improvement on her third try to squeak into eighth.

"Yes!" Mason pumped the air with his fist.

Tam squinted at him. "That lousy throw for Rockjan."

"Not her best, sure," he said. "But it puts her into round two. She gets three more tries."

Bhaaj felt too tense to speak. The officials disqualified Rockjan's fourth attempt when she fell after she threw, which happened a lot when she used so much momentum, but this time she couldn't stop her leg from hitting the foul line. Her fifth attempt was valid, but her worst yet. When she came up for her last throw, she remained in eighth place, last among the remaining finalists.

"Eh," Shiv said. "Eighth not bad."

"It'd be our best ever in javelin," Mason said. He didn't sound happy, though.

Bhaaj recognized Rockjan's look. She got it when she wanted to crush her enemies. Except this time her opponent was a line in the grass. She took off running hard, strong—*there*. With a shout, she threw the javelin and fell again, except this time she didn't lose control. Bhaaj never saw the official raise the white flag because the view switched to the field, showing the javelin coming down, down, down—and it hit the ground, its point digging deep while people ran out to measure it.

"It's more than ninety meters!" Mason yelled. "That will put her in fourth—*ho!*" His next shout came so loud, athletes from other teams turned to look. In the same instant, Rockjan's score came up in holo-numbers hanging in the air. It wasn't quite as good as her first throw, but that made no difference. Either would have given her the same result.

"A bronze! She got the bronze!" Mason bellowed. "*Look!* Hot damn!"

Laughter rolled through the athletes, and someone said, "Language, Coach."

Relief flooded Bhaaj and another emotion, one that came not only from her, but from her baby as well, as her daughter picked it up and reflected it back to Bhaaj. Unlike with negative emotions, Max made no attempt to protect her child's mind when joy washed through her mother.

"Look!" Strider said. "There's Lamp!"

Someone switched the display to show the sprinters at the starting blocks. The 100-meter finalists stood cool and calm while a commentator introduced them and holos played above their heads. Lamp didn't crack a smile, but nothing could hide his pleasure at being part of the group.

Within moments, the starter boomed and the sprinters took off. Lamp came off the block well and ran a hard race, one of his best. It finished almost as soon as it started, just a few seconds. He came in sixth out of eight.

"Yah!" Strider beamed as if he'd won the gold. It was, Bhaaj realized, one reason her dust gang formed such a strong unit. Their support of each other extended beyond winning. The commentators barely mentioned Lamp as they enthused over the three medalists, but Strider saw what they neglected, that his achievement also deserved celebration.

"Got to go." Strider rose to her feet. "Got 400 finals later today. With Angel."

Tam also stood up, shifting her weight back and forth. "I go practice for ten kay finals."

"With Wild," Shiv said.

"Yah." Dice looked smug. "We in a lot of finals."

"You're all doing an incredible job," Mason told them.

They are, Bhaaj thought. He hadn't realized the most amazing thing, though. Dice referred to the team as *we*, an acceptance of the city runners as part of their group. She laid her hand on her baby bump. *Maybe we're making you a better universe after all.*

"I found out more about Hyden's Kyle tests," Max said.

Bhaaj paused on her walk back to her cabin. If Max was speaking out loud, he must have determined nothing in this area could hear them, either human or tech. He understood her well, even realizing that right now she felt more like talking. Thinking took too much energy. With a sigh, she sat on a scrolled bench by the landscaped path, with blue flowers nodding in the grass. It was all so pastoral. Not a prickly stalk in sight.

"Yah?" she said to Max. "You know more?"

"Yah," he answered, his tone a perfect copy of hers.

"Oh, Max. Don't make fun of me."

"Actually, I was trying to make you laugh." He sounded troubled. "You should be happy."

"I am." She managed a smile. "It's just this gravity. I didn't think I'd notice it so much." She rubbed her lower back, which ached despite her top physical condition.

"Is this a good time to talk about Hyden?" Max asked.

"Sure. Is he safe?"

"Yes. He's with his bodyguard. That wasn't my news, though."

"What's up?"

"I can't find his mother's true genetic profile. It's better hidden than even I can hack."

"That's your big news? You're having trouble breaking the law?"

"I haven't broken any law." Then he added, "I can't."

Bhaaj slowly stood up. "How is that news?"

"For two reasons. Number one. I don't think she's his real mother."

She started walking again. "Great. We've a team full up with illegitimate sons of rich people."

"Neither Kiro nor Hyden are illegitimate," Max said. "Both their fathers were married at the time of their births."

"It was a joke, Max." The day felt lovely, warm and full of sunshine. If only the baby would stop kicking—ah, no. Bhaaj stopped and groaned as her daughter ramped up her efforts. "Hold still, little one."

"Is it the baby?" Max asked.

"She's trying to run a sprint inside of me."

"I think you're having Braxton-Hicks contractions."

"Say what?"

"False labor. It happens when your body is preparing to give birth."

"Oh." This whole pregnancy business felt odd. She'd expected to resent losing some of her physical autonomy, but she didn't really mind. It all felt different, unexpected for a former military officer, martial arts teacher, and now a coach. But it was, well, *interesting*. She felt a bond to the child. Although she didn't look forward to the actual birth, she didn't plan on being a wimp. If she could survive combat, she could give birth the natural way.

"I'm not in real labor, right?" she asked. "It's too soon."

"Yes. You're fine," Max said. "False labor is normal. But let me know if it keeps up."

"I will." She resumed her walk. "What's the second?"

"The second what?"

"Reason. About Hyden."

"Oh. Yes. I think his real mother is more powerful than the socialite Zaic Laj married."

"She's no featherweight." Bhaaj had always considered social status its own form of power.

"I can't break into her records. Whoever protected them used some of the best security I've ever encountered. Why? Maybe to protect a big secret."

"Oh, Max. That's hardly evidence that Hyden's mother isn't his mother."

"It's not just that. Hyden's genetic records look odd. He doesn't have the Raylicon swirl."

"The what?"

"It's when the hair on your big toe grows in a swirl."

"Oh." That sounded as exciting as watching traffic during rush hour. "Everybody has that."

"Not everyone. But his parents do," Max said. "Almost everyone on Raylicon does, given the inbred gene-pool. You and Jak do, and so will your child. The trait is dominant. You only need one copy of the allele for the trait to manifest."

"Yah, but Max, that could just mean his parents each have only one copy, and he didn't get it from either of them. Besides, I've seen Hyden with his mother. There's no doubt he's her kid. I even heard her joke once about giving birth to him."

"Perhaps a doctor implanted her with his embryo. She might not know he isn't her child. That hair thing is so minor, most people don't notice it."

"Seriously?" Bhaaj rubbed her back as she continued walking. "Taking an embryo out of one woman and implanting it in another without her knowledge has so much wrong with it, I wouldn't know where to start. It's unethical, immoral, and difficult."

"Yes." He sounded relentless. "But not impossible."

"Well, I don't find it credible. Even if it were true, who is Hyden's mother?"

"One other person on the Raylicon Olympic team lacks that genetic trait."

"Really?" Her curiosity stirred. "Who?"

"Azarina Majda."

Ho! Bhaaj stopped stock still on the path. *Are you trying to say Hyden's mother is a Majda?*

Taking his cue from her, Max answered via her biomech instead of out loud. **Yes. If it's true, it explains a lot. All Majdas are minor Kyles, and Lavinda Majda is a full Kyle.** He seemed genuinely excited. **Having Hyden tested secretly for Kyle traits makes perfect sense in that context.**

You think Lavinda is his mother? Bhaaj didn't buy it. She knew Lavinda best of the three Majda sisters. She couldn't imagine the colonel having an illicit affair with Hyden's father. If Lavinda ever strayed outside her arranged marriage, she'd take a woman as her lover.

Not Lavinda, Max said. **However, twenty-five years ago, Zaic Laj served on a committee to attract new corporations to Cries. That committee also had a Majda rep.**

Who?

Vaj Majda.

Holy shit. That's a huge leap, Max.

I don't believe divine excrement is involved. But yes, it's big.

What a thought. In the antediluvian universe of the Majdas, women could have affairs, but they'd never admit it or acknowledge a child conceived of such a union. Had Vaj committed such an indiscretion in her youth? If she'd cared for Zaic, she might have wanted her son, even loved the unborn child. The Majdas had access to the best possible medicine anywhere, enough that Vaj could have even secretly arranged for another woman carry the embryo to term.

Like Hyden's mother.

Vaj Majda had four legitimate children with her husband, all younger than Hyden. Goddess, could Hyden be her firstborn? So much suddenly made sense, including Vaj's heightened interest in Scorpio. It also explained her increased support of the track and field team after Hyden joined, the fortunate coincidence that put a Majda judge into position to decide Hyden's petition for emancipated minor status, even Vaj's willingness to speak on behalf of Ruzik and Kiro rather than see the team weakened by allegations of impropriety.

Bhaaj considered the thought. *You still think Abber Isles was Zaic's mistress?*

Their private communication from twenty years ago implies it.

Bhaaj didn't ask how he knew their private communication. *It wouldn't surprise me. Maybe Zaic had trouble dealing with what happened with Vaj Majda. He couldn't talk to his wife about it, so a few years later he turned to someone else, the person who tested Hyden for Kyle abilities. Vaj Majda is a minor Kyle, so Zaic would have reason to think Hyden might be as well.*

You think he told Abber Isles that Hyden is Vaj Majda's child?

People say a lot of things they shouldn't in pillow talk.

It would explain why his father didn't forbid Hyden to compete until after he qualified for the Olympics. If Abber Isles is his spy, Zaic probably knew she'd be at the Games.

Ho! If Vaj and Zaic arranged to have Zaic's wife implanted with the fetus in secret, and his wife believes Hyden is her own child, then yah, Hyden's father wouldn't want his son anywhere near Abber Isles. I'd bet she's the only person he ever told.

No wonder Vakaar is extorting millions from Zaic.

Yah and nahya, Bhaaj said. *I mean, sure, it would explain why he'd pay so much and for so long. But how the hell would Hammerjan Vakaar know?*

Hyden's mother had a drug problem years ago.

Yah, but even if his mother knew the truth about Hyden, which I doubt, she wouldn't tell the Vakaars. Bhaaj shook her head. *No one could squeeze her over the drugs, either. After she got clean, she never made her addiction a secret.*

Even so. If she bought from Vakaars, that's the link between Laj and the cartel.

Any trail to show that?

Nothing. But Zaic Laj has the resources to cover it up.

Keep looking. See if you can find more.

Will do. Also, Mason is trying to contact you.

Put him on. Mentally, she made herself change gears from PI to coach.

Her gauntlet comm buzzed and she tapped it on. "Heya, Mason."

"The 400-meter finals start in fifteen minutes," he said. "I thought you'd want to be here."

She did want to join them in the lounge. Right now, though, her cabin was only a few meters away, and she wanted to sit down even more.

Max, she thought. *Are there holo-screens I can access in the viewing lounge?*

Yes, several. You can sign into them with your coach's account.

She spoke into her comm. "Mason, I'm at my cabin." Making it true, she walked to the door of the rustic dwelling. "I'll join you as a holo."

"Sounds good. See you in a few."

It only took moments, once she was inside the cabin, to link to a holo-screen in the lounge. Her holo formed next to Mason, glowing from the play of lasers across a screen behind her. Word of their medals had spread, and athletes from other Raylicon teams joined them to watch, including gymnasts, fencers, archers and the one person who'd qualified in cycling.

Mason grinned at Bhaaj, or more accurately, at her holo. "Look at you."

Even as she smiled, her gaze shifted to the display above the largest dais in the lounge. It showed the sprinters crouched down, their feet in the starting blocks. The instant the starting orb sounded, they exploded into motion, including Angel and Strider. For one glorious moment Angel led the pack. Then a woman from the Iquar team, last year's gold medalist at the Interstellar Track and Field meet, surged past her. Angel battled for second with a man from the Parthonia team and another from an Allied team. Strider was in seventh, gaining on a man in sixth.

With the 400-meter only one lap around the track, it seemed only moments before they were sprinting down the final stretch. Angel had fallen into fourth, but at the end she kicked as if drug punkers with machine guns were in pursuit. Iquar finished first, then the man from Parthonia. Leaning forward, Angel crossed in almost a dead heat with the Allied runner. Strider came in battling another sprinter for sixth. A second later, a holo of the results appeared in the air: Angel had won the bronze and Strider had come in seventh.

Bhaaj realized cheers had erupted through the Raylicon team. She'd turned the sound down, but when she upped it, she heard Mason bellowing, "*Another* medal! Way to go, Angel! And look at Strider. *Look!*" He waved his gauntlet at Bhaaj, or at least at her holo. It showed the overall track and field rankings—with Raylicon in thirteenth place.

He grinned. "Top ten, maybe?"

"Wouldn't that be a hoot?" Her glee faded. "Except we don't have anyone in the high jump or the decathlon, and those results haven't yet factored into the standings. It's going to push us down on the list, especially since the decathlon counts so heavily."

"True. But the marathons count more, too, and we've strong competitors in those." He spoke in a confidential tone. "We need to get some of these kids training for the decathlon."

"Agreed." Bhaaj had wondered about Rockjan for exactly that. She could climb and jump like nobody's business. Although she hadn't made the Olympic cutoff for the royal marathon, she'd come close, and she was even better at middle distances, like the 1500-meter in the decathlon.

"I'm going out to watch the medal ceremony by the track," Mason said. "Meet me there?"

"I'll try." Bhaaj wanted to, but the baby kept kicking. "Or I may go see Doctor Izaka."

Worry replaced his smile. "Problems?"

"I'm good." Dryly she said, "I'm just eight months pregnant."

"I'm glad you're having the baby here," he confided. With that, he turned his attention to a man who had approached him, a recruiter wearing the colors of Parthonia University.

Relieved to let Mason handle matters, Bhaaj stopped being a holo and sunk back onto the couch. The recruiter was one interested in Shiv and Dice. Although they'd never seen Parthonia, she suspected they'd like it there, too. Foreshires and Parthonia had the most successful terraforming of any Imperialate colonies, with mild seasons and beautiful landscapes.

Closing her eyes, Bhaaj tried to rest while her baby did calisthenics. When the door clicked across the room, she lifted her head to see Jak coming into the cabin.

"Eh, Bhaajo." He looked inordinately pleased. "What a day!" With satisfaction, he added, "I could run one hell of a betting pool here. It'd do even better than the ones that Dara has going for me in the Top Mark. Everyone here dismisses our team. It gives our athletes great odds."

"For flaming sake," Bhaaj said. "Don't you ever stop gambling?"

"I never gamble anymore. Too easy to lose." He grinned. "I just run it for all the marks who want to lose their money to me."

She spoke wryly. "If I don't watch out, you'll have people betting on the sex of our kid."

Regret came into his voice. "I had to close that pool. I let that one out of the bag."

"Jak!"

He dropped down to sit next to her. "How's the little one?"

Her voice lightened. "She thinks she's competing, too. Kickboxing."

Although Jak smiled, it didn't reach his eyes. "Do you need help?"

"Nahya. It's just practice contractions." Then she added, "This is actually kind of fun."

"Fun?" He blinked. "Really?"

Bhaaj tried to explain what she didn't fully understand herself. "Now that I don't have morning sickness that lasts all day, I feel good most of the time. Tired, but not a bad tired. It's like when your muscles ache after a good workout. But when all this work is done, it isn't for a medal or a solved case or more muscles. It's a new person. Part you and part me."

"Poor thing," he said. "She never got to choose her parents."

"We aren't *that* bad." Then she added, "But blast it, Jak, if you start teaching her how to calculate odds before she can even talk, I'll have your hide."

He grinned. "I'll wait until she can talk."

Laughing, Bhaaj grabbed one of the plush couch cushions and thumped him over the head.

"Ho!" He pulled the pillow away from her. "Not *that* tired, I see."

She did feel better now that she'd rested. Or maybe her spirits had improved because he'd showed up. "Come on. Let's go watch Angel get her bronze."

They headed out together. When they left the cabin, the lovely day shed its light on them. The sky had even cleared enough to look blue instead of gold.

"You want we get a cool-cart?" Jak asked.

"Nahya." Bhaaj turned her face up to the gentle sun. "Got time to walk."

"Air is good today."

"The city is using those high-end weather machines to clean it up."

"You know, I listen a lot up in the stands. It's amazing how much you can learn."

She turned to him. "Like?"

"Like some athletes on other teams have specialized health meds that filter out air particles."

"All meds do that, especially here." It was one reason the Foreshires Olympic committee required athletes to have updated health nanomeds.

"Yah, but what they're talking about, it's like meds on steroids."

She couldn't help but laugh. "You do realize that, medically, that statement makes no sense."

He smiled. "You know what I mean. They cram every aid they can into the meds their athletes use."

"And they didn't get marked for violations?"

"Not according to what I, uh, overheard."

Right. She'd seen him pinch her beetle spy-drone this morning. "Spill."

"Ever since they knew the Olympics would be on Foreshires, other teams have worked on new filters in their health meds," Jak said. "A few had athletes disqualified at smaller meets because they got the balance wrong, but they fine-tuned the meds until they had the best possible hack for these Games."

"It's not illegal." She and Mason would have done it too if they'd had the funds and hadn't been so busy convincing the Undercity athletes just to accept meds. "Costs a lot, though."

"Maybe Raylicon will get new supporters after these games."

"I hope so." Bhaaj thought of the Majdas, then of Zaic Laj. "Jak."

"Yah?" He studied her face. "What's up?"

"You hear a lot in the Top Mark. Even the softest gossip in the Whisper Mill."

"Maybe." He waited.

"You hear anything stealthy about Majda twenty-five years ago?"

"I don't know. Too long to say."

"How about Zaic Laj?"

"Not recall." He regarded her curiously. "Why?"

"Got more. Is private."

"I ken." He used the words and tone that told her it would go no further than him.

They were in an area Max had already determined was secure. So she said, "Max thinks Hyden is the illegitimate son of Vaj Majda and Zaic Laj."

Jak laughed. "Good jib." When she didn't smile, he stopped. "You're joking, yah?"

"Nahya."

"Then your EI needs an upgrade."

"He's part of me," Bhaaj said. "We've evolved together for more than twenty years. If he needs an upgrade, then so do I."

Mischief touched his voice. "Not sure I could handle an upgraded Bhaaj." His gaze lit up. "Zaic Laj and General Majda? Goddess, that's freaking delicious."

"Not delicious," she said. "What if Hyden has trouble here? It not only affects him and his parents, but the House of Majda, too."

"You're sure about this?"

"Hell, no." Then she added, "But so much makes sense."

"You have Hyden protected, right?"

"Duane is on the job. Olympic security, too."

"And these Balkers?"

Bhaaj grimaced. "They're a crime syndicate with ties to offworld drug rings, not only to us, but also to the Earthers and Traders. That's how they knew about Dice and Shiv."

Jak's worry returned. "Need bodyguard for those kids, too."

"Yah. Duane took care of it."

"You think Hyden is the reason Hammerjan Vakaar is extorting Zaic Laj?"

"I just can't see how Hammerjan would know."

Max spoke. "Actually, I may have found a link. Abber Isles."

"Again?" Bhaaj asked. This woman certainly got around. "She has links to the cartels?"

"Just Vakaar," Max answered. "Hammerjan used her Kyle secret testing service for Dice, the same service Gwen Caballo and Zaic Laj used for their sons."

"How did Hammerjan know about a secret lab on Foreshires?" Bhaaj asked.

"Before the cartel war, Vakaar was working to extend their offworld contacts."

"Drug contacts," Jak said. "That has nothing to do with Dice's Kyle abilities."

"True," Max said. "But the contacts still existed."

Bhaaj thought of the Balkers. "Those ties might still be in place."

"Probably," Max said. "But I get the sense Hammerjan hasn't followed up on them."

It fit with what Bhaaj had seen. "The cartel is spread too thin." She paused, wondering if that was the only reason. "I'm not sure Hammerjan wants to follow up on her mother's work."

Jak spoke. "You asked if I heard whispers back then. Not Zaic or Majda, at least not that I recall. But Vakaar? Yah." His voice had an odd quality, as if he felt he'd lived too long and seen too much. "If a punker tried to leave the cartel, Hammer Vakaar called them traitor. And traitors died."

Bhaaj thought of Kiro's father. "Even her own son."

"Hammerjan must have known."

It made an ugly, gruesome sense. "Hammer would force her to witness the death, make her daughter see firsthand what'd happen if she ever tried to leave."

"Hammerjan isn't Hammer," Jak said. "Kajada is different now, too. Maybe for this new generation, family supersedes even cartel loyalty."

Bhaaj spoke quietly. "That's all Dig ever wanted from her mother. Loyalty. And love." Instead, Jadix Kajada had turned their lives into a nightmare. As a teenager, Bhaaj had always defied Jadix. Every time, Jadix had her minions beat the holy hell out of her. Had Bhaaj not left Raylicon, Jadix would've eventually killed her, enraging Dig, starting a war between mother and daughter. Bhaaj doubted anything could have saved Dig from the cartel, but at least the way it happened, it was Hammer Vakaar who murdered Jadix, not Dig committing matricide.

"Goddess," Bhaaj said. "The sins of the mothers come back to haunt their daughters."

Jak laid his palm on her arm. "Dig broke the cycle. For her daughter."

She put her hand on his. "And for us."

He spoke with a gentleness he showed no one else. "Come on. Let's go watch one of this new generation's leaders get her Olympic medal."

The medal ceremony went well. When the haunting music of the Trader anthem soared over the stadium for their gold medalist, it raised hairs on Bhaaj's neck, but nothing could take away her joy. Angel stood on the podium, her head lifted as she received her bronze, and the Raylicon team cheered, all of them, Cries and Undercity athletes alike.

No other crises arose. The usual requests for verification had already come up, as at any major sporting event. The Skolians wanted proof that the Allieds hadn't engineered their male athletes for upper body strength. All the men came back clean, as they usually did, though every now and then the tests caught someone for steroid use or biomechanics disguised as human tissue. Mostly, all those gorgeous muscles were real. Not that Bhaaj noticed. Really. She didn't.

Yah, right, Bhaaj told herself. Of course she noticed. The Earth male physique appealed to something innate within her. None of them would ever surpass Jak in her view, but it wasn't coincidence that one of the male sexual icons among her people was the massive warrior that a queen had to conquer. Of course, it always came with the conquering part, at least in Skolian literature. The Earthers couldn't care less; they liked their men big and strong, and to the hell with what the rest of the universe thought.

Earlier, Earth had asked for verification that Angel was female. Although Mason had it ready, Bhaaj didn't see how anyone could have any doubt. Angel was a beautiful woman by any standard, Skolian, Allied, or Trader. She resembled an historical Earth icon named Priyanka Chopra known for her acting and stunning looks. The Earthers, however, claimed Angel ran like a man called Usain Bolt. Far from anger at the challenge, Angel seemed honored. At first it puzzled Bhaaj, until she watched recordings of Bolt. Yah, she saw why Angel considered him the greatest sprinter ever, even in this modern age where the top athletes could beat his records. When he'd competed, no one had health meds, advanced medical treatments, or modern coaching techniques.

Or genetic manipulation. Supposedly that never happened. Yah, right. Many teams chose athletes based on genetic characteristics, pushing it to the edge of the rules just like they pushed it with their health meds. In a sense, Mason had done the same, recruiting Undercity athletes from a population that had selected for faster people over thousands of years. It was no wonder athletes got stronger and faster every decade. Female runners on Earth caught up with female runners from offworld, male weight lifters from offworld caught up with male weightlifters from Earth, and on and on while humans found ever more ways to optimize their athletic prowess.

The Aristos did it better than most, which was why they tended to dominate the Games even with only four teams, huge ones, but still, only four out of the hundreds that competed. Bhaaj tried not to dwell on it. She wished Aristos didn't exist, but they did, and nothing would change that reality. At least they hadn't conquered the Skolian Imperialate, despite their stronger military. They wouldn't as long as Skolia maintained its advantage in the Kyle sciences. It would be even better if the Allieds would quit being so blasted neutral and become their allies, but at least they hadn't allied with the Traders.

No matter how she looked at it, though, that made it no easier to have the Traders trounce them in track and field year after year after year.

CHAPTER XXVII
Marathons

"They put them both at the back," Mason grumbled, sprawled on a couch in his cabin. "Tam in the royal and Dice in the climb."

Bhaaj sighed as she settled on the sofa across from him. Everyone else had gone off to celebrate. They had good reason; so far, the track and field contingent had done better than anyone expected. They'd earned five medals: two silver, with Ruzik in steeplechase and Tam in the ten kay; and three bronze, for Angel in the 400 meter, Azarina in the 1500, and Rockjan in javelin. They'd placed nine others in the top ten, including Angel in the 200, Wild in the ten kay, Lamp in both the 100 and 200, Zee in the 200, Shiv in both the 1500 and 5000, Strider in the 400 and Jon Casestar in discus. If they included the top twenty, Azarina placed in the 5000, Hyden in the ten kay, Kiro in the 800, and Tanzia in the 100-meter hurdle. Only four events remained: the 4×400 meter relay, the climb, and the two marathons.

"You look pensive," Mason said.

Bhaaj focused on him. "Sorry. I was thinking through our rankings."

"Let's see..." He flicked his finger through holicons above his gauntlet. "After the decathlon and the big jumps, we dropped to nineteenth. We moved around a bit... we're in fourteenth now, and that's before the marathons and Dice's climb." His pleased look turned to a scowl. "Except for the lousy starting placement they gave him and Tam."

This time Bhaaj didn't mind. "It's fair. Tam had the slowest qualifying time for the royal. And after Dice's problems with his security harness at North-Metro, he barely qualified."

"Yah, but neither of those things are real," Mason stated.

"Of course they're real," Bhaaj said.

"I mean they aren't a genuine representation of how well either Tam or Dice can do."

"Yah, but it's what we have. Once our kids have interstellar rankings, it'll get better."

"I know it doesn't really matter in the royal," Mason admitted. "No one has ever finished this course in under six hours, and people run it every year in different meets. A small delay at the start shouldn't matter."

Bhaaj thought about Dice. "The climb favors people who can scale cliffs, not fast starts."

Mason scrolled through his holicons, then groaned. "Not *this* again." He looked up. "We're getting more criticism for putting Kiro in the 4×400 relay instead of Angel."

She raised her eyebrows. "You said the same thing about Kiro at first."

"That was before I saw how well Strider's group works together." He squinted at her. "I swear, it's surreal. It's like they're one mind instead of four."

"They are one, in a sense. They're empaths. They attune to each other."

"Well, whatever it is, it works." He stood up. "Come on. Let's go watch."

She got to her feet, feeling clumsy. "In the coach's lounge, yah?" They had nice couches.

"Yes, sure. I know you need all the rest you can get."

Bhaaj glared at him. "I most certainly do not." She felt as strong as ever. Just heavier.

Mason smiled. "You know your tough-gal exterior doesn't fool me."

Would that he never had to see that side of her. "Yah, well, let's go." With that, they set off to view the last events of the Games.

Just as they reached the coach's lounge, Mason's comm beeped, followed by a buzz on Bhaaj's gauntlet. Puzzled, she brought up the message. In the same instant that Mason said, "What the blazes?" Bhaaj said, "Hell no!"

Mason swung around to her. "They can't do that!"

"It's another Aristo stunt." After the failed Highton Privilege business, the Aristos knew the officials wouldn't unconditionally accept their objections to the Undercity. This new challenge, however, could turn into an unmitigated disaster.

Mason ordered a cool-cart and had it ready at the closest exit from the stadium. As soon as they boarded, it whisked them toward the countryside, that idyllic stretch of meadows where the royal marathon would start. It only took five minutes to reach the starting area, but it felt like an eternity. As soon as Bhaaj and Mason disembarked, officials escorted them to a white tent with tassels bearing the Olympic logo hanging from its eaves.

Inside, Tam Wiens stood with four officials, two from the Olympic committee and two from the Quaelen team. Relief flooded across her face as Bhaaj entered with Mason. She sped over to them. "Not ken! Why they say I can't run?"

Before Bhaaj could respond, the officials joined them. She recognized the Olympic reps, the referee Lyra Mollin from the steeplechase protest, and Tarj Hawkson, the empath who'd read *The Ascendance of Eube*. Although she didn't know the Trader officials, the woman had rust-red eyes that showed her partial Aristo heritage. Her badge read Quaeljan Vala, naming her as the legitimized daughter of an Aristo woman called Vala Quaelen. The man looked pure Aristo, and his badge said Vitar Kaliga, after the Kaliga Highton Line.

Vala spoke to Mason and Bhaaj. "You are coaches for the Raylicon track and field team?"

Mason watched her warily. "That's right." He turned to Lyra Mollin. "What's the problem?"

Lyra motioned at Tam. "The Quaelen team objects to athlete Wiens on medical conditions. They don't allow empaths to run in contests."

"What the blazes?" Mason said. "What are you talking about?"

Bhaaj didn't get it, either. "Being an empath isn't a medical condition."

"We never allow providers to compete," Vala said flatly. "It is immoral. How can you subject her to such a crushing experience?"

"What crush?" Tam said. "I fine." She turned to Bhaaj and Mason. "Games people ask me to explain. Want my med records. I not ken. So they comm you."

"This makes no sense," Mason said. "Being a Kyle operator isn't a medical condition, no more than having brown hair, hairy legs, or red eyes."

Vala watched him as if he were a bug creeping across the floor. "That you lack the proper concern for your athletes is your crime, not ours." She spoke to Lyra. "This is an appalling offense."

Bhaaj frowned. Normally an athlete wouldn't be present during a challenge. Given that the Traders framed this as a medical condition, the officials needed Tam to answer their questions, but she had no more idea what they meant than anyone else.

"The Olympic rules don't forbid empaths," Lyra Mollin said.

Vitar Kaliga spoke with disdain. "Atrocities like this are perfect examples of why taskmakers should never run major events without proper oversight."

"Taskmakers?" Lyra asked. "What do you mean?"

Tarj Hawkson, the other Olympic official, said, "It means slave. That's how they view us."

"This isn't the Eubian Concord," Lyra told the Traders, her voice cold. "We're free citizens. The rules and policies of the Olympics supersede your laws or customs."

"If your rules allow providers to compete," Vala said, "then they need to be changed."

"Why?" Tarj asked. "So you can justify how you enslave and torture empaths, and also refuse to let them come here, a place where we don't allow that behavior?"

Kaliga's tone turned icy. "You need to show more respect."

Tarj visibly tensed, but he didn't rise to the bait. Nor did he give Kaliga the other result he'd expect as an Aristo, a groveling apology. He just regarded them both with a neutral expression.

Lyra spoke warily. "It isn't our intent to offend. However, nothing prohibits empaths from participating." Her voice became firm. "You're asking us to set a sweeping precedent with ramifications for the entire interstellar athletic community. We can't make such a change only a few moments before a major race."

"If you learned that coaches were beating an athlete to make her compete," Kaliga asked, "would you similarly ignore our protest?"

"Of course not." Lyra glanced at Mason, then spoke to Kaliga. "Are you making such a claim against the Raylicon coaches?"

"Absolutely," Vala told her. "It is horrifying that they are forcing this young woman to run."

"For fuck's sake," Tam said. "No one force me to do shit."

Not helping! Bhaaj thought. Tam glanced at her and just barely nodded.

"Listen to that." Kaliga motioned at Tam. "She can't even speak a coherent sentence."

"We would *never* force a runner to compete," Mason said. "This is a falsehood you've created with no basis in the truth."

Lyra turned to him. "Do you have medical papers showing that Goodwoman Wiens is cleared to participate as an empath?"

"Why would we?" Mason asked. "Nothing anywhere, in any competition I've ever known, has required such a clearance."

"Lyra, listen." Tarj Hawkson said. "This is wrong. Aristos torture their providers because it provides them pleasure. That's literally why they're called providers. They inflict some of the worst atrocities you can imagine on Kyle operators, exactly *because* they're empaths. They don't want Kyles to compete because they oppress them beyond anything you can imagine."

Kaliga sighed. "How did this melodramatic boy become an Olympic official?"

Lyra's gaze on the Aristos never wavered. "Goodman Hawkson is an experienced, respected official." Turning to Tam, she asked, "Has anyone used violence against you during these Games or any others? Anyone, from any team?"

"Yes." Tam indicated the Aristo reps and spoke in Flag. "Quaeljan Vala and Vitar Kaliga. Their minds are attacking mine. It hurts me, and they like that. It gives them pleasure."

"You must calm yourself, girl," Vala said. "Getting histrionic will only make you ill."

"Wiens is telling the truth," Tarj Hawkson said, "They're doing exactly what she says. I can feel it, too. They're trying to intimidate her into withdrawing from the race."

Lyra raked her hand through her hair. "These are serious allegations." Glancing at Tarj, she tilted her head toward the other side of the tent. "We need to talk."

As the two officials withdrew, the Traders also stepped back. Bhaaj struggled not to let her anger boil over. The Aristos had known from the start that empaths competed for Raylicon. Why single out Tam? Ruzik was also in the race, a stronger empath, and they never mentioned him. Neither he nor Tam posed a threat to Kryx Quaelen, the runner everyone expected to win.

I don't think they're worried about Kryx Quaelen, Max thought. **It's Jaibriol Kaliga.**

He's the other Aristo from the Quaelen team in the royal marathon, right? Bhaaj thought.

Yes. He's expected to come in eighth or ninth.

That will help their team ranking, especially with Kryx Quaelen's gold.

Exactly. It looks like the Quaelen team will rank first and the Iquar team tenth. However, that assumes Kryx wins and Jaibriol Kaliga comes in ninth or better in the royal.

And Tam could beat Jaibriol Kaliga! No wonder Vitar Kaliga had shown up. In the nepotism-fueled empire of the Traders, Jaibriol was probably a relative.

As Lyra and Tarj came back, the two Quaelen reps rejoined them. Lyra spoke to them both. "Before we give a ruling, we need to know why you waited until now to bring this up. Given the timing, it looks as if you are deliberately targeting Tam Wiens."

Vala met her gaze. "We didn't know until now that she was an empath."

"What do you mean?" Tarj said. "You know the moment you meet one of us."

Kaliga sighed. "Please do not get hysterical, boy. Contain your overwrought fantasies."

Tarj spoke with laudable restraint. "I'd suggest we avoid inflammatory language."

Lyra regarded the Traders coldly. "I honor Goodman Hawkson's calm, well-founded input."

"And what of decency?" Vala asked. "Of course we had no idea Wiens was an empath. Otherwise, we'd have raised this issue before."

"That's not true," Tarj said. "During the complaint made by the Iquar team against Raylicon, they referred to Coach Bhaajan as a provider. We have a holo-vid of that meeting."

"Major Bhaajan is a coach, not a competitor." Vala glanced at Bhaaj with an odd look. For one instant, her mask of arrogance slipped, revealing something far uglier, a hunger that chilled. In that moment, Vala murmured, "A coach creating more providers for us, hmmm?"

Bhaaj stiffened. *Max! Are you protecting the baby's mind?*

Yes. I'm also protecting yours.

"For heaven's sake," Lyra said. "Nothing prohibits a coach from being pregnant."

"It should," Kaliga told her. "Given the vulnerability of providers and the great value of their offspring in the markets, it was a crime to let Major Bhaajan serve in the military and an even worse crime to let her come here, in this condition."

Well, that was stupid, Bhaaj thought. Kaliga had just metaphorically shot himself in the foot.

"In the *markets*?" Lyra stared at him with horror. "Babies are *not* commodities."

Bhaaj spoke calmly. "They didn't bring this up because they're suddenly concerned for our welfare. They did it because if Tam Wiens beats Jaibriol Kaliga, the Quaelen team could come in second in the overall team rankings after Metropoli A."

Vala regarded Bhaaj as if she wanted to scrape her off her shoes. "We didn't bring it up before because you did such a good job hiding your filthy practice of coercing empaths."

"No one coerced me to do anything," Tam said.

Lyra spoke carefully to Tam. "Would you like to talk to me in private?"

"What for?" Tam asked. Then she added, "And yes, I know, you think if anyone is coercing me, I'll be afraid to tell you the truth in front of them. I don't need to talk to you in private because no one is forcing me to do anything."

"Of course she says this in front of the people who control her actions," Kaliga said.

Tam ignored him, speaking to Lyra and Tarj. "I *asked* you to bring my coaches here."

Lyra nodded to her, then turned to the Trader reps. "If your people have such concerns, why have you never mentioned them before? You could have done so decades ago."

"You've never even hinted at it," Tarj said.

"Empaths are exceedingly rare," Kaliga said. "Among my people they never compete. We had no reason to believe other teams allowed such an abomination."

"You don't want your providers here because you're afraid they'll ask us for sanctuary," Bhaaj said. "But you like it when our empaths compete. You *want* to interact with them." She thought of Dice and Shiv, and the Balker links to offworld drug rings, including some in Trader territory. "You figure if they come from the Undercity, they might even be foolish enough to let you recruit them."

Neither Vala nor Kaliga spoke, they just stared at her, but Bhaaj felt their reaction. They hadn't expected her to figure it out. Then Vala said, "My dear, you are clearly under stress and have let your imagination get the better of you."

Oh, fuck you, Bhaaj thought.

Lyra frowned at the Traders. "If you didn't realize Raylicon would allow an empath to compete, how did you know about Tam Wiens?"

"She told Kryx Quaelen," Kaliga said. "This morning."

"That's ridiculous," Bhaaj said.

Tam gave her a look of regret. "Is true." To Lyra, she said, "I was talking to another runner during our warm-ups. Kryx Quaelen heard. He made 'small' talk with us, and somehow the subject of empaths came up. When he claimed empaths weren't strong enough to run, I said I ran just fine."

Mason scowled. "In other words, he tricked you into revealing it so they could bring this protest and claim it was the first they knew about our team having empaths."

Lyra glanced at him with a flash of hope. "Can you prove that?"

Mason opened his mouth, closed it, then said, "No."

With a look of apology, she said, "I'm sorry. But if this is potentially a serious condition, one that could lead to severe or life-threatening injuries, either physical or mental, then until we've had a chance to consider it in depth, I think we may need to remove Tam Wiens from the race."

"That isn't fair," Tam said. "I did nothing wrong. I'm fine."

"I truly am sorry," Lyra told her. "We don't understand enough about the duress empaths can experience. Until we do, we can't make a ruling. If we had proof the Quaelen team brought this protest only for discriminatory reasons, we could rule in your favor. But we've seen none."

"No, wait!" Bhaaj said. "Can you get the holo of our team when we gathered during the Opening Ceremonies outside the stadium? We need the part where Kryx Quaelen stopped to talk to us, just before his team entered the stadium."

Lyra glanced at Tarj. "Do you have that footage?"

"Let me see..." He unhooked a tablet from his belt and brought up many holos, flicking his fingers through them like a maestro. Within moments, a vid appeared above the tablet. It showed Kryx Quaelen striding past the Raylicon team—and stopping.

"Goddess, you're all providers," Kryx said. "So many of you."

Someone said, "Enough!" out of view. Then Bhaaj appeared in front of her athletes. "My greetings, Lord Quaelen."

It amazed Bhaaj now to hear the courteous tone she had used, given how much she'd wanted to punch him. In the holo, she said, "Thank you for your notice."

His voice turned hard. "Is this how Foreshires Hold shows esteem to its Olympic guests? By letting people address a Highton with such massive discourtesy?"

"My apology if I caused offense," Bhaaj said.

"Ah, Coach Bhaajan," he said. "Or should I say Major, hmm? I understand you fought against my people during your military service. But you bring life, too, don't you?" He lowered his voice. "Making little dust vermin. How nice of you, to create more providers that can someday come under the umbrella of our glorious empire." He waited a moment, then frowned when she didn't react. "You do know your spawn is an empath, right? I feel it."

"I've heard enough," Lyra said. As Tarj switched off the holo, she turned to the Eubian reps. "Lord Quaelen clearly knew from the start that the Raylicon team included empaths. Yet he never said a word to us in protest, not about *any* of them." She tilted her head at Tam. "Until now, when suddenly he wants this particular runner dropped from the race."

Vala lifted her chin. "He says otherwise."

Lyra spoke firmly. "The IOC does not accept Highton Privilege."

Tarj spoke tightly. "What did he mean, 'create more providers that may someday come under the umbrella of our glorious empire'? You can't take our citizens back to your territory."

"Why would we want to?" Kaliga sounded incredulous. "We

already have two trillion people. Yours are more trouble than they are worth, both literally and figuratively."

An edge grated in Mason's voice. "We aren't products for sale."

Neither of the Traders responded, they just looked at him with impassive faces.

Lyra glanced at Tarj, and he gave a slight nod. Turning back to Traders, she said, "It is our decision that Tam Wiens be allowed to compete." She took a breath. "However, if the Eubian Concord wishes to submit a petition that the IOC prohibit empaths from participating in future Olympics, we will take it under consideration."

Neither of the Traders looked happy—but for some reason they let it go.

After a short silence, Tam said, "Can I go back to the warm-up?"

"Yes, go ahead," Lyra said. "We thank you for your cooperation."

Bhaaj focused on the Traders. Rather than anger, she felt... satisfaction? She understood then: No matter how the ruling went, they won. Either they stopped Tam or else they upset her enough that it affected her ability to run.

Except they didn't know Tam. They'd tried to deny her this race—and she'd remember.

The royal marathon only started a few minutes late. A hint of dawn showed in the sky, the light on the horizon dimmer than the rings in the sky. One hundred sixty men and women gathered at the start, with the top-seeded runners at the front and the lowest at the back, including Tam.

Bhaaj and Mason watched from the coach's area. The athletes started with no fanfare, headed along a country road wide enough for six runners to go abreast, though they spaced themselves out more. Tam moved gradually through the pack, working her way toward the front.

Andi Jinda hadn't qualified for the Olympic royal, but then, no one had expected her to, including Bhaaj. Still, it relieved her that Tam had one less problem to worry about here.

The two Aristos, Kryx Quaelen and Jaibriol Kaliga, ran with the leaders. It didn't surprise Bhaaj that they'd ended up on the same team. All its members came from Eube's Glory, the capital world of Eube, but the coaches worked hard to curate the group. Jaibriol Kaliga had long competed with military teams, earning a reputation as a top marathoner. He conveniently got a posting on Eube's Glory just in time to work with the Quaelen Olympic team. Today he led the pack, and Kryx Quaelen ran behind him, protected from the brisk winds by the barrier of Jaibriol's body.

"Jaibriol Kaliga is pacing them," Mason said.

"Yah." Bhaaj shrugged. "He'll eventually drop back to let Quaelen take the lead."

"Assholes," he muttered.

She somehow managed a slight smile. "Don't let the kids hear you say that."

"I wanted to say a lot worse to Kaliga and Vala. Why aren't you furious?"

"I am angry. But Mason, my people get stuff like this all the time, including from Skolians."

"I have to admit, when I recruited Angel, I had no idea." He regarded her with a guilty look. "I'd be ready to blow apart the atmosphere if people treated me that way."

She spoke wryly. "If I'd gone ballistic every time it happened, the army would've dishonorably discharged me almost as soon as I enlisted."

He regarded her with curiosity. "Was it hard to become an officer?"

Bhaaj grimaced. "Every time I took the tests for the program that promotes enlisted soldiers into the officer ranks, I aced them. And every time, they turned down my application. The only reason they finally accepted it was because someone went too far."

"Too far? What do you mean?"

It was a moment before she answered. "I was injured in combat and caught behind enemy lines with another soldier, a guy in my battalion." Bitterness edged her voice. "Hell, Mason, we were drowning in the Hizar mud flats on Xizar II. A helo managed to reach us, but they only had room for one person. The soldier trapped with me said they should take me instead of him, that I wouldn't survive otherwise. The pilot said no 'Undercity vermin' was worth leaving him behind. He tried to refuse, but she outranked him. She ordered him onboard, and they left me to die." The words sounded so calm, so unlike the shattering battle and desperate screams that day.

Mason stared at her. "That's horrific!"

"Well, I didn't die." Despite her attempts to stay calm, her pulse spiked. "I fucking crawled on my stomach across the battlefield, with bombs, jumbler beams, and lasers everywhere. I got through it alive because in all that chaos no one bothered with one dying kid dragging herself through the mud." After a pause, she spoke more evenly. "It took hours, but I got back to base. I told the CO what happened, and the guy who hadn't wanted to leave me behind backed me up. When I filed a case against the pilot, the scandal exploded. To make it go away, the brass quit blocking me from the officer's program." With grim satisfaction, she added, "They expected me to fail out. I graduated at the top of my class."

Mason fell silent, one of the few times she'd seen him without words. Then he said, "You are an impressive woman, Daughter of Bhaaj."

"Eh." Her face felt warm. Deflecting, she said, "What do I call my kid, eh? Bhaajanjan, daughter of daughter of Bhaaj." An old joke, but it was all she had now.

Mason's voice lightened. "How about Jakjan?"

"Hey." The mother's heredity generally got priority, or at least it had in her time. It wouldn't surprise her if people used "jan" with a man's name nowadays; the young always came up with new ways to defy the sexist traditions of their elders. Jak might get a kick out of the idea. She smiled, relieved to turn away from her combat memories. "You never know."

He chuckled and the tension eased. "The classic starts in the city. We should get back there."

"The Traders better not try to stop Angel, too."

"I doubt they will. Only one Aristo is running in the classic, and Angel isn't likely to beat him." Then he added, "I did warn her not to mention being an empath."

They left then, off to the next event.

The classic marathon started without fanfare. Two hundred and forty runners gathered at the start in the city center. A magnificent tower rose behind them, a mirrored spire that reached toward the heavens with the spectacular rings arching across the sky beyond its grandeur.

Although both marathons would end at the stadium, the classic took far less time. Even if stragglers came in later than the other runners, hours would still separate its finish from the royal. During that break, the final track and field event in the stadium would take place, one of the most popular in the Games, the 4×400 relay.

After the classic started, Bhaaj returned with Mason to the coach's lounge and sank gratefully onto a sofa. In response, her daughter gave a mighty kick.

"Ungh," Bhaaj muttered, ever articulate.

Mason settled next to her. "She trying to run a marathon too?"

Bhaaj laughed. "Or kickbox." A diffuse sense of contentment came from her daughter, nothing specific, just a forming brain that detected no problems within her contained universe.

"See you in a bit." Mason settled back on the couch and pulled on his VR helmet.

Bhaaj lowered her own helmet. *Max, link me up to the classic.* She'd already checked on Hyden and Tallmount. *How's Angel bearing up?*

Here you go.

A scene formed, so vivid it felt real. She was running along a wide street in Eos City with waist-high barriers on either side. People crowded behind the barriers, some real, some avatars created to make the sim more exciting. Looking down, she saw her feet—Angel's feet—pounding the road. A breeze wafted against her face. The air smelled mostly clear, with the barest powdery scent of ring-dust.

Good sim, Bhaaj thought.

Easy to connect with, too, Max said, his version of beauty.

The sim relaxed Bhaaj. She could enjoy running without expending energy. It felt blissful, soothing... sleepy...

"Agh!" Bhaaj muttered. Angel had just stumbled on a crack. She recovered immediately, and probably barely noticed, but the simulated version of her mishap jarred through Bhaaj.

Angel was passing a series of water stations. When she reached the Raylicon table, she grabbed a bottle without pausing. Bhaaj felt its ridged surface as if she held it herself. Although she couldn't feel the water going down Angel's throat, she did experience a cooling balm as Angel poured the rest over her head. It felt so real, it surprised Bhaaj that she didn't get wet. The up-close-and-personal sim made it harder to watch the race, though, since she only saw it from Angel's perspective, as modeled by the EI controlling the simulation.

End sim, she thought.

The scene went dark, and she pushed back her visor, finding herself back in the lounge. It had gained more coaches, those who specialized in marathons. The big dais in the center of the room displayed the classic, and a smaller dais closer to her sofa showed the royal.

Max, activate the feed in my subs for the royal broadcast.

A woman's voice came to Bhaaj's ears. "—Xi Aio from Metropoli A is running the royal today instead of the classic. He's tucked in there right behind Vanya Longbow, with Kryx Quaelen of Eube's Glory and Manuel Rodriguez from Earth behind him."

"This is a formation we've seen before," the man said. "These four in the lead. Longbow is favored for silver here, but of course the man to watch is Kryx Quaelen. In the past few years, he has consistently blasted through what has become one of the most popular events in all human-settled space."

"Absolutely," the woman said. "Ultramarathons offer a dramatic showcase of our ability to adapt to varied planetary biospheres, putting this sport in the forefront of interstellar athletics."

The scene shifted to a pack of runners behind the leaders, including an Aristo in Quaelen colors and three other runners.

The view focused on a woman at the front of the chase pack. "Canda Azi from the Imperial Fleet team is currently in fifth," the male announcer said. "She took ninth in the last Olympics, but she's improved since then. Does she have a shot at the bronze? It's too early to tell. Many runners lose steam later in this grueling event."

"The fellow behind her is Jaibriol Kaliga from the Quaelen team," the man said. "Although he's a newcomer on the interstellar stage, he's made a strong showing among his own people."

"Good for him," Bhaaj grumbled. She hoped the Aristos were right to worry about Tam, because after that "disqualify empaths" business, it would be gratifying to see her beat Kaliga.

The commentators talked about various runners until finally the view shifted again to a place farther back in the race, this time showing Ruzik loping along. "Ruzik of the Dust Knights is one of the three Raylicon runners in this event," the woman said. "Although he comes from the weakest team, he made a good showing in the Metropoli meet, coming in seventh there."

"Blast it." Mason pushed back his visor. "Why do they always feel compelled to say how bad our team is? Hasn't anyone noticed we're in fourteenth place?"

"If Ruzik can maintain his pace, he might finish reasonably well here," the man said. "His teammate Tayz Wilder also made a strong showing in the North-Metro meet, coming in eighth." The holo-scene morphed to show a new group of runners, with Tayz well ahead of them.

"Wilder has a promising record," the woman said. "Last year, rumor claimed stronger teams were recruiting him, that he would leave Raylicon for a team that offered him more challenge. Then suddenly the rumors went silent."

"It's obvious why," the man said. "Raylicon's performance here is unprecedented. The influx of Undercity runners into their ranks has changed everything. These kids can *run*."

"And 'kids' is right," the woman said. "It's a young team. The other Undercity runner in the royal, Tam Wiens, is just twenty. Only three athletes in Raylicon track and field have even reached the age of majority. This team may not have many medals, but they're racking up a good number of top-ten finishes, and these youngsters have plenty of Olympics in their future."

"Thank you," Mason said. "*Finally* someone notices."

"Yah." It pleased Bhaaj. Her daughter, too; their littlest team member had ramped up her kicks. *You're a strong one,* Bhaaj thought. *Already making a ruckus.*

The holo-vid on the main dais morphed into a new scene, showing three runners in the classic marathon. "—now in the second hour of the race," a female announcer was enthusing. "Fina Caster is in front, with Karanja Njoro close behind and Ruv Muzeson in third."

"The big question is will Njoro take gold," the man said. "Hailing from the country Kenya on Earth, he's medaled in every race he's done in the past two years, including gold at the Boston Marathon."

"Fina Caster has a history of doing well on Metropoli," the woman said. "However, she seems more affected by differences in gravity and atmosphere here."

"The Eubian, Ruv Muzeson, is a question mark," the man said. "He started winning bronze medals last year and continues to improve."

The view morphed to runners Bhaaj didn't recognize, while the commentators enthused, criticized, or gossiped about them. Eventually they focused on a group that included Angel. After commenting on the other three, the male commentator said, "And of course the big surprise here is Angel of the Dust Knights, the bronze medalist in the 400-meter sprint."

"Who would have expected it?" the woman said. "The only runner in Olympic history to medal in a sprint race and then finish a marathon at the same games."

"That's *if* she finishes," the man said. "She's currently fourteenth, but no way can I see her holding on to that position in this elite field."

"My prediction?" the woman said. "She'll drop out. Sprinters don't train for endurance."

"She did win gold in Selei City last year," the man said, "It's a lower-ranked race, though, not an elite competition. Let's see... I have her stats from the Open. Huh. Interesting. Her pace now is almost exactly what she had at this point in that race. Who knows? Maybe she'll finish."

"Maybe." The woman didn't sound convinced. "The training is different. Concentrating on sprints affects your distance ability. She may have trained on distance for the Selei Open, but she switched to sprints here."

"What?" Bhaaj said. "Angel never trained for the Selei City Open."

"Really?" Mason asked. "I'd assumed she did."

"No more than anyone else in the Undercity. We just run distance every day."

The view changed, showing other athletes Bhaaj didn't know. After a moment, Mason said, "How are Hyden and Tallmount doing?"

"Here," Max said. The scene on the small dais in front of them changed, showing six runners, including Hyden. "He's currently nineteenth out of two hundred and thirty-seven. Helyne Tallmount is forty-fifth." The scene switched again, this time showing Tallmount as she passed two runners. "Make that forty-third," Max added.

"Two hundred and thirty-seven?" Bhaaj had thought two hundred and forty entered.

"Three had to drop out," Max said. "Two from injury and one got sick."

"Goddess," Mason said. "Angel is ahead of both Hyden and Tallmount."

"Yah, but Hyden always picks up speed in the last hour," Bhaaj it abuse to let empaths do sports. Or something." She sounded baffled.

"*Abuse?*" The man's voice hardened. "Has anyone pointed out what Aristos do to their empaths? The word 'abuse' is far too mild."

"You served in the navy, didn't you?" the woman asked. "Did you encounter Aristos?"

"Unfortunately." He sounded subdued. "I had the misfortune of seeing firsthand how they treat empaths. I still have nightmares about it, twenty years later." Then he added, "I can't see why they'd want her out of the race, though."

"It is odd," the woman said. "Everyone seems afraid of this runner, but it isn't clear why."

"She was doing well on Metropoli before her injury." The man paused. "And there's those fan-vids showing that practice race she did on Metropoli. She almost beat Bayonet."

"Bayonet wasn't trying," the woman said. "Still, it will be interesting to see what happens."

When the commentators went on to gossip about other runners, filling time, Mason said, "They underestimate Tam."

"Yah." To herself, Bhaaj thought, *They have no idea.*

said. "He's got a shot at the top ten. Helyne maybe top twenty. Angel tends to run at a steady rate, but with her body so primed for sprints now, I wouldn't be surprised to see her slow down."

"Except for that kick she always does at the end," Mason said, sounding hopeful.

Bhaaj had her doubts. "We'll see."

Max suddenly said, "They're talking about Tam in the royal."

"Switch feeds," Bhaaj said. "Restart it where they talk about Tam."

"Here." The scene on their small dais morphed into three runners slowly going uphill on a dirt path. One was walking. None, however, were Tam.

"—and they're on the first of several big inclines," a man was saying. "It's a steep slope with a total gain of about two hundred meters."

A woman came into view, running at a steady lope. "That's Tam of the Dust Knights," the female commentator said. "She's run that way for two hours, never faltering, taking water or food at the help stations but never stopping."

"She's tackling this hill the same way. Or trying." The man sounded doubtful. "She still has four hours on this course. If she keeps pushing this hard, she'll hit her limit on energy reserves, the 'wall' as people say, and she'll need to drop out."

"I'm not so sure," the woman said. "She finished on Metropoli, just barely in time to qualify for the Olympics, but she managed even on a sprained ankle."

"Maintaining her current position doesn't seem likely, though," the man said.

"Well, yes," the woman admitted. "I have to agree, particularly given her inexperience."

"Inexperience," the man said. "Exactly the right word. A more seasoned runner, like yourself back in the day, would know how to manage the pace and conserve energy."

"It's an important balance," the woman said. "To be honest, I'd like to see her finish, given her story. The Trader team tried to get her disqualified because she's an empath."

"What?" The man's tone changed, turning tense and angry. "I've never heard of that."

"Nor has anyone," the woman said. "Apparently they consider

CHAPTER XXVIII
Going the Distance

"And there he is, Karanja Njoro, coming out of the tunnel and onto the track!" the male announcer said. "What a triumph for Earth! Njoro is about to crush the Olympic record for the classic marathon. He's run a blazing race today."

Bhaaj and Mason stood in the coach's area near the finish line, watching Njoro do his final lap around the track with the applauding crowd calling out their delight.

"He's going to beat the two-hour mark!" the woman cried. "No other athlete has done that on a heavier gravity world like Foreshires Hold. And there he goes—yes! It's gold for Karanja Njoro, at one hour, fifty-eight minutes, and sixteen seconds! What a run!"

"Nice job," Bhaaj said. They stayed back while Njoro's coaches hugged their jubilant athlete and handed him the flag of Earth, which showed a white silhouette of humanity's home world surrounded by olive branches on a blue background.

"Under two hours, and in this atmosphere," Mason said. "That truly is impressive."

"Hyden talked to him at the Boston Marathon," Bhaaj said. "He said Njoro is a nice guy. Humble. He's from a rural area on Earth and runs on country roads all the time."

Another swell of applause came from the crowd as the male commentator said, "And there she is, Fina Caster, headed for her first Olympic silver!"

The two commentators also enthused for the bronze winner, and to a lesser extent for the fourth and fifth place runners. Bhaaj was paying more attention to her gauntlet's mini-feed, which showed Hyden loping through the city, toward the stadium. The feeds cut out when he entered the tunnel into the stadium and came back on when he emerged onto the track, supposedly because holo-cams couldn't get a good signal inside the tunnel. Bhaaj didn't believe it. The media techs did it to add excitement to the finish, as each athlete burst into the open when they exited the tunnel.

As Hyden finished his lap and crossed the finish line, the female commentator said, "That's Hyden Laj in eighth place, his highest rank ever in an interstellar meet and a personal best for him, including his Boston run on Earth, even with its biosphere better suited to human athletics."

"His eighth-place finish is another feather in the cap for Raylicon," the man said. "Given the youth of these athletes, they have an incredible future. Are we seeing the birth of a track and field powerhouse? Raylicon is the team to watch."

You better believe it, Bhaaj thought as she and Mason waved to Hyden. He grinned and waved back, then continued walking around in the finish area, regaining his breath.

"All that trouble he had," Mason said. "All the complications, the grief, the pain when his father tried to crush his dream, getting to Boston, going to court, the danger and the bodyguards and the tension—it was all worth it for this moment."

"Yah." In honor of Hyden, Bhaaj added, "Yes," in the same dialect he spoke, Skolian Flag with a lilt from the upper city area of Cries where he lived.

Hyden came over and hugged them unabashedly, his clothes wet from water.

"Fantastic," Mason told him in the same moment as Bhaaj said, "Good job!"

Drawing back, Hyden smiled. "Thanks. Both of you." He nodded to them with a respect Bhaaj had never thought he'd show the Undercity when she first met him.

The male announcer was saying, "Here is Ruv Muzeson, the top Eubian in this event."

Looking out, Bhaaj saw Muzeson break into the sunlight from the tunnel, followed a few moments later by a dark-haired Allied man.

"Muzeson is racking up a ninth-place finish for the Eubian military team," the woman said. "Yamamoto from the Alpha Centauri team with the Allied Worlds isn't far behind, in tenth."

"Angel just went into the tunnel," Mason said, watching his gauntlet feed.

Bhaaj nodded, too tense to speak.

"Look at this!" the female announcer exclaimed as Angel burst out into the sunlight. "Angel of the Dust Knights is in eleventh place. What a feat for a sprinter!"

"It's incredible," the man said—and then he shouted. "Ho! She just *kicked!*"

"It's the Undercity kick!" the woman enthused. "She's *sprinting* to the finish line!"

"Eh," Bhaaj said.

"I don't believe it!" Mason said. "Bhaaj, Hyden, *look.*"

Angel ran hard around the track, gaining on Yamamoto, gaining, gaining, coming down the final stretch, there! She pulled even with him, so close to the end—and with a final burst of energy, she crossed the finish line in tenth place.

"This is a first!" the woman yelled while the crowds cheered the exciting finish. "A *sprinter* just finished in the top ten of the classic marathon!"

Angel was gasping as she staggered around the finish area. A medic spoke to her, but she shook her head the way she always did when she told someone she felt fine. She did take the water they offered, gulped some down, and then poured the rest over her head. Bhaaj noticed all her runners did that, Undercity and Cries alike, drinking some and then pouring the rest, a joyful act that celebrated the wealth of drinkable water, enough that they could even dump it on their body without guilt.

Angel came over to them, breathing hard. "Eh," she managed.

"*Incredible!*" Mason grabbed her over the barrier and hugged the flustered Dust Knight. "What a feat! I'm so incredibly proud of you!"

"Angel!" Hyden grabbed her as well, hugging with gusto.

Bhaaj grinned at Angel, who stared at her over Mason's shoulder with a panicked look. No one ever hugged the powerful, dangerous dust ganger that way, except Mason and Hyden didn't know that, so they continued to do the unimaginable.

"Eh," Bhaaj told her.

It took Angel a few moments to untangle herself from Mason and Hyden, and by then even she was laughing. She started grinning again, her breathing less strained.

It seemed hardly any time passed before the commentators announced Helyne Tallmount's entry into the stadium. She finished nineteenth, also her best time ever, higher up in the rankings than anyone expected, including herself.

"Good job, Helyne!" Mason enthused as they gathered together. "Three runners in the top twenty. *Three*. Excellent! Superb! Wowzing!" His words tumbled over one another.

"Wowzing?" Hyden asked and they all laughed.

"I'd have liked to beat Muzeson, too," Angel confided.

"Yah." Bhaaj agreed, not only for Angel, but also on the general principle that the Traders had treated them like garbage here, and it annoyed her immensely that they were going to come out on top, with the most medals and the highest ranking.

Even so. The commentators had it right. These games were just the beginning for Raylicon.

"Bhaaj and Mason," Max said. His voice came between the gusts of wind blowing over the seats where they waited in the stadium, watching the relay runners prepare for their finals. "They're talking about Tam again in the royal. I can put it on the holoscreen at your seats, if you'd like."

Bhaaj said, "Yah, good," even as Mason said, "Great! Yes! Play it from wherever they started talking about her." Despite his words, Bhaaj heard his unease. They never knew what slant the commentators would take on their athletes.

The flat screen at their seat activated, and a holo-vid appeared above it showing a solitary runner on a trail with a sheer white cliff on her right. The wind whipped back her hair as she ran up the slope. The sheer drop-off on her left made it look as if nothing protected her from that chasm of air, but regularly placed poles, almost invisible, glistened in the sunlight, the only sign of the transparent force-fence that would stop runners from falling. Far below, great waves beat against the cliff, their breakers spraying water and foam high into the air as they crashed against the rocks. The sun shone in the golden sky, and the rings arched across the heavens like a bridge to paradise.

"Goddess," Mason murmured. "What a lovely place to run."

"She seems in the zone," Bhaaj said. Tam was gazing out at the ocean, which stretched to the horizon, her face a study in bliss. Today, she witnessed what, for her, was a miracle: limitless water that thundered against the cliff and stretched on and on, to the rim of the world.

"This is one of the longest inclines," the female commentator was saying. "By the time they finish it, the runners have gained more than three hundred meters of elevation."

"The total change in elevation for the royal is two thousand meters," the man said. "About six thousand five hundred feet, and that doesn't count the cliff climb. The steepest section is yet to come, with a dirt path through the Harkovian Forest at a demanding incline of *eighteen* percent, followed by the Harkovian Ascent, a climb of fifty meters up a sheer cliff. And I do mean *sheer*. The surface is rough, sure, but it goes up in a vertical wall. It's the most grueling section, one that defeats at least three or four competitors every time."

"Wiens' last cliff climb was a disaster," the woman said. "At Metropoli, she needed extra precautions with the security harness, which slowed her down, and then she had to struggle up the cliff without putting too much weight on her injured ankle."

"Whether or not she can climb when she's in good shape remains to be seen," the man said. "Scaling a cliff can stymie even the best athletes. The Harkovian Ascent uses skills different than a distance run, and it's the nemesis for many a would-be royal marathoner."

"So far, after four hours, Wiens has maintained her pace," the woman said. "It looks good in the stats, but that isn't likely to last. Experienced ultramarathon runners take it easier on steep ascents to let their bodies recover and may walk in the most grueling sections. Wiens hasn't even slowed."

"Well, it's put her in eleventh place," the man said. "It's tempting to say this newcomer might shock everyone and reach the top ten."

"The Harkovian Ascent will be a challenge," the woman said. A display of numbers appeared above Tam, glowing against the magnificent landscape, giving times for the leaders, including Kryx Quaelen and Vanya Longbow. "Wiens is running faster than Longbow now and about equal to Quaelen," the woman added. "But that may only last until she hits the infamous wall of fatigue. And then? It could end her dream of finishing one of the most demanding royal marathons known anywhere, both for the Olympics and in the many other meets that use this course."

"It's a different story for Quaelen," the man said. The view shifted, showing Kryx Quaelen running in a forest where golden rays of sunlight slanted through a green canopy and patches of golden sky showed through the overhead foliage. Shimmerflies danced in the air.

"That was all they had to say about Tam," Max said.

"All right. You can turn it off." Bhaaj had no desire to hear everyone rhapsodize about how Kryx Quaelen was the greatest marathoner humanity had ever produced. Pulling the VR helmet over her eyes, she said, "Can you put me with Strider's relay team?"

"Here you go," Max said.

Bhaaj abruptly found herself in lane six at the starting block with Zee. She looked around at the other runners, all from Zee's view. With the staggered starts, she couldn't see much. She wished she could talk to Zee or bring in her beetle-bot to monitor the race right next to the members of the Raylicon relay team. Of course she couldn't; the rules forbade coaches from doing anything that might give their athletes an unfair advantage.

Bhaaj pushed back her visor and once again found herself in the stadium. Out on the track, the Starter called out commands, runners took their positions—and boom! Off they went, with Zee hurtling off the block.

"Yes! Good start!" Mason said. "Come on, Zee, keep it strong, get out in front."

It seemed only moments before Zee came pounding into the end of her lap. Kiro waited in her lane, poised, barely looking back. Zee slapped the baton into his outstretched hand, and he took off so smoothly, they seemed two parts of a single, primed machine. For all the commentators who'd criticized them for not putting Angel on the relay, that perfect baton switch said it all.

Kiro sprinted around the track at a sure-footed pace, jockeying for position. He passed the sixth-place runner just before he handed the baton to Strider, another beautifully coordinated switch. The fourth-place runner wasn't so lucky; her baton hit an edge of the outgoing runner's hand. They recovered almost instantly, but it gave Strider a few seconds to surge ahead of their team, too.

Strider ran hard, faster than Bhaaj had ever seen her sprint. Strong and sure-footed, she gained on the runner in third. They were nearly neck-and-neck when Strider reached Lamp and passed him the baton, again perfectly. Lamp took off like lightning, tied for third. The crowd in the packed-to-overflowing stadium roared as Lamp burst into the infamous Undercity kick—

And sailed past his rival into second place.

As Lamp crossed the finish line, he raised both hands in the air, still clutching the baton, and his shout reverberated like the bellow of a triumphant warrior. Mason was yelling at Bhaaj's side. They had both jumped to their feet, though Bhaaj had no memory of doing it. As they scrambled down to the railing, Mason kept saying, "Did you see? Did you *see!*" Out in the finishing area, Lamp, Strider, Kiro, and Zee were hugging each other now, Lamp still gasping for breath.

"Yes!" Mason yelled from the barrier. The relay team members all turned, then ran over to them. As Bhaaj draped the Raylicon flag over their shoulders, they laughed and gulped in breaths, all of them, her *why-the-hell-we-run-in-circles?* athletes, overjoyed at how gloriously they'd just run those circles.

Right before the relay medal ceremony started, Max thought, **They're talking about Tam again.**

Show us after the ceremony. Bhaaj stood with the wind blowing her hair while officials gave the bronze winners their medals and Foreshires Memory Scrolls. Then came Raylicon's moment. With a pride so full she hardly knew where to put it, she watched them drape silver medals on Zee, Kiro, Strider, and Lamp. They stood with their heads raised, their arms around each other, their joy obvious despite their attempts to look impassive. Kiro didn't even try. Bhaaj had no doubt that broadcast after broadcast would show the tears running down his face as he accepted his Olympic medal.

"—now in eighth place, Wiens is approaching the most demanding portion of this course, what runners call the Harkovian Hammer," the man was saying. "With only about an hour left in this race, she has to surmount what seven runners ahead of her have already conquered, a continual incline of eighteen percent followed by a climb of fifty meters up a cliff face."

Bhaaj watched intently, sitting alone in a corner of the coach's lounge, while Mason went off to do administrative biz. The place had been almost empty, most coaches either in the stadium or busy with tasks, but now they were trickling back to watch the royal finish. Many people considered it the most spectacular event, at least the parts where the hours-long run didn't become tedious. Spectators loved the dramatic landscapes, the inclines, the Harkovian cliff, the sheer beauty of the trails, and especially the finish, when the athletes entered the stadium vying for the gold or, as the hyperbolic commentators put it, becoming "The Best! Distance runner! In all! Humanity!"

Bhaaj sighed. Sometimes all the Olympic hype gave her a headache. Seriously, how could every race have something qualify as the *best we've ever seen!* Still, she did feel the excitement, especially for the classic, her own event, and for the royal, with its punishing eighty kilometers.

"So far the Hammer hasn't defeated anyone," the woman was saying. "Kryx Quaelen conquered it outright, achieving a record time in his ascent."

"I've never seen a marathoner climb that slope with such speed," the man enthused. "Usually they rely more on their safety harness, letting it support their weight so they can ease the strain on their body as they climb. That slowed down both Vanya Longbow and Xi Aio, currently in second and third. In contrast, Quaelen barely seemed to notice his harness."

"Yes, but it's good he had it," the woman said. "That place where he lost his footing—if the harness hadn't caught him when he started to slide, he could have lost all his progress, even injured himself in a fall."

"Historically, we see the most problems here for this course," the man said. "The Hammer has inflicted severe injuries, even a few deaths on athletes who refused the harness."

"It takes time to put it on," the woman said. "Even with race officials to help. Given the extent of Quaelen's lead, though, it won't matter even if someone manages it faster than his ascent."

"Enough already about Quaelen," Bhaaj grumbled.

Eventually they got back to Tam. "Wiens is partway up the Harkovian incline," the woman said. "She's still running hard. The question now is how much this high elevation will slow her down." The holo-vid showed Tam loping up a steep path into the upper reaches of the forest. The trees had become smaller, more widely spaced, and the scraggly bushes no longer had flowers.

Wimpy plants, Bhaaj thought.

Why? Max asked. **Tam will pass the timberline on the cliff. Above that, no plant life grows in this region.**

Foreshires has a wimpy timberline. I mean, seriously? On Raylicon, native plants grow fine at elevations a lot higher than this. She'd seen cacti-patches in regions on Raylicon that would have killed this pretty but puny Foreshires greenery.

A lot of factors cause a timberline, Max answered. **Not enough water, too much wind, cold temperatures. Low oxygen levels can damage root systems. Plants on Raylicon are adapted to survive more severe conditions than here.**

Yah, well, the same for our athletes.

That's the hope. Max still sounded concerned. **However, Tam has never tried a course like this. It would be grueling even with just the cliff, and she's going to hit that climb after she does one of the steepest inclines on any royal course.**

Of course she's tried courses like this. Bhaaj didn't know if she was trying to convince him or herself. *We get less oxygen at lower elevations on Raylicon than Foreshires has in those mountains. And some of our cave-ins in the Undercity are harder to climb than that cliff.*

You could make a comparison. Max didn't sound convinced.

If Bhaaj hadn't known better, she'd have thought he felt worried. Hell, maybe she didn't know better. He did such a good job emulating emotions, she couldn't tell the difference anymore. He had good reason for his cautions. This course went through the mountains, with even its lowest point at an elevation of two thousand feet. At the top of the Harkovian Ascent, Tam would be more than nine thousand feet above sea-level, a situation she'd never seen in the Undercity.

"Wiens is *still* pushing too hard." The man sounded frustrated. "Why doesn't she use common sense? She'll push herself right into the hospital!"

"I have no idea what to think anymore," the woman said. "We keep saying she's pushing too hard, that she'll flame out. For *five* hours we've said that. And *look* at her. She looks like she's in the zone."

"Of course she is," Bhaaj commented to the mostly empty lounge.

"She's more than halfway up the Harkovian incline," the woman continued. "Here's her stats!" The view panned out until Tam was a small figure running through the starkly beautiful panorama of the towering Harkovian mountains with only a few stunted trees around her. A display appeared above her, glowing with numbers, not just hers, but also for other athletes.

"I see what you mean," the man said. "Wiens is now the fastest runner on the course. She started slower than any of the seven people ahead of her, but as with most royal marathons, runners tend to slow down by this point in the race."

"Except not Wiens," the woman said.

"I have to admit, I've never seen anything like this," the man said. "Many athletes can't deal with these high altitudes. Some have trouble walking. She just keeps running."

"You have to remember she comes from Raylicon," the woman said. "It has the lowest concentration of oxygen in its atmosphere of any world where humans can live without a breathing apparatus. Visitors sometimes report having to use oxygen tanks just to go outside."

"True," he said. "But toward the top of the Harkovian Cliff, she'll hit the point where the oxygen has dropped to dangerously low levels. Even if she can manage without sagging too much in her safety harness, she'll have to move more carefully just to breathe."

"I've seen athletes pass out on that cliff," the woman said. "I only climbed it once, twenty years ago, and I barely reached the top. Without oxygen at the aid station up there, I don't know that I could have kept going."

"And you won the gold that year!" the man said. "What an accomplishment!"

"Yah, good," Bhaaj grumbled. It was impressive, she agreed, but she wanted them to talk about Tam. In such a lengthy race, though, they needed to get chatty to fill time.

Eventually the man said, "Wiens is almost at the cliff. How do you think she'll do?"

"She had serious trouble with the only other cliff she's tried," the woman said. "We don't know how much of that came from her injury, though. The temperature here may help, too. Raylicon is *hot*. Some claim people live in the Undercity because it's cooler. The mildness of this biosphere works to her advantage."

"There is that," Bhaaj acknowledged. On Raylicon, even at midday when slicks stayed inside their climate-controlled buildings, her people carried on as usual in the cooler Undercity.

The view of the Harkovian Mountains narrowed until Tam's figure filled the screen. She'd always favored bleaching her hair white, and now it glowed in the sunlight, brilliant against the brown of her skin. She'd had her short locks styled at a trendy boutique in the Olympic Village so they swept across her forehead and curled down her neck. The small gold hoops in her ears sparkled in the sunlight. Her black eyes seemed huge in her face and tilted slightly upward. No wonder the broadcasters were concentrating on her image. She was a spectacularly beautiful woman running in a spectacularly beautiful landscape.

Bhaaj also recognized her look. Tam was off in her own world, aware of her surroundings but blissfully in her head, lost in her agile, creative mind. If Bhaaj hadn't known better, she'd have thought Tam wasn't at her top speed even now. But she did know better. Even Tam had her limits.

"And here it is, that moment everyone waits for in this race," the man said. "Wiens is the eighth runner to reach the Harkovian Cliff. We've had plenty of excitement from the first seven. The big question now: how fast can she scale a sheer cliff face?"

"We know at least some Undercity runners can climb," the woman said. "Dice Vakaar won a silver medal earlier today in the ten kay climb, the sixth medal for the Raylicon team, all silver or bronze, but still an incredible achievement for this underdog team."

"These Undercity athletes are like nothing anyone expected," the man said. "Their presence has pulled up the entire team, pushing the other runners to strive for better results."

"Just you wait," Bhaaj said. They'd barely grazed the surface of talent among her people.

"Wiens is at the harness station—what the *hell?*" the man said, forgetting the prohibition against cussing on sports broadcasts. "Tam Wiens just blazed past the harness team waiting to strap her into the apparatus. She didn't even slow down!"

"Eh," Bhaaj said. She'd wondered if Tam would take the harness. None of the Undercity runners liked it, but no one wanted to suffer the same result that had almost kept Kiro out of the Olympics, a slip that would send them sliding out of medal contention, maybe even lead to injury.

On the Harkovian Ascent, it could kill you.

Tam kept going, the same way she approached any barrier in the Undercity. When she reached the cliff, she grabbed a jutting spur of rock, hauled herself up without pause, setting her feet on the wall, and then repeated the process for the next handhold. The view moved out, getting wider as she scrambled up the cliff, fast and certain, with a skill she'd honed her entire life.

"I can't believe it!" the female commentator cried. "She's *flying* up that cliff."

"Eh," Bhaaj told them. *Flying* was another exaggeration the commentators liked. It was true, though, that Tam climbed swiftly with the grab-jump-haul technique their people used, a method honed for speed so you could catch someone who tried to escape by going up a difficult slope, or that you could use to escape your own pursuers. The better you managed it—without falling—the more likely you'd survive to fight another day. And Tam did it better than anyone else.

But fifty freaking meters? The climbs at most meets were only a tame fifteen meters. Some doubled that to thirty, but a fifty-meter climb was rare even in a royal marathon. Tam took the cliff as if it were nothing, scaling it with confidence. She went even faster than when she'd climbed the shorter, gentler cliff in Mason's Olympic qualifier. She must have been practicing on her own in the Undercity or out in the desert at night.

"I've never seen an ascent this fast," the man said. "Look at her times! This puts her even farther ahead in her average speed compared to most of the other runners—no, wait! *NO!*"

In that instant, Tam's hand slipped on the wall, and she started to slide down the cliff. Bhaaj froze, her entire body going rigid. *Nooooo!* Tam was gaining speed—

With an audible grunt that the orb monitoring her progress caught and transmitted, Tam tensed her fingers into claws, a method they all used in the Undercity—one that failed as often as it worked. Spreading out the contact between her body and the cliff, using not only her hands, but her feet, knees, elbows and even her stomach to press against the wall, she slowed her descent with friction. Without pause, she whipped up one hand, dug her fingers into a crack in the wall—

And resumed her climb.

"HO!" the female commentator bellowed. "That could have been a fatal slip! But she *stopped* herself. She's *climbing* again."

"I can't believe it!" the man shouted. "She only lost a couple of seconds. Look at her go!"

"Goddess," Bhaaj muttered, adrenaline crashing through her system. This was far more excitement than anyone needed.

"She doesn't even seem fazed!" the woman cried. "She's almost done!"

In the same instant that Tam's hand slapped on the top edge of the cliff, she launched herself up with so much power that her body flew into the air as she vaulted over the top. She landed on level ground beyond, a move Bhaaj had seen a hundred times and more in the Undercity, a final leap to shave off more time, but out here in the open, in the streaming sunlight with majestic peaks in the background, it looked far more spectacular.

With barely a pause, Tam took off running, pounding past the aid station. She grabbed a water bottle and energy bar that people held out for her, but she didn't stop to use the oxygen mask another volunteer offered. Instead, she ran along a path without a plant in sight, headed down to more human-amenable altitudes.

"Look at her times!" the female commentator shouted. "She's closing in on Jaibriol Kaliga in seventh place. He lost a lot of time on that ascent, and Wiens *gained*."

"Saints almighty, she *still* looks strong," the man said. "What a runner! What an athlete!"

"Gods," a woman said in the lounge, close to Bhaaj. "Did they check that girl for biomech oxygen filters in her body?"

Startled, Bhaaj turned around. Coaches from other teams had gathered on sofas or chairs, others sitting on the floor. Mason was also here, on a stool not far away. Before Bhaaj could react to the woman who made the crack about biomech, Mason said, "Enough! The officials have checked my athletes again and again. Not only do none of them have augmentation, but until they joined my team, most didn't even have health meds."

"It's true," a woman sitting on the floor said, turning down the feed. "My Docker's Haven team was at the meet where the Metropoli teams tried to make those allegations. The panel not only cleared Raylicon in every case, but they recommended giving the athletes better meds."

"It's amazing," another man said, nodding with respect to Mason and Bhaaj. "You've found a gold mine in these runners."

"Both literally and figuratively," someone else said, evoking a ripple of amusement.

"Well," Bhaaj admitted, pleased by their unexpected support. "Not literally gold, at least not here. But they're young. And they love to run. They've a great future."

"And there are more of them!" Mason said. "A lot more." With a wry smile, he added, "I just have to convince them and Coach Bhaaj to get them on the team."

"Look!" Another coach motioned at the feed. "Wiens is closing on Kaliga."

Turning back, Bhaaj realized Tam had come within view of Jaibriol Kaliga, running down a rocky path bordered by stunted trees and bushes. For the first time she showed signs of strain; going downhill could hurt even more than uphill. She still went fast, though, using the descending slope to increase her speed as she gained on Kaliga. More than strain, her face showed determination. This Aristo came from the people who'd tried to deny her this run.

Someone turned up the feed in time for another, "It's *incredible!*" from the commentators.

"They should just put that statement on a loop and keep running it," someone said, followed by a sprinkling of laughter. People were more relaxed now that the Games had almost finished, with only this event remaining and then the Closing Ceremonies.

"There it is!" the female commentator said as Tam pounded past Jaibriol Kaliga. "Wiens has moved into seventh place!"

"And Raylicon has more coming up," the male commentator added. The holo changed to a man running through the thinning forest prior to the Harkovian cliff. "Ruzik is in fourteenth. He's kept up his pace well, not as fast as Wiens, but strong and steady."

"And Tayz Wilder," the woman added as the scene changed to the lush forest of the lower slopes. "Last year he was the only Raylicon athlete who did the royal. He came in thirty-eighth, the best finish ever back then for any Raylicon runner. He's currently in twenty-second. His average time has slowed on the second half of the race, but he's kept a good clip and shows no sign of hitting the wall. He'll pass more runners if he keeps this up."

"It will be a huge upset if Raylicon places three people in the top twenty," the man said. "With the extra weight given to the royal, especially the top ten, this could move them up in the overall track and field ranking. They're currently in twelfth."

"You can't help but wonder," the woman mused, "what would have happened with the 4×400 relay if they'd put Angel there instead of in the classic, where she had no chance of a medal."

"It's hard to say," the man answered. "Relays aren't just about speed. It also depends on how well a team works together. It was like poetry in motion watching the Raylicon team, almost as if they knew each other's thoughts."

"Who knows," the woman said. "The Eubians complained about letting empaths compete. Maybe they had ulterior motives."

"I wouldn't be surprised," the man said. "The Eubians have raised their ability to predict an athlete's performance to an art. They might have realized how well Tam Wiens could do." The view switched, showing Tam running past flowering plants as she reached gentler elevations.

"Kaliga needs to make the top eight," the woman said. "If he does, then along with Kryx Quaelen's gold, the Quaelen team will make a full sweep in track and field honors, including the most medals, most golds, and top rank overall."

"Wiens pushed him back to eighth, but that won't take away the Aristo edge," the man said.

A man among the coaches in the lounge said, "True. But still. She's beating the Aristo."

"Gods, the way they talk," another coach said. "It's like we're insects they want to step on."

"It's appalling," someone else said. "How can they claim it's abusive to let Kyle operators compete when they *torture* empaths?"

Bhaaj hadn't realized the news about the challenge to Tam had become so public. She understood why the IOC let it, though. That way, when Eube submitted their motion to bar empaths from the

Olympics, no one could accuse the IOC of hiding anything. And Eube would make the challenge, of that Bhaaj had no doubt, especially given that in their view, Tam had just humiliated Jaibriol Kaliga.

As the marathon continued, the commentators focused on other runners, mostly Quaelen, Longbow, and Aio in the lead. Bhaaj's attention drifted. She leaned back on the couch. So tired...

Bhaaj, Max thought. **Wake up. Look at the holo-feed.**

Eh? Groggy, she lifted her head as Max turned up her ear subs.

"—she's now in fifth place!" the male commentator was saying. "What a showing from Wiens. And she's gaining on Avery Ocal, the fourth-place runner."

"We've been doing calculations," the woman said. "If Wiens keeps up this pace, she has a chance of coming in fourth."

"No medal, but an enormous feat for Raylicon," the man said. "It will move them up in the rankings. The big question: can they make the top ten?"

"Not at these Games," the woman said. "Every team with athletes in the top twenty here will see a boost in their scores. According to my EI's calculations, Raylicon will come in twelfth, with a chance at eleventh if Wiens finishes fourth."

"It's still astounding for a team that usually gets no medals. Their coaches must be ecstatic."

"Well, yah," Bhaaj said. "Very pleased. But not surprised."

Mason grinned at her. "Is this where I can say 'Eh'?"

She laughed. "Absolutely." They'd still have to battle the Traders over empaths, but Bhaaj doubted Eube would win. Even if the IOC did rule in their favor, they couldn't make it retroactive. No one had ever needed to register as a Kyle for the Olympics, and no record existed of who was or wasn't an empath. Some people didn't know themselves. The challenge might go for seasons, even years, but Tam would keep her standing for these Games.

As the race neared its finish, more people came to the lounge and joined the crowd around the holo-dais. When Tam passed Avery Ocal, moving into fourth place, the commentators went back to exulting over her run. Someone noted that the stats now running continually over Tam in the display showed her speed had increased again, just barely, but enough to notice.

A chill went through Bhaaj, shivering up her spine. Sliding closer to where Mason sat on a stool by the couch, she spoke in a low voice. "I've seen Tam do this before."

He glanced at her. "Do what?"

"She's going to sprint."

"With what energy?" he asked amiably. "Maybe a bit at the end. But not enough to matter."

"I suppose." She'd never done a full marathon with Tam in the Undercity; they usually had different places to go, so they'd run for a while and then separate. The few times she'd finished with Tam, though, she'd had a hard time keeping up, and Bhaaj could do the Undercity kick as well as anyone. Then again, she'd never seen Tam try it after six hours of exertion.

The top runners had entered the city, following the route where the classic had finished a few hours earlier. Vanya Longbow was within distant view of Kryx Quaelen down the long avenue, but he had too much of a lead for her to overcome. Farther behind, Aio came on in third place. He looked exhausted, and his speed had slowed, but usually at this point of the race, the next runner would be far enough behind that someone in his position didn't have to worry.

Except today.

The view panned out, showing all three leaders followed by chase trucks, bots, and cool-carts—and Tam. She was only a few meters behind Aio now, and gaining rapidly. When someone turned up the feed, it came with a burst of words, the two commentators talking over each other, "—possible she'll take a *bronze*?" the woman said.

"I don't believe this," the man shouted. "*Tam Wiens just passed Xi Aio!*"

"A first!" the woman exclaimed. "A runner from one of the most underprivileged slums in settled space, a virtual unknown with just one limping royal under her belt, and she's in position to *medal* at these races."

"Her stats say it all," the man said. "She's faster now than either Longbow or Quaelen."

The woman spoke in a calmer voice. "But look at the EI calculations on those stats." She sounded disappointed. "For Wiens to catch Longbow, she'd need to speed up even more and maintain it until the end of the course. That isn't likely to happen."

"I'm not making any more predictions," the man said. "Wiens has defied them all."

Mason nudged Bhaaj's arm. "Let's go to the stadium."

"Yah." Bhaaj stood up with him, aware of several other coaches getting up as well.

They didn't have far to go from the coach's lounge to the finish area outside, but the walk seemed to take forever. Bhaaj felt so wound up, she no longer noticed her fatigue. A few people glanced her way; even with her lean build and loose clothes, anyone could tell she was pregnant now. She doubted they cared. They all strode through the coach's tunnel and out into the windy afternoon. Her pregnancy did have one advantage. The people in the finish area moved aside to let her right up to the barrier that separated them from where the runners would finish.

Holo-displays in the stadium showed the three leaders running through the city. Even before Bhaaj turned up her ear subs, she could read the stats for Tam. She'd sped up again, less than a hundred meters now from Vanya Longbow.

Voices swept over her. "—rumor says the Dust Knights train in a killing environment," the woman was saying. "People in the Undercity face threats of death from their living conditions and the brutality of their lives every day. Are we seeing the product of that forge, humans able to survive what most of us would consider impossible? Because make no mistake, Tam Wiens is doing what no one believed could happen. She *does* have a chance of passing Vanya Longbow and wrenching that silver away from the runner everyone expected to claim it."

"The three leaders are almost to the stadium!" the man said "Quaelen is about to enter the tunnel—look! Another first! We're seeing the feed from *inside*." And indeed, the scene shifted, showing the interior of the wide tunnel that led from outside the stadium into the track area.

Quaelen gave the barest nod to the officials at the tunnel entrance as he passed them. Holo-cams, media orbs, and cool-carts crammed with people came with him. He kept running, his aristocratic face set with determination. Bhaaj recognized his tells from other Aristos she'd interacted with.

No, not tells, she thought. *Admit the truth. He's close enough now that you're picking up his mind.* He knew he was about to win what most people considered the most prestigious distance race in existence. Humanity would exalt him as the best runner in history—and he expected it as his due. He considered himself godlike, and as such this win and the accolades that would follow belonged to him. Period.

"Longbow sped up!" the woman cried as the view switched to Longbow entering the tunnel. "If Wiens thought she had a chance at a silver, Longbow just made short work of that hope."

The scene changed again, showing Quaelen bursting into the sunlight, onto the track. The crowds in the packed stadium went nuts, not just the Eubians who had scored permission to come here, but also the Skolian and Allied audience as they cheered Quaelen's phenomenal achievement. Not far behind him, Vanya Longbow ran into view, and the roar from the spectators swelled. It buffeted Bhaaj, both the noise and the onslaught of so much excitement. But she didn't barrier her mind, leaving it open as she tried to sense Tam through all that chaos.

"Wiens is on the field," the female announcer said. "Only a few seconds behind Longbow. At this point, no way exists for her to catch up—*Holy shit!*"

In the same instant that the announcer shouted her broadcast-prohibited words, the crowd screamed and the male announcer yelled, "The Undercity kick! Gods-all-freaking-mighty, Tam Wiens just gave us that end-of-race sprint that has become notorious at these games!"

"It's impossible! Where does she get the energy?" the woman exclaimed. "Wiens just passed Longbow! Wiens has moved into second place! She's demanding that silver!"

"Look at her face!" the man said. "If any expression ever defined the word fierce, that's it!"

Bhaaj *felt* it blazing in Tam's mind. Everything Tam had dealt with, Quaelen's people trying to deny her this race, the accident on Metropoli, everything the runners had endured to get here, the deprivation and poverty of the Undercity, the fight to stay alive that had defined her life before she joined the team, her unrelenting struggle with gender dysphoria, the pain of losing her parents, then losing her siblings to the violence of the aqueducts and killing diseases that doctors in Cries could have treated if they hadn't refused to see

Undercity patients—it all went into her face as she set her sights on Quaelen.

"She's doing it!" the announcers yelled. "She's going after the undisputed king of the royal marathon!"

As Tam and Quaelen headed down the final stretch, the woman shouted, "The stats tell it all! She doesn't have enough time to catch him—he'll get there a few seconds earlier—LOOK AT THAT! Wiens kicked *again*. Saints almighty, she kicked again!"

As the announcers yelled, as Mason yelled, as every coach around them who'd ever endured Aristo arrogance or cruelty yelled, Bhaaj stared. Huge screens all over the stadium showed holos, mostly of Tam gaining on Quaelen, but some of Bhaaj and Mason as well, Bhaaj with her mouth agape, something she'd never done before in her life.

TAM, GO, she thought. *YOU CAN DO IT!* She wasn't a telepath, but in a moment like this, with enough ferocity, maybe, just maybe, she could reach Tam.

From somewhere distant, or maybe it seemed that way because of her lower Kyle rating, she sensed other minds, Ruzik, Angel, Kiro, so many others. *Tam, you got this! Go. GO!*

As the crowd and the announcers screamed, Tam closed the gap with Quaelen. He shot one look at her when she pulled even with him, and if hatred could have killed, Tam would have died in that instant. Whatever she felt of that explosive attack from his mind, she showed no sign. In defiance of every torture and suppression the Aristos had ever inflicted against their empaths, Tam surged across the finish line—

One step ahead of Kryx Quaelen.

Bhaaj no longer heard the crowd, no longer felt the force of their minds or voices. She couldn't even hear Mason screaming with joy as jubilant Skolian officials held him back so no one could take away Tam's medal by claiming her coach acted out of bounds. Bhaaj's focus narrowed to one person.

She thought, simply, *Tam. Good job.*

Tam turned from all the people crowding around her, the officials and medics and everyone else, and looked straight at Bhaaj. She nodded. Bhaaj nodded back. And it was done. In the Undercity, that one exchange surpassed all the yelling from everywhere else.

Stats continued to evolve as other runners came in—with another roar from the crowd when Ruzik entered the stadium in tenth, coming as he did from the now acclaimed underdogs of the Games, and similarly when Tayz Wilder came in at eighteenth.

Tam was walking back and forth in the finisher's area, holding the Raylicon flag high above her head, facing the crowd as they shouted with joy that one of their own had wrested gold from the Eubians. She even smiled in the roar of their approval, though she looked confused as well as elated. Bhaaj felt her response. It was triumph, yes, but something more, a stunned sense that finally, *finally* things had gone right in a life that had beaten her down from birth. A deep sense of affirmation glowed within her, beneath all the excitement and adrenaline.

After the top twenty runners came in, the displays all over the stadium changed to show not only the medal winners and the athletes finishing the royal, but also the top ten teams in track and field. The medal count would always be the ultimate honor at the Olympics, but the team rankings had become well respected. With Tam taking gold and Quaelen getting silver, it changed the standings just enough so that despite Iquar's eighth place finish, the Metropoli A team edged into first, with the Quaelen team in second.

Raylicon came in tenth.

For the first time in history, not only at the Olympics but for any major sports tournament, Raylicon ranked in the top ten for track and field. They didn't come close to the powerhouses, those teams from worlds with populations in the billions like Metropoli and Earth, or the endlessly curated Quaelen team, or those from major government centers like Parthonia or Eube's Glory. Raylicon had only one gold, and in terms of total medals for all sports at the Olympics, they were in fiftieth place—but for a team that almost never won even a single medal, their results today obliterated their previous finishes.

For Bhaaj and Mason and their team, it was the sweetest victory.

CHAPTER XXIX
Koyo

Angel leaned against the console in the living room of the cabin she shared with Ruzik and smiled at her husband, relaxed for the first time in she didn't know how long. It was done. They'd finished the Games, and with good results.

Ruzik smiled. "You look like those purple fluff-pups that jump in the meadows."

She stretched her arms. "They not get Olympic medals."

He laughed more easily than she'd heard from him in many tendays. "Not fast like us."

"Yah." Angel went over to him. "We go party at pub, eh?"

He pulled her down onto the bed. "In a bit."

"Hmmm." Angel agreed.

Sometime later, as they lay together, Ruzik said, "Maybe get up."

Angel yawned. "In a bit."

A while later, he sat up and rolled his shoulders. "Should go now. Gets dark."

Angel squinted at the window they'd left with the curtains open. The Harkovian Mountains showed in the distance, on fire with the brilliant reds and pinks of sunset, which also glowed on the rings, vibrant and intense. "Lot of colors," she said.

"Thick air," Ruzik said. "Lot of dust."

"Pretty." Angel sat up next to him. "You go to pub, yah? I join soon." She motioned at the console, which included the Kyle station Bhaaj had arranged for her. "Got to do check."

He frowned. "Not work now."

"Just make check. Worried."

"Why?"

"Holo-vid person say Dice Vakaar. Want to make sure is okay people know his name."

Ruzik nodded. "Meet you at party. Not be long, yah?"

She kissed him. "Not long."

After they cleaned up and dressed, Ruzik headed for the pub that lay a kilometer outside the city, out in fields of waving cloud-grass. Most people were taking cool-carts, especially runners from the marathons, but he'd probably jog there. She would too, if she wasn't too long in the web.

It took only moments to access the Kyle and enter the "office" she'd created. Sometimes she used Undercity scenes, which felt right for prowling the web. Today, she chose her office in Selei Tower, except the view had rings in the sky and those outstanding sunset colors.

Maze formed in her office, morphing out of the air, an androgynous figure with stylish white hair and small gold hoops in their ears, snazzy creased pants, a black vest with silver accents, and black shirt. Angel rarely knew how her EI would choose to present; she'd left it up to the code.

"Eh," Angel said. "You decide yet if you man or woman?"

"Not sure," Maze said.

"You want me call you Him, Her, They, or It today?"

Maze considered the question. "It."

"You sure? Sound like thing. How about They?"

"Not plural today."

"'They' not always plural."

"Yah. Ken. But I like 'It' today. Some other time I am They. Or Her. Or Him."

"You ever decide on one?"

"Why have to decide?"

Good point. "Can be what you want." Maze kept evolving, in some ways becoming more like her, in others not so much. For one, Angel always felt female. Unless she doubted it without realizing it? She'd asked Tam if it that was possible, but Tam didn't think so given that Angel liked being female, especially with Ruzik, who in Angel's view qualified as the ultimate man. Maybe her EI's fluid gender choices had more to do with her own fluid choices regarding the rest of her identity. Was she Undercity, above-city, telop, athlete, what? Bhaaj said she could be all those, which seemed okay, except it meant one hell of a workload. Sometimes she wanted to go back to the days when she was just a Dust Knight protecting her circle. Mostly, though, she loved her life. All that work brought good stuff, like medals and access to the Kyle.

"You do stealth today?" Maze asked.

"Yah. The usual."

Except not quite "the usual." When Bhaaj had insisted she tell her mentors how she prowled the Kyle in secret, it had annoyed Angel. *Not their biz*, Angel told her.

You got bargain with them, Bhaaj answered. *They make you telop. You work for them. Have to tell. Not bad thing. Might surprise you.*

So Angel let them know. The more she said, the stronger their reaction: she scared the hell out of them—and they loved what she could do. They *wanted* her to, as they put it, "use her skills to access unusual places for novel excursions." Yah, right. The Pharaoh's Army made her a spy. That sat fine with her. She hadn't liked Aristos even before the Games, and after all the shit they'd thrown at Raylicon, she'd gladly spy on them. Of course, she also spied on the Kyle Division, but she didn't mention those details. She suspected they had some idea, though, so she moved with care. The result? They let her do her biz, and in return she did her best for them.

Today, she had another matter to attend. In one holo-vid, a reporter had said, *We know at least some Undercity runners can climb. Dice Vakaar won a silver medal...*

"Maze," she said. "You get my neural stuff?"

"Your what?"

"Neural firings. You get them?"

"You mean your thoughts about Dice?"

"Yah. How that reporter know he Vakaar?"

"Not know."

She frowned. "We go look."

"Where start?"

"Games shadow mesh."

The office faded, replaced by a nighttime scene bathed in light from the rings. They stood on a forest path, one with stunted trees and rocky ground. Angel walked along, studying the place.

Not so shadowed here, she told Maze. Technically, their communication always came as thought. The Kyle apparatus read the firing patterns of her neurons, interpreted them, and sent Maze the signals, then turned its response into neural firings that her brain interpreted as thoughts. In the virtual sims the Kyle created for their minds, though, their exchanges came as either speech or thoughts. By "thinking" to Maze now, she activated a higher level of her security code.

This outer shell of shadow mesh, Maze said.

Dice Vakaar, Angel thought.

A patch of cloud-grass shook, then grew until it came as high as her mid-calf. Wisps of Kyle code waved within it. Kneeling down, Angel brushed her hand across the grass. Glimpses of Dice came: climbing a cliff, laughing, eating a steak, Shiv's face. Eh. Lot of stuff with Shiv.

Nudging the grass aside, Angel dug her fingers into the gravelly soil. In response, it turned into rock. Not good. The shadow mesh fought her entry. *Need shovel,* she thought. *Not too big. Discreet. Good spy shovel.*

Here. A digger formed in her hand, a skinny trowel the length of her lower arm.

Too long, Angel thought. *Too thin.* She envisioned the tool she wanted.

Done, Maze answered. The trowel morphed, shortening and widening while she gripped its handle. It glistened silver and black in the ringlight.

Good. Angel dug into the ground, and the trowel cut through the rocks, deeper, deeper...

The scene around her faded, then reformed as a shadowed tunnel, not stone, but metal, black or dark blue, with conduits running along the ceiling and circuit diagrams on the walls.

Angel headed down the hall. *Keep lookout for traps.*

Not touch walls, Maze warned.

Make me cloak. Head to foot, not heavy. Cowl for head. She envisioned the details, giving specs for Maze to apply to the shroud routines she'd developed. A long cloak formed on her, as dark as the deepest parts of the aqueducts where no crystals formed.

Doors here? she asked.

Ahead. Look where this tunnel cross other.

Angel continued on, checking the walls, ceiling, and floor, looking for tricks or trials the tunnel might use against her. She remained dark. Hidden.

At an intersection with another tunnel, Maze said, **Here.**

Angel checked out the intersection. The cross tunnel ran at a slant to this one. Its right-hand branch looked promising, with glowing circuit diagrams that hinted at activity. The walls to the left stayed dark, just the barest trace of circuits, so dim she could barely see them.

Angel turned left.

Within a few steps down this new tunnel, its walls leaned inward toward her, their shadows hardening in the darkness.

Not like this, Maze thought.

That the point, Angel thought. *Tries to hide. Not fool me.* She kept going. *Any doors?*

Were some. They move. Now gone.

Angel kenned the process. Moving portals around the shadow mesh made it hard to reach them unless you had the code that specified how their locations changed. *Paint,* she told Maze. Stopping, she faced a wall. *Here. Blue code.*

A paintbrush the color of blue azurite morphed into existence in front of Angel. She pointed at the wall, and the brush whisked over it, painting long blue swaths.

Nothing happened.

Wrong color, she decided. *Try red.*

The brush morphed into a stubby red brush. It whisked away the blue and painted in red.

Nothing.

Angel scowled. *Purple.*

A slender purple brush replaced the red, cleaned up the wall, swept out new paint—

An arrow appeared in the air, glowing deep purple.

Eh. The arrow pointed back the way she'd come. She retraced her steps, and the arrow moved with her—

Until it stopped and morphed into a door.

Open, Angel thought.

Nothing happened.

Traps on door? she asked.

Many, Maze answered. **All over. Not touch. Set off big, loud alarms.**

Nahya. A secret door wouldn't shout its presence, not if its builder knew their biz. *Traps fake. A trick.* Laying her hand on the door, she pushed—

The portal swung open into a wild place. Angel walked into a nighttime bazaar full of purple lights that managed to make the place look poorly lit even though they hung in strings all over the endless cavern. Avatars were everywhere, some cloaked, some in glittery nightclub digs, and others who weren't human but creatures with circuits for faces, features of animals on human bodies, or beings more cybernetic than human.

Eos shadow market. Angel had wondered when she'd find it. She'd been too busy to look before, more concerned with preparing for her events. *Put me in work digs.*

Her cloak disappeared, replaced by Undercity trousers and a muscle shirt torn in places that revealed her scars and virtual cybernetic tattoos. The clothes fit tighter than in the Undercity, and the rips showed too much of her abs and body, better matching the sexed-up clothes people wore here. Everyone looked gorgeous, including the animal or cyber hybrids. A lot of people used avatars based on athletes from the Games, many of them altered to fit whatever their creator liked.

You already here, Maze informed her, sounding amused.

Eh? Angel found herself looking at herself, a version wearing even fewer clothes than the real her, just a glittery skirt that barely covered her ass and a crop top that fit so tightly, she wondered how whoever made that avatar expected her to breathe.

In fact, now that she looked, she saw more versions of herself hanging out, buying drugs and other shit or doing body-biz with Ruzik avatars. And not-Ruzik avatars, too. Ho! Some creepzoid had an Angel avatar getting hot for a cybernetic dragon-lion.

Too weird. Compared to all these avatars, hers was so boring, it hid her as well as the cloak.

You want we find Dices? Maze asked.

Plural of dice is dice.

That mean if Dices fall in love, they love self?

Angel smiled. *That an EI joke?*

Maybe. Not sure how to make jokes.

You good. And yah, find me Dices. She continued on, mingling with the crowd. It didn't take long for her to get fed up with embarrassing sims of Ruzik, herself, Tam, Kiro, Zee, Lamp, and anyone else someone wanted to have sex with. These people had crazy-shit imaginations, some so far out that she didn't even get what they were doing. At least no one noticed her, with the fake Angels so much more enticing than the real one.

Not like this, she thought.

You want leave? Maze asked.

Want find Dices. None?

Sex-bot Dices. You want see?

Angel sighed. *Nahya.*

One not same as others. Maze nudged her along a lane that wound into a hidden region of the bazaar behind the back walls of darkened buildings.

Shooter four, Angel thought. A smart-gun appeared in her hand, the icon for one of her best security mods. She made it look like Bhaaj's EM pulse gun, except this one committed mayhem against code instead of people. Keeping her back to the wall of a building, she crept along the lane.

"—you better get me more," a man was saying up ahead.

Angel stopped. The shadows left barely enough light to let her see a sexed-up bunny-girl talking to an avatar that resembled Dice, but taller and much more muscular, like a weight lifter. He had an Undercity look, scars and tats, also cyber-diagrams embedded in his skin that flashed as they downloaded code onto his body. His cybernetic arm ended in a smart-sword that gleamed. Although Angel doubted Dice would slow himself down by building such a huge physique, he'd probably like an arm like that if sports rules didn't forbid it.

Make me new gun, she thought. *Tougher. Part of me.* Her arm changed into a cybernetic limb with even more tech-mech than her real gauntlets. The gun, bigger and uglier now, became part of her arm.

"I don't have more bykes," the sex-bunny cooed at the mega-Dice. "You cleaned me out."

"No bykes, no bliss." Dice leaned closer, invading her digital space. "Unless you got something else for me, hmm?"

Angel scowled. Dice wouldn't pull this shit, especially not for bliss, which was so addictive to Kyle operators that going into withdrawal could turn them psychotic.

"Oh no," the sex-bunny purred. "You're so evil." She sounded delighted. "What do you want from helpless me?"

The mega-Dice leered at her. "Come here, little one, and I'll show you."

They playing, Maze thought.

Yah. Angel still felt like blasting them with her cyber-gun, but she didn't protest when Maze morphed her arm back into a normal limb. She didn't care about their sex stuff, but it worried her that the guy used a Dice avatar to sell drugs. People knew.

Angel edged back into the shadows. *Do deeper dive on the fake Dice and bunny bimbo.*

Easy, Maze told her. **Two kids from Earth. They hear Dice called Vakaar. Even on Earth, people know Kajada and Vakaar names.**

Dice get bad rep? Both he and Shiv were settling on terms for an athletic scholarship, with Bhaaj as their liaison. They also had some lucrative sponsorship offers. Nor were they the only ones; the Raylicon team had captured the imagination of the public. No more stealing images of Undercity athletes to promote stuff for free. The offers Angel had received startled her. Power-Run had already paid Ruzik for using his image in their ads, and they wanted a sponsorship contract with both him and Angel, saying they made a "photogenic couple," whatever that meant.

Do people think Dice and Shiv work for cartels? Angel asked.

Some reels call Dice a drug boy, Maze answered. **One say Shiv drug girl. But slicks think all Undercity kids druggies. That why they test you again and again.**

We need put comments in sim worlds, holo-games, smash-pads, dup-dens, all that. She considered the thought. *Say how it inspires that Dice and Shiv climb out of bad stuff, make better life, go to school. Role models. Make people say, "Great feel-good story, show best in people."*

Yah. Take care, though. Not want people ken it come from you.

How I make sure?

I can do.

Good. Make vid saying Games give Undercity kids way out. It was true. Drugs created a crushing weight in the aqueducts, and Dice and Shiv *did* want a new life. Neither were Knights, so they hadn't sworn off drugs, but if they'd used before, they'd stopped when they joined the team.

Not have vid to use. Maze paused. **Got bits from when media talk to Dice. You want I make reel with bits and pieces? I can put it on new account. Call self Dust-Fan.**

Yah. Good. You fan of Dice. Of Shiv. Say they inspire. Make sen-tee-men-tal vids.

Can do.

Good.

Found other Dice thing.

Thing? Or avatar?

Thing. Hidden. Backdoor. Had to go through big maze to find. Got me into place near where Bhaaj had Max look.

Near where Bhaaj and Max look? What that mean?

When they look into Hyden.

She didn't see what Hyden had to do with the cartels. *I thought you say this about Dice.*

Yah. And Kiro. You want look?

Kiro? This sounded odder and odder. *Show me.*

A distant light appeared. Angel found herself in an alley bordered by dark buildings with a faltering lamp at its far end. Voices whispered, languages she didn't recognize. The air had an aging metallic quality, like someone had set up this place and then locked it tight, until over the years it became crusted with secrets.

A figure ran past Angel and darted into a nearby recess. Startled, she turned—

The blow came from behind. Even as Angel staggered, she spun around and grabbed for her attacker. They weren't where she calculated; they'd run up the wall, ignoring gravity. When she went after them, someone else jumped out from a window and shoved her off the wall. She flew into the air, but as she sailed away, she glimpsed their face, human-shaped, but metal.

Angel somersaulted and landed on the wall of a building across the alley, her body parallel to the "ground." She had no idea what these buildings hid; she wanted that door at the end. When its light flickered again, she took off running toward it along the wall. Someone dropped through the air in front of her. As she collided with them, they both sailed off the wall and crashed to the ground. This time she got a strong grip on her attacker and hurled them away. In the strange gravity, they went high and far, then twisted around so they could land on the roof of a building.

The other attacker jumped down on Angel, and she battled it with eerily magnified punches. They weren't literally fighting; she was trying to reshape the evolving code protecting that distant door with its flickering light, and these mesh-mods wanted to stop her. Her coding tricks became tykado moves she used against the metal-faced guardians. This time when she spun toward them, she kept whirling, around and around. She adapted faster than her attacker expected and dodged their blow, then grabbed the guardian and whirled it high into the air.

In that same moment, the second guardian appeared at her side and hefted her up, preparing to hurl her back the way she had come. Angel twisted, pulling them with her, and they flew through the shadows. She threw the guardian to the ground, fast but not too hard, nothing explosive that would wake up more of these dodgy mesh-mods. She needed finesse here more than power. In silence, she bent her legs and jumped into the air, going high, high, high. In the alley below, the second guardian re-formed, walking "upside down" under the eaves of a roof.

As Angel came down, she blew hard on the guardian, a silent blast of wind. They fell off the eaves and tumbled down as if moving through a heavy liquid. After they hit the ground, they slowly rose to their feet next to the other guardian. They'd become distorted, stretched long and thin, weakening their underlying structure.

Angel landed on the mesh-mods with weight but no noise. Both vanished, then re-formed a few paces away from her. Their motions were jerky now, instead of smooth. She blocked their blows, careful. Covert. Quiet.

Under the onslaught of Angel's rewrites, the mesh-mods slowed and slowed, until finally they stopped. She left them sitting together in the alley, back-to-back, slumped in a heap.

Angel ran for the door at the end of the alley. Its light flickered out when she reached it, but she could see the doorknob, an ornate construction with an antiqued quality, its many ridges making swirling designs.

She opened the door.

✧ ✧ ✧

Bhaaj sent out two of her beetle-bots to monitor the area so she and Jak could walk to the pub in privacy. They only had about a kilometer to go, an easy stroll along a path by the country road. The air felt warm and clear, and the rings graced the darkening sky in a luminous arch.

"Hyden want go to pub party later," she commented.

"Should," Jak answered. "Clinks go with him?"

"Yah. His bodyguard and Duane." To be safe, Duane still had a bodyguard on Shiv and Dice, and also another for Azarina. Finally Bhaaj could relax and enjoy the evening.

Max had a different idea. They'd walked about two thirds of the way to the pub when he announced, "I have more news on Gwen Caballo."

Bhaaj sighed. "Not now, Max."

"Oh. All right. Shame you won't know it when you see her. I heard some family members are joining the athletes later at the pub. Including Kiro's parents."

"All right," she grumbled. "What is it?"

"Angel did a deeper mesh dive," Max said. "Guess what she found? Gwen Caballo isn't a data analyst. Actually, she is, but that's not all."

"It doesn't surprise me." Of course Abyss gave Caballo a better position as she gained seniority. They should have promoted her even more by this time, given how well she obviously did her job. "I don't see why that's crucial enough to disturb this lovely walk."

"Gwen Caballo founded Abyss Associates," Max said. "She owns a significant percentage of the company, not a controlling share, but more than any other single person. She's also the CEO."

"Say *what?*" Bhaaj came to an abrupt stop. "That's impossible."

Jak stood next to her. "Abyss has a CEO. I forget their name, but it isn't Gwen Caballo."

"That person is a front," Max said. "A figurehead."

"I doubt it," Bhaaj said. "It's fraud to give a fake name for the CEO of a public company."

"True," Max said. "Gwen Caballo has the power without the title. Her contract with the official CEO requires they follow her directives if she chooses to step in. She doesn't often, but she can override their decisions if she wants. The board can't remove the CEO without her approval. And there's more. She owns a private holding company with no public listing, so her name doesn't appear. That company owns her stock and votes on the Abyss board. Almost no one knows, not even her son, but in all except name, Caballo controls Abyss Associates."

Bhaaj squinted at the air. "Is that legal?"

"Yes. She's brilliant," Max said. "And she hid it all remarkably well. She's as good a hacker as me." He seemed astounded that a human could rival his ability.

"No wonder that family is so fucking rich," Jak said.

"You need to watch out, Bhaaj," Max added. "Angel found a backdoor into Caballo's holding company when she searched the Foreshires shadow mesh. She isn't as experienced as Caballo, but she's just as smart, and she's getting into risky places."

"I'll talk to her." Angel had gone beyond what anyone could control, but she had good sense and listened to people she trusted. "What was she doing in the shadow mesh?"

"Damage control," Max said. "People know Dice and Shiv are cartel. Angel didn't want bad press for them, so she started positive rumors about how they rose above their origins, the nobility of it, all that. People seem to love the Undercity-kids-make-good thing."

"Ah." Relief swept over Bhaaj. "Good."

"What does that have to do with Abyss?" Jak asked.

"Maze found a link between Dice and Hyden Laj."

"I'm not sure how that connects to Gwen Caballo." It was Hyden's father who coveted Abyss, not Hyden. "And who the hell is Maze?"

"Maze is Angel's EI," Max said. "Even experienced EIs wouldn't normally have found the link. Maze did because of Angel. She knew about your work with the team, both for Hyden and for Dice. So in the Kyle, she ended up close to Hyden's father and Dice's family."

Unease washed Bhaaj. "You mean she found out why Hammerjan is extorting Zaic."

"Not exactly," Max said. "I think Hammerjan figured out that Kiro is the true Vakaar heir. My guess as to why she kept it secret all these years? She's protecting her brother's son."

It didn't surprise Bhaaj. Hammerjan didn't have her mother's murderous psychotic edge. "But how does that connect to Zaic Laj?"

"Twenty years ago, Laj's wife got in trouble buying drugs from Vakaar. In helping her get clean, Zaic had to pay off Hammerjan. It would have stopped there, except Hammerjan asked him about Kyle testing. She probably figured if anyone could tell her how to get Dice secretly checked, Laj would know. He gave her his contact on Foreshires Hold."

"Ho!" Jak said. "Is this the inescapable Abber Isles again?"

"That's right," Max said. "Isles had a private business, testing kids for Kyle abilities whose parents wanted it kept secret. Gwen Caballo, Zaic Laj, and Hammerjan Vakaar all used her service."

Bhaaj finally understood. "Zaic probably thought that would put Hammerjan in his debt, at least enough to keep her away from his wife. But he miscalculated. Slicks have no idea how well our wizards ride the meshes. Hammerjan must have had her cyber-riders do deep searches on both Isles and Zaic. *That's* how she found out about Hyden."

"That implies she knows truths about both Kiro and Hyden," Max said. "Gwen Caballo started Abyss just before Kiro's birth. It's her legacy for him. I'll bet you Hammerjan is making Zaic's life even more miserable lately because he's trying to rob Kiro of his inheritance."

"Nahya." Bhaaj's pulse suddenly spiked. "*NO!*"

"It is strange," Jak said. "Delicious, in fact. But hardly the end of the world."

A surge of adrenaline swept Bhaaj. "Max, do you have a recording of when I talked with Dice and Shiv about their meeting with the Balkers?"

"Yes. What do you want to hear?"

"When Dice said the word 'koyo.'"

Dice's voice floated into the air from her comm. "Not sure," the youth admitted. "They want information about 'elitist CEO koyos.'"

"Koyos." Panic surged in Bhaaj. "It's *plural.* Jak! What if they know about Kiro? And Dice is *leaving* Raylicon." She stared at him. "That makes Kiro both the Abyss *and* the Vakaar heir. He's even more valuable to the Balkers than Hyden."

CHAPTER XXX
To Keep the Peace

The party was in full swing by the time Kiro arrived with Zee, Lamp, and Strider. Usually he avoided crowded places, but with the four of them together, all buffering each other, it felt fine. The room brimmed with their teammates, many of them friends now. It felt good. Raylicon had thrived, and they were part of that achievement.

Music played with a good beat that made Kiro want to dance, except of course he couldn't with so many people around to see. He could run races with hundreds of billions of people watching, but he felt too self-conscious to dance in a club. The proprietor kept the lights low, using blink-holos in the air like a wash of sparkles, luminous enough to let him see other people, but not in a lot of detail. Maybe he'd dance later.

Kiro took Zee's hand, and she smiled. Without the team, he'd never have met the woman he loved. He didn't know what would happen, how he and Zee would work things out, but tonight he had no worries. They'd find a way.

Athletes crowded the pub, some with family members. He'd come early to enjoy this time with his friends before his parents arrived and things got awkward. Did his father know the truth? He'd always mentioned Kiro's offworld cousin to explain his son's curly hair. Kiro wasn't convinced his cousin even had curly hair, that it wasn't just something he'd done for fashion. He sort of saw the resemblance, though not as much as when he looked at images of himself and Dice together. No one else seemed to see it beyond his general "Undercity look." If his father had ever noticed, he'd never given any sign.

I am his son, Kiro thought. Whatever his genetics, the father he knew was the man who had raised him. They had problems, sure, but Kiro had never doubted his father loved him.

He pushed a curl out of his eyes. Everyone saw him as Undercity now, not only because of his look, but also because people considered him part of Strider's "clique." Right, clique. A polite name for dust gang, but what the hell. They never asked him to break the law, just help protect their circle—his circle—from gangs trying to pinch their food and water. The better he learned to fight, the better he held his own. Sometimes they tumbled with other gangs just for sport.

Dust Knights *did* train to do harm, but only if no other choice existed. Although Kiro had tried a few classes at the Cries Tykado Academy, he didn't go back despite how well he'd done there. At the Academy, they learned form over function and never expected to use their skills. He preferred the Knights, especially now that they'd promoted him to the class with Strider, Zee, and Lamp. He still couldn't fight as well as them, but he was learning, and it came easily given his other athletic training.

"Hyden not here," Zee commented as they headed to the bar.

"Not around much," Kiro said as they reached the table with drinks. Tonight they could bypass the sweet stuff without alcohol and enjoy the real thing.

Lamp held up his fluted glass. "Too pretty, eh?"

Strider laughed. "Slicks."

Kiro regarded her curiously. "Your father is glass blower. Make more beautiful glass than these." He used a three-syllable word to honor her father's craft.

"Yah," Strider said. "Is true."

Zee looked around nervously. "Eh."

"What?" Kiro asked.

"You see parents?" Zee asked.

"Not yet." He gave her a reassuring look. "They like you. Promise."

"They think I dust rat."

"They not that way." At least, he hoped not. His mother would like Zee, but who knew about his father. Nial had made a special effort to be here, though, getting other pilots to take his flights. It meant more than Kiro knew how to say. His parents enthused about all his events, even the 800-meter where he hadn't made the finals. His mother had secured excellent seats in the stadium, close enough that after Kiro had a good run, he'd gone to hug them over the barrier. They watched all the stories about him on the holo-casts. Many reels showed him with the relay team; in a few he and Zee had touched in ways suggesting they were more than friends. Embarrassingly, one reporter caught them kissing. His parents must know by now that his girlfriend came from the Undercity, yet neither had objected. He hoped that boded well.

Kiro relaxed against the bar, sipping his drink and watching athletes from all over human-settled space socialize. Zee stood next to him, with Strider and Lamp on the other side, four people, one unit. They didn't need to talk; their silence felt right.

And then it didn't.

The air seemed to tighten. Kiro stiffened. What the—

"Nahya," Strider said, as if her denial covered the entire bar.

"What—?" Lamp said, his face strained.

"Not like," Zee said.

Then Kiro saw them. Aristos. Three had arrived, Kryx Quaelen and two Iquar women.

"Time to leave," Lamp said.

"We got right to be here," Zee said. "Same as them."

"Not want be here now," Strider said.

The Aristos moved among the other athletes as if they belonged at the party. Although no one Kiro knew had invited them, no one had invited him, either. He'd heard about it, so he went. For all he knew, other people here thought the Raylicon team had crashed their party.

More Trader athletes came, all taskmakers. The Aristos ignored them. The only time they deigned to notice was when Kryx Quaelen told one athlete to get him a drink. The guy made quick work of the task, and he even freaking bowed to Kryx as he handed him the glass. Kiro grimaced. He'd hate being on a team where he had to act as if he worshiped its captain.

The Aristos kept to themselves, watching other athletes dance. The club owner put on new music, inspiring stuff from some sports movie Kiro vaguely recalled. The story had mostly revolved around athletes trying to sleep with each other. They never trained. They spent all their time getting high or fall-over drunk and then missed their events after they stayed out late the night before. They didn't do squat about their raging hangovers because supposedly the competition rules didn't allow them to have health meds. It was too much bullshit, and Kiro had quit watching halfway through the movie. He did like the music, though.

With the Aristos paying attention to the dancers, their effect on Kiro receded. He still felt uncomfortable, though. Glancing at Zee, he asked, "Go outside?"

"Yah." She regarded him warily. "We meet parents there?"

"Not yet." They wouldn't come until later tonight, tactfully giving him time with his friends first. "But not worry, eh? It fine."

"Eh." She sounded unconvinced.

Outside, no lamps glowed in the night. Kiro could still make out the flowering bushes and cloud-grass because the rings shed radiance over the night. In their light, Zee looked even more lovely. No one else had wandered out here yet, so they had privacy. They found a secluded bench on the side of the building beneath a flower-draped arch.

"Pretty," Zee said.

"Yah," Kiro agreed.

Zee touched his cheek, and Kiro took her into his arms.

Except something felt wrong...

With a start, Kiro looked around. Even as Zee drew back, he jumped to his feet, ready to fight. He didn't think about it until he was already standing. Zee had risen, too, tensed at his side.

Kryx Quaelen stood a short distance away, watching them.

What he want? Zee thought.

Not know, Kiro answered. They could just ask, but he had no idea how to talk to someone who considered himself a deity.

Quaelen spoke in a friendly voice, using Flag. "My greetings. A pleasant evening, yes?"

"Eh," Zee told him.

Kiro would have smiled at her one-word conversation, except Quaelen's approach left him tense and confused, as if he balanced on a mental cliff above the chasm of the Aristo's mind. He barely managed to say, "Um, yeah. Nice night."

"I enjoyed watching your team in the events," Quaelen said. "Raylicon did well this year."

Zee stiffened, and Kiro felt her fists clench at her sides as if they were his own hands.

Zee, nahya, he thought. *We here for peace. Show honor.* He had no wish to show Quaelen anything; Kiro just wanted him to leave. But this moment, this golden night outside a pub, offered testament to why the interstellar Olympics existed, to bring together the far-flung multitudes of humanity and find a common ground with good will instead of combat. *Not fight,* he thought. *But guard mind, yah? Make walls.*

Yah, she answered, her thought fading as she fortified her mental barriers. Kiro did the same and his sense of the Aristo receded. It still felt miserable, but less intense. That also meant he lost touch with Strider and Lamp, but he could pick them up again after he and Zee escaped Quaelen.

"Thank you," he said to the Aristo, "Your team is amazing." It was true. Although the Quaelen team had come in second in track and field, in terms of medals overall they'd ranked first.

"Yes. We are." Quaelen paused. "But this seems new for Raylicon."

"I suppose." Kiro wondered what he wanted.

The Aristo tilted his head, watching them as if they were valuable livestock. "It's a shame you have to compete for the worst team in the Olympics."

"Seriously?" Kiro didn't know whether to get angry or laugh. "It's an honor to compete on any team." Then he added, "Besides, we aren't the worst in track and field." They'd even beaten the Iquar team, which came in eleventh.

Quaelen waved his hand in dismissal. "Tenth place? It means nothing. You ought to be embarrassed, not honored."

Kiro had an odd sense from the Aristo, as if it never occurred to him that they might find his comments offensive. In his view, he honored them immensely just by allowing them to be in his presence. He thought they ought to feel terrified even to speak to him.

Ass-byte, Zee thought.

Yah. Kiro had no disagreement.

Quaelen was watching them closely. "You know," he said. "I've heard rumors that some of your athletes are talking to university recruiters."

"I wouldn't know." Kiro did know, given that Dice and Shiv had told him, but he'd never reveal that to someone who believed he should be ashamed of his team.

"Other teams recruit as well," Quaelen said.

Kiro blinked. "What?"

In his too perfect voice, the Aristo said, "You could run with the best team in all humanity."

Kiro stared at him, stunned into silence. Given that this Aristo's team currently had the most medals, and that many people considered the Olympics the highest sports event, Kiro could only run with "the best" by joining the Quaelen team.

Panic swept Kiro, bringing back his voice. "I'm not, uh, looking for any sponsors."

"Why would you need one?" Kryx said. "You could live in absolute luxury, never worry about work again, never have duties except to prepare for your meets." His gaze took in them both. "You would never again lack for water or food. No poverty. No crime. No sickness. You'd have the highest standard of living possible."

"Except what?" Kiro ground out. "We'd be providers?"

"It is an unimaginably great honor," Quaelen said. "The highest elevation you can attain."

Not ken what he mean, Zee thought.

Kiro was losing his battle to stay calm. His voice cracked. "You *torture* your providers. You *own* them, make their lives a living hell. Forever."

What? Zee asked.

Slaves. In his panic, Kiro slipped into his own dialect. *He wants us as his slaves. To hurt us, like he does with his mind, but much, much worse, physically and mentally.*

Quaelen sighed and his gaze took on a glazed quality, as if Kiro and Zee's reaction created a high for him better than any drug. "Your suffering elevates you," he said. "In return we would give you anything, train you with an expertise beyond anything you could know anywhere else. And you're so young. You would win medal after medal for many years to come, including the gold. And you'd do it with the best team humanity has ever known."

"Yeah, sure, right," Kiro said. "Even though you don't allow empaths to compete."

"I'm sure we could find an accommodation," Quaelen said, his voice smooth.

Zee spoke flatly. "Nahya."

"What did you say?" he asked her.

"Never," she told him. "We got good team. Not want shit with yours."

A frown creased his face, interfering with whatever high he had wrenched from them. "You will not speak to me in that manner."

"Fuck that," Zee told him. "This how I talk."

Zee, stop! Kiro thought. *He's a powerful man. Even here, in our territory, he could find ways to make you pay for insulting him.*

Quaelen narrowed his gaze. "This is what happens when providers are allowed to live free of control and guidance. You call yourself human, but you act like animals."

Those were his words—but what he wanted to say flared with such intensity in his mind that Kiro caught it despite Quaelen having no Kyle ability. *You will pay for that, my pretty little scum. You who are too low even to lick my feet with your Undercity tongue. Someday you will scream and scream and scream until you beg me to forgive your every insolent word.*

Zee froze, staring at Quaelen. As the effect of his mind on theirs intensified, their barriers weakened, breaking down. The Aristo responded to their fear with—

Pleasure.

He spoke in a deceptively kind voice. "I have no wish for us to be enemies. Think about my offer. You needn't live in Undercity squalor. It won't matter that you have no education. You don't need it. I can give you everything you've ever dreamed of attaining."

Kiro said nothing, just looked at Quaelen, his face impassive.

"We got our own school stuff," Zee told him. "Like it fine."

"I'm sure you think so." Quaelen's voice took on a hypnotic resonance, like an invitation to the riches of the universe. "You would never have to study again. Just train for the Olympics. And provide your services to the Aristo who chooses to elevate you."

Kiro scraped out the word that shouted in his mind. "No."

"Don't decide yet," Quaelen said. "Let me host you at our reception—" He stopped, his gaze going to a point beyond Kiro's shoulder.

Jumping at the interruption, Kiro turned. A man and a woman who looked like security officers had come up to them. Both had the Abyss logo of the Raylicon sun on their uniform.

They stopped by Kiro, and each gave him a slight bow. "My greetings, Goodman Caballo," the woman said. "Your parents asked us to fetch you."

Relief flooded Kiro. "Thank you. Are they in the pub?"

The man motioned toward the darkness behind the pub, where the only light glimmered on a few strings hung in trees. "They set up a surprise for you. Shall we go?"

"Yes, of course." Turning to Quaelen, he said, "Thank you for your offer." It terrified him, but these Games were about peace, togetherness, and all that, so he used his best diplomacy.

Quaelen glanced at the officers, then at Kiro. "I hadn't realized Abyss Associates helped sponsor your team."

"They always have." More this year than in the past, but Kiro didn't elaborate.

Zee seemed almost as uneasy with the Abyss escort as with Quaelen. She'd been that way ever since she learned his parents wanted to meet her. Except... despite her barriers, Kiro sensed more. This fear felt different than her flustered unease about his family.

"Eh." Kiro took her arm, watching her face. "We go, yah?"

The woman from Abyss came up alongside Kiro. "Just you," she told him.

That made no sense. His parents expected Zee. They wanted to meet her, especially since he'd never brought home a girlfriend. Hell, he'd never *had* a girlfriend before, just casual relationships that never went anywhere. He expected Zee to step back, withdrawing after this insult, having her fears about his parents verified. Instead, she watched him, studying his face.

Quaelen considered the Abyss officers, his gaze puzzled, his forehead furrowed. When his attention became less concentrated on Kiro, the onslaught of his mind eased, and Kiro could almost see him as just another athlete close to his own age, someone interested in making friends. Almost. Then Quaelen's focus returned to him, and with it the full force of his mind.

"Are you all right?" Quaelen asked.

Kiro knew his concern came because of the security officers, not his effect on them. "Yes, fine, thank you." He didn't miss Quaelen's flash of irritation, as if Kiro had insulted him despite his courtesy. Quaelen expected far more, though what, Kiro had no idea.

Glancing at Zee, Kiro tilted his head toward the garden behind the pub, indicating they should both go with the officers his parents had sent. She shook her head, the barest motion.

Trust me. He laid his hand on her arm. *My parents not insult you.*

Her thought came faintly. *Guards wrong. They fake.*

The female guard removed Kiro's hand from Zee's arm. "I'm sorry," she said. "We need to go. Your mother had an emergency and asked us to get you."

"An emergency?" Kiro stepped back from her. "What are you talking about?"

"His mother?" Quaelen spoke in his cultured voice. "Why would a man from the Undercity have a mother who provides him with corporate bodyguards?"

Good question, Kiro thought. He tapped his gauntlet comm, but it wouldn't respond. "I don't understand why I can't get a comm signal. This area should be full of them."

Zee motioned to the pub. "We go back inside, yah?"

"Yes." Distracted by so many people and their conflicted or disguised emotions, Kiro took Zee's hand and stepped away from everyone. She had it right; the Abyss officers seemed off. Cold.

"I'm sorry." The Abyss woman moved in front of them, blocking their escape. "Goodman Caballo, you must come with us."

"He told you no." Quaelen came up beside Kiro. "He and this young woman may do as they wish." His tone had taken on a cool assumption of authority that Kiro responded to on an instinctual level. Then he thought, *NO*. Still holding Zee's hand, he tried to step around the Abyss guard. When the woman raised her arm to block him, he brushed her elbow—

And it gave the slightest ripple.

Normally he wouldn't have noticed, especially not out here with only ringlight to lighten the evening. But he'd become so focused on the guard, he saw that telltale shift.

"Hey!" Kiro jerked away from the woman. "You've got a holo-mask." She was hiding her true appearance by using a screen produced by her clothes and holo-dust on her face. He and Zee had to leave, *fast.* They needed to get back inside the pub, surrounded by the safety of many people.

Still holding Zee's hand, Kiro strode around the officers, escaping both them and Quaelen—

And the male officer grabbed Zee from behind, swinging her away from Kiro.

"Ho!" Zee's shout rang through the air. She twisted hard, using a tykado move, and hurled the guard around, then jammed her knee against his leg and flipped him to the ground. In the same instant, the second guard grabbed for Kiro. Reacting on instinct, Kiro kicked out, getting her in the torso. As she staggered back, he glimpsed Zee knocking down a third officer. She had no qualms about punching him; she hauled off the same way she would have with any gang attacking them in the Undercity.

The Abyss woman came at Kiro again, but even as he lunged away, someone new barreled into him, he couldn't tell who, just that they felt heavy. And *strong.* They threw him down and tried to trap him, but he rolled away faster than they moved. The night careened around him, stars and rings, and then a glimpse of Quaelen with a Trader bodyguard pulling him away, their faces confused.

Kiro scrambled to his feet and went after the fake Abyss woman, keeping the second man in his sights. And a third! When they came at him, he twisted, turned, grabbed their arms, and pushed their legs, driven by desperation to move faster and with more strength than he'd ever managed in practice. All the weight lifting he'd done paid off as he threw one of them to the ground.

"Get him," the woman said, her voice hard and low. "And get rid of that Undercity bitch. This was supposed to be easy."

Kiro whirled and kicked again. He didn't know who stood behind him, but his mind sensed them and his body responded. Grabbing the guy, Kiro threw him as hard as he could manage.

The other two kept coming. They caught Kiro and took off running, dragging him through the grass toward the back of the pub. Using their weight against them, he unbalanced the man on his right, but even as the guy stumbled, a third person caught Kiro from behind. As they pulled him behind the building, two men and a woman in Abyss uniforms, he glimpsed Zee fighting two more Abyss guards. Where the blazes did they all come from? He kept struggling, using tykado moves to try wresting free from his three captors.

"Damn it," someone said. "Where'd a rich fucker like you learn to fight?"

Kiro, run! Zee's thought shouted in his mind, no longer muted by shields. *They Balkers!*

For one instant he saw the scene through her eyes, that she was on the side of the building, fighting two supposed Abyss officers. The vision shattered as someone yanked Kiro's arms behind his back. They locked his wrists together and hauled him through the hip-high grass. Damn! With no mesh signals here, no one inside knew that he and Zee needed help.

Strider! Kiro shouted the name in his mind. *Lamp! Come fast!* He had no time to figure out if he'd reached them, caught in his struggles with his captors. Although he couldn't pull free, he did unbalance all three of them, sending everyone crashing to the ground, including himself. The ugly crunch of tech-mech hitting a boulder sounded by his ear—and he found himself staring into a man's face, one of the supposed Abyss officers, except now he looked different, hard-edged, with a cold stare.

"Fuck it all to hell," the man said. "He's seen me."

The woman heaved Kiro to his feet. "We've got to get out of here."

They broke into a run, their hands clamped around Kiro's upper arms. Kiro went limp, forcing them to work harder. Even if he couldn't use his arms, he could slow them down.

"Help!" he shouted. "Back here—"

His voice cut off as one of his captors punched him. Kiro reeled, his sight going dark for an instant. Then it cleared enough to let him glimpse a large vehicle looming by the country lane. A holo-van. The lamps on the road had gone out, leaving the van hulking in the shadows. His captors dragged him toward the vehicle—and yet another fake Abyss woman sprinted past them. When she reached the van, she swung open the doors.

Kiro gasped in a breath. "*Help—*"

One of his captors socked him in the face. "Shut your fucking mouth."

As Kiro groaned, Zee's presence flooded his mind; she was still fighting. He was alone back here, except for his captors. No one could stop these people from taking him, and he'd seen at least one of them, which was almost surely fatal.

"Who is that?" a new voice suddenly said, a girl it sounded like.

One of his captors stumbled and the other two jumped back, jerking Kiro with them. In the same instant, three kids sat up in the cloud grass, two girls and a guy, athletes Kiro vaguely recognized from the Parthonia team. They held a small bong with smoke curling up its ornate snout, and the scent of a drug called crackers-dream drifted around them.

"What are you doing?" one of the girls said in the same moment the guy said, "I know that kid. He's from Raylicon," and the other girl said, "Hey! You're hurting him."

"Damn it, get rid of them," one of the men holding Kiro said.

With his adrenaline raging, Kiro's time sense seemed to crawl. As if in slow motion, the woman out on the road, the one standing by the van, raised what looked like a Mark-5 submachine gun. She aimed at the three confused kids, about to end their Olympics careers forever.

A dark figure barreled into the woman, and her shot went wild, an explosion of sound that tore apart the night. Someone screamed, someone else shouted, and a third person swore.

Kiro's captors started dragging him again, urgency blazing in their minds. They'd expected an easy extraction, not this confused mess against trained fighters. The person who knocked over the woman by the van, a man in dark clothes, was wrestling her for the gun, using a mix of tykado and the ugliest street fighting Kiro had seen. This was no "sport;" that man meant to kill.

Kiro struggled harder, hoping to stall his captors so the trio of athletes could escape. As they jumped to their feet, Kiro shouted, "Run!" one of the girls yelled, "Come on!" and the guy with her bellowed, "We can't just leave him with them!"

The man holding Kiro threw him to the ground while the woman let go of him and drew her gun, an ugly EM-pulser. Moving with what Kiro perceived as an eerily slowed quality, she sighted on the frantic trio of athletes sprinting toward the pub, their bodies outlined in ringlight. Her intense thought came through to Kiro: *Easy, one, two, three, and they're gone.* Beyond her, by the van, the other fake Abyss woman lay on the ground. A figure stood over her—a tall, lean man in dark clothes and heavy gauntlets.

Jak.

He loomed over the Balker, holding her submachine gun. While one of Kiro's captors pinned him to the ground, the other man aimed at Jak. It happened with excruciating slowness, though Kiro knew, somewhere in his desperate thoughts, that they were all moving fast, Jak even with enhanced speed.

Then someone more distant said, "That's their fucking coach, the preg one."

The fake Abyss man aiming at Jak put his finger on the ignition stud on his weapon, about to turn Jak into exploding plasma—

Jak fired.

He stood with his feet planted wide as he whipped his gun across the scene with surgical precision, first catching the man aiming at him, then the woman sighting on the three fleeing athletes, then the man holding down Kiro, and then a Balker Kiro couldn't see, whoever had shouted about Coach Bhaaj. Jak never hesitated, shooting like a trained assassin. Bullets tore apart the ground only a handspan away from Kiro, spraying dirt and grass over his body.

Stunned, his mind reeling from the deaths, Kiro struggled to his feet. Jak ran toward him in a surreally fast sprint, a blur of motion. Almost as soon as he moved, he had reached Kiro.

Still gripping his gun, Jak said, "You all right?"

"Yah," Kiro lied, gasping.

The moment Kiro spoke, Jak set off again, headed around the pub. Kiro went after him, going as fast as he could manage with his hands locked behind his back.

As Bhaaj strode along the country road, she kept trying to get her gauntlet comm to work. "Max, what's wrong? This area usually gets great reception. I can't reach Kiro or anyone, anywhere." Jak had gone on ahead when they realized the danger to Kiro, using his enhanced biomech to run at double or even triple the speed that even the best Olympic sprinters could manage.

"I can't link with Jak, either," Max said. "Someone has set up jammers in this entire area, blocking communication."

"Keep trying to break through." Max had tricks he'd developed over the decades. "See if you can get medical help out here, too." She didn't know yet if anyone had any injuries, but she'd rather be wrong and have to apologize for overreacting than end up having to mourn because she didn't react enough.

Spurred by her growing unease, Bhaaj tried to jog, but she struggled with her extra weight. She needed more strength. *Put me in combat mode.*

No, Max answered.

What do you mean, no? You have to if I tell you.

Yes. However, it will override your body's instinct to choose the behavior best suited to carrying a nearly full-term child.

Yah, well, if someone attacks, and I can't protect myself, that damn well isn't the best way to protect my kid, either.

If you're threatened, combat mode will automatically activate. You sure you want it now?

Bhaaj wanted to run hard and fast. She had to make sure her athletes were all right. But she couldn't risk the well-being of her daughter. *Jak must've reached the pub by now.*

Yes, he should have arrived.

All right. Don't activate my biomech. She stopped as her daughter gave a hearty series of kicks. Or maybe it was that Braxton-Hicks thing, the fake contractions. When it eased, she set out again, striding toward the pub. It was visible in the distance, bathed in ringlight, a solitary building like an island in the billowing cloud-grass. A few strings of glow-lights lit the area. She'd expected partygoers to be outside, socializing. Instead—nothing.

"Any success with my comm?" she asked.

"Still nothing," Max said.

As Bhaaj approached the building, she saw what looked like people fighting in the shadows. She notched up her speed, nearly running.

A voice suddenly called, "That's their fucking coach, the preg one."

Bhaaj had no time to react before someone lunged at her.

Combat mode on, Max thought.

As her enhanced reflexes cut in, Bhaaj dodged her attacker, then grabbed the woman's arm and swung her to the ground. In the same moment her would-be attacker shouted, one of the people fighting a few paces away stumbled forward. Bhaaj had one lightning instant to see his uniform, one she'd never mistake even in this dim light—that of a military Aristo bodyguard.

"Lord Quaelen, run!" the man shouted in Highton. "*RUN!*"

Bhaaj had no time to figure out why the blazes someone was fighting an Aristo's bodyguard. The woman she'd thrown had jumped to her feet again. In her accelerated state, Bhaaj could see every detail of the woman's motion, her stumble for balance, her fist pulling back, her intent to strike Bhaaj in the abdomen. Fury swept over her when she realized the woman intended to attack where she figured it would do the most damage, injuring or even killing Bhaaj's child.

Compelled by an instinct greater even than her fear of anyone, Bhaaj went after her attacker. It didn't matter that she couldn't use tykado well with her body so heavy; she could still punch with the power and speed of the combat-level system in her bio-enhanced body. The woman tried to dodge, but she couldn't move fast enough. As Bhaaj's fist pounded into her attacker's shoulder, the woman screamed and a great crack burst through the air. She collapsed to the ground—and her reaction hit Bhaaj's mind *hard*. Her meds and neural system protected the baby's mind, but they didn't have enough left over to shield her as well, and the woman's pain from her shattered shoulder crashed through Bhaaj.

In her heightened state, even that shock couldn't slow down Bhaaj. The Aristo's bodyguard was fighting a man wearing what looked like the uniform of an Abyss security guard. Harsh and silent, their struggle took them hurtling through the cloud-grass. With a grunt, the Trader officer went down again—and this time he didn't get up.

And then Bhaaj saw the other person here.

Kryx Quaelen.

Someone had thrown the Aristo to the ground, and he was struggling now to his feet, his face contorted with pain. When the Abyss man who'd knocked out Quaelen's bodyguard saw Quaelen standing up, he drew his EM-pulse gun. Compared to Bhaaj's accelerated state, he seemed to move through invisible molasses. She felt an ugliness in his mind, the chill of a hired killer.

She spun back to the woman she'd knocked down—yes, there, she had an EM-pulser. Bhaaj grabbed it even as the woman groaned, then whirled back to face the Abyss killer.

The man was raising his gun, aiming at Quaelen. "Fucking Trader demon." Hatred saturated his voice. Quaelen stared in disbelief as he realized he was about to die a horrible, miserable death.

"*Noooooo!*" To her augmented hearing, Bhaaj's cry seemed drawn out in the night. If this man assassinated a Highton Aristo in Skolian territory, that would end all the hopes for peace engendered by these Games. It would look like an act of war, not the current muted war between the Imperialate and the Traders, but a full-on conflict. Moving in a blur, she whipped up her stolen pistol and fired. The noise of the shot battered the night, and the Abyss man seemed to explode with the force of the bullets. He didn't scream; his life ended before any sound left his throat.

The man's death crashed through Bhaaj's mind, agonizing. *NO!* Someone was shouting at her. She couldn't hear—baby was in distress—*must protect*—

Bhaaj groaned as pain wracked her body. Doubling over, she fell to her knees in the grass.

"—have to get help!" Max was shouting.

Someone else was talking, Zee it sounded like. "Aristo—they try to kill him—"

A man suddenly knelt next to her. "Bhaaj!"

Looking up, seeing Jak, she barely managed two words. "Baby... coming."

Grabbing her hand, he raised his head and shouted, "Get help! She's having the baby."

"Kiro?" she whispered.

"I'm here, Coach." That came from her other side.

She turned to see Kiro crouched next to her, his hands behind his back, with Zee standing behind him. "Alive?" Bhaaj asked them, one of her stupider questions, but what the hell.

"Yah." He even managed a smile, which disappeared as fast as it came. "Balkers—didn't expect fight. Thought—could just lead me away." He was talking too fast, his words spilling over themselves. "Was mess. We saw their faces. Three other athletes, we all saw—they meant to kill everyone—ransom me—then kill—"

"Kiro, slow down." As Bhaaj's contraction eased, she said, "Thank goddess you're alive. What about the others?"

"Jak saved the three kids behind the pub." He took a ragged breath. "And me."

When Kiro shuddered, Bhaaj knew he'd felt the deaths of his kidnappers. "And Kryx Quaelen?" she asked. "I'd swear I saw him here."

A man spoke above her in perfect—albeit uneven—Highton. "I am alive."

Lifting her head, Bhaaj saw him a few steps away. He met her gaze and spoke words that never, in a million years, would she have expected to hear from an Aristo. "Thank you, Major."

Bhaaj started to respond, to say what she had no idea, but instead she groaned as another contraction swept over her.

Raising his head, Jak called out, "Where are the medics? They should be here already!"

"Contractions too close—" Bhaaj managed.

"Royal, what's wrong?" Jak asked. "What should I do?"

"Just stay with her," the EI said. "Be helpful."

"Helpful *how?* I've no clue how to deliver a baby."

A commotion came from nearby—and then more people surrounded Bhaaj, talking firmly, telling everyone to move back. People hefted her onto an air stretcher. When they took off running, with the motorized stretcher humming between them, Bhaaj groaned. It felt like a huge vise clamped her body, tightening until she couldn't breathe, couldn't think, couldn't do squat.

"Her contractions are too close together," Max was telling someone. "She has biomech in her body. She had to accelerate into combat mode to save Lord Quaelen. And the heavier gravity here has given her problems. It's pushed her into premature labor."

"Up now!" a man called, and they lifted Bhaaj into a waiting vehicle.

"You can't come with us," someone else was saying.

"Good gods," a woman said. "You can't bring a *machine gun* in an ambulance."

"Here." Jak's voice faded as if he'd turned around. "You take it."

"Uh, yah," Zee said, sounding disconcerted.

"Sir, you can meet us at the hospital," someone else was saying. "We're taking her to—"

"Damn it, I'm her husband," Jak interupted. "The baby's father."

"Let him come," Bhaaj managed.

More noise, and people were moving fast, setting up medical equipment where Bhaaj lay on the stretcher. Then Jak was next to her, taking her hand.

"Eh," Bhaaj told him. As the contraction eased, she heard the hum of the ambulance driving. "Balkers?" she asked. "How many?"

"Eight, maybe." Jak spoke in a harsh voice. "They not ken how well Kiro and Zee fight."

Bhaaj groaned as another contraction built in her. "The kids—?"

"They okay." In a dark voice, he added, "Balkers not know Undercity. Five get shot. Cops take others. Not sure how many."

"Why not sure?"

"You go into labor."

"Oh." Bhaaj didn't know where to put all this. "You in trouble, Jak. Me too."

"Aristo say you save his life. Is huge. You hero. Me? Not know. Kiro, other athletes, they ken what happen. They tell key clinkers." He grimaced. "I hope."

"You save their lives." Bhaaj yelled as another contraction hit her. "*Ah, damn!*"

"You need to move back," a woman told Jak. "The baby is coming."

"Nahya!" Bhaaj told the air as Jak moved away and a medic took his place. Looking up at the woman, she said, "I *can't* do this now. Got to check—my runners—ah, naaaaahya!" She shouted as the contraction wrung her body, ignoring her insistence that it stop.

"She's fully dilated," someone was saying. "Coach, you need to push!"

"I thought she was an army major," someone else said.

Bhaaj didn't care what they called her, she *had* to push. With a grunt, she went full force into the process women had been doing since time immemorial, or whatever. How the blazes had the human race survived—ah, *noooooo.*

"I see the head," someone called. "Come on, Coach, you're doing great. Keep pushing!"

So Bhaaj kept on, silent now in her efforts. Again the contractions—this baby was coming fiercely—

"There!" someone said. "She's in a good position—here we *go!*"

A huge wail split the air, as if someone with the world's most powerful lungs had just announced her irate response at her unceremonious entry into the universe.

"Her stats look great," someone was saying at the same time as the woman leaning over Bhaaj said, "Congratulations, Major Bhaajan. You have a healthy baby girl."

Bhaaj managed a shaky smile. "Got a loud girl."

Someone laughed, and then they were putting the child in her arms. Bhaaj cradled her body, aware of tears running down her face. Leave it to her daughter to find such a dramatic entrance into life. The universe had better be ready, because her daughter would hit it by storm.

The medic moved and Jak took her place. "Eh," he told Bhaaj.

She meant to glare at him for being the cause of all this shouting and pain, but instead she spoke in a gentle voice she never used with anyone else. "She did well, eh?"

"Yah," he whispered. "She and her mother both."

CHAPTER XXXI
Homecoming

"—and the Highton Line of Quaelen formally expressed their gratitude to Major Bhaajan for saving the life of the Quaelen heir at risk to her own child," the holo-cast continued. "That unprecedented announcement is the first time in the history of Imperialate and Concord relations that the Hightons have in any way thanked an Imperialate military officer, either current or retired."

"Great," Bhaaj muttered. Of all the things she'd liked to have become known for, saving the life of an Aristo ranked close to the bottom of the list. Still, she was glad he'd survived. Goddess only knew what would have happened if the Balkers had killed him. She felt grateful that Max and her nanomeds had shielded her daughter's mind from the deaths, but she'd never forget. As much as she wished she had Jak's ability to compartmentalize combat from the rest of his life, it had never worked that way for her.

"Turn that down, yah?" she asked.

Someone muted the newscast. Earlier today, people had poured into her room after the docs cleared her for visitors. When the medical staff saw the entire Raylicon track and field team crowding around her bed, they told everyone to leave. After some back and forth, they agreed to let Mason, Ruzik, Angel, Tam, Azarina, Hyden, and Duane stay. The police had Jak at the station. Mason soon had to leave, to take care of administrative biz, but then Kiro showed up, coming from his own room, still in his hospital smart-smock with purple bruises on his face, accompanied by Strider, Zee, and Lamp.

Kiro's parents came, too. They stayed back and stood by the wall, giving their son space with his friends. They seemed disconcerted by Strider's gang. Gwen smiled at Zee when the young woman glanced her way, though, and with a startled look, Zee smiled back. Nial projected confidence with everyone, which Bhaaj supposed he had to do, given his glamour job. However, she also sensed his bemused acceptance of Kiro's friends. After having mercenaries beat and almost kill their son, his parents seemed more willing to accept the Undercity kids, who came off far better in comparison, especially given how Zee had fought to defend Kiro.

Feeling less groggy by then, Bhaaj didn't growl at anyone, so either the medics didn't notice that more people had crowded the room or else they pretended not to. Kiro's parents did see when one of the nurses glanced around with concern, and they soon left, going to check out of their hotel. Everyone else sat in chairs around Bhaaj's bed, avidly watching news-holos about what had happened last night at the pub.

Bhaaj settled the baby in her arms, shifting the sleeping infant. In her youth, before she'd left the Undercity to enlist, some of her friends had already had children, so she'd become used to holding a baby. For the team, though, it had taken a while for the novelty of seeing their coach with a kid to wear off. They'd finally settled enough to stop oohing and aahing and let her daughter sleep.

A nurse came by, pretending not to see all the people gathered around the bed. Stepping past Lamp, she went to Bhaaj. "Sorry, I need to take the baby for a short bit. We have to run more tests, make sure her premature birth isn't causing her problems."

Bhaaj had expected the nurse earlier. They seemed to trust that she'd let them know if the baby needed anything, though. Gently, she gave the infant to the nurse, startled at how odd it felt to have her arms empty. "She okay?"

The nurse smiled. "She's doing great. A real fighter, this one." That evoked a ripple of laughter from the gathered members of the team, making the nurse blink with confusion.

Strider explained. "Her hoshma, she a mean rumble-round. Crush bad quaz, all dust."

"Uh, oh." The nurse squinted. "Of course."

Bhaaj smiled at her and even meant it. "She means I'm a good fighter, too."

The nurse gave her a gentle look, then went off to take care of the sleeping infant.

Tam had lost interest in babies, her attention fixed on the holo of Kryx Quaelen above the dais in the room. "He look fine," she grumbled. "No one hit him. Not like Kiro and Zee and Bhaaj."

"What, you want him get hit?" Although secretly Bhaaj agreed, she left it unsaid.

When Tam just slanted a look at them all, Kiro laughed, then winced.

"You sure you okay?" Bhaaj asked him.

"Yah." He touched the bruising around his eye. Already, with his top-notch meds on the job, the injury was fading. "Is nothing."

"Docs say they beat you up bad."

He shrugged. "I fine."

Bhaaj suspected he hurt a lot more than he admitted, but she said nothing more.

The holos shifted, running some algorithm the room's EI used to figure what they all wanted to see. This new scene showed a guy interviewing a woman from the IOC. Although Bhaaj couldn't hear them, she could tell the woman had just said, *Tam Wiens*.

"Eh," Tam said. "Turn up."

The woman's voice came into the room. "—officials for the Quaelen team made the announcement a few moments ago."

The scene morphed into a man with rust-red eyes wearing the colors of the Quaelen team and a coach's badge. A woman from one of the larger media conglomerates was interviewing him. "After a great deal of consideration," the man said. "It is our decision to withdraw the Quaelen challenge to the presence of empaths at athletic meets."

"Is this because Coach Bhaajan saved the life of Kryx Quaelen?" the reporter asked.

"The decision is one our Highton sponsors have chosen to make," the coach answered. "You may interpret it however you please."

The reporter blinked. "But can you give specifics—"

The Trader man held up his hand to stop her. "The Line of Quaelen does not choose to say more." With that, he nodded curtly and took his leave.

"Ho!" Tam said. "I can't believe they dropped their challenge."

Bhaaj blinked at the sound of Tam speaking Flag. Then again, she'd had plenty of practice since she beat Kryx Quaelen. Everyone wanted to interview her.

"Aristos ken that you the best runner," Lamp said. "Afraid you might beat Kryx."

Tam grinned. "They right."

The others laughed, more relaxed than Bhaaj had seen them in ages. Then Zee moved her hand in dismissal and said, "This Kryx person, he try recruit me and Kiro for his team."

Bhaaj stared at her. "He *what?*"

Kiro spoke dryly. "He told us we'd be rich beyond our wildest imaginings, that we could have whatever we wanted, and we'd be part of the greatest track and field team ever known."

"He talk a lot," Zee said.

Bhaaj spoke harshly. "And did he tell you what else would happen? That you'd become slaves? *Providers?*"

"Yah." Zee growled the word. "He say if we pro-vi-ders, it raise us up."

"I can't *believe* it," a man said from the doorway.

Bhaaj looked up with a start. Mason stood there, looking ready to blow holes in the sky. "I cannot *believe* it," he repeated. "What do you think they'd do if we tried to recruit their athletes, convince them to defect to the Imperialate? They'd scream to high heaven, claim we were violating every treaty our governments have ever managed to work out together."

"Quaelen not care." Zee spoke his name as an insult, because he made no attempt to keep it to himself. "Think we be happy to let him hurt us."

"Ass-byte," Strider stated.

Mason came over to Bhaaj. "We'll put in a complaint as soon as possible—"

"Mason, no." She laid her hand on his arm. "Let it go."

"How can I let it go?" He stared at her with incredulity. "It violates every understanding between ourselves and the Traders about these Games."

She spoke quietly. "They've dropped their challenge to empaths competing."

He looked as if he'd run into a wall. "You're kidding."

"It's true. They've spoken to the Olympic committee."

"Because you saved Quaelen's life."

"In part." She exhaled. "Or maybe they just wanted to stop Tam from competing yesterday, and now it doesn't matter." She spoke bitterly. "Even if they don't admit it, they know it gives them an advantage to compete against empaths. Our discomfort strengthens them and hurts us."

He spoke firmly. "We need to make sure our kids never fall for a pitch like that."

Strider snorted. "We not stupid, no matter how much they think so."

Mason nodded to her. "You ought to go to university, too. You've all got what it takes."

"Not want." She paused. "Not for now. Maybe someday."

Lamp spoke in Flag. "A recruiter from Parthonia University took Dice and Shiv 'to breakfast' this morning." He smirked. "They want give big scholar boats."

Bhaaj squinted, wondering if it he'd get annoyed if she corrected him about the scholarships. Whatever her expression, it provoked a peal of laughter from Lamp.

"I ken scholarship, Coach," Lamp told her.

"Eh," Bhaaj said.

"So you got name for baby?" Zee asked.

"Not sure," Bhaaj admitted.

Zee laughed. "Call her Bhaajanjan, eh?"

"Ha, ha," Bhaaj growled. "Old, old joke."

"Eh," Ruzik said. "Turn up newsfeed. That's the cop who took Jak."

A reporter's voice rose into the air. He was standing with a woman in the uniform of the police force for all things Games-related. "Thank you for appearing, Chief. Have the authorities made a ruling about the deaths of the mercenaries killed or injured during the attack last night?"

"We've taken statements from everyone involved and looked at what holo footage we managed to glean," the chief said. "The mercenaries never expected the Raylicon athletes to fight back, let alone so well. These Dust Knights—they're an elite fighting force in the Undercity. They live by a Code of Honor as binding as the code that Jagernauts follow. The adults are black belts in tykado."

"And great athletes," the reporter enthused. "I understand that Coach Bhaajan founded the Dust Knights."

"I can tell you this," the chief said. "She and her husband saved the lives of our athletes. If not for their bravery, our community would be mourning now instead of celebrating the Games."

"Eh," a man commented from the doorway. "You hear? We brave." He sounded amused.

Bhaaj looked up to see Jak leaning against the doorframe of the entrance to her room. Her shoulders came down from a tensed position she hadn't even realized she'd taken until she let it go.

"I not brave," she told him. "Just pissed off. Big-time."

As Jak came over, Mason stepped back, out of respect yah, but Bhaaj sensed his fear. Even the Undercity kids moved out of Jak's way. They all knew the saying, that you never messed with Mean Jak, but they'd never experienced its truth before last night.

"So." Bhaaj looked him up and down. "Key clinks let you go."

"Yah. They agreed, I had no choice." He spoke dryly. "They also told me to get off Foreshires. They've ruled my actions necessary to save the athletes, but they don't like me, to put it mildly. They were going to take me straight to the starport and put me on a flight to Raylicon, but for some reason they changed their minds and let me come see you."

"Eh," Angel commented.

Bhaaj slanted a look at her. "What you do?"

"Do?" Angel regarded her with innocence. "Not ken what you mean."

"Haven't you seen the reels?" Azarina lifted her wrist band, where holos twirled above its screen. "Jak, you're everywhere! People keep forwarding these reels that fans of our team made about your heroism, defending your wife and unborn child at great personal risk."

"Yah," Tam said. "And who this Hood guy? They say you Undercity Robin."

"Robin Hood is an Earth legend," Hyden said. "A bandit who steals from the rich and gives to the poor."

"So." Lamp nodded. "Mean Jak."

"Hmmm," Bhaaj said, looking at Angel. "I wonder who spread all those stories."

"It looks like it started spontaneously." Kiro was flipping through holos that floated above his wrist band. "People were playing with sims in virtual spaces, getting to be Jak and save the day, until the sim went viral." He glanced at Bhaaj with a look of apology. "Apparently that's a lot more appealing than rescuing a Highton Aristo. No one wants to play that sim."

"Trust me, I wouldn't either," Bhaaj said. She'd saved Quaelen's life because she had to, but she never wanted to be in that place again.

"Hey, look at this one." Strider raised her tech-mech gauntlet. Amazing how fast the Undercity kids figured out how to link into the offworld media meshes. "Says Jak bad-boy sexy." The holos above her gauntlet showed views of Jak in his black leather glowering at a reporter who kept dogging him for quotes about the Undercity athletes.

Bhaaj blinked at Jak. "You sex symbol now?"

He smirked at her. "Could be."

As everyone showed off Jak-hero sims they'd found, Bhaaj looked across their heads at Angel and nodded her thanks. Angel nodded back. Enough said.

Jak came to the bed while the others enjoyed the game of finding Jak-sims. He spoke in a low voice. "I still need to leave, before the authorities find a reason to arrest me."

"We only planned to stay so I didn't go into labor in space. That doesn't matter now." Bhaaj thought about the nurse tending to their child to make sure she didn't have any problems. "Let's see what the medics say. If they clear our daughter to travel, maybe we can go back with the team." She glanced at Mason. "You think we can reschedule our flights?"

"I'll look into it," he said. "Let me know what the doctors say."

"Will do," Bhaaj told him.

It was time to go home.

The crowds at the Raylicon starport were like nothing Bhaaj had ever experienced. The mayor of Cries showed up, along with a contingent of city officials decked out in crisp suits, and also a police honor guard. Officers in dress uniform from Majda Security showed up as well, not just to greet the team, but also to guard the woman who stood in their midst, the second of the three Majda sisters, Corejida, the financial genius of the family and Azarina's mother.

Holo reporters floated orbs everywhere, and the spheres created feeds as the athletes trooped into the starport lobby. Everyone cheered and the athletes all grinned, not just the track and field team, but the other Raylicon competitors as well, basking in the glow of having a team that for once hadn't come in close to last. They waved at family and friends, their faces lit with excitement. Many of the Undercity kids looked disconcerted, but they were growing more used to commotions. Some even enjoyed the attention.

Shiv and Dice stood together, discreet but no longer avoiding each other. They had full scholarship offers from both Parthonia and Eos Universities. How they planned to tell their parents, Bhaaj didn't know, and she prayed it didn't end in violence. *Be careful,* she thought to them. *Take care in what you say.* As much as she understood that they'd wanted to see their families one last time before they left home, possibly forever, nothing could take away the risks they faced.

Bhaaj walked with Jak, resting their baby in a sling on her hip. Holo-casters tried to crowd them, asking, asking, asking questions. Mercifully, Duane kept them back. When athletes wanted to talk with the reporters, he let them by, but when they shied away, Duane was suddenly in the way with a contingent of officers he'd trained himself.

As people clumped into groups, greeting each other, hugging, doing all the stuff people did at arrivals gates, Bhaaj glanced at Jak. They needed to escape—except then she saw a couple coming toward them, two people who'd taken a private star yacht home from Foreshires and arrived on Raylicon only a few hours before the team. Kiro's parents.

Gwen and Nial approached slowly. When they caught Bhaaj's look, Gwen tilted her head as if asking a question. Bhaaj nodded, laying her hand on Jak's arm.

"Eh?" He glanced at her, distracted. He lived in the shadows; all this hoopla unsettled him.

"Kiro parents," Bhaaj said.

"Eh." He stayed put as Gwen Caballo and her husband joined them.

"Congratulations." Kiro's father beamed at them. "What a great showing."

"We're so proud of Kiro," Gwen said. "Of the whole team."

"Kiro's an incredible young man," Bhaaj said. Beyond his parents, she glimpsed Kiro with Zee and the others. He was trying to watch her talk to his parents while at the same time pay attention to the people greeting him.

Faintly, like a distant whisper on the wind, his thought came to her. *He doesn't know...*

I ken, Bhaaj thought. If Nial ever learned his son's true parentage, it wouldn't be from her.

Gwen spoke directly to Jak. "I don't know how we can ever thank you."

"If you hadn't intervened," Nial said, "We'd never have seen our son alive again."

Jak looked excruciatingly self-conscious. "Glad he's all right."

Gwen smiled at the baby sleeping in the sling. "You've a lovely child."

"Yah." Bhaaj agreed. Odd, that she had happened to give birth to the best-looking kid in the Imperialate. In her more rational moments, she thought her daughter didn't look all that different from anyone else's baby, but no matter. She settled the sleeping girl more comfortably.

"Kiro seems happy," Jak said, which was about the extent of his ability at small talk.

"More than happy." Joy showed in Gwen's face. "He's wanted this all his life."

"He has a great future ahead of him." Bhaaj meant it. Kiro had surpassed everyone's expectations, including his own.

They continued chatting, casual and careful. Whatever accommodations all these people would find with their secrets—Gwen Caballo and her husband, Hammerjan Vakaar and the cartel, Zaic Laj and Vaj Majda—those life-changing truths were theirs to keep or tell. Vaj Majda had hired Bhaaj to look into the Scorpio takeover of Abyss Associates, and Bhaaj had done her job. She'd never tell Vaj that she'd figured out why the Majda Matriarch had more interest in that one deal than in the multitude of other financial matters conducted by the Majda financial empire. Hyden might never know his true heritage, but neither would he ever live with the beyond-the-pale constraints of a Majda prince. If Scorpio conquered Abyss, then Vaj had ensured that her firstborn son received what would become—after Majda— the most powerful corporate legacy on Cries.

Whether or not Hyden wanted that legacy was a question only he could answer.

Although neither of his parents had come to greet him, Bhaaj suspected they wouldn't have even if they'd celebrated his participation in the Olympics. Zaic Laj rarely went into public, given the way people mobbed him, either out of hero-worship or hatred. Maybe he and Hyden could work things out, maybe not. Either way, Hyden's life had changed forever.

She and Jak talked a bit more with Kiro's parents, and Bhaaj even enjoyed it. She'd never have imagined it in her youth, but being a mentor suited her. It meant more than she knew how to express that her Dust Knights had futures to look forward to beyond the crushing poverty of their lives in the Undercity.

Taken literally, the title *Arches* did describe this area of the Undercity. Even so. Bhaaj had always thought that calling this great cavern *Arches* was like calling the vast, magnificent deserts of Raylicon *Sand*.

The Arches weren't centrally located in the Undercity. Set off from the canals used by the Knights or the cartels, but still higher than the Deep, they offered one of the less visited places for her people. It helped preserve their beauty. Whoever had designed these ruins had created one of the greatest wonders on Raylicon, second only to the ruins of the city Izu Yaxlan in the desert above.

Arches filled the cavern. Built from stone, in row after row of sculpted beauty, they offered a magnificent feat of architecture that had survived for more than five thousand years. Tiles in tessellated mosaics covered the stone in borders and circled their great columns. The Undercity sculptors who maintained the arches kept them in their original glory, passing down the knowledge from generation to generation. Painted with glossy enamel, they glimmered in the dark and burst into rich colors when bathed by light. Blue, violet, purple, gold, they made the cavern radiant.

Today strings of tiny white lights also hung on the arches, creating a wash of sparkles as if someone had taken stars from a nebula and brought them here. Naturally occurring crystals embedded in the rock glittered as well, until light filled the cavern, turning it into a miraculous place unlike any other on Raylicon or beyond. And it was theirs, only theirs, a place you could only find if you lived in the Undercity and knew it well.

Today Bhaaj dressed in Undercity clothes, her best trousers and a blue shirt with embroidered hems. Jak wore black, all his best. Their circles showed up in their best as well, come to celebrate. Bhaaj's closest friend, Dara, had even decked out the baby resting in a sling on Bhaaj's hip, tailoring soft clothes for her, with handwoven lace.

Dara stood with Bhaaj as her first. Gourd, the giant of a man who stood as Jak's first, had been part of their dust gang in their youth: Dig Kajada, Jak, Bhaaj, and Gourd. Many others joined them today, including athletes from the Raylicon team, Dust Knights who hadn't gone to the Olympics, and many more from their circles. Bhaaj's cousin, her only living blood relative, arrived with a contingent from the Deep.

In today's unprecedented proceedings, General Vaj Majda had come to the Undercity for the first and possibly only time ever, standing back with her hand-selected bodyguards, including Duane. Her sister Lavinda Majda stood at her side, a figure better known to Bhaaj's people, one who made them more willing to accept the Majda Matriarch in their midst. Azarina Majda stood with the Raylicon team, but near her family.

Kiro stayed with Strider's gang. None of the above-city athletes had brought anyone from Cries besides themselves. This gathering remained limited to a select few. Hyden stood side-by-side with Kiro. Although Bhaaj doubted either of them would mention the corporate battle that had gone on between their families, she sensed Kiro's gratitude. In an unprecedented and unexpected move, Hyden had voted the many Abyss shares he'd so laboriously accumulated *against* the takeover. So it was that by the barest margin, Abyss defeated the takeover and survived the financial warriors of Scorpio.

The Majdas and the city athletes, however, weren't the most startling guests. Deep in the shadows, two groups remained apart from everyone else. Hammerjan waited back there with her lieutenants; on the other side of the cavern, well separated from Vakaar, Cutter Kajada stood with her people. To honor their decisions, that each chose to let their heirs leave Raylicon and attend college, Bhaaj had invited them. She hadn't expected either to show up given that she asked them to come only if they felt they could be in the same place without violence. Although their attacks against the Dust Knights had stopped after Bhaaj arranged the bargain where Dice and Shiv brought more supplies to their families, the cartels remained bitter rivals. Each stunned her with their response: they would come and they wouldn't fight.

Digjan—the daughter of Dig Kajada—stood with the Kajadas, who remained her family even though she'd left years ago to become a starfighter pilot. She used her military leave to come today as Bhaaj's niece, not by blood but by ties that went just as deep.

Nor would Bhaaj forget that moment when Hammerjan Vakaar met Kiro's gaze—and nodded to him. One nod, nothing more, but that moment said it all. Hammerjan knew the truth and never intended to act on the knowledge. She gave Kiro what she couldn't give her brother, Kiro's father: the freedom of his own life.

Today the Undercity and Cries witnessed a first in their history, not the well-hyped firsts of the Games, but one unlike anything else ever known. Undercity bards had already composed songs to pass down the generations about this gathering. For reasons that honored, baffled, and gratified Bhaaj, they had all come today to celebrate with her and Jak.

The religious leaders in the Undercity had no formal background, but rather a spirituality they gave to the people. Dara's husband Weaver was one such leader. Bhaaj and Jak stood before him, and he offered each pure water from crystal goblets he'd created himself. Bhaaj and Jak intertwined their arms so she could sip from his goblet and he from hers. And they drank. Together.

"As you do," Weaver said. "Do you also say?"

"Yah, say," Bhaaj answered, in the same moment that Jak replied, "I say."

"Good." Weaver nodded to them both, then grinned. "You together now. Always. Yah?"

Bhaaj smiled at Jak. "Always."

She thought he'd grin. Instead, he watched her with a rare look, an intensity he showed only her, a look she'd seen just twice before. The first had been decades ago when she left the Undercity to enlist. The second had been years ago when he admitted he'd loved her his entire life and she had told him the same. Today was the third time.

He said only, "Yah. Always."

Someone played a lyder-flute, its clear tones floating through the cavern in the hauntingly beautiful chords of "The Lost Sky." The music flowed as everyone shook leather strips with tiny bells, the sound shimmering in the cavern. It was done, then, what Bhaaj and Jak would always consider their true wedding, not one for officials or records, but for them and their circles.

And so the Undercity and Above Cities also witnessed a marriage and a birth of a different sort, the glimmerings of what could someday be a future they shared together.

TIME LINE

Circa 4000 BC	Group of humans moved from Earth to Raylicon
Circa 3600 BC	Ruby Dynasty begins
Circa 3100 BC	Raylicans launch first interstellar flights; rise of Ruby Empire
Circa 2900 BC	Ruby Empire declines
Circa 2800 BC	Last interstellar flights; Ruby Empire collapses

✧ ✧ ✧

Circa AD 1300	Raylicans begin to regain lost knowledge
1843	Raylicans regain interstellar flight
1866	Rhon genetic project begins
1871	Aristos found Eubian Concord (a.k.a. Trader Empire)
1881	Lahaylia Selei Skolia born
1904	Lahaylia Selei Skolia founds Skolian Imperialate and becomes first modern Ruby Pharaoh
2005	Jarac born
2111	Lahaylia marries Jarac
2119	Dyhianna Selei Skolia born
2122	Earth achieves interstellar flight with inversion drive

2132		Allied Worlds of Earth formed
2144		Roca Skolia born
2161		Bhaajan born and abandoned at Cries orphanage
2164		Bhaajan runs away from orphanage and returns to Undercity with Dig Kajada
2169		Kurj Skolia born
2176		Bhaaj tries to enlist in army but is too young ("Children of the Dust")
2177		Bhaaj enlists in army; they send her to school ("Children of the Dust")
2178		Bhaaj finishes school, becomes emancipated minor, ships out with army
2182		Bhaaj makes jump to officer ranks
2197		Bhaaj retires from army as a major and returns to Undercity on Raylicon
2198		Bhaaj moves to Selei City on world Parthonia and works as PI
2203		Roca marries Eldrinson Althor Valdoria (*Skyfall*)
2204		Eldrin Jarac Valdoria born (*Skyfall*) Jarac Skolia, patriarch of the Ruby Dynasty, dies (*Skyfall*) Kurj Skolia becomes Imperator (*Skyfall*) Lahaylia Selei Skolia dies, followed by the ascension of Dyhianna Selei Skolia to the Ruby Throne

2205	Bhaaj returns to Raylicon. Hired by Majdas to find Prince Dayj ("The City of Cries" and *Undercity*) Bhaaj establishes the Dust Knights (*Undercity*)
2206	Althor Izam-Na Valdoria born; Bhaaj hired to solve killer jagernaut case (*The Bronze Skies*)
2207	Del-Kurj Valdoria and Chaniece Valdoria born Major Bhaajan hired to solve the vanishing nobles case (*The Vanished Seas*)
late 2207	Major Bhaajan hired to solve technocrat case (*The Jigsaw Assassin*)
2208	Carnelian rash threatens to wipe out Down Deepers (*The Down Deep*)
2209	Undercity athletes begin training with Cries track and field team (*Gold Dust*) Havyrl (Vyrl) Torcellei Valdoria born
2210	Sauscony (Soz) Lahaylia Valdoria born Olympics on Foreshires Hold (*Gold Dust*)
2219	Kelricson (Kelric) Garlin Valdoria born
2220–2222	Eldrin and Althor change warfare on planet Lyshriol ("The Wages of Honor")
2223	Vyrl and Lily elope and cause a political crisis ("Stained Glass Heart")
2227	Soz starts at Dieshan Military Academy (*Schism*)
2228	First war between Skolia and Traders (*The Final Key*)

2237	Jaibriol II born
2240	Soz meets Jato Stormson ("Aurora in Four Voices")
2241	Kelric marries Admiral Corey Majda
2243	Corey assassinated ("Light and Shadow")
2258	Kelric crashes on Coba (*The Last Hawk*)
2255	Soz meets Hypron during New Day rescue mission ("The Pyre of New Day")
early 2259	Soz meets Jaibriol (*Primary Inversion*)
late 2259	Soz and Jaibriol go into exile (*The Radiant Seas*)
2260	Jaibriol III born, aka Jaibriol Qox Skolia (*The Radiant Seas*)
2263	Rocalisa Qox Skolia born (*The Radiant Seas*) Althor Izam-Na meets Coop ("Soul of Light")
2268	Vitar Qox Skolia born (*The Radiant Seas*)
2273	del-Kelric Qox Skolia born (*The Radiant Seas*)
2274	Radiance War begins (also called Domino War)
2276	Traders capture Eldrin; Radiance War ends (*The Radiant Seas*) Jagernaut Jason Harrick crashes on world Thrice Named ("The Shadowed Heart")
2277-8	Kelric returns home (*Ascendant Sun*) Dehya coalesces (*Spherical Harmonic*) Kamoj and Havyrl meet (*The Quantum Rose*)

	Jaibriol III becomes emperor of Eube (*The Moon's Shadow*)
2279	Althor Vyan Selei born
2287	Jeremiah Coltman trapped on Coba ("A Roll of the Dice") Jeejon dies (*The Ruby Dice*)
2288	Kelric and Jaibriol Qox sign peace treaty (*The Ruby Dice*)
2298	Jess Fernandez goes to Icelos ("Walk in Silence")
2328	Althor Vyan Selei meets Tina Santis Pulivok (*Catch the Lightning*; rewritten as the Lightning Strike duology)